HER DARKEST NIGHTMARE

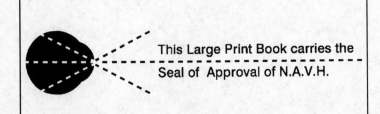

This Large Print Book carries the
Seal of Approval of N.A.V.H.

HER DARKEST NIGHTMARE

BRENDA NOVAK

WHEELER PUBLISHING
A part of Gale, Cengage Learning

GALE
CENGAGE Learning·

Farmington Hills, Mich • San Francisco • New York • Waterville, Maine
Meriden, Conn • Mason, Ohio • Chicago

LIBRARY OF CONGRESS CATALOGING-IN-PUBLICATION DATA

Names: Novak, Brenda, author.
Title: Her darkest nightmare / by Brenda Novak.
Description: Large print edition. | Waterville, Maine : Wheeler Publishing, 2016. | Series: Wheeler Publishing large print hardcover
Identifiers: LCCN 2016033497 | ISBN 9781410494801 (hardcover) | ISBN 1410494802 (hardcover)
Subjects: LCSH: Large type books. | GSAFD: Suspense fiction.
Classification: LCC PS3614.O926 H47 2016 | DDC 813/.6—dc23
LC record available at https://lccn.loc.gov/2016033497

Published in 2016 by arrangement with St. Martin's Press, LLC

Printed in Mexico
1 2 3 4 5 6 7 20 19 18 17 16

HER DARKEST
NIGHTMARE

Prologue

Kill one and you might as well kill
twenty-one.
— MARK MARTIN, BRITISH MURDERER

When she came to, Evelyn Talbot could hear nothing. She couldn't see anything, either. Darkness had fallen, and the shack, where she lay on the cool dirt floor, didn't have electricity.

Or . . . was she no longer in the shack?

Her thoughts were fuzzy. . . .

Maybe she was *dead.* She'd been expecting death, been thinking that, unlike most people, she wouldn't live long enough to graduate from high school. If she was alive, there would be pain. There'd been plenty of that in the three days Jasper Moore had held her captive in this place. Yet, in this moment, she felt . . . nothing.

That made no sense.

Unless she'd dreamed the whole thing.

7

Was it all just a terrible nightmare? Would she wake up and go to school to find Jasper hanging out near her first-period class, lounging against the wall along with some of the other guys on the baseball team, talking about where they should eat dinner before prom?

She imagined telling him that she'd dreamed he killed Marissa, Jessie and Agatha — all three of her best friends. They'd have a good laugh, blame it on the horror movie they'd seen together not long ago, and he'd sling his arm around her neck and draw her in for a kiss, which would fix everything, put her world right.

But the brief flash of hope that shot through her didn't last. Her own bed didn't feel like the lumpy, hard-packed earth. Even the old mattress they'd dragged out here when they first found this place and made it their secret hideaway didn't feel *that* uncomfortable. As soon as she inhaled, she could smell smoke and remembered Jasper tossing a lighted match on some kindling he'd gathered from the forest. He'd sat there, on one of the stools they'd also brought to this place, for what seemed like forever, smoking a joint. He'd never smoked weed before, at least not around her, and they'd been together for six months. But *this* Jasper Moore wasn't the boy she'd known; *this* Jasper Moore was a monster.

While he studied her, she hadn't dared to so much as twitch. She'd kept her eyes closed, couldn't see what he was doing. But she'd had the feeling he was watching her carefully, waiting to be sure she was dead.

Since he'd released her from the rope he used to tie her up, she'd had the use of her hands. It had been all she could do not to use them to staunch the blood pouring from her neck. She could hardly keep from gurgling as she breathed — and the smoke that thickened the air made those shallow breaths even more difficult. She'd thought she might suffocate if she didn't bleed to death first. But gut instinct had told her that her last and only chance depended on convincing him he'd finished the job he set out to do when he slit her throat.

"That'll teach you to mess with me, bitch," he'd muttered when, at long last, he walked out, leaving her to the fire he'd started to destroy the evidence.

Once he was gone, she'd tried to get up, but she must've blacked out. It had been light then, light enough that she'd pictured him hurrying home so he wouldn't be late for baseball practice. He'd attended school while keeping her out here. When he returned each night, he'd laugh and tell her how frantic the whole community was to find her and her friends — even what various kids and teachers were saying at school — as if he found it quite thrilling. He'd talk about the prayer circles, the yellow ribbons, and the anxious news reporters who were hounding everyone she knew for the smallest detail. When she asked him how he was able to keep slipping away to come back to the shack, he'd explained that he told everyone he was going out searching, too. The worried boyfriend was a part he claimed to play well, and she had no doubt of it. He could play *any* part.

He'd certainly fooled her.

If only someone would realize he wasn't sincerely upset and take a closer look at him! But that would never happen. With his chiseled face, athletic body, sharp mind and rich parents, he was so convincing, so believable, so unlikely a killer. No one would *ever* suspect him of committing a crime like this.

Squeezing her eyes closed, she struggled to staunch the tears that welled up. That he could betray her love in such a terrible way was the worst of what she'd suffered. But she couldn't focus on the heartbreak. That would only make her situation worse. She had to concentrate on *breathing* or maybe she'd simply . . . stop.

The fire must've burned itself out. She had no idea why it hadn't consumed her *and* the shack, as Jasper had intended, but below that acrid scent she identified the sweet, cloying smell of decaying flesh. The stench had been getting worse, more stomach churning every day. Jasper had said it made him hard to have her friends watch, with their sightless eyes, what he did to her. He said they were all just hanging out together, having fun like old times — except her friends had finally shut their big mouths.

What he'd done to them made her skin crawl. How he talked about it, with such relish, was almost as bad. She couldn't escape the vision she'd seen when she'd come looking for him — and surprised him while he was posing their bodies like mere mannequins. He'd said he killed them because they tried to make her break up with him by telling her he'd hit on Agatha at a party a week ago — as if their loyalty somehow made all of this *their* fault. He'd said he wouldn't allow *anyone* to cause trouble for him.

He'd claimed he hadn't been planning to kill *her,* but he certainly hadn't acted as though he minded, as though she was any

11

different or more special to him than they were. As a matter of fact, the more pain he caused her, the happier he became. The torture had ignited something in him, changed him. She'd never imagined anyone could be like that.

But she wasn't dead yet. If she could smell what she could smell and feel what she could feel, the darkness was simply that — darkness. And her muddled thoughts? Whose thoughts wouldn't be muddled after what she'd suffered? She had to fight the heaviness that dragged at her limbs and seemed to slow her heart, fight for her life. At least she didn't have the fire to contend with. Good thing she'd been on the floor, below the smoke, or she probably would've died.

If she could make it to the highway, maybe she could flag down a passing motorist.

Lifting a heavy, unwieldy hand to her throat, she felt the stickiness of her own blood. She was lying in a pool of it. But the gaping slash in her throat wasn't her only injury. She had a broken leg — it was crooked, which left little question — and had various other injuries. She could see out of only one eye and, in three days, hadn't eaten anything except the gross substances he'd forced down her throat while enjoying the humiliation he caused.

Did she have even half a chance?

It was too late, she decided. No one could be expected to survive what she'd endured. She should use her last moments on earth to scratch a message into the dirt so that her family would know it was Jasper who'd killed her. At least then he wouldn't get away with it.

But the thought of her parents created such a tremendous longing — and empathy for how they would feel to find her so badly used and broken — that she managed, with massive effort, to sit up. When she didn't pass out again, she took heart and, feeling for something solid, grabbed Jasper's stool to help drag her to her feet.

That was when the pain started. Why it suddenly rushed upon her out of nowhere she couldn't begin to guess. But the moment she came upright, her entire body screamed out in protest. And when she put pressure on her leg — oh God! She nearly lost consciousness.

Focus! Keep standing! Push the pain away! Think of only one thing — what to do next!

That was getting out of the place where her friends had been murdered — where he'd asked them to meet him so they could have a "private talk."

She feared Jasper would somehow realize the shack hadn't burned and come back to investigate. But if she was going to live, she had to move *now*. In five minutes, or less, she might not have the strength or the presence of mind.

Considering the agony of every footfall, Evelyn had no idea how she managed to stagger through the rain-drenched woods. She wasn't even sure she was moving in the right direction. It didn't matter that she'd traversed the small path to the shack at least a hundred times. There was greenery everywhere, and it all looked the same. She could be going in a circle, but she had to keep moving, keep struggling — had to find someone to help her.

Not until she was in the road did she realize that she'd reached her goal — and then it occurred to her only because a car horn sounded as a vehicle came at her. The blast was intended to get her out of the way, but she couldn't take another step, couldn't even raise her arms to signal her distress.

She heard the brakes squeal as the driver swerved to miss her, heard the crunch of gravel as the car came to a stop. Then she crumbled and would've died right there on the dotted yellow line separating the two lanes of pavement if not for the man who came rushing toward her, shouting, "Oh my God! What *happened* to you?"

1

We are all evil in some form or another.
— RICHARD RAMIREZ, THE NIGHT STALKER

Twenty years later . . .
He'd kill her if he could. He'd attacked her once before. She had to remember that.

Dropping her pen on top of the notepad she'd carried in with her, Dr. Evelyn Talbot slipped her fingers under her glasses and rubbed her eyes. She hadn't gotten much sleep last night; she'd had another of her terrible nightmares. "The plexiglass is there for a reason, Hugo. It will always be between us. And we both know why."

This wasn't the answer he'd been hoping for. Impatience etched lines in his handsome face, with its wide forehead and innocent-looking brown eyes, but he was careful not to raise his voice. In fact, he did the opposite: he lowered it in appeal. "I won't lay a hand on you, I swear! I just have

17

to tell you something. Come over to this side so I can whisper. It'll only take a minute."

It would take even less time for him to get his hands around her throat or put her in the hospital, like he did when she first met him at San Quentin.

Reclaiming her pen, she replied in the same measured tone she always reserved for her subjects. "You know I can't do that. So say what you have to say. Do it right here, right now. We've been going around and around with this for two weeks."

He twisted to look up at the camera being used to monitor his behavior. Whenever she met with an inmate, a correctional officer in a room down the hall viewed the proceedings on closed-circuit TV. The inmates thought they were being watched for security purposes, but these sessions were also recorded. The video enabled her to study the nuances in their body language, which was, in addition to their speech patterns, the focus of her research.

"I *can't,*" he insisted. "Not in front of the cameras. I'm a dead man if I do."

Someone had him convinced. She believed that much. Although, with the way her subjects lied, she could easily be wrong. Maybe he was making it all up. "But *who* would harm you?" She leaned closer. "And how?"

Evelyn had been studying Hugo Evanski since Hanover House opened three months ago, in November. He'd been among the first of the psychopaths transferred here, had scored a whopping 37 out of 40 on the Hare Psychopathy Checklist, or PCL-R. But to look at him or talk to him no one would know he was capable of murder. From the beginning, Evelyn had found him to be intelligent, tractable and, for the most part, polite. He was even helpful, when he could be.

The thought made her a bit uneasy, but if she had a friend among the psychopaths she'd come to Alaska to analyze it would be Hugo. Maybe that was why she was tempted to trust him, even after what he'd done before and everything else she'd been through.

"I was right about Jimmy, wasn't I?" he said.

A month and a half ago, he'd warned her that another inmate was planning to hang himself with a sheet. If not for Hugo, Jimmy Wise would be dead.

"Yes, but you didn't demand I risk my life to get that information."

"Because Jimmy was no threat to me!"

19

"So who is?"

Squeezing his eyes closed, he tapped his forehead against the glass.

Evelyn waited.

"What can I do?" he asked when he spoke again. "How can I get you to believe me? To give me just a moment of privacy?"

He'd strangled fifteen women and he'd injured her. That meant there was *nothing* he could do, because she wasn't stupid enough to put herself in jeopardy.

"I'm sorry," she said. "I truly am."

His gaze fell to the four-inch-long scar on her neck. "It's *his* fault."

She touched the raised flesh. She supposed, in a way, Hugo was right. But she found it amusing that he assumed no personal responsibility for his own behavior the day they met. She could've pointed that out but was more interested in what he hoped to tell her. "Yes."

Getting up, he paced the length of the small cubicle that comprised his half of their meeting space — what constituted her "couch." "I would never let anything happen to you," he said, "not if I could help it."

"And what happened at San Quentin?" This time she couldn't resist. . . .

"I didn't know you then. Things are different now."

Were they *really*? That was the question.

"I appreciate the sentiment," she responded, but that didn't mean she'd change her mind.

He stopped and pivoted to face her. "You don't understand. *You're not safe.* None of us are."

The intensity of his voice and expression made the hair on her arms stand on end. Was that what Hugo was hoping to do? Frighten her?

She had to admit it was working — but only because he'd never taken this tack before January 1. And he seemed so convinced, so sincere.

Apparently, even *she* could still be taken in. . . .

Grabbing her pad and her pen, Evelyn stood. "I'm afraid we'll have to end our session early. You're so obsessed with . . . whatever it is that's causing your agitation we can't make any progress."

"Wait!" He rushed the glass. "Evelyn . . ."

When she gaped at him for using her first name as if they were familiar enough for him to do that, he reverted to the usual formalities.

"Dr. Talbot, listen to me. Please. This prison houses psychopaths, right? Men who take lives without hesitation or remorse."

She made no reply, didn't see where one was necessary. He was stating information they both knew to be accurate.

"I'm trying to tell you that" — he glanced at the camera again — "not every killer at Hanover House is locked up."

This was the last thing she'd expected. "What are you talking about?"

"That's all I'll say. Unless . . . unless you can give me a chance to speak to you in private. I'll explain what I know, what I've seen and heard. And I won't hurt you. *I'm trying to help!*"

Evelyn refused to listen to any more of this. Clearly, Hugo was hoping to gain some type of control in their relationship by acting like her protector at the same time he chipped away at her peace of mind. No way would she allow him to do that. At just sixteen, her life had nearly been taken when she fell in love with a man like Hugo. After becoming a psychiatrist eight years ago, she'd devoted her life to unraveling the mysteries of the remorseless killer. She knew more about the psychopathic mind than anyone else in the world, except, maybe, Dr. Robert D. Hare, who had developed the PCL-R and had been researching the same subject for nearly thirty years. But, sadly, even she didn't know as much as she wanted, not nearly enough to protect the unsuspecting.

"We'll meet at our regular time day after tomorrow," she told Hugo. "Do what you can to relax. You're growing paranoid."

She walked out, but he didn't let it go at that. "You'll see," he called after her. "You're going to wish you'd believed me!"

With a sigh of bone-deep exhaustion, Evelyn tossed her notepad on her desk and slid into her chair.

"What's wrong? Another headache?"

The sound of Lorraine Drummond's voice at her open door brought Evelyn's head up. "No, I just left a session with Hugo Evanski."

Lorraine, who'd answered an ad in the newspaper when Evelyn and the warden began staffing the center last September, was heavyset, in her mid-fifties and recently single. She had a small house in Anchorage an hour away, two grown children and no education beyond high school. She hadn't even worked until her divorce, but she was doing a terrific job of running the center's food service program.

"Since he came here, Hugo's been perfect. You told me that yourself."

"He's changing. Acting strange."

23

"Why not pass him along to Dr. Fitzpatrick or one of the others? Give yourself a break?"

"Dr. Fitzpatrick is already using him for some of his studies — and has been since we opened. I can't ask him to do more. Not since Dr. Brand quit and Dr. Wilheim came down with the shingles. We're barely managing without them. Who knows how long it'll be before we can find someone to replace Martin and Stacy's able to come back to work?" Besides, Evelyn felt duty bound to carry the heaviest load. She was largely the reason they were all stuck in the middle of nowhere with thirty-seven of the worst serial killers in America. The other 213 inmates were also diagnosed as psychopathic but were in for lesser crimes and would one day be released.

"You could if you wanted to," Lorraine insisted.

"I don't want to. There're only four other productive members of the team right now. I can handle him." The men she'd come here to study manipulated her constantly, or tried to. Why should she expect Hugo to be any different? Especially with the way their first meeting had gone?

"He's very nice whenever I see him in the dining hall." Lorraine put a sack lunch on the desk. She came over to the mental health wing quite often to make sure Evelyn had food to eat, regardless of the meal.

Evelyn peeked in at her lunch: carrots, an apple, a cup of chicken noodle soup and a chocolate-chip cookie. "You can't trust nice." *Jasper had once been nice, too. And look what he did.*

Lorraine adjusted an earring that was hanging too low. "Dr. Fitzpatrick says everyone dons a mask. With psychopaths, that mask is more like a mirror. Whatever they think you want to see, that's what they reflect back at you. They're empty."

No, not empty. Evelyn didn't believe that for a second. She'd once seen the bared soul of a psychopath, stared into his eyes in a way Dr. Fitzpatrick never had and, God willing, never would. The men they treated were far from empty; "empty" was too synonymous with "neutral, harmless." If she were a religious person she might substitute "soulless" and find it quite fitting, but she hadn't been to church in over a decade.

"They know how to blend in," she corrected. "How to appear as emotionally invested as those around them. They're wolves in sheep's clothing, which is why they're able to cause so much pain and destruction." And why the truly caring individuals involved in their lives usually suffered for it.

Lorraine seemed to measure Evelyn more closely. "Are you sure it's only Hugo that's got you down? You look . . . frazzled."

And it was only Monday. Not a great way to start out the week. "I didn't sleep well last night."

"Why don't you go home and lie down, get some rest?"

Evelyn waved her off. "It's not even noon."

"Listen, this place won't fall apart if you take a couple of hours. Everyone admires your commitment — no one more than me — but you'll run yourself into a brick wall if you don't slow down."

Evelyn shook a daily vitamin from the bottle she kept in her desk and tossed it back with a drink of water. "Don't be so dramatic. I'm fine. And I *can't* leave." She checked the clock hanging on her wall. "Our new inmate will be here any minute."

"Anthony Garza? I thought he wasn't due until four."

"Weather report says we've got another storm coming in. So they caught an earlier flight. You didn't get the message?"

Lorraine adjusted her hairnet. "I haven't checked my e-mail this morning. I've been too busy in the kitchen."

"One of the federal marshals called just before I met with Hugo. The plane's already landed in Anchorage." Because of the amount of security required to move the high-profile killers they often received, arrivals were always a big deal. The entire on-site staff was alerted . . . just in case — although Lorraine's presence wasn't as high a priority as the warden, the COs and the mental health team. The last thing they needed was for someone to make a careless mistake that would result in an escape or injury. As the first institution of its kind, Hanover House was perceived to be a radical new approach to the psychopathy problem, which meant they had to prove themselves professional and effective or risk losing the public support they'd worked so hard to achieve. Just because Hilltop hadn't mounted much resistance to having a maximum-security mental facility built on the outskirts of town — nothing like the other locations the government considered — didn't mean they wouldn't rally at the prodding of an inciting event. For the most part, the locals who weren't working at the center seemed to be reserving judgment, but they weren't welcoming her or her brainchild with open arms, especially Amarok, the handsome Alaska State Trooper who was about the town's only police presence.

"What do we know about Garza?" Lorraine asked.

That question made Evelyn uncomfortable. The inmates at Hanover House were hand selected for the type of crimes they'd committed and the behavior they exhibited. That was one of the details that made their institution unique, besides the friendly name ("House" instead of "Prison") and the focus on research and treatment as opposed to simple incarceration. But Evelyn had chosen Garza because he was so difficult to handle. Had the team been asked to weigh in on some of the details, as they probably should've been, they would've rejected him on the grounds that he was too antagonistic to be considered for their program. Not only had he attacked every cellmate he'd ever had; a year ago he'd nearly killed a guard.

But Evelyn thought that anger, that level of hatred and vocal interaction, might bring insights they'd been missing so far.

"We know he killed the first three of his four wives. That he's egocentric, feels no real human attachment, has delusions of grandeur and lies like a rug." She straightened her blotter. "He also has a penchant

28

for self-mutilation, but that's another thing."

"How'd he murder his wives?" Lorraine's expression suggested she didn't really care to know but had to ask.

His file lay on the corner of the desk. Evelyn had read the documents inside it several times. She slid it over and flipped through the pages as she spoke. "He didn't do anything uniquely gruesome. Knocked them out with a hammer before setting the bed on fire."

"He did that to all three?"

When she came to a picture of the burned remnants of a mobile home, Evelyn paused. She hated to imagine what'd happened to the poor woman who'd been inside, but couldn't stop the heartbreaking images that flashed before her mind's eye. "Yes."

"He wasn't afraid *three* fires would raise his chances of being caught?"

Evelyn managed a shrug as she closed the file. She had to keep some distance between her emotions and what she encountered every day or she would never survive this job. Even if she couldn't maintain that separation, she faked it. Otherwise her colleagues would be all over her — cautioning her, giving advice, telling her she was taking the job too seriously. What she didn't understand was how they could take the men and issues they dealt with any less seriously, how they could look at their jobs as just a nine-to-five grind. "He killed each one in a different state, and he nearly got away with it. Was only tried two years ago, five years after the death of the last woman. By then, he was separated from his fourth wife. I guess he found something that worked and stuck with it."

Lorraine made a clicking sound with her tongue. "Amazing that these cases aren't connected sooner. What about the last wife? Why didn't he kill her?"

"Courtney Lofland? I have no idea." Evelyn set the file aside. "She's remarried and living in Kansas."

"Lucky girl. I bet you'd love to talk to her, see what she has to say about Garza's behavior."

"I've already sent a letter," Evelyn said with a smile.

Lorraine shook her head. "I should've known. With you, no stone goes unturned."

Evelyn ignored the reference to her diligence because she knew the compulsion she felt had turned to obsession long ago. "If she agrees to be interviewed, I'll fly out there and meet her."

"And get away from all this?" Lorraine spread her arms to indicate the sprawling two-story complex, of which Evelyn's office comprised only a small part of the third wing.

Outside, snow was falling so heavily Evelyn could no longer make out the Chugach Mountains. They'd had sixty inches since she arrived in September, and it was only January 13. "It'd be nice to feel the sun, warm up," she admitted.

"I wish I could go with you. I haven't been much farther from home than the prison."

Evelyn pulled her gaze from the window. "You'd have to fight off the mental health team first. They'd all love to return to the Lower Forty-eight." Homesickness was what had driven Martin Brand back to Portland, where he was from. It wasn't easy adjusting to such a hostile environment. The echoing halls, clanging doors, occasional moans and crazy-sounding laughter were hard enough to cope with. Add to those realities the long, dark winter and lonely evenings spent with more files and psychology journals than people, and the memories of countless conversations filled with blood-curdling details, and saying life here was harsh went well beyond the weather.

"Will you take one of them along?" Lorraine asked.

Evelyn shook her head. "We don't have

the funds. I'll be lucky if the Bureau of Prisons approves *my* ticket."

"So who'll be working with Mr. Garza?"

"Who do you think?"

"Not you — you're already juggling a lot more than the others. As it is you don't get time to think about anything besides your patients."

Evelyn offered her a rueful smile. "Maybe you haven't noticed, but there's not a lot to do in Hilltop besides work, especially this time of year."

"You could get a social life."

"Which would include . . . what? Drinking at the Moosehead?"

"Why not?"

Evelyn had gone there once last summer, before Hanover House even opened. Amarok had taken her. She'd had a good time, but she tried not to think about that.

"You never know what kind of guy you might meet," Lorraine added by way of enticement.

She rolled her eyes. "Truer words were never spoken."

"I meant that you might run into someone fun and interesting, not dangerous."

Like Amarok. Surely Lorraine had heard the rumors about them. Or maybe not. As with so many other members of the staff, she lived in Anchorage and commuted to work. Didn't socialize with the locals. "There are no guarantees."

"Glenn would go with you."

Glenn Whitcomb, one of the COs, had taken it upon himself to look after the both of them, as well as some of the other women who worked at Hanover House. When he could, he walked them out of the prison, carried anything that was heavy or helped scrape the snow off their cars. "Glenn faces the same drive you do," she said. "He doesn't need to be staying here in Hilltop any later than his work requires."

"Why not? What's he got to go home to? His married sister? He needs to find a mate, too."

"He'll meet someone eventually." Regardless, she couldn't become any friendlier with him. She could sense how much he admired her, had to be careful. Getting too chummy with a guard wasn't professional and could undermine her authority at HH.

"Come on," Lorraine said. "You have to overcome the past at some point."

She was spitting Evelyn's own words back at her. "I've made peace with my past. I'm happy as I am," she responded, but she knew she bore more scars than the one on her neck. After the attack, she'd spent nearly a decade in therapy.

"You'd rather be single for the rest of your life?" Lorraine asked.

Suddenly realizing that she was hungry, Evelyn pulled the carrots out of the sack. Maybe if she ate something she'd get her second wind. "I don't need a man. I've filled my life with other things."

"Psychopaths?"

"A *purpose,*" she said, tearing open the plastic. "And to fulfill that purpose, I can fit one more inmate into my schedule."

Lorraine tsked. "You're pushing too hard. Driving yourself right over the edge."

"I appreciate the warning — and the lunch," she said. "What would I do without you in all of this? But I'm okay. Really. So . . . did Glenn's uncle get your security alarm installed?"

Lorraine gave her a look that let her know she recognized the deliberate change in subject. She allowed it, however. "Last week. That high-pitched tone that goes off when I open the door about makes me jump out of my skin."

Evelyn chuckled. "You get used to it." She could speak with confidence, because Glenn's uncle had also installed one in her house. She found the sound quite comforting.

"I guess it's a wise thing to have."

"It is." Especially because Lorraine's husband had moved out six months ago and she was now living alone. Evelyn thought it might provide her with some peace of mind — once she became accustomed to how it worked.

"I'd better get back downstairs before all hell breaks loose," Lorraine said. "But I wanted to ask you . . . have you heard anything from Danielle?"

"Connelly? The gal you hired to help in the kitchen? Not yet. Why?"

"She didn't come in this morning."

"Have you tried calling her house?"

"Of course. Over and over. There's no answer."

"Are you sure she didn't talk to the warden or another member of the team? Maybe she's sick. Maybe she turned off the ringer on her phone so she could get some sleep."

A knock interrupted, right before her assistant, four-foot-nine Penny Singh, poked her head into the room. "Receiving just called. Anthony Garza has arrived."

"Thank you."

"Did you plan to talk to the marshals?" Penny asked.

"Of course." Evelyn felt it was important

to thank the escorts. Sometimes they had warnings or other information to convey. She also made it a habit to meet with every single inmate as soon as he received his jumpsuit and other essentials so she could create his chart, make some initial notes on his attitude and psychological state and whether he was likely to be a problem.

"You'll have to hurry," Penny prodded. "They can't wait. They're worried about missing their flight, are afraid they'll get snowed in."

Evelyn couldn't blame them for being antsy. With the monstrous cold fronts that rolled through Anchorage, getting snowed in was a real possibility — and it could mean they'd be trapped for a week or longer. "I'm coming." She turned to Lorraine. "About Danielle — can you get away long enough to drive by her house?"

"Not during work hours. Not when I'm short staffed. But I'll stop on my way home."

"Perfect. Call me if for some reason she's not there."

Lorraine nodded as Evelyn brushed past. But it wasn't fifteen minutes later that Evelyn forgot Danielle. While the staff in Receiving checked Garza in, she met with the marshals in the warden's conference room. What they had to say about Anthony made her nervous. So she was already on edge when, right after they left, the intermittent honk of the emergency alarm sounded, punching her heart into her throat.

2

I always had a fetish for murder and death.
— DAVID BERKOWITZ, THE SON OF SAM

They'd had to sedate him. That was what the marshals told Evelyn before they left. They said he was so difficult and dangerous, to himself and others, that the only way to get Garza safely from one place to another was to medicate him. A registered nurse at ADX Florence in Colorado, where he'd been incarcerated before, had administered three hundred milligrams of Ryzolt four hours ago. There was a note on his chart.

But the tranquilizer had worn off by the time he arrived at HH. According to the COs in Receiving he'd come in slightly agitated and, despite his chains and cuffs, quickly grown violent, going so far as to head-butt an officer. At that point, someone had sounded the alarm while others wrestled Garza to the ground and replaced his cuffs with a straightjacket, further restricting his range of motion. Now he had four officers flanking him instead of two. They'd just dragged him into the holding cell across from her and had to support him so he wouldn't trip on his ankle chains because he wouldn't settle down. He was raving like a lunatic, threatening to dismember anyone he came into contact with.

"I won't stay in this godforsaken place!" he cried. "You'll all be fucked if you make me. Do you hear?"

"Should we take him to his cell?" It was Officer Whitcomb who asked. He obviously doubted she'd be able to get anything meaningful out of Garza when the man was in such a state, and she had to agree. She'd been about to suggest they take him away and give him a chance to cool off. But the second Mr. Garza realized she was on the other side of the glass, he fell silent and went still.

"Who are you?" His dark eyes shined with anger-induced madness as they riveted, hawk-like, on her.

The first thing she noticed was that those eyes were too close together, his nose was slightly crooked and he had a wide face with almost no chin. A little bit of facial hair or

39

even longer hair on top would've made those things less noticeable. But with his head shaved . . .

Still, she wouldn't call him *ugly* — just average.

Prepared for an unpleasant encounter, should it go that way, Evelyn fixed a placid expression on her face. She couldn't, wouldn't, show this man how unsettled he made her. If he thought he was the first to use intimidation, he was sadly mistaken. Even the sudden reversal in his behavior came as no surprise. Sometimes the men incarcerated at HH reminded her of actors in a play with how quickly and easily they could slip in and out of whatever character suited them best.

"Ah, you're coherent after all," she said. "So what have you been doing, Mr. Garza? Putting us on notice that you're no one to be messed with?"

He didn't answer the question. *"Who are you?"*

She put on the glasses she used to alleviate eyestrain and jotted a note on his chart. *Low frustration tolerance. Possibly disorganized thinker and yet . . . seems more calculating than that. Aggressive when fearful or uncertain or presented with unfamiliar stimuli —*

"Hey! I asked you a question!" He half-dragged the COs along with him so he could shuffle up to the glass.

The guards started to yank him back, to show him that he'd better not get out of control again. No doubt they were angry about before. One of their fellow officers had been shuttled off to Medical nursing a broken nose because of Garza hitting him with his head. But, lowering her clipboard, Evelyn motioned for them to leave him be. She was here to study, not punish. That distinction was important to her own humanity. "I'm your new doctor."

"No, you're my next victim," he said. Then he made kissing noises and smiled, revealing the jagged, broken front teeth he'd gotten from gnawing at the cinder-block wall of his last cell.

Evelyn tried not to let the threats she received trouble her. On the whole, considering how frightening and explicit the inmates could get, she coped with what she heard pretty well. Some threats were to be expected when dealing with the worst criminal element in America. And she could usually understand the behavior, even if understanding didn't equal justification. Many of the men she dealt with attempted to gain control in a world where they had no control by inducing fear in others. That gave them power, to a degree. Or sometimes they threatened her simply because they wanted to be despised if they could no longer be admired, wanted to at least *matter.*

But even after she'd left Hanover House for the day, she couldn't erase the disturbing image of Anthony Garza and his evil smile from her mind. While he might've been showing his displeasure with an unwelcome transfer in the only way he felt he could, she was convinced there was more to his "next victim" comment than a desire to frighten her. Something about him and their brief exchange carried an air of authenticity that confirmed the suspicion she'd had when his file first came across her desk. Maybe he'd killed so many of the women he'd been married to in order to avoid nasty divorces, for revenge because they were planning to leave him or for the small amount of insurance money he stood to gain. But he was, at heart, a lust killer — someone who took human life simply for the pleasure of it.

Which made her wonder if he'd murdered more women than just those three.

She was willing to bet he had —

"You going to pay for that?"

A deep voice jarred her out of her thoughts. She'd been standing at the coffee machine, absently stirring the cup she'd poured several seconds earlier. She wasn't anxious to head back out into the cold. The storm had hit full force, dropping the temperature to twenty below.

But it wasn't the cashier who'd confronted her. It was the Alaska State Trooper she'd briefly dated over the summer — if a couple of meals, one kiss and several telephone calls could constitute "dating." His name was Benjamin Murphy, but the locals called him Sergeant Amarok. He'd told her he'd received that nickname — Inuktitut for "wolf" — in grade school after some bully picked a fight with him. Apparently, he'd won that fight. He looked like he could win just about any fight.

Only twenty-nine, Amarok was wearing a heavy coat that made his shoulders appear even broader than usual and a hat with flaps designed to protect everything but his vivid blue eyes. She could see the rest of his face only because he hadn't bothered to close the part of the hat that covered his jaw and mouth.

Considering the ice crystals caught in his dark beard growth, he looked as if he could use something hot himself, if only she'd get out of the way.

Because things had ended badly between them, she smiled in an attempt to be friendly. "Would you haul me off to jail for stealing a couple of swallows?"

He didn't return her smile. He angled his head toward the blizzard wreaking havoc beyond the cheerful music and bright lights of Quigley's Quick Stop. The storm had hit later than expected, enabling her to delay her departure from Hanover House until nearly nine o'clock. Thanks to a satellite dish she had Internet service, so she could work at home. But a heavy snow like this could, and often did, knock it out. And she didn't really enjoy being there. As comfortable, even fashionable, as her little cabin was, the place was too quiet. It made her feel completely cut off — especially during a blizzard, which could potentially interrupt her phone service, too. There weren't any cell towers out here to provide an alternative. She didn't even own a smartphone anymore; she'd sold hers before moving to the remote outpost of Hilltop.

"Might be tough hauling you anywhere in this," he said.

"Good thing you have a snowplow on your truck." He also had four-wheel-drive, off-

44

road tires, a row bar, a winch and enough emergency supplies to last a week or more in such weather. Police officers in these parts had to be prepared for every eventuality.

He removed his gloves and motioned to his vehicle, which was parked next to her BMW. "*Had* a snowplow. The hydraulic lift went out early this afternoon. A shovel doesn't do me much good if I can't lower it."

She could see that he'd left his truck running. He'd turned off the headlights so they wouldn't shine into the store, but his windshield wipers remained hard at work, swishing in quick time as they struggled to keep up with the swirling snow.

She should've left *her* engine running — wipers, too, she realized. She hadn't been thinking of the practicalities when she stopped for coffee and some cereal for breakfast in the morning; she'd been too caught up in Anthony Garza and what he might have done. Not only that, but it was habit to turn off her car and take the keys. People in Boston didn't leave their vehicles running if they wanted to have a vehicle when they got back.

"That's bad luck," she said.

Seemingly unconcerned about the state of

his dark hair, he took off his hat and scratched his head. He was confident, probably knew he was sinfully attractive regardless of what his hair looked like. Or, after she'd disappointed him so completely, he didn't care what she thought one way or the other.

"It's not bad luck for me," he said. "I get to go home instead of working all night. It's bad luck for everyone else. Without a plow, I can't help clear, which means it'll take Phil that much longer to do it alone." He studied her for a few seconds with an intense expression, one that gave her hope he might show some sign of softening, of forgiving her. But that didn't happen. "You might want to head home before the roads become impassable, in case he hasn't covered that side of town in a while. It won't be a priority, since there's just you and a couple of other folks out that way. He'll plow the more traveled routes first."

Which meant it might already be too late.

She should've built her cabin closer to everyone else. When she'd chosen the location, there hadn't been any snow on the ground. And she hadn't considered how lonely it would be living apart from most of the rest of Hilltop's residents. She hadn't known them so she hadn't thought it would matter. She'd only considered the serenity and the view and the fact that she might want a break from the other doctors.

"Right." She lifted her cup in a salute. "Have a nice evening."

He nodded, then watched her pay for a box of Frosted Mini-Wheats and her coffee. She could feel his eyes boring holes into her back as she ducked her head and stepped into the weather and felt as self-conscious as she always felt these days when she accidentally ran into him.

She was wearing snow boots and a heavy coat, but she'd left her hat at the office. She had a terrible feeling she was going to regret not going back for it when she got behind the wheel and pushed the start button and nothing happened.

"Come on. You're only three years old. And you certainly cost me enough," she muttered to her car, and tried again.

The starter wouldn't so much as turn over. What was wrong? The battery? The alternator? Something else? How could her Beamer have fired up so easily at HH but not now? She hadn't been in the store that long. . . .

With a curse, she smacked the steering wheel and leaned back. The snow covering her windshield left her in complete darkness, except for the dim glow of her instrument panel. And it was so cold. Even out of the wind. Cold and dark. This place was always so damn cold and dark!

Take a deep breath. Calm down. Try again.

She did, but with no better results. Then she really began to worry. It wasn't as if she could call Triple A and wait in the warmth of the store. Triple A didn't have service out here. Why would they? There weren't enough people to make it profitable. But if she didn't get her car started soon, she'd never make it home, not in a storm like this and not with only one plow in operation.

"Damn it!" She was going to have to go back into the store and ask Amarok to help her. But she didn't really want to do that. She remembered his thinly veiled disapproval when she first came to town, his opposition to the institution and his skepticism of her goals, her car — almost everything related to her. He didn't want her bringing a bunch of serial killers to his hometown. He'd all but asked her to stay the hell away. Then they'd started seeing each other and he'd come around, to a point. Until he wanted more than she could give him and everything fell apart.

Squeezing her eyes closed, she pinched the bridge of her nose while she gathered herself together. Then she braced for another blast of icy snow, opened her door — and nearly hit him. The sergeant had already come out. It looked as if he'd been about to knock on her window.

"Sorry!" She had to raise her voice above the howl of the wind. "Didn't mean to —"

"What's wrong?" he broke in, getting right to the point. He didn't want to be out in the storm any longer than he had to be. Evelyn felt the same.

"Car won't start."

"Why not?"

She shouldn't have left the prison without her hat. But by the time she'd realized she'd forgotten it, she'd been too lazy to pass through security again, figured she could survive a quick dash to her car. She was paying for that decision now, just as she was paying for keeping her BMW instead of trading it in for a truck. "The ultimate driving machine" wasn't built for this kind of weather. "Don't know. Started fine at the center."

"Let me try." He waved her out of the driver's seat, but she didn't see how he'd be able to do anything more than what she'd done. Maybe he wanted to hear what happened when he punched the starter button. . . .

The engine made no sound, same as with her.

"Get in the store!" he snapped as he reached for the lever that would open her hood.

Thanks to her gloves, it wasn't easy to hold the hair out of her face, but she tried. "What can you feasibly do in a storm like this?"

"Without more light? Most likely nothing."

"So . . . what if we can't get it started?"

"I'll give you a ride and we'll deal with this tomorrow."

If the storm was even over by then. She could be stuck indefinitely at her house with only Sigmund, her cat, for company.

Just in case that possibility became a reality, she went inside and loaded up on more cold cereal, some cans of soup, cookies, crackers — anything she could find that looked remotely appealing. The cashier, Garrett Boyle, a grisly old widower who lived in the back of the store, raised his scruffy eyebrows when she began emptying his shelves, but stocking up on food made her feel as if she was protecting against the worse.

Amarok came in, stamping snow off his boots, just as Garrett was ringing her up.

"Any luck?" she asked.

Amarok frowned. "No, and I can't tell what's wrong. But I'm not much of a mechanic. I've certainly never worked on a Beamer. You don't see many of them in Hilltop."

She was pretty sure only she and a few of the other doctors drove luxury cars. But she didn't do it to be ostentatious. Her small sedan wasn't even one of the more expensive models. Instead of trading it in, she'd kept it as a security blanket of sorts. By moving here she was giving up every other aspect of the life she'd built in Boston. She hadn't been ready to part with her car, too. The idea of that had felt too final, as if she'd never be able to leave Alaska if she did.

"I hope I can find someone to fix it," she said.

"You will. Tomorrow. Come on, I'll take you home." His gaze dipped to the groceries in her arms, then shifted to all the others piled on the counter. "Don't tell me there's nothing to eat at your house."

"Other than a year's supply of cat food, there's nothing to eat at my house," she said. "As you know, I'm rarely there."

He shook his head. "You don't belong in Alaska."

"Excuse me?" She blinked up at him until

he glanced away.

"Never mind." He lifted a box out of one sack. "At least you bought donuts. Those are pretty imperative in an emergency."

He was playing off his first comment so she wouldn't pursue the "You don't belong in Alaska" statement. "They'd be better than going without," she said.

"I'd have to agree with you there. Let's go." He grabbed the four bags she couldn't carry and toted them to his truck. She followed, letting him break the wind, but her face and ears were numb before she could even get in and close the door. Fortunately, he'd left the heater running along with the engine and wipers.

"Why do you live in this godforsaken place?" she asked.

"I was born here," he said as if she didn't already know. Then he got on his radio. "Phil, this is Amarok. Do you copy?"

"I copy, Sergeant . . . ," came the static-filled response.

"How's the removal going?"

"Not so . . . can't keep . . . on my own."

"Just do your best."

". . . Going . . . long night."

"Listen, Phil, when's the last time you were over by Dr. Talbot's place?"

"Dr. who?"

The radio crackle increased, making it difficult to decipher his words. "Talbot. The woman who runs Hanover House."

Nothing. No response.

"Talbot. Do you copy?"

"Yes, Sarge. Haven't . . . More than I can do . . . But I finished that road that leads to where the other shrinks live up the hill, if that helps."

It didn't, but Amarok didn't say so. "Any chance you can get over her way?"

"Not unless you want . . . people stranded . . . this side of town."

"No. That would only make things worse. Thanks."

". . . keep . . . what I'm doing?"

"Roger that."

Evelyn eyed Amarok as he hung up. "No plow?"

"No plow," he repeated.

"What does that mean?"

"It means we'd be crazy to head over to your place and risk getting stuck in drifts that have to be three or four feet high by now."

She gripped her purse tighter. "You don't think we can get through? Even with chains?"

"I'd rather not try. I wouldn't want to wind up in this all night; would you?"

"Definitely not." He made a good point, but . . . "What else can we do? Head back to Hanover House?"

"The prison is even farther out."

"But I'd have to go all the way to Anchorage to get a motel."

Popping the transmission into reverse, he started to back up. "That's not possible, either. You'll have to stay at my place."

She felt her jaw drop. *"What?"*

He stopped the truck and gestured to the pay phone attached to the side of the building, which she could barely see, thanks to the snow. "This isn't some ploy on my part. If you'd rather get out and call one of your doctor friends, feel free."

With the possible exception of the sixty-three-year-old Stacy, who was sick, she didn't really have any doctor friends. She had professional associates. They were unfailingly polite to each other, but she wouldn't feel comfortable imposing on them. Running a place like Hanover House could get difficult with so many egos involved. She suspected some of her colleagues resented how hard she pushed them and the rest of the staff. It was almost as if they thought she was trying to upstage them when she was merely determined to get results. "I've made a friend who lives between here and Anchorage," she suggested, thinking of Lorraine.

"Closer to here or closer to Anchorage?" He almost had to shout to be heard over the voices that were cutting in and out on the radio, the whir of the heater, the chug of the motor and the wail of the storm.

"Closer to Anchorage," she admitted. *A lot* closer to Anchorage.

His eyebrows slid up. "That's your closest friend?"

She glanced away. "I don't socialize a great deal, which I'm sure comes as no surprise to you."

"By choice," he pointed out.

She let her breath go in a silent sigh. "I'm sorry, Amarok. If you want me to apologize again, I will."

"I'm not asking you to apologize. I'm not asking you for anything. I'm just saying, if a friend in Anchorage is your best alternative, you'll have to stay with me whether you like it or not."

"I'm fine with it, as long as . . . as long as you don't mind."

He didn't try very hard to make her feel welcome, but she supposed she should be happy for what reassurance he offered. "I don't mind. Not if you plan on sharing."

He didn't specify what.

3

I didn't know what made people want to be friends. I didn't know what made people attractive to one another. I didn't know what underlay social interactions.

— TED BUNDY, SERIAL KILLER, RAPIST, KIDNAPPER AND NECROPHILIAC

Evelyn was a little drunk. She suspected Amarok was, too. He sat below her, his back against the couch on which she lay, as they started on a second bottle of Salmonberry Wine, a local favorite. The alcohol had mellowed him and made her talkative, maybe *too* talkative, but she couldn't remember when she'd had a better time, especially with nothing but Led Zeppelin playing in the background, a fire raging in the hearth and a man she barely knew for company. With the storm pummeling the house and flame the only light in Amarok's cabin-like living room, it felt as if they were camping on the very edge of civilization.

"I can't believe we ate all the junk I bought." She groaned, gazing at the candy bar, chips and cookie wrappers strewn on the floor.

"We didn't eat it *all*. We skipped some of the cold cereal and the soup."

"But we must've consumed three thousand calories *each*. Actually, I think *you* consumed twice that much."

He lifted his big shoulders in a shrug. "Saved me from cooking dinner."

She laughed, feared it sounded more like a giggle, and forced herself to stop. When was the last time she'd *giggled*? Maybe never. Unless it was before Jasper Moore revealed his true self. She tended to measure her life that way. Before the attack and after.

"Besides, Makita helped." He whistled to his dog. "Didn't you, boy?"

Amarok's Alaskan malamute, who was dozing by the fire, lifted his head to acknowledge his master, causing the tag on his collar to jingle.

"He'll probably be sick tonight," she mused.

"Nah. He'll take a big dump and be fine."

She shifted on the couch. When they first got home Amarok had provided her with some sweats, but the heat of the fire had caused her to peel them off. Now she was dressed in an Alaska State Trooper T-shirt and a pair of boxers, with a fuzzy throw blanket to cover her bare legs. "Still, we should've opted for a salad. I can already feel the fat clogging my arteries."

He held up his glass and gazed at the liquid inside. "How often do you let yourself eat as many Twinkies as you want?"

"Never."

"So don't worry about it, Doc. You can go back to eating salad and measuring the dressing tomorrow."

She'd essentially come to the same conclusion. It was almost as if she'd left her Hanover House persona in the spare bedroom where she'd hung her suit. For the past couple of hours she'd been talking and laughing and feeling like a regular woman. She'd also been ignoring the fact that she and Amarok had a little history together — and, to her relief, Amarok was doing the same. The escape alone was enough to make her feel drunk. "I don't measure my dressing!"

"You're the measuring type."

She leaned up on her elbow to take another sip of wine. "Meaning what? I'm . . . OCD? Too politically correct? A pain in the ass?" She had colleagues who would agree with him no matter which answer he picked, but he made up his own response.

"Uptight. Smart. Out to set the world on fire."

Diplomatic though his answer was, she didn't get the impression being "out to set the world on fire" made him any less angry with her. She guessed it was just the opposite — part of what frustrated and disappointed him. "And you don't like it."

"You've created a human dump in my backyard. I don't like *that,* and I've never made a secret of it."

"So you're holding a grudge?" she asked, and she hoped he understood she wasn't just talking about their difference of opinion on Hanover House.

"Still trying to decide," he said.

"Well, I think it's time you forgive me."

"How do you know I haven't?"

"You're kidding, right? With the way you scowl at me if you ever happen to see me?"

"Scowl?"

"Yes. You could definitely be a little *friendlier.*"

He brought one leg into his body and rested the hand with the wine on his knee. "And I think *you* could be a little friendlier. The only reason I scowl is because every time I look at you, *really* look at you, your eyes dart away."

"No, they don't."

He drained his glass and leaned forward to pour. "They just did."

That had much more to do with how he affected her on a sexual level, which was why she'd broken things off. She couldn't handle the feelings he evoked, what those feelings made her want. "Stop. You don't like me anymore. That's the problem."

"I don't like what you've done. To my town or to me. It's not the same."

"To *you*? I tried to be honest!"

"You gave me some bullshit about friendship and then you avoided me. You have some sort of idiotic hang-up with my age."

It wasn't idiotic. She was thirty-six and he was only twenty-nine. She was too old for him! She'd mentioned that, too, when she'd told him she didn't want to see him anymore, but that had only been part of it. "Seven years is a lot."

"That's an excuse and you know it."

She narrowed her gaze. "So you're going to treat me like I'm not welcome in Hilltop? Say things like you said at Quigley's?"

He didn't apologize. "You *don't* belong here."

Alaskans even had a name for people like her, who weren't from Alaska and didn't know how to live there. She'd heard it before: cheechak.

"This is my life's work!"

"You don't need to be studying psychopaths. What you suffered when you were sixteen, and then this last summer, has you so frightened of men you can't trust 'em anymore. Why make it worse?"

"I can trust the right people," she said.

"You couldn't trust *me.* That was the problem. I'm a cop, but I'm still a man and, as far as you're concerned, that makes me one of the bad guys."

"So you don't even want to speak when we see each other?"

"You know what I want."

"I can't handle a romantic relationship."

"I think you can. It's time to get past what happened to you."

She wished he had the right of it. Part of her still craved the connection she'd felt with Amarok. She hadn't bailed out because she wasn't interested in him. She'd always wished she'd had some warning where Jasper was concerned and felt it only right to be honest about her own psyche. "Three days of rape and torture leaves a mark that doesn't fade much, not even with time. And last summer, when I was abducted again, that just . . . brought it all back, returned me to the very beginning of the climb." She ran her finger over the raised flesh of the scar on her neck.

"You don't ever regret breaking it off with me?"

There were times she did, but, given her limitations, there were other times she felt relief. She almost expressed how torn she was but knew that wouldn't make things any easier. For his sake, she had to remain decisive. "No, I did the right thing."

He nodded. "Okay, I'll leave it at that."

"Thank you." She'd warned off other men over the years, too, had destroyed every chance she'd ever had to be with anyone who excited her. She justified it by telling herself she was protecting those who might be hurt or disappointed by her limitations. But she knew she was ultimately protecting herself.

Amarok had actually gotten closer to her than any of the others. For a short window, she'd felt like she *could* overcome the past, with his help. But then Jasper resurfaced and . . . As much as she sometimes craved a sexual relationship, especially with Amarok, she just couldn't cope with all that held her back.

She lifted her glass for more wine. If they weren't going to obtain any sexual gratification, she figured they might as well enjoy what they could and keep drinking.

"Why'd he do it?" he asked. "What could a guy possibly get out of torturing you — or anyone else?"

Her mind went back to the first attack. She'd worked so diligently to distance herself from those three days when she was sixteen, but ever since last summer it was harder to put that incident in perspective. Her emotions and her memories were just too close to the surface. "He was a sadist. And a sadist derives sexual pleasure from hurting others."

"That'd be the clinical definition."

"You're looking for more?"

"You *knew* this guy."

She downed the rest of her wine. They'd talked about this before, but the question remained and would remain until her research or someone else's could provide the answer. *Why?* That was what everyone wanted to know — her most of all. "I can't explain on that level, even after all my studies. Not really. That's part of the problem."

"You loved him. You told me that."

"I did. Even worse, I thought he loved me. But he was incapable of true emotion."

He poured for her. "If he wanted to kill you, why didn't he do it in the beginning?

Why bother pretending?"

"Until that point, he'd probably only fantasized about killing. He hadn't actually crossed the line. Besides, it was foreplay. It's the building of excitement that makes the climax so enjoyable."

She hadn't meant to create a double entendre. In her office, she might've said the same thing to almost anyone. But in this setting, it came off totally different.

Luckily, his dog distracted them both by coming over to lick her hand. It was almost as if Makita understood her pain and was offering his sympathy, which made her smile as she scratched under his collar.

Amarok broke the silence. "Last summer, I wanted to ask but didn't . . ."

Assuming it would be another difficult question, she swallowed hard. "What?"

"Had you slept with Jasper before it happened?"

"Yes. He didn't rape me because he couldn't get it any other way." Another reason Jasper's behavior had been such a terrible betrayal. She hadn't withheld anything from him, not her virginity and certainly not her heart.

"That's what I hate most," he said with a grimace.

Feeling cold again, she adjusted the throw

blanket. "I don't follow."

"He took all the things that were meant to be good and twisted them into something painful." He turned toward her, and this time she didn't glance away. She let him study her, risked having him see whatever it was he was hoping to see — as well as what she was afraid he'd figure out: that nothing had really changed, despite their last conversation. She may have pulled away, but he still had the power to arouse her in spite of her fears and scars.

"The only sexual experience you have occurred with someone who purposely destroyed your trust by torturing and raping you for three days," he added in disgust.

Jasper with an electric cord. Jasper wielding a knife. Jasper holding the pillow he'd used to deny her oxygen. The memories flooded Evelyn's mind before she could stop them.

Amarok cursed when he noticed her flinch. "Sorry. I shouldn't have brought it up."

"It's okay."

"I can't help thinking — never mind." He shook his head.

"What?" she prompted.

He hesitated.

"What?" she said again.

"I should've thrown up a roadblock, mounted some resistance to having Hanover House in the area instead of letting the mayor and everyone else who wanted jobs for the community talk me out of fighting your pet project."

"Then we never would've met."

"Exactly."

She winced. "You regret *knowing* me?"

A change came over him, as if he was suddenly taking note of every nuance of her expression and body language. "Not knowing you would make my life easier. I'd be lying if I said the thought of you, of us, didn't cross my mind just about every day." He tipped his glass her way. "More than once. So yeah, I guess I wish we'd never met. Then I wouldn't know what I was missing."

She hated that he felt that way, had never wanted to negatively impact his life. "Well, maybe you'll get rid of me sooner than you think. Tonight, when my car wouldn't start I was tempted to make my plane reservations back to Boston."

"Your parents would like that."

So would her sister; they all wanted her to come home. But she wouldn't, not until Hanover House was thriving and she had someone else who was equally committed to what she'd created ready to take over. After what Jasper had done, she was in it for the long haul.

Amarok poured himself another drink. "And when you leave, we'll be stuck with what you created: Hundreds of psychopaths living within a few miles of all we hold dear."

"Those psychopaths have to be held somewhere."

"They didn't have to be held here."

"Some claim psychopathy is on the rise, Amarok. According to the statistics, four percent of the population could be classified with the disorder — that's one in twenty-five! With numbers like those, chances are most of us will run into at least one in our lifetime."

"Having Hanover House in Hilltop might guarantee it for the people here."

"Still. It's a step in the right direction. Knowledge is power. Psychopaths make up only twenty percent of our prison population, yet they perform over half of all violent crime. And they are very difficult to detect. That means it's not just *my* problem."

"We haven't had a murder in Hilltop in a decade."

"Considering all the security measures at HH, the community is as safe as ever."

He frowned but didn't answer.

"Anyway, let's not argue. Let's talk about something else."

"Fine. Feel free to change the subject."

"I will."

"To . . ."

"How's your father?" These days his father lived in Anchorage, where he and his new wife exported seafood for a living.

"Doing great."

"And your mother?"

He shrugged.

"She still in Seattle?"

"I guess."

"You don't know?"

"Haven't talked to her."

His mother left his father when he was only two and took his twin brother to Seattle with her. Although Evelyn could see why he might feel as if she'd played favorites when she left him behind, he'd told her it wasn't the abandonment that bothered him as much as the fact that he hadn't known he had a sibling, let alone a twin, until he turned eighteen and received a call from Jason. "When's the last time you heard from her?"

"She called a couple of months ago."

"From Seattle?"

"I couldn't tell you. I didn't pick up."

"And you didn't call back?"

68

"I've been busy."

"You mean you can't forgive her."

"It's not that. She hated Alaska, was miserable here. I can understand why she might leave. Everyone has the right to find their own happiness and all that. I can even understand why she'd think it was fair to take one son and leave the other. But she's been gone for twenty-seven years. And we had no contact until Jason reached out. I don't know her that well, so it makes for an awkward conversation." He yawned, checked his watch and stood. "It's late. We'd better get to bed. If the storm lets up, tomorrow will be a hell of a day."

The way he'd handled her questions about his mother told Evelyn he didn't care to talk about her. "Because of the cleanup?"

"And whatever damage it leaves in its wake."

"What if it doesn't let up?" She almost hoped it wouldn't. She may have told him she didn't want a relationship, but the attraction she felt hadn't gone anywhere. She couldn't say she'd be disappointed by the prospect of spending another day here, with him.

"Then we put everything off until it does."

She finished the last of her wine. "Thanks for taking me in."

He extended a hand to her, and she let him pull her up. "You're a pretty onerous houseguest, but I'm managing. And you did provide dinner." A flash of teeth told her he was smiling, but shadow obscured the finer details of his expression.

He started to let go of her, but she curled her fingers through his, and he hesitated as if her response surprised him. It surprised her, too. She'd indicated she wasn't a good romantic option.

Looking down at their entwined hands, he moved his thumb over her palm in a seductive circle. "You realize you're giving me conflicting signals."

"I do," she said, but couldn't seem to let go. Despite how she'd discouraged him in the past, she was suddenly burning with the desire to be touched by him.

He stared into her eyes for several seconds. Then he bent his head and pressed his lips against hers. She could tell he was taking it one second at a time, didn't have a lot of hope she'd allow him to kiss her very thoroughly, but she was pretty sure she felt what any normal woman would feel when being kissed by a man she found so attractive. No fear. No desire to flee. Just a heady euphoria, as if his mouth was twice as intoxicating as the wine.

Was it because she was already drunk? If so, she didn't care. Not if it made this possible.

His lips moved so lightly over hers she found herself leaning into him for something deeper, more satisfying, but he seemed to be holding himself on a very tight leash.

"I like that," she whispered.

Emboldened by the compliment, he parted her lips and touched her tongue with his as if he couldn't quit without a taste. Then he stepped back and let her go. "You've had too much to drink. Let's get you into bed."

A noise woke Evelyn. At first, she thought it had to be the weather. The storm still raged. Huge gusts of wind whistled through the eaves, bending the trees against the house, making just as much racket as before. Ensconced in Amarok's spare bedroom, which smelled like her aunt Dot's attic since it was hardly ever used, she was warm and comfortable enough that she almost rolled over and went back to sleep. But then she heard the whine of a dog and the low murmur of a man and realized that Amarok was up, taking Makita out. She couldn't imagine how much trouble it would be to perform such a routine task living in Alaska,

71

but thanks to the bears and the wolves Makita couldn't go out alone — not at night. The sounds in the hallway indicated Amarok was suiting up, as he would have to, for Makita's five-minute stint in the great outdoors.

Having a dog here required more sacrifice than other places. She empathized as she pictured the sergeant stepping into the cold. Makita was likely feeling the results of the human food they'd let him eat, she realized. But then her thoughts turned to the evening they'd spent together and how much she'd enjoyed it. She hadn't experienced such fulfilling companionship since . . . since she'd been with him last summer, she decided. Amarok was . . .

She wasn't sure how to describe him. His own man. Self-assured. Easy to be around. Calm on a level she could probably never reach. Somehow time with him assuaged the gaping wound in her soul — the one she'd finally accepted as something she'd always have to live with. Essentially, he'd shown her what the cessation of that old pain could feel like.

Then there was his kiss and those few seconds of uncertainty when the contact could've turned into much more. She could still taste him, feel the sensation of his lips moving, firm yet soft, against hers.

Those moments had been exhilarating. So damn exhilarating the memory alone was enough to make her mouth water.

By the time he came back in, Evelyn was lying on her back, wide awake, and staring at the ceiling. She'd slept off the alcohol, but the longing that'd flared up during those hours by the fire hadn't gone anywhere. Having all her faculties restored only made her *more* aware of the sergeant, because there was no false euphoria to distract or mollify her.

Her body was prepared for him. The thought of Amarok's skin moving against hers made her so sensitive she could feel her pulse between her legs. But what about her mind? The emotional damage she'd suffered had been far greater than the physical damage, more lasting, too. She wasn't sure she could muster the amount of trust making love would require. Since Jasper, she'd rarely been tempted to try.

So why now? After she'd told Amarok no last August?

Maybe it was his willingness to let her stay on a cold, snowy night when she couldn't get home. Or the way he'd broken off the kiss when he could've kept going.

He'd admitted to wanting her. But she'd

warned him away. What would he do if she went to him now? Would he play it safe and reject her? Or would he gamble?

Even if he accepted her in his bed, being able to have sex again wouldn't miraculously heal her. She had no delusions about that. It would, however, be a small step forward, one her therapist had encouraged her to take years ago.

Dared she be so bold? What would happen if she initiated contact but couldn't go through with it?

She'd ruin what small recovery they'd made in their friendship tonight.

Maybe she should settle for that one kiss. Wait and see if a deeper, more intimate relationship developed over time.

But it'd already been twenty *years* since she'd been with a man. She was usually so guarded no one could get through her defenses. Amarok had tried once and been rebuffed.

She thought of her suit hanging in the closet. In the light of day, when she returned to her normal self and her normal job, those inhibitors might snap back into place. Then what could've been would never be.

Amarok went into the bathroom. The toilet flushed and the floor in the hall creaked beneath his step. He was heading back to bed. If she didn't act right away, it'd be too late.

4

Every man to his own tastes. Mine is for corpses.

— HENRI BLOT, PARIS'S SLEEPY
NECROPHILIAC

The moment she touched his bare back, Amarok froze. Evelyn was certain he'd heard her approach, that the whine of her door as she opened it had given away her presence and her proximity, because he didn't seem startled. He did, however, seem unsure of how he wanted to respond to this little meeting in the middle of the night.

"You warm enough?" he asked without turning.

"Yes."

"Then why are your fingers so cold?"

She dropped her hand in case they were also uncomfortable or unwelcome on his skin. "I guess I'm nervous."

She hadn't imagined this being quite so

awkward. Not after last summer and that memorable kiss tonight. But without the help of alcohol they had nothing to smooth over the damage she'd done.

Fear that he might reject her, if only to give her a taste of her own medicine, made her wonder why she'd left her bed. It was completely out of character for her to be so forward. She honestly didn't know him that well, had stopped what had started between them almost as soon as it'd begun. Yet she couldn't bring her feet to carry her back to her own room. She wanted him whether it was awkward or not, whether he was too young for her or not, whether it would be difficult or embarrassing when she ran into him after tomorrow.

Finally, he swung around. She couldn't see him in the dark hallway, but she could tell where he was and which direction he was facing by his voice when he said, "I didn't mean to wake you."

How should she respond? She had no idea. Didn't he know what she wanted? Couldn't he guess?

Of course. Which meant he must not be interested, or he would've given her some indication. "Is that a no?"

She heard him sigh, then rub the beard growth on his face.

"It should be," he said.

"Because of that grudge you're carrying?"

"Because I've never been with anyone who's experienced anything even remotely close to what you have. I don't want to hurt you, don't want to bring back bad memories or do anything else that'll cause you to shut down or lump me together with the bastard who hurt you."

That was a lot of words for him. Obviously, he'd been thinking about the situation, had understood all along what she was offering. "I know you're not him."

"I want more than that."

"More than what?"

"The two of us together — I see it as wild and a bit out of control. Messy, you know? I want to be able to go with what I feel, to trust my natural impulses. It can't be good if I'm second-guessing my every move. No one would enjoy that."

"Of course." She felt silly for expecting him to forget that she'd already bailed out on him once. Why would he keep trying with her when he could have a much less complicated woman at the snap of his fingers? Men outnumbered women here two to one, but the sergeant could have his pick of the lot. "That wouldn't be any fun. I understand."

She started to move away, but he caught her arm. "No, you don't. I'm not worried about me. I already know what good sex is like. I want *you* to feel it, to experience it, to enjoy human intimacy as it should be — not be subjected to some watered-down version where I'm half-afraid to touch you. That would only convince you that you're not missing anything, make you happy to hide behind the defenses you've thrown up."

"And why would you care if that happened?"

"Because you've been robbed of what you should've had and you deserve better. Everyone does."

"So . . ."

"So I'm not interested in having sex with you if you're simply going to suffer through it. Does that make sense?"

She swallowed hard, wished — for the millionth time — that she wasn't damaged in this area. "It does. But . . . I can't make any promises, Amarok. You know this would be my first time since . . . then. I don't know what to expect from my own body. It could get uncomfortable, end badly. You need to be aware of that. You'd be smarter to play it safe." She lowered her voice. "But . . . some risks are worth taking. I guess that's what you have to decide — if this is one of those risks."

When she said that, he stepped close enough that she could feel his breath fan her cheek. "I'm aware of the possible payoff, Dr. Talbot. Hence my dilemma."

Her stomach hardened into a tight ball of energy. "Well? What are you going to choose?"

"Depends."

"On what?"

"Are you ready to spread your legs for me?"

He was testing her, talking dirty to see if it threatened her. It didn't. She liked the guttural tone to his voice, the evidence of his desire, but . . . he hadn't touched her yet. She had no idea how she might react to the weight of his body pressing her into the mattress or some of the other things that could remind her of the ordeal she'd been through.

Standing on tiptoe, she kissed his jawline, his lips. "Just thinking about you makes me wet."

Her voice was so husky she almost didn't recognize it, but she'd spoken the truth, and he seemed to like it. She heard him suck air between his teeth as his hands slid down her arms. "Let's see how wet," he said, and those same hands slipped into the boxers he'd loaned her.

She tensed up when he touched her. She would've thought he'd take it slow. But she got the impression he wasn't about to give her time to think, to reconsider. His mouth covered hers as he slid a finger inside her, and instead of fighting him, instead of feeling overwhelmed or defenseless, as she'd feared, she felt as if her bones were melting and was happy to have them do so.

"There you go," he coaxed when her hand guided him deeper. "You can trust me. I won't hurt you, Evelyn."

Tears filled her eyes. She wasn't sure why, because he didn't frighten her; he turned her on. She was breaking through some sort of barrier that'd kept her from the real world. At last, she was back, experiencing everything she'd been missing for twenty years.

"That's . . . good," she breathed. "No, that's *great.*"

The pleasure intensified when he lifted her shirt. "No kidding," he murmured, circling the tip of one breast with his tongue. "You're doing fine. You taste like heaven. And you feel even better."

When he removed her clothes, she wasn't even tempted to resist. She didn't mind

81

when he carried her to the bed, either. He acted as if there were no more decisions to make, no room for reason or fear. And strangely enough, she believed him. His mouth, his hands, were everywhere, suckling, touching, arousing.

"You're too young for me," she said, repeating the thought that was floating out there, somewhere in her mind.

Laughing softly, he used an additional finger. "I'm old enough to give you what you want."

Makita whined every so often. He seemed interested in what was going on. She even felt his wet nose brush her leg once when he got up to investigate. But having the dog as a witness didn't bother Evelyn. She doubted he could see much more than she could, which was nothing. He had to be able to smell them, though. The scent of sex, heady and ripe, seemed to be everywhere. On her. On Amarok. On the bedding.

Sex *was* messy, she thought, gloriously messy. But she didn't care about that, either. Maybe Trooper Murphy was seven years younger, and maybe they had nothing in common, but this was an accomplishment, a release, one of the best moments of her life. And it was happening in remote Alaska, in the place she'd cursed almost every day since coming here.

Amarok didn't seem to notice that his dog had followed them into the room. He was too focused on her, too determined to bring her to climax. This was nothing like what she'd experienced with Jasper — even before the violence, when they were first experimenting. It hadn't been *bad* back then, but there'd been more fumbling than pleasure. Now that she understood how lonely life could be going solo all the time, how close she'd come to shutting off her own sexuality, she valued the sensations pouring through her that much more.

"I'm shaking," she whispered.

"I've noticed," he said.

"But it's a crazy good kind of shaking."

"I can tell." He fed off her excitement, and she fed off his.

"Take me now." If they joined quickly, she'd have less chance of building up any resistance to the idea, less chance of backing out. She wanted to make sure it didn't boil down to that.

He let her strip away the snow pants he'd donned to go outside and removed his own shirt.

The first time his bare chest touched hers, she got butterflies. But then his erection pressed against her stomach and she experienced something else, something akin to fear. She was sure it would ruin everything, but after he put on a condom he didn't roll her beneath him as she expected. He let go of her and shifted onto his back. "I'm ready when you are," he said.

He expected *her* to take charge? Could she do it? Could she go through with it?

Her heart threatened to pound right out of her chest as she straddled him. She could feel his hands gripping her thighs, guiding her, encouraging her. But when his hard shaft brushed her bottom she froze.

"You're almost there," he said. "You've got this."

He didn't act as if he'd press her if she didn't want to continue. That helped. He was being careful to make sure she retained some power in this exchange, some control.

"I want you," she whispered. That was true in spite of the fear, in spite of her sudden resistance.

"Then you know what to do," he said. "Or you can wait. It's your choice. There's no rush."

Did he really think they'd have another opportunity? She had no faith in that. She had to finish this tonight, while she was out of her element. She was *so* close.

But no matter how hard she tried, she

couldn't make herself take him inside her. A sudden rush of panic paralyzed her as quickly as a shot of succinylcholine chloride.

"Amarok?" she choked out his name as if he could help her, but she wasn't sure what he could do. Encouraging her would only make things worse. She was already breaking into a cold sweat, felt as if she were somehow outside of her body watching the previous excitement unravel in the most disappointing and humiliating way.

"It's okay," he whispered. "It doesn't have to happen now."

She'd failed. She'd wanted it so badly, but the memories were too much for her. Even if she wasn't thinking of Jasper consciously, even if she was doing everything possible to convince herself there was no connection between what had happened so long ago and what was happening now, there was resistance on such a base level she couldn't overcome it.

Tears rolled down her cheeks as she climbed off him. She wanted to head back to her room, where she could recover alone, but he caught her hand.

"Stay."

"I'm sorry. I knew this could happen —"

"And you warned me. It's fine. We'll sleep. Come here." He coaxed her into lying down. Then he pulled her up against him. "You're okay." He spoke in measured tones, as if he was talking her down off a cliff or handling a spooked animal. She was embarrassed, but the gentleness of his voice and the security of his embrace helped.

Eventually, the panic ebbed and she could breathe normally again. She wanted to thank him for his understanding and patience. This had to have been the worst sexual experience of his life. She hated being responsible for it. But by the time she could speak without breaking into tears, which she definitely didn't want, he was asleep.

"Sergeant, you there? Sergeant? Please copy. We got a problem here."

Amarok's radio woke them early the next morning. Although they hadn't had intercourse, they were lying tangled in each other and the sheets, with Makita at the foot of the bed, keeping their feet warm.

"Don't tell me it's morning," Amarok mumbled.

Evelyn was just groggy enough not to mind that they were both naked. "Without a clock, how would I know?" It wasn't as if they could judge by the sun creeping around the blinds. This time of year, Hilltop received only about five hours of daylight.

"It *can't* be morning. I just closed my eyes." He curled around her as if he'd doze off regardless, but the radio crackled again.

"Hey." She jiggled his arm, which lay across her middle. "I think someone's trying to reach you."

"Right. I know that." He stretched as he grew more coherent. "What's the storm doing?"

She lifted her head to listen. "I'm guessing it's over. I don't hear anything —"

"Sergeant? Do you copy?"

"— except your radio."

"Shit," he said, and yawned.

"Sergeant, it's Shorty. Come back."

She leaned up on her elbows. Shorty owned the Moosehead. He was also a Public Safety Officer, during the summer. "You planning to answer?"

He shoved his head under a pillow. "Haven't decided yet."

The pillow muffled his words, but she picked up most of them. "He sounds desperate."

"Yeah. That's why I'm hesitant," he said, but he tossed the pillow aside and got up.

Once he managed to extract himself from the bed, he didn't stop to dress. He strode into the living room, where she heard him

87

respond. "This is Sergeant Amarok. What's up?"

"Um . . . not sure, Sergeant. But . . . I think you'd better get down here."

The emergency in Shorty's voice caused Evelyn to sit up.

"Where's here?" Amarok asked.

"The Moosehead."

"What's wrong? Has the snow caved in the roof?"

Evelyn thought that was a good guess, but Shorty denied it.

"No, sir."

"Then what? Spit it out. I'm not in the mood for games."

"This is no game, Sergeant. We found something. I'd tell you what if I could. But . . . I'm afraid to guess. Just come, okay? Come quick."

When Amarok returned to the bedroom he no longer seemed sleepy. He flipped on the light and dressed with an economy of movement that belied his earlier exhaustion.

"What's going on?" Suddenly self-conscious, Evelyn pulled the blankets up to her neck.

"I have no idea. But they'd better not be hauling my ass out in the cold to look at a giant icicle."

"Do you think it could be that innocuous?" Knowing she had 250 of the most dangerous men in America housed not far away, she couldn't help but feel a trickle of anxiety, especially after her odd session with Hugo. Surely nothing had gone wrong at Hanover House.

Shorty had mentioned finding "something" at the Moosehead. That meant this had nothing to do with her.

She hoped.

Amarok nudged his dog out of the way and sat on the bed to put on his boots. "No. But whatever it is, I'll take care of it. Get some rest."

"You'll let me know what's happened, though, won't you?"

"I'll check in as soon as I can."

"Okay." She put some lift in her voice for his benefit. But she couldn't go back to sleep. As soon as he left, she yanked on the sweats he'd given her and tried to use the phone. She wanted to see if everything was okay at the prison. But there was no service. The storm had probably knocked over a pole, just as she'd feared it would.

Glad she had self-replenishing food and water dishes for her cat, since she hadn't been able to make it home, she paced the living room. She assumed the sergeant would return sooner rather than later, but one minute ticked away after another. An hour passed, then an hour and a half.

Evelyn showered, dressed in her suit since it was all she had, and made eggs and coffee — only to sit and watch the clock for another hour after she did the dishes.

"Where the hell is he?" she grumbled. "It's almost noon."

Makita got up and came to her as if she'd been talking to him. "It's okay, boy. He'll be back," she said, but she was growing so damn anxious. What could be keeping him? Had he forgotten she was stranded at his place without a vehicle?

For the first time since Lorraine had been in her office yesterday, Evelyn thought of Danielle Connelly. The new girl was safe, wasn't she? Lorraine would've called if not — providing the phones had been working when she went by.

Taking a deep breath, Evelyn crossed to the front door and peeked out at a white world. Snow was still falling, but gently. She was considering pulling on some gear, taking one of Amarok's flashlights and trying to walk to the trooper post or the Moosehead when she saw the glint of a single headlight and heard the whine of a snowmobile coming down the street. He was home. It had to be him; his closest neighbor lived half a mile away.

"Took you long enough," she grumbled while he parked. As cold as it was, she waited on the stoop, the door closed behind her so she wouldn't let all the heat out of his house.

"What is it?" she called as he waded through the snow covering the walk.

He didn't answer. That bothered her.

What is it? she asked, louder. He looked even better to her now than he had yesterday, but she hated to acknowledge that. She was too humiliated by their aborted attempt to make love.

When he reached her, he opened the door and waved her back through it. "Come on inside."

"Amarok?"

He seemed hard, aloof. The man he'd been before he'd held her through the night. They were back to being almost strangers.

"Is there any way one of the crazy bastards you've got over there at Hanover House could get out?" he asked after yanking off his hat.

You've got. She heard the accusation in that statement but didn't respond to it. "No. Absolutely not. It's a maximum-security mental health facility."

"Which means it houses a lot of dangerous men. You're sure there're no breaches in security? No chance anything could've . . . happened?"

Again she thought of Hugo. *You're not safe. None of us are. . . .* Could he have been right? Again? "Almost positive. Why?"

"You need to make sure everyone's accounted for."

"Take me there and I will, but" — she wet her lips — "first tell me what's going on."

He wiped his face with his sleeve. "Someone's been murdered."

Evelyn's blood ran cold. She must've gone pale, too, because he insisted she sit down. "Who is — er — was it?"

"We don't know yet," he said. "All we found was a woman's head. And it was beaten beyond recognition."

5

We serial killers are your sons, we are your husbands, we are everywhere. And there will be more of your children dead tomorrow.
— TED BUNDY, SERIAL KILLER, RAPIST, KIDNAPPER AND NECROPHILIAC

The man in the bathroom stared down at his hands. He couldn't get the blood out from under his nails. He opened the medicine cabinet, looking for a toothbrush he could use to help with that, when a knock came at the front door.

"Hey!" a male voice called out. "Stan, it's Ian. Open up. I have some scary shit to tell you."

His pulse doubled as he shut the medicine cabinet. What now? He preferred not to be seen in Stan's house. That was the whole reason he'd parked down the street and waded through the snow despite his hurry to get cleaned up.

Someone must've spotted the bathroom light even though he'd been careful to leave the rest of the house dark. . . .

Quickly wiping his hands, he checked the mirror to make sure he'd gotten the blood spatter off his face. There was some more pounding at the door, but he told himself not to panic. Panicking would only get him caught.

"Stan? You on the shitter or what?" Ian yelled. "Open the damn door!"

Grabbing the knife he'd brought with him, he hurried to the front and peered through the peephole. It looked as if Ian was alone, but he couldn't be too careful. In such a small town, it was tough to do anything without notice, especially as an "outsider." Outsiders were watched closely — and one remained an outsider until he'd circulated among these people for a year or more. So it was a major accomplishment that, so far, he'd managed to get away with . . . well, *murder.*

Had he not been so tense, he might've chuckled. For once, that cliché wasn't just an expression.

His luck could always change, however. He was so amped up on adrenaline he was still shaking. Chopping a human body to pieces had that effect on a person. It was a risk for him to encounter anyone; any hint of strange behavior could raise suspicion.

So what was he going to do? Ian seemed determined to get a response. Should he open the door and stab the guy? Or wait to see what he wanted?

When Ian put a key in the lock, there was no more time to think. He opened the door. "What's up?" he asked, keeping the knife ready but out of view as he leaned casually against the frame.

The other man blinked at him. "Whoa! *Who are you?*"

"A friend of Stan's." That was the name Ian had used for the homeowner or tenant, wasn't it? He was pretty sure he'd heard correctly.

"So am I," Ian responded. "I live next door." He tried to peer into the house. "Where *is* Stan?"

How the hell would *he* know? He'd chosen this house out of desperation. The way it was shut up, he'd assumed its occupant was gone for the winter — or at least gone for a while. He'd been relieved when he broke in through the back and found that he didn't have to overpower anyone else, that he'd managed to find shelter from the storm. "Not home."

"So his father hasn't improved?"

He measured the other man in his mind. Should he go for the heart? Or the throat? Which would be quicker? " 'Fraid not."

Confusion created lines in Ian's forehead. "I'm a little stunned to find someone here. Did he say you could stay? Because, if he did, he didn't mention a word of it to me when he asked me to look after the place."

"No, he doesn't know I'm here. Last night the roads were so bad I couldn't get anywhere else. And I knew Stan wouldn't mind if I grabbed some shelter until it passed." He tried to appear confident, as if this weren't anything unusual. At least part of what he said was true — he hadn't been able to use the roads, or he would've been able to wash up at home.

Folks in these parts had to pull together sometimes. That wasn't unusual. . . .

The tension in Ian's body eased. "Oh, of course he wouldn't mind. I almost didn't make it home myself. Where the hell were the plows, right?"

"That's what I kept thinking." Except he'd actually been glad that there didn't seem to be anyone about.

"In a storm like that, a guy's got to do what a guy's got to do. But . . . I don't think I've ever seen you before. . . ."

"Really? I met you down at the Moose-head once — when Stan and I went in for a drink." That was probably the most brazen lie he'd ever told, so he was shocked when it seemed to work. Ian's expression cleared. There was even a hint of chagrin in his voice when he responded.

"Oh. Sorry 'bout that. I was probably too damn drunk to remember."

This was going better than he'd antici-pated, but he kept a tight grip on the knife, just in case. "No worries. What else is there to do in the winter but have a few beers?"

"You said it."

He dipped his head to peer out past Ian, at the sky. "Well, now that the weather has cleared a bit, I'd better get going. . . ."

"You need a lift?"

"No, thanks. My truck's not far." He didn't say exactly where. It was bad enough that Ian had seen *him.* No way did he want Stan's neighbor to have a description of his vehicle, too. "It was easier to park and walk in that mess than to keep driving."

"Of course. But be on the lookout. It sounds as if we've got some trouble in town."

"What kind of trouble?"

"Shorty, down at the Moosehead, just called. Told me someone's been murdered."

He rocked back a little, as if this came as the shock it was expected to be. *"Who?"*

"Some woman who hasn't been identified."

He'd done all he could to make identification difficult. "They catch the guy who did it?" He felt that was the next logical question; it might also shed some light on what he had to watch out for.

"No. But it's got to be one of those ghouls from Hanover House."

"The *psychopaths?*"

"Of course. One of 'em must've gotten out. Who else could it be?"

He shook his head. "I have no idea."

Forever conscious of the trooper at her elbow, Evelyn was careful not to slip on the melted snow others had traipsed in. As they passed through security and hurried down the hall to the elevator, she told herself to calm down, but she couldn't help being apprehensive. She didn't want to be responsible, even by extension, for any kind of violence, most especially such a grisly murder.

No matter what Amarok thought, the chances that anyone at Hanover House was involved had to be very slim. She didn't care what Hugo said. Security here was as tight as any other level 4 facility. And they were prepared for bad weather, had all kinds of backup systems. It wasn't as if they hadn't understood where they were building the institution.

But almost immediately she learned that there *were* some problems. Despite the dorm rooms in the second wing that housed additional COs during the most difficult months, the staff was overtaxed. This was the biggest storm they'd faced since opening and most of them were new at corrections. The officers she and Amarok passed informed her that the added manpower hadn't been enough. Some people had been working for eighteen hours. But, given the fact that their emergency systems had been untried until now, the situation could've been much worse. They'd fine-tune it.

"The roads aren't easy to navigate, but they've been cleared." She mentioned this to Amarok as they made their way to the administration offices even though he'd seen the roads for himself, had been driving on them. She wanted to point out that the prison's beleaguered staff would soon have the replacements they needed.

But he didn't respond. He couldn't seem to stop frowning long enough to speak, and given what'd happened — between them and with the murder — she couldn't blame him.

Dr. Timothy Fitzpatrick was the first to greet them. They encountered him as he stepped out of the administration area. Obviously, he was on his way somewhere, most likely to a session with a prisoner. As soon as he saw her, he opened his mouth as if he had something specific to say but stopped short when he noticed the sergeant.

"Is there a problem?" he asked, glancing between them.

Evelyn breathed a sigh of relief. If there'd been an escape in her absence, Dr. Fitzpatrick would have initiated this conversation much differently. Second to her, he'd had the biggest influence in bringing HH into existence. Without his support and willingness to buy in to her vision — even move to Alaska to help make it a reality — she doubted Hanover House would ever have gotten past the concept phase. "I'm sure you've met Sergeant Amarok, Tim," she said.

"Not formally," Fitzpatrick replied. "But I've seen him around. I've heard of him, too. He's almost a folk hero in Hilltop, isn't he?"

"He's certainly well-liked." She thought Fitzpatrick could take a few lessons from

Amarok on how to win friends and influence people, but she knew he'd be shocked if she said that.

"What brings him to Hanover House?"

Unsure of how much Amarok wanted her to reveal, and assuming he'd fill in if he chose to, she said, "There's been an incident in town."

The fifty-year-old Fitzpatrick shoved his glasses higher on his prominent nose. "What kind of incident?"

"The kind that leads me to believe one of your boys might've gotten out last night," Amarok said. "Or maybe someone disappeared a day or two ago and he hasn't been missed for whatever reason."

"That would be impossible," Fitzpatrick scoffed. "We do a head count morning and night."

Evelyn had indicated as much on the drive over, but Amarok didn't seem to put much store by that.

"A count might make escape unlikely — doesn't make it impossible," the sergeant said.

Despite the work they'd been able to accomplish together, Fitzpatrick's prickliness made him one of Evelyn's least favorite people. The self-importance that rang through his tone didn't seem to endear him to Amarok, either.

"It's not as if we have thousands of inmates here, Sergeant," he said with a grating laugh. "I think we'd be able to tell if someone went missing."

Tall and imposing in an Abraham Lincoln sort of way, Fitzpatrick was used to establishing quick superiority over those around him. His arrogance came from being highly intelligent and knowing it. But Amarok hardly seemed intimidated, and that didn't surprise Evelyn. The men she'd met in Alaska were a breed apart from those in the Lower 48. Because they lived such a rogue existence, they relied almost exclusively on their own opinions — and that was true of no one more than the sergeant.

"Sorry if I'm unwilling to take that on faith, Dr." — Amarok's eyes flicked to the nameplate attached to his lab coat — "Fitzpatrick. You have two hundred and fifty of the most dangerous felons in the country located in this facility — a facility that is new and untried. For the most part your staff is just as green. Figure in the storm as a distraction and we have to make sure every single inmate is present and accounted for."

"This must be serious." Fitzpatrick adjusted the paperwork on the clipboard he carried. "What type of incident are we talking about? An attack of some kind?"

"Murder." The gravity in Amarok's voice gave that word the proper emphasis.

As expected, Fitzpatrick's face registered surprise. Nothing ever happened in Hilltop. But he quickly rallied. "Who was killed?"

"Don't know yet," Amarok replied.

"Then what are you doing *here*?"

The sergeant's eyes narrowed. "I have people working on identifying the victim. But there are some . . . peculiar challenges that lead me to believe it might take a while." He didn't expound on what those challenges were, and Evelyn didn't jump in to do it for him. "Since there's no way to bring a dead person back to life, I'm trying to make sure we don't overlook the obvious and wind up losing someone else, someone we could have saved by being proactive."

Fitzpatrick gave a little shrug. "Fine. Check whatever you want, but it'll be a waste of time. Where would one of our inmates go even if he could get out? We're in the middle of nowhere."

When he said "nowhere" as if he meant "the biggest hellhole on earth" a muscle jumped in Amarok's cheek, and Evelyn regretted behaving similarly last night, when she'd been frustrated and upset that her car

103

wouldn't start. No wonder the sergeant didn't like Hanover House or those who ran it. Their attitudes were offensive to the locals, as were their very vocal opinions that the places they came from were so much better than Hilltop.

"He means they've all been shipped in and aren't familiar with the area." Evelyn hoped to soften Fitzpatrick's words but knew she'd wasted her breath when Amarok's eyes cut to her.

"I know what he means."

If her fellow doctor realized he was being rude, he didn't apologize. He pressed on in the same condescending manner. "How would an escapee survive the cold, Sergeant?"

"Maybe he didn't," Amarok responded. "Maybe he's as dead as his victim by now. But there's always the chance that he's obtained help and is perfectly alive."

Skepticism etched deep grooves in the older man's forehead. "Who'd help him?"

"A Good Samaritan who thinks they've encountered a lost stranger, for one."

Evelyn's mind immediately reverted to Hugo's words: *Not every killer at Hanover House is locked up.* Was it a strange coincidence that he'd come up with that on the eve of the first murder in Hilltop in over a decade? Or did he really possess pertinent information?

Was there some way he could even be *responsible* for it?

"I don't care what you think," Fitzpatrick was saying. "Whoever you're looking for isn't one of ours. There's no way any of our inmates could get out."

"Maybe they couldn't do it on their own," Amarok responded. "But surely friends, girlfriends and family come to visit."

"Very few," Fitzpatrick replied. "These men don't have much contact with the outside world, not since being sent here."

"What about a staff member?" Amarok asked. "Friendships start. Relationships build."

Fitzpatrick shook his head. "Absolutely not. They know what's at stake."

"Such things have happened before, in other prisons. People act crazy for love. Or money. Or a thrill. Or any number of reasons."

"You need to broaden your search, Sergeant." Fitzpatrick remained unmoved. "The men locked up here aren't the only ones capable of murder."

Amarok came right back at him. "They're the only ones I know who have already proven their capacity."

"You've been very clear about your unhappiness with our presence in your community." As usual, Fitzpatrick enunciated every syllable perfectly. "You don't want us here. But you won't be able to blame what happened on Hanover House."

This wasn't going anywhere. Evelyn jumped in before the animosity could get worse. "We'll order another count. That's all there is to it."

Fitzpatrick's attention slid over to her. "Sure, accommodate him. Why not? We have nothing to worry about." He stalked off, but Evelyn called after him.

"Everything else okay?"

"Of course." The way his gaze riveted on the sergeant made it clear that his next words were intended for him. "Hanover House has been running like a top since the day we opened."

The hostility apparent in Amarok's body language made Evelyn wonder what she'd been thinking when she'd slipped out of her room last night. Maybe he was as attractive as sin, but they were worlds apart in every other way. He didn't believe in what she did, didn't even want Hanover House in the area.

"Please excuse Dr. Fitzpatrick," she said when he was gone. "It hasn't been easy to

106

establish HH. He's understandably defensive of what we've created."

"He's a pompous asshole," Amarok muttered.

Evelyn feared he viewed her the same way — or that the other locals did. She, too, was a cheechak. Ignoring his derogatory comment, she motioned him toward her office.

Along with the other doctors' assistants, Penny had a cubicle in the reception area. She couldn't speak to them because she was on the phone, but she waved. As Evelyn waved back, she wondered if her assistant noticed that she was wearing the same outfit she'd had on yesterday and couldn't help feeling as if the lack of fresh clothes somehow advertised the fact that she'd gotten intimate with Amarok.

Regardless of what her guilty conscience suggested, she had bigger things to worry about than a random, once-in-a-lifetime close-but-no-cigar hookup with a younger man, even if he was an important official in Hilltop and someone she was likely to bump into time and again.

"I'll call the warden and have him order a count." She straightened one of the chairs across from her desk. "Take a seat. We'll have an answer in no time."

Amarok didn't do as she suggested. He

prowled around her office, making her even more nervous.

"Is this Brianne?"

Finished dialing, she looked up to see him holding a photograph of her and her younger sister. "Yes. She and I went to Italy when I finished my undergraduate work."

"What part?"

"Rome, Florence, Venice, Milan and Tuscany."

"Just the two of you?"

"Yes." Out of the corner of her eye, she spotted a note on her desk. Judging by the chicken scratch, Fitzpatrick had left it. *What the hell is going on with Anthony Garza? Are you crazy? Why didn't you fully explain his history?*

That must've been what her colleague had been looking to discuss with her when they bumped into him. But it wasn't Garza who concerned her right now. It was getting the warden to do a count. And figuring out how Hugo could've predicted something like this.

She wasn't getting a response on the phone, so she expanded on her answer to Amarok. "We spent two weeks there. It was fabulous. Have you been?"

"No." He didn't elaborate, which led her to believe he'd never left Alaska.

Crumpling Fitzpatrick's note, she tossed it in the wastebasket. For some reason, Warden Ferris wasn't picking up, and she was hesitant to use the radio for this.

"You went to Harvard, right?"

She didn't remember ever talking about her education with Amarok. They hadn't spent that much time together. And she didn't care to discuss it now. She was afraid she might sound snobbish, especially after the superior way Fitzpatrick had behaved. But refusing to answer would make her education even more of an issue. "Yes."

"Thought so." He whistled. "An Ivy Leaguer."

Did she detect a trace of sarcasm? "My parents were big on education." She hung up and tried the warden again.

"They must've been wealthy, too, to afford a school like that." Amarok arched an eyebrow. "Or did you put yourself through?"

"I helped, but they paid for the bulk of it. I'd say they're . . . affluent but not necessarily *wealthy.*"

He chuckled as he returned the picture to its place on her credenza. "There's a difference?"

"It's subtle." Where the heck was Ferris?

"I'm amazed that, after the attack, you were able to pull yourself together enough to concentrate on your studies."

His words made her self-conscious about last night. Although he'd been patient, he couldn't have been pleased with the way their encounter had turned out. "Getting past the attack wasn't easy. But the curriculum challenged my mind and kept me occupied. Gave me a purpose, a way to fight back. That helped."

"You wanted to climb inside the mind of the guy who attacked you."

"The *boy*." She was about to pick up the radio when she finally heard a hello. It wasn't the warden who'd answered. Her call had finally been routed to Dede, his administrative assistant. But at least Evelyn had someone on the line.

When Evelyn made it clear what she needed, Dede put her on hold long enough to track down Ferris.

"Something wrong?" the warden asked when she eventually made contact.

She told him about the murder in town. He told her that no one at Hanover House could've gotten outside the walls. And she felt reassured but told him to count, anyway.

"No problem," he responded. "Give me fifteen minutes."

The silence stretched while they waited. Having lost interest in the limited number of personal belongings she had in her office, Amarok crossed to stand at the window. "How do you do it?"

She perched on the edge of her chair. "Do what?"

"Deal with the kind of scum you deal with day in and day out?"

"You already know. I'm looking for answers. Not only for me, for other victims."

He grimaced. "There's no way to explain crazy."

"These men aren't crazy. They're narcissists who exhibit anti-social behavior. Some do so in extreme ways, but they're legally and psychologically sane."

"Anyone who can murder someone and hack that person into pieces — like what I saw this morning — is insane as far as I'm concerned."

She folded her hands in her lap. "Conscienceless, yes. But I'm not studying psychotics. These aren't people who hear voices that tell them to kill or don't know the difference between good and evil. They simply have no real understanding of emotion, can't truly connect with other humans. They do whatever benefits them, whatever interests them, and they feel perfectly justified. The real problem is that psychopaths are more common than most people think."

"You already told me — they make up four percent of the population. But I'm having a hard time believing it. That'd be a hell of a lot of serial killers."

"Fortunately, not every psychopath is a serial killer. Some are subclinical, meaning they don't break the law. They don't worry too much about what is ethical, however. They are liars and manipulators, often wife abusers, bullies and cheats if not swindlers, robbers and rapists. They all leave pain and anguish in their wake. It's a complex problem; there's so much yet to learn."

"And you think facing your past every single day is the only way to solve the problem?"

She'd had critics challenge her choices before. Heck, *Amarok* had challenged her before. "Who else would be more dedicated? More driven? Besides, in my opinion, it's always better to face your fears."

"Even though you're putting yourself in harm's way."

According to the clock on her wall, it'd been ten minutes since she'd spoken to the warden. But she was already antsy. Now that she was in her own environment, she wasn't sure she cared to deal with the sergeant and his skepticism. He made her react on so many levels. Regardless of the chasm that stood between them now, it was difficult not to think about last night and how powerful and liberating it had felt when they first touched. Already she wanted to try again.

That worried her as much as everything else.

"Someone has to take the job, assume the risk," she said. "It can't always be the next person in line."

"It could be a man."

Attitudes toward women hadn't changed here as much as other places in America. "So you're as sexist as some of the other guys around here?"

"Merely practical. These guys should have to confront someone their own size if they get out of line."

"It's not always about what's practical." She tucked a lock of hair behind her ear that'd fallen from the tie holding the rest back. "Think of the damage Jasper has probably done over the past twenty years. The damage he's probably *still* doing. He's out there . . . somewhere."

"So you're empowering yourself."

She could feel him examining her scar. "If that's how you'd like to look at it."

"How hard are they searching for the bastard?"

"They're doing everything they can. I check in religiously with the detectives back home, to keep prodding. And not just since last summer. I always have. It's been a long time since they've had any solid leads, though."

"What about hiring a private investigator?"

She chuckled humorlessly. "I've hired an army of them over the years. They've never been able to come up with anything solid, either. The one I'm working with now believes Jasper left Boston after the attack last summer and went to Aruba. But he hasn't been able to confirm it."

Pale yellow sunlight limned Amarok's profile as he turned toward her. "Have you tried contacting his parents? They're the ones who helped him get away the first time, aren't they? A boy that young wouldn't have had the resources to disappear on his own."

She believed they had. So did the police. The detective on her case just hadn't been able to prove it. "It always helps to have rich parents. But they wouldn't talk to me before, and they won't talk to me now."

"Would 'rich' fall under 'wealthy' or 'affluent'?"

He was needling her, but she ignored it

and gave him a straight answer. "Wealthy. Wealthier than my parents." She had no doubt Jasper's parents had gotten him out of the country or, at a minimum, out of the state that first night.

It was difficult to tell what Amarok was thinking. He studied her so intently she couldn't help but glance away.

"If you wouldn't mind, I'd like to take a look at your file," he said.

He'd asked her the same thing last summer, and she'd put him off. "Out of general curiosity?" She straightened her desk so she'd have an excuse not to meet his gaze, but he waited until he had her full attention.

"Let's call it professional interest."

"Sorry." She cleared her throat. "I'd rather you not have access."

His eyebrows knitted, showing his displeasure. "Why not?"

"The boy I loved slit my throat and left me for dead. I've never been more vulnerable in my life. That makes the details pretty . . . personal, for lack of a better word." It was the sexual torture that made it extremely private, but she didn't say so. Why raise the level of his curiosity? "It's not something I want random cops going through just for the hell of it."

His jaw hardened. "Is that what I am? A random cop?"

Hardly. She couldn't look at him without remembering last night. But that was the problem. He made her long for things she could never have. That was why she'd backed away after their brief romance last summer, too. "You'd like nothing more than to shut down Hanover House and send us all packing, including me. That doesn't make you my friend."

"You didn't mind being my friend last night. Maybe we didn't have sex, but we came damn close to it. I can still smell you on my fingers."

The heat of a blush warmed her neck. "That was . . . that was an isolated incident."

"It didn't change anything?"

"No. But . . . I appreciate how you handled the . . . situation. It was . . . nice of you."

He winced at her halting words. "Don't thank me for being decent!"

Her phone rang. Eager to put an end to the conversation, she snatched up the handset.

"We've laid eyes on every last inmate," the warden informed her.

"Even Hugo?"

"Were you particularly worried about him?"

She cleared her throat. "No. Never mind. Thanks." Exhausted, Evelyn hung up and dropped her head in her hands. "We're in the clear."

"Glad to hear it." As Amarok turned to go, he nearly collided with Penny, who appeared in the doorway.

"Dr. Talbot?"

"Yes?"

Her assistant glanced at the trooper, blushed and smiled. Then she couldn't seem to quit looking at him even though she wasn't speaking to him. "The kitchen just called. They need some help down there."

"What do you mean?" The warden ran the prison. Evelyn, with Fitzpatrick second in command, ran the mental health team and managed all the studies. Although the mental health team often collaborated with those who ran the prison side of the institution — had helped with the initial staffing of HH and often consulted on how to respond to various problem inmates — this was something the warden would ordinarily handle. Was he unavailable again?

She'd just talked to him. . . .

"They're in a mess without Lorraine. They called to see if you know whether or not she's coming in."

Evelyn rose to her feet. "She's not here?"

"Not yet."

"How did anyone get breakfast — or lunch, for that matter?"

"We called in Kathy Olsen and Patrick Bolen. They managed without her, but they've been running all morning and can't keep up."

"What about the new girl, Danielle Connelly? She's not here to help?"

"I guess not."

A cold unease spread through Evelyn. "Have you tried calling to see where Lorraine is?" The question felt like an echo. She'd asked Lorraine the same thing about Danielle yesterday and had never learned what'd kept the girl from work. . . .

"The phones are still out. We can only call internally."

That meant Lorraine could be snowed in. Or be sick and unable to let them know. But, storm or no storm, it seemed odd that Danielle hadn't shown up for two days in a row.

The concern on Amarok's face indicated he'd taken note of the fact that they had a couple of people missing. Evelyn guessed he was thinking what she was thinking: What if Hanover House had supplied the victim instead of the perpetrator?

The possibility that they'd lost Lorraine,

or Danielle, particularly in such a horrible way, made Evelyn's heart race. Her first impulse was to track Danielle down, then drive to Anchorage to check on Lorraine. If the BMW wouldn't start, she'd get the sergeant or someone else to take her.

But what if she couldn't find one or both women? Absence didn't necessarily equate with death. They could've stayed over with someone last night like she did. . . .

The best way to figure out whether the victim was one of her employees wasn't to spend hours searching. Not when there was a far more efficient method available to her.

As repulsive as it sounded, she had to take a look at the severed head.

6

I actually think I may be possessed with demons, I was dropped on my head as a kid.
— DENNIS LYNN RADER, BTK KILLER

Dr. Evelyn Talbot had caught Amarok's eye — and his full attention — the moment she started coming to town. She was a beautiful woman. But she was also someone who wouldn't last long in a place like this. Other than her work, which kept her in constant danger and served as a perpetual reminder of the trauma she'd suffered, there wasn't anything in Hilltop to hold her. He'd always believed she'd stay, at most, five years before heading back to warmer climes.

Now that they'd had such a violent murder and she didn't have the usual army of police and detectives to rely on, he thought she might go back a lot sooner.

Noticing a light sheen of sweat on her upper lip, he adjusted the heat even though he wasn't sure there was any correlation. She was sweating because she was nervous. Her silence said as much.

"You okay?" he asked as he drove.

She continued to stare at the road ahead but nodded.

"You should take that off." He gestured at the coat she had buttoned up to her neck.

"I'm fine."

"I need to warn you about what you're going to see. It won't be easy."

"I've seen dead people before."

That was true. She'd seen her friends. Jasper had attacked and killed three other girls before dragging Evelyn off to an abandoned shack — not that Amarok knew exactly how that had all played out. They hadn't discussed it — he wasn't sure she could — and he'd been only nine years old when those murders occurred. He didn't remember what was reported at the time, and the articles he'd looked up once he learned a psychiatrist who'd once been a victim of a brutal assault was coming to town and bringing a bunch of psychopaths with her didn't include the level of detail he was searching for. Even the anchors who had hosted Evelyn on TV during her big push to build Hanover House provided only a short biographical summary.

He wanted to delve deeper. The more interested he became in her, the more he craved all the answers. But he didn't have them yet. The only thing he could say for sure was how deeply the past had affected her. He'd felt it come between them last summer — and then again last night. That meant her medical training and experience in corrections might not amount to shit when it came to this. Being confronted with a severed head, especially one that had been abused to such a degree, would disturb *anyone.*

"You're white as a sheet," he said. "And we're not even there yet." Not only that, she was sitting so rigidly it looked as if the slightest bump might cause her to shatter.

"I'll be okay."

It sounded as if she was trying to convince herself, not him. But he had to trust her to handle what lay ahead. She could possibly identify the victim.

"Where is . . . where is what you found?" she asked as they arrived at the outskirts of town.

That she couldn't bring herself to be specific made him glance over again. "In the back of Shorty's SUV. He agreed to deliver it to the State Medical Examiner in

Anchorage for me. But I radioed him. He's coming back to meet us."

She tapped her fingers on the armrest attached to the door. "So we'll meet him somewhere?"

"At my trooper post."

Silence.

"We'll just take a quick peek out in front." He didn't want her to think they'd be carrying the body bag into the office. Peering into Shorty's SUV would be gruesome enough.

Again, she made no comment.

He lowered his visor to keep the sun from reflecting off the snow. The storm had moved on almost as quickly as it had hit, but the weather could worsen at any time, obliterating any evidence the killer might've left behind and making it impossible to find the rest of the victim — if they had any chance of doing that in the first place.

When they passed The Dinky Diner, Amarok's stomach rumbled. He hadn't eaten. But he couldn't take the time to stop. "How well do you know the woman who runs the kitchen at Hanover House?"

"I let her stay with me for a couple of weeks in October when she and her husband were splitting up. She was" — her voice broke, but she gained control — "sort of like a second mother to me."

"She's not the one you were thinking of staying with last night. . . ."

"Yes." The word, when she uttered it, was barely audible.

"And Danielle?"

"I don't know her as well. She moved to Alaska a few months ago to pursue a relationship that began online, but . . . it didn't work out. I don't think she's planning on staying long-term. If only for the money, she'd leave right away."

"You hired her knowing she was a short-timer?" He hoped a bit of small talk might put Evelyn at ease, but it seemed to have no effect.

"Her job didn't require much training. Lorraine talked the warden into it. She was like that, always took in strays."

Edging to the far right of the road, he slowed to allow a car coming from the opposite direction to squeeze past. "Danielle's been missing since yesterday?"

"I don't know that she's *missing*. She didn't come to work. Lorraine was going to check on her. That's all I can tell you."

"What does Danielle look like?"

"Long dark hair. Dark eyes. Young. Pretty."

A girl fitting that description had been

drinking at the Moosehead last weekend. He remembered because she'd hit on him several times. "And Lorraine?"

"Short hair, dyed a reddish brown."

He bit back a curse. "Was she middle-aged?"

When Evelyn winced but nodded, he turned down the radio. "Listen. . . ."

The hollow misery in her eyes gave him a front row seat to her suffering. "What?"

He tightened his grip on the steering wheel. Damn it, this . . . shit, this violent shit, was what he'd hoped to avoid when he'd tried to rally the citizens of Hilltop to fight the construction of a maximum-security prison so close to their homes and families. If not for the silver-tongued mayor, Amarok wouldn't have backed down. Then this never would've happened. He felt certain of it. Not here.

Evelyn wouldn't have come to town, either. But that was good, like he'd said last night. Then he wouldn't have started fantasizing about a woman who would only leave him, even if he managed to develop a relationship with her.

"It's not Danielle," he said as gently as he could.

Tears slipped down her cheeks, but he supposed she was still holding out hope,

125

because she didn't succumb to her grief until they reached his post.

When Shorty opened the hatch of his SUV and unzipped the plastic covering what rested inside, she whispered, "Lorraine." She would've sunk to the ground if he hadn't caught her. But she didn't dissolve into a puddle of tears or get sick. She came up kicking and swinging — at the vehicle, the telephone pole beside it, the mounds of icy snow piled at the curb, anything within range.

When he grabbed hold of her to stop her before she could injure herself, she even tried to hit *him.*

"Where could the rest of her be?" Her knuckles were bleeding and her toes were aching, but Evelyn finally felt calm. She stared out at the snow-draped trading post–style buildings that lined Main Street, working to put what she'd seen behind her, while the sergeant drove her to her car. Thanks to the murder, he had a lot yet to do, so Jack Call, who owned a small repair shop one street over, was meeting them at Quigley's to be sure she could get her Beamer started.

Briefly, Amarok studied her before returning his gaze to the road. She guessed he was trying to reconcile the woman who'd wanted

126

to make love to him last night with the crazy person who'd just lost control and wouldn't stop fighting until he hugged her so tightly she couldn't get her arms up or gain enough distance to land an effective kick. "I have no idea," he said. "But I'm hoping that will change. Soon."

So was she.

Seeking consolation in the mundane, Evelyn forced herself to take particular note of the progress the locals had made in getting back to normal life. Hilltop handled the many storms that rolled through so well, so quickly. According to dialogue that'd come through on the sergeant's radio, even the phone lines were back up.

But one thing wasn't the same and never would be. . . .

Evelyn flinched as the image of Lorraine's head, with all its contusions and bruising — and one missing eye — conjured in her mind. That sight would haunt her for the rest of her life, just like the equally gruesome memory of finding Marissa Donovan, and two more friends, covered in blood, stripped naked and erotically posed. After twenty years that vision hadn't faded one bit, and probably never would.

"Shock value," she muttered.

Amarok unzipped his coat. "What'd you say?"

It hurt just to draw breath. She wasn't sure why. "That was what the killer was going for: shock value," she said, louder, more certain. "What's worse than finding a dead body?"

He didn't answer, but she could tell he was listening.

"Finding a body part," she filled in. "And what's worse than stumbling across an arm or a leg?"

"A head," he replied. "I get it. And I'm sure it adds insult to injury to remove one or both eyes."

"Exactly."

"But there was no 'stumbling across' this. The killer put her head on a broom handle and stuck it in the snow at the back door of the only bar in town."

"Because he didn't think he could get away with doing it at the front."

"And if you're right, if he was going for effect, it's a bit more sinister to do it in an alley."

"Very Jack the Ripper–ish," she agreed. "Which arouses a great deal of fear."

When he rubbed his jaw, she guessed he was as tired as she was and felt guilty for keeping him up as long as she had last night. Hilltop, and Lorraine, needed him so badly today.

"You're very familiar with the type of person who would do this," he said.

"I should be." She'd been studying and interviewing killers, serial and otherwise, for over a decade. And that was in addition to her personal experience. Not only had she been victimized by a murderer, she'd also been in love with one, which gave her a much closer look at the behavior and the reality.

"You could be valuable to the investigation — if you stay."

"If I *stay*?"

"Last night, you mentioned buying a ticket home."

"I wasn't completely serious. I've still got a lot of work to do here." Even if she were ready to give up, she wouldn't leave Hilltop without doing everything possible to make sure that whoever killed Lorraine was put behind bars. Maybe Jasper had gotten away with what he'd done to her and her friends. He'd gotten away with what he'd attempted last summer, too. But the individual who'd caused Lorraine's death would not go unpunished.

Amarok's tire chains clanked on patches of heavily salted pavement as he turned into the parking lot where her car sat beneath a foot or two of snow.

Jack was waiting for them in a tow truck with his "Call Me!" logo on the side. A plume of exhaust streamed out of his tailpipe as he let the engine idle. He looked busy with paperwork or maybe a call on the radio.

Evelyn wanted to let the sergeant get on with his work, but she had one more question. "What about Danielle?" she asked. "I can tell you realize what this could mean for her."

When Jack looked up, Amarok waved to let him know they'd seen him. "I'm heading to her place right now to have a look around, make sure she's safe."

"You won't find her."

"How do you know?" he asked with a scowl.

She opened the door and got out. "I can feel it in my gut."

7

Even psychopaths have emotions if you dig deep enough but then again, maybe they don't.
— RICHARD RAMIREZ, THE NIGHT STALKER

Jack got her car started by tightening a few cables and hoses, then giving her battery a jump while she watched from inside the convenience store. After that, Evelyn headed to HH. She was still wearing the clothes she'd had on yesterday and it was late afternoon, but she couldn't go home. She had to talk to Hugo, see if he had any knowledge of the murder or if what he'd said had simply been some bizarre co-incidence. While she was there, she also needed to break the news of Lorraine's murder to everyone who knew her at the prison. Evelyn felt she should be the one, but it wasn't going to be easy. Everyone loved Lorraine, especially Glenn Whitcomb, the CO who tried so hard to look out for her. He'd never really had a mother — had been raised by his older sister since their father died when he was twelve — which was probably why he and Lorraine had become so close. Evelyn couldn't imagine how hard he was going to take her death. . . .

She hoped someone at Hanover House had heard from Danielle. Maybe Danielle was safe. She could've come by the money she needed and left for the Lower 48 without giving notice.

But, in her heart, Evelyn believed otherwise.

By the time she pulled into the parking lot, it was already dark. Earlier the temperature had warmed a few degrees, but the wind had kicked up again since, adding a chill factor that made it colder by the second — so cold that the air itself felt like a thousand needles pricking her eyes, her nostrils, her lips.

At least it wasn't snowing. Evelyn didn't think she could take another storm on the heels of the last one — not while knowing how much it would hinder Amarok's ability to figure out what'd happened to Lorraine and catch her killer.

"You bastards." She glared through her windshield at the giant stone edifice that housed so many remorseless killers. "I will figure out why you do what you do and how to stop you if it kills me." And she knew that someday it might. She'd had a few close calls over the years. Nothing on the scale of what'd happened with Jasper the first time, but there'd been his second abduction as well as other incidents. Like that one at San Quentin with Hugo. She'd also had a felon she'd given a psych evaluation to show up at her house in the middle of the night once. Her neighbors heard the commotion and called the police before anything could happen, but she still didn't know how he'd found her. When asked, he told the police and media that she'd slipped him her address.

She switched off her headlights and, with a sigh, carried her coffee inside. She'd call a meeting with the mental health team before alerting the rest of the staff. Given the fear this would cause in the community, they should develop a unified approach to answering the questions that would arise, maybe put out a press release stating their profound sadness, their support of local law enforcement and their belief in the security of the institution. Also, while she had so many behavioral experts in the same room she planned to discuss the type of killer who could have done this, in case they could come up with some detail or tip that would help Amarok, if not a full psychological profile.

But she couldn't get even a few of her fellow doctors together. Of the six who'd started with her at HH in November, only five remained — four registered forensic psychologists and Dr. Tim Fitzpatrick, who was a psychiatrist like her. Stacy Wilheim, the only other woman on the team, was out sick and probably would be for some time, given how long it took to get over the shingles. Preston Schmidt had called to say he wasn't coming in because of the storm. And Dr. Fitzpatrick, Greg Peters and Russell Jones were conducting an experiment together that tried to determine whether male psychopaths were aroused to a greater or lesser degree by the same stimuli as other men.

Finding the offices deserted reminded Evelyn that she'd broken her own appointments. Storm or no storm, some of her patients would be upset. For the most part, therapy sessions were their only break from the tedium of prison life. But working in corrections meant they simply stayed in their cells instead of meeting with her. No harm done. She'd get back into her routine tomorrow — not that it would ever be the same without Lorraine coming in with lunch or some other snack.

Since there was no possibility of gathering the mental health team for an advance meeting and it was Glenn's day off, Evelyn decided she'd call Glenn, then go ahead and make a general announcement of Lorraine's death.

Should she send a mass e-mail? Or use the PA? She couldn't put it off. If she did, word would spread before she could say anything.

She decided to use the PA, then follow up with an e-mail for those who weren't at the prison. She grabbed the phone to call Glenn but never got the chance to dial. Dr. Fitzpatrick barged into her office, followed closely by Penny, who'd been trying to intercept him.

Evelyn hung up the handset and stood. "It's okay, Penny," she said. "You can shut the door."

Obviously put out that Fitzpatrick hadn't bothered to let her announce him, Penny shot him a sullen glance but did as she was told.

Assuming he'd come to talk about the murder, Evelyn squared her shoulders. She hoped she could tell him what she'd seen and what it might mean without tears. But it wasn't the sergeant's visit he had on his mind.

"I can't believe you!" he railed. "What were you thinking when you arranged to have Anthony Garza transferred here?"

She wasn't prepared to defend herself on this. Not right now. She'd been second-guessing that decision ever since Garza had hurt one of the COs. But she couldn't let the dominating Fitzpatrick know she had doubts. She'd lose the power she worked so hard to protect, which would seriously limit her ability to be effective in this environment. "I was thinking he'd be beneficial to our research. What else?"

"Oh, come on," he said with a sneer. "If that were true, you would've put him forward in our last meeting. Why did we discuss Pop Humphries and Saul Weber and all the others but not Anthony Garza?"

Closing her eyes, she rubbed her temples, then dropped her hands and looked at him again. "Because I didn't want to be shot down."

"Exactly! You knew what we'd say! You knew we'd reject him —"

"He scored a perfect forty on the Hare, Tim."

This was significant, and she knew he'd

have to view it as such. Most people with no criminal background scored a 5 or a 6. Inmates who weren't psychopaths usually scored in the early twenties. Anyone who scored over 30 was officially diagnosed a psychopath. But a perfect 40? That was rare.

Unfortunately, her announcement only set Fitzpatrick back for a moment. "I don't give a shit if he got a perfect score! You had him transferred here without disclosing everything about him. That isn't our policy, Dr. Talbot."

"You would have done the same if there was a certain subject you were looking to study," she said. They each had some discretion — or, at least, that was what she had intended when she initially formed the team. The Bureau of Prisons hadn't created any restrictions.

"No." He shook his head. "I wouldn't have broken the rules."

Because he was the one making them! He'd been busy creating as many policies and procedures as possible. He claimed he wanted the power at HH to be vested in the entire mental health team, but he had so much influence over the other doctors, he was essentially taking control.

"We can learn a lot from him," she insisted.

"Have you heard what he's been doing all day?" he countered.

Did it really matter? At *this* moment? She had to call Glenn, break the news to him, then tell everyone else that Lorraine was dead. With the intensity of the emotions that were flying around, she preferred to fight one battle at a time. "How could I have heard?" she said. "I've been gone." He was more than happy to inform her.

"He's been carving your name in his arm with a sharpened toothbrush. Said he wouldn't quit until you agreed to see him. But you weren't here to take care of the problem you invited into our facility."

"So what did you do?"

"We warned him, several times, but he kept at it until we had to send him to the infirmary. Once he was bandaged up, we put him in a straightjacket to keep him from hurting himself any worse and didn't take it off until just a few minutes before you showed up."

You're my next victim. . . . Remembering Anthony's unnerving, wild-eyed look and the way he'd focused on her, Evelyn felt behind her for her chair. He was a problem. As difficult as it was to face, he was probably a mistake. From the beginning, she'd had a strange feeling about him, a sense of having found what she'd been searching for. But she wouldn't be the first to be blinded by impatience and drive.

Either way, she didn't appreciate Fitzpatrick trying to make her out to be such a renegade when it was only *his* rules she'd flouted. Who'd put him in charge, anyway? No one. Yet he got more demanding and less easy to mollify the longer they were in Alaska.

And today she wasn't in a position to do battle with him. She was more worried about Glenn and how he was going to take the news of Lorraine's death, and Hugo and what he'd tried to tell her yesterday.

"We've had other inmates do similar things," she said. "Nearly forty of our patients are serial killers. They often fixate on us."

"He shouldn't even be here! He could skewer our findings."

"He's a psychopath like the others." She'd had HH built so they could study any psychopath they pleased. . . .

"He has a whole host of other personality disorders, too. You create too complex a cocktail and there's no way to tell which disorder is causing which behavior. We've been over this. I haven't evaluated him, but from what I've seen today, he could even be a little psychotic."

The coffee she'd drunk to keep her going was making her jittery. Breakfast at Amarok's now seemed like a long way off. "He's *not* psychotic. His file intrigued me, okay? I've added him to *my* roster; he shouldn't affect you at all."

He pointed a finger at her. "We're not working in isolation here. We're compiling data on similar subjects, and he's too different."

"Says you! You don't even know that he's too different."

"It's obvious! He has to go back."

"Because I didn't get *your* permission?"

"The team's permission."

"That's bullshit. Anyway, it's not possible for him to go back. Maybe several months down the road, but not now. Transfers cost a fortune, especially a transfer way up here." Even after several months, she doubted ADX Florence would be happy to have him returned. He was so difficult, so disruptive, they'd been eager to let someone else worry about him for a change. The warden had told her he frightened the nurses, the medical staff, even some of the COs.

She could see why. He frightened her, too. Of all the inmates she'd dealt with, Garza was the one who reminded her most of Jasper. Physically, they were opposites — one dark and threatening, the other a preppy all-American boy. But inside . . .

Fitzpatrick shot her a snide look. "That's what you were counting on."

"I never guessed I'd have to rely on it, Tim — never dreamed you'd act as you're acting now."

"You knew I'd reject him. You were trying to force my hand."

"Fine. If that's the way you view it, yes. I have a subject you don't want at HH. So what?"

"You wouldn't even have HH if not for me!"

"I've been very aware of that, which is why you've gotten away with so much. I've been careful not to pull rank on you — out of respect for what you've achieved professionally and out of the gratitude I feel for your support — but I *am* in charge here."

Now that she'd come out swinging, he stepped back and seemed to reconsider pushing her up against that metaphorical wall. "Why is this particular inmate so important you'd risk everything we've accomplished?"

She wasn't risking anything. She was trying to shed more light on the psychopathy problem and that meant studying as many killers as she could.

She located Garza's file in the stack on her desk and handed it over. "See for yourself."

He flipped through the pages but was still frowning when he looked up. "He killed three of his wives to collect on their life insurance policy. What's so damn intriguing about that? In the context of what we deal with, that's nothing. Maybe if he'd skinned them or eaten their eyes for breakfast or —"

"Keep reading," she broke in. "It's the cases he *hasn't* been convicted for that piqued my interest."

He folded his tall, bony frame into a chair and, this time, he read for several long minutes. Then he said, "Detectives in Utah believe he might be the Porn Poser?"

"Yes. You've heard of those crimes?"

"Of course. They received a great deal of media attention five or six years ago."

"There were six deaths in all. The killer has never been caught."

He slid the file onto the corner of her desk. He was calming down, but his anger had only disappeared beneath the surface — since she wouldn't allow him to harangue her without fighting back. "What makes you believe it's Garza?"

"He lived in the area, no more than an

hour from each of the victims. He worked at the ski resort where one of the bodies was found. And the killings stopped once he went to prison."

"That's it?" Sitting forward, his sharp chin jutting out, he slapped his leg for effect. "That could all be coincidence! A lot of people go skiing in the Salt Lake area. What about forensic proof?"

She propped her elbows on the desk and watched him over the steeple of her fingers. "If there was any forensic proof he would've been charged. The lead detective's the one who tipped me off."

"And how did that happen?"

"I called to see if those cases had ever been solved."

Fitzpatrick tapped his foot as he considered her response. "Nothing escapes you."

By the sarcastic way he said that, she decided it wasn't a compliment. "I've dedicated my life to this cause. Why would I be less than thorough?"

"There are other ways to describe your behavior."

"If you're suggesting I'm obsessed, I admit it."

He shook his head as if he was stymied and had nowhere to go with that statement, which had been her intent. "Fine," he retorted. "You suspect Garza's the Porn Poser. What does that mean? Why are you hung up on some unsolved murders in Utah? You're trying to solve murders now in addition to studying psychopaths?"

His smug expression was difficult to tolerate. She clenched her jaw. "It was the way the killer positioned his victims that drew my attention, Tim. Although I've followed this case from the beginning, I was an outsider looking in. It wasn't until recently that the detective gave me any details." Once she'd built up a little bit of credibility. When she'd first contacted Green, she'd been working at her own small treatment center in Boston eight years ago, where she'd gotten her start, and had yet to make a name for herself in psychiatry.

Fitzpatrick pulled a handkerchief from his pocket and blew his beak-like nose. "So what? Why so much interest in the positioning behavior?"

She was surprised he couldn't guess. "Jasper did something similar when he killed my friends."

Shoving the hanky back into his lab coat, he startled her with a bark of laughter. "Oh dear."

Offended by his response, she straightened her spine. "What?"

"You *know* what. You're using everything I've helped you create for your own purposes."

"My own purposes? We're studying psychopathy here, and Anthony Garza is a psychopath. He fits the profile, so I've done nothing wrong. And even if you think I have, I've never made a secret of the fact that I intend to find the psychopath who nearly killed me. That's what enticed me into this field to begin with."

He came to his feet. "But that isn't the understanding we had when we joined forces. Hanover House is supposed to be about something bigger than one person's experience."

She rose to help compensate for his tremendous height advantage. He'd gone outside their initial understanding, too, when he'd cornered her in her office and tried to kiss her one night when they were both working late in December. As far as she was concerned, *his* behavior had been worse, because it had been awkward to work around him ever since, especially when he asked her out a week later as if he could get her to change her mind. "If I have the opportunity to learn from someone who has the same behavioral pattern as Jasper, I'm going to take it."

"But don't you see? It's such a long shot that Jasper and Garza have anything in common. And going about it the way that you did, behind our backs —"

She couldn't argue this anymore. Not when Lorraine's murder made a far greater impact than one more serial killer at HH. "Tim," she interrupted. "Lorraine's dead."

His eyes widened. *"What?"*

"You heard me."

It took several seconds for him to find his voice. "The woman who runs the kitchen? That's why she didn't show up today and we had to call in Kathy Olsen?"

"That's why. She was the murder victim the sergeant came here about."

"He's sure?"

"I'm the one who identified her." She couldn't help but shudder as she described what the killer had done. She'd dealt with the perpetrators of such violence for so long she sometimes felt numb to even the worst atrocities. But not today. Having such a personal connection to the woman who'd been killed removed the professional buffer that protected Evelyn in other cases and brought back all the heartbreak of losing her girlfriends in high school.

"I'm sorry," he said. "I know you were

close to her. Do they have any idea who did it?"

"None," she said dully.

Agitation replaced his earlier pique, and he began to pace. "That's unfortunate. Her murder will shock the whole community, make them suspicious of us, unfriendly —"

His concerns were valid. She'd have to consider them eventually. But Evelyn couldn't bear to hear what the killer's actions would do to HH right now. She hadn't gotten over the shock of what the killer had done to Lorraine. "We'll deal with that later."

The edge to her voice let him know he'd struck a nerve. "Have you told anyone else?" he asked, softening.

"I was just about to call Glenn. He should hear first, since they were so close. Then I'll make the announcement."

"Okay. I'll . . . put together some safety tips. E-mail them to the staff and make them available to the general public."

"Thank you. That will help."

He headed to the door, but she stopped him. "I'm sorry you're unhappy about Anthony Garza, Tim. But I honestly believe he might be valuable to our research."

"I understand that," he said, looking back at her. "I don't agree with your tactics.

147

But . . . somehow we'll make it work."

"I appreciate your flexibility. I really do."

He opened the door.

"One more thing," she said.

Again, he hesitated.

"Can *you* make the announcement about Lorraine? I don't — I don't want to break down on the loudspeaker." Just having the conversation they'd had made her feel perilously close to tears — and she still had to call Lorraine's closest friend at HH.

The sympathy in his eyes gave her a glimpse of Tim the Educated Psychiatrist instead of Tim the Driven, Hard-Headed and Opinionated Pain in the Ass she so loved to hate. "Of course."

"Thank you. Just give me a few minutes to call Glenn."

"Buzz my office when you're ready."

Evelyn breathed a sigh of relief when he was gone only to have a fresh deluge of tension tighten the muscles in her back and neck as she dialed.

"Hello?"

"Glenn, this is Evelyn."

"Oh, hi. What's going on?"

She could hear the surprise in his voice. She typically didn't call him at home. "Do you have a second to talk?"

"Sure. Is everything okay at HH? Are you

148

short staffed or something?"

If he were going to be called in, that call probably wouldn't come from her. But she could see why his mind would go in that direction. "No. This is . . . this is about something else, something terrible."

His mood changed instantly. "Whoa, are you *crying*?"

She sniffed. The harder she tried not to break down, the more the tears came.

"What's wrong?" he asked before she could even answer. "Did we have an incident at the prison? Just tell me what you need, Dr. Talbot. I'll come right away."

"I don't need anything, Glenn. I merely . . . felt like I should . . . tell you that" — she gripped her forehead — "Lorraine's dead."

Silence.

"I'm sorry, Glenn."

"Th-that can't be true," he stuttered when he finally spoke.

"I wish it *weren't*. God, how I wish it weren't, but —"

"What happened?" he broke in. "Was it a car accident? I've been telling her about her tires. The tread's nearly gone. I should've gotten on the phone and found her some new ones myself. Why didn't I do that?"

"It wasn't a car accident."

His voice grew thicker with tears. "What else could it have been? She wasn't sick, was she? She never said anything to me about being sick."

"Someone killed her."

Another shocked silence met this statement. *"Who?"* he cried at length.

"We don't know yet." Evelyn thought about the way Lorraine had been found, but she couldn't bring herself to tell Glenn about that. She figured he could look into the situation a bit more himself. By now the whole town had to be talking about Lorraine's murder. He didn't live in town, probably didn't even know anybody from Hilltop who didn't work at the prison, but whatever happened locally filtered over to Hanover House fairly quickly.

"Could it have been her ex?"

Evelyn hadn't even considered that. What she'd seen seemed too brutal for it to be anyone who'd ever loved Lorraine. Because of her line of work, Evelyn could only imagine the person responsible being a lust killer. But that flew in the face of the usual reality. Generally, "overkill," as it was called, suggested the perpetrator knew the victim and a great deal of emotion was involved in the attack.

Lorraine had just gone through an acrimonious divorce, one in which her ex hadn't been happy about her taking half his pension. Could he have gotten angry enough to kill her?

Maybe, maybe not. But the mere suggestion gave Evelyn hope that they weren't looking at a psychopath, despite the level of brutality she'd seen — that Lorraine's murder would be more easily solved than she expected and Danielle would soon be found alive and well. What reason would Lorraine's ex-husband have to murder Danielle?

"I hope so," she said.

"You *hope* so?" he echoed.

"It's better than the alternative."

"What's the alternative?"

"I'd rather not go into that."

"Can you tell me *anything* else?" he asked. "How'd it happen?"

"I'm afraid I can't discuss the details. I just . . . I wanted to make you aware, before you heard from someone else."

"I appreciate that," he said, and, a few seconds later, Evelyn was off the phone.

She gave Fitzpatrick the go-ahead. Then she listened as his voice rang through the institution, somber and austere.

He did an admirable job. She had to hand it to him. He expressed sadness, asked anyone who might have any idea who did the terrible deed to contact the police and warned everyone to leave the prison in pairs, especially in the winter when it was so often dark. He closed by saying what a great woman Lorraine was and giving examples of her many kindnesses.

Evelyn couldn't have managed so eloquent a eulogy. Not in her current state. She was battling the effects of too little sleep and food and too much caffeine and grief. Calling Glenn had been hard enough.

She should go home. But first she had to talk to Hugo.

8

If the blue meanies are going to get me
they'd better get off their asses and do
something.

— THE ZODIAC KILLER

The first thing Amarok noticed was the
warmth of Danielle's small duplex.

"Hello?" he called out.

No one answered him. He figured if Danielle were home she would've come when
he knocked. He'd had to break a window to
get in, but . . . it didn't hurt to make the attempt to be polite. He didn't want to invade
her private space, was still holding out hope
that he would find her as alive as she'd been
when she gyrated against him at the
Moosehead not long ago, trying to get him
to dance with her.

As he stood in the entry, he heard the
heater kick on. Anyone who was going away
for an extended period would turn that off,

he thought. Especially in Alaska. Yet her duplex had to be a toasty seventy-five degrees.

The warmth put him on edge. He'd been hoping to find the place cold and empty so he could believe she'd moved back to the Lower 48.

"Danielle?" he called again. "It's Sergeant Amarok with the Alaska State Troopers."

Nothing. No movement. No response. At this point, he was no longer expecting it.

After putting some forensic booties over his shoes, he pulled off his hat and heavy gloves, shoved them in the pocket of his coat and ventured inside. He'd thought he might find a bloody murder scene. But it didn't smell like death. It smelled like rotting garbage, which was exactly what he encountered when he rounded the corner and flipped on the light — a large black trash bag stuffed to overflowing. If Danielle had been home over the past day or two, the stench would have forced her to take it out, no matter how much she hated going into the cold.

What he found on the table was even more interesting. There were two goblets and two plates with the remnants of a meat loaf, mashed potatoes and green bean dinner. She'd had company. A rose hung wilting in an old mason jar. Not many people bothered with a centerpiece unless they had someone they were hoping to please or impress, someone they were excited to see — like a date.

"Who'd you invite over?" he murmured as, careful not to touch anything, he walked around to the living room and gazed at the photograph sitting on top of an old TV. That picture showed Danielle with three other girls. They were dressed in Halloween costumes and were laughing, holding drinks.

He hoped Lloyd Hudson, her closest neighbor, could tell him who she'd been with before she went missing. That would at least give Amarok a place to start. Lloyd was an unmarried pilot. In the warmer months he flew hunters and fishermen into the more remote parts of the state, but he didn't work much during the winter. He might've been home when Danielle was entertaining, might've heard or seen . . . something.

Lloyd wasn't around now, though. Amarok had checked.

The bedroom and bathroom weren't nearly as clean as the kitchen and living room, which again gave Amarok the impression that she had prepared for an evening with someone special. . . .

In the bathroom, he noticed that her makeup was spread out on the counter. Her toothbrush sat on the edge of the sink, but it wasn't wet, so she hadn't used it that morning. Most women would pack those toiletries, even if they were going somewhere for only one night — further evidence that she hadn't taken a vacation or returned to her home state.

Her purse made it all unequivocal. He discovered that in the bedroom, on her nightstand.

"Shit," he murmured, and pulled on the pair of latex gloves he'd brought with him so he wouldn't mess up any forensic evidence. She had less than twenty bucks in her wallet and a debit card. Other than that, he found some cheap jewelry in the bottom of the bag, lip gloss, a brush, some coupons, a whole handful of condoms and an appointment book filled with male names. Mike, John, Bill, Big Jim, Tim — there had to be thirty such entries and they all had an annotation: "A laughable 3." . . . "A solid 5." . . . "A pathetic 4." . . . "Maybe 3.5." . . . "A decent 6."

What was this?

He would've caught on sooner if there weren't so many. But the past three months were filled with the same thing. There was one almost every day — on some days there were as many as five or six. A few of the names repeated, but not a lot and none with any consistent regularity. Amarok was still wondering what the heck she'd been keeping track of when he saw that under one man's name she'd written: "A full 8 inches!!!"

The exclamation points — and the condoms — gave it away.

Hugo wasn't nearly as talkative as normal. He sat in his seat on the other side of the glass, drumming on the desktop as if he was listening to music in his head.

"Hugo?" Evelyn prompted. "Are you going to answer me?"

The rhythmic thumping stopped. "I tried to tell you."

"Tried to tell me what?"

He glanced at the camera and remained mute.

"You no longer want to help me?"

Standing so fast he knocked over his chair, he glared at her before approaching the glass. "How can I help you if you won't trust me?"

She *couldn't* trust him. This guy had murdered fifteen women. It was ridiculous of Hugo to be irritated by her inability to forget that, but psychopaths often acted as if their past deeds weren't a big deal, as if others who found them horrendous were overreacting. Psychopaths dismissed murder as easily as most people dismissed neglecting to send a thank-you card.

Or they played the martyr.

Evelyn would never forget seeing a taped interview of Diane Downs, a psychopath infamous for killing her three young children because they stood in the way of her latest love interest. When asked about her children's deaths, she said that they were the "lucky" ones compared to her with the pain she had suffered from the self-inflicted gunshot wound in her arm.

"You know trust isn't possible for me," Evelyn said. "And you know why."

"Then you might as well let me go back to my cell." He headed for the door in anticipation of being met by his escorts, but she stopped him.

"Did you know Lorraine, Hugo?"

When he turned back, his eyebrows knitted into a solid line. "Of course. She worked in the kitchen; I saw her almost every day. Why else would I be upset? Do you think I have *no* feelings? That I don't care if she's dead? She was nice. Nicer than just about anyone."

Since he really *didn't* have empathy for others, Evelyn was impressed. His grief seemed real. Although psychopaths had a cognitive sense of emotion — they quickly learned to mimic others, which helped this missing element go undetected — they often struggled to come up with a normal response to certain stimuli. They occasionally laughed, for instance, when recounting their crimes and only sobered when the person they were telling tipped them off that they were acting inappropriately. Or they'd claim to feel regret or remorse in one sentence, but in the next they'd chuckle while recounting details of the "stupid" expression on their victim's face as he or she died. Hard though it was for regular people to fathom, there'd been a number of studies to back up psychopaths' complete lack of empathy. Evelyn had performed several herself. True psychopaths were so extremely egocentric that any grief they felt was grief for their own personal loss.

Maybe that was what was going on here. Maybe Hugo realized that Lorraine had made Hanover House a more pleasant place to be. Or it could be that he hated whoever killed her and feared he was losing at some sort of power struggle. Without love or duty or compassion to motivate behavior, psychopaths often felt the desire to prove their superiority to others, to come out on top or *win.*

"Lorraine was my friend," he said.

When Evelyn didn't respond, he grew cross.

"Aren't you going to say anything?"

"I'm thinking." Of whether or not she could continue this session. She had no patience today, no reserves. Hugo, who'd become one of her favorites despite the violence of their first meeting, suddenly seemed no better than her other, less endearing patients.

"Well, could you think a little faster?" he snapped. "I'm pouring my heart out here."

What heart? Those two words nearly came to her lips — another sign she was in no shape to deal with the inmates. With effort she bit them back.

"You know why he picked *her,* don't you?" Hugo went on.

She clasped her hands in her lap. "No, I'm afraid I don't."

"Because you loved her," he said as if it were obvious. "This is all about you."

More likely Hugo was attempting to play on her past again. "Who's *he?*"

"Forget it." He waved her question away. "I won't tell you now. You'll just have to figure it out for yourself."

"And you're acting this way because . . ."

"I'm sad! You're sad, aren't you? You loved Lorraine. You must feel like shit, must be *this* close" — he showed her his fingers less than an inch apart — "to breaking down."

It was true. She was teetering on the edge. She couldn't accept that Lorraine was gone, couldn't equate the person she'd known with what was left of her body. She felt like crying again, but she couldn't. Not in front of him. He would only interpret tears as a sign of weakness.

"For the most part you've been sounding more angry and indignant than sad," she pointed out.

Tensing, Hugo stepped back. "Because I could've kept Lorraine from being murdered. *You* could've stopped it. If you would've listened to me."

Evelyn couldn't help but flinch when he put the blame on her. She desperately hoped that he wasn't right. "Is that a sympathetic thing to say to me, knowing, as you do, that Lorraine was one of my closest friends?"

"It's true, so I don't care. You're letting me down just like my bitch of a mother!"

Evelyn spoke through her teeth. "You mean the mother who sends you a weekly care package? *That* bitch?"

He could tell he'd been acting inappropriately again, so he tried to pass it off. "Stop twisting my words."

Evelyn shook her head as she stared at him.

"What?" He didn't seem to realize that she wasn't twisting anything, just noting the contradictions so common in his language. One day, he loved his mother, said she was the best woman in the world. The next, she was a bitch, with nothing in between to trigger the change.

"I thought you were different, better," he went on. He hadn't liked her little head shake, knew it signaled disapproval. "But you're as frightened and weak as all the rest."

"Is that so?"

"Yes! Who are you to act superior? Like you have everything figured out?"

Now that he was attacking her, trying to make her feel unworthy of the love and devotion he'd reserved for her, she was seeing, once again, a glimpse of what Hugo was like when he was disappointed. A glimpse of what she'd seen at San Quentin. A glimpse of what the women he'd strangled might have seen before he killed them. But what upset her was that she *did* feel a measure of guilt for "causing" this negative turn in their relationship. Apparently, she'd responded to the protective comments and effusive compliments he'd paid her in the past in spite of everything she knew about him and psychopaths in general.

It was amazing how convincing they could be. No wonder so many people — wives, children, girlfriends, friends and unsuspecting strangers — were taken in. And yet, when she looked at this meeting objectively, she could see how he was making it all about him — *his* disappointment, how she'd let *him* down — when *she'd* just lost one of her best friends. In that moment of insight, he grew quite transparent, revealing the egocentricity Evelyn had found to be so common among those who scored high on the Hare.

She needed to quit noticing, quit analyzing. Today she was here to glean whatever information he possessed on the murder, if, indeed, he possessed any. That was all.

"You're saying it was someone at Hanover House who killed Lorraine?" she asked, trying a different tack.

A knock interrupted. Then Steve Jacobs, a CO, poked his head into Evelyn's side of the room. "Dr. Talbot, Dr. Fitzpatrick asked me to find you."

Reluctant to take her eyes off Hugo, she barely glanced over. "What does he want?"

"He says you need to meet with Anthony Garza before you go home. I guess he's causing trouble again. He's telling everyone he won't quit until he sees you."

They could put him in a straightjacket or give him a sedative. They had ways to force him to calm down. But Fitzpatrick was making a point. He wanted her to know that she'd really blown it by bringing Garza to Hanover House, wanted to make sure she felt it.

"Fine. I'll meet with him next." She said that mostly to get rid of the distraction, but sending off Officer Jacobs did her little good. No matter how many times she asked Hugo who he thought had killed Lorraine or how hard she prodded him, he wouldn't say another word.

Because he was lying, she decided. That was what psychopaths did.

9

You feel the last bit of breath leaving their body. You're looking into their eyes. A person in that situation is God!
— TED BUNDY, SERIAL KILLER, RAPIST, KIDNAPPER AND NECROPHILIAC

It was Anthony Garza's turn behind the plexiglass. He stared at Evelyn for maybe fifteen minutes, but she refused to be the first to speak. Garza had demanded this meeting. She was giving it to him, but she wasn't about to initiate the conversation. Either he had something to say or he didn't.

Apparently, he just wanted to waste her time.

Tired of his game playing, she stood to go — and that was when he broke the silence.

"Hell of a storm, huh?"

Even in cuffs and chains and an orange jumpsuit, with bandages on his arms and broken front teeth, he sounded like a normal, rational individual, someone she might've chatted with on an airplane. But that was calculated behavior, designed to make her lower her defenses.

Wrapping her arms around her clipboard and hugging it to her chest, Evelyn returned to her seat. She liked being able to jot a few things down if she wanted. Doing so gave her an excuse to look away from her patient when she needed to regain her emotional equilibrium or keep various statements in perspective. But it wasn't necessary to take notes for the sake of being able to remember what was said and done. She always video-taped her sessions with the inmates, and this one was no exception. From the way Garza kept glancing at the camera in the corner of the room, even smiling as if pandering to an audience, she guessed he was well aware of that.

"You bloodied your arm with my name just to be able to say to me, 'Hell of a storm'?"

He ducked his head, acting abashed. "Figured it was a good icebreaker."

At five-foot-eleven, he wasn't particularly tall, but he wasn't short, either. He had a few physical assets she hadn't paid much attention to in their first meeting — a nice golden skin tone and, by all appearances, a powerful build. Other than his teeth, which he'd destroyed since being incarcerated, there was nothing overtly frightening about his looks, nothing that would warn others he was dangerous.

Evelyn imagined some women might even have found him handsome when he was younger. Not that he was old now. The paperwork she'd received listed his fortieth birthday as Valentine's Day.

Valentine's Day. For a wife killer. Wasn't that ironic.

"I'm not here to discuss the weather," she said flatly.

When he realized that his attempt to charm her had failed, his mood shifted. Eyes shimmering with the hatred he'd momentarily concealed, he stood and stepped up to the glass. "Then what do you want from me, Doc? There must be some reason you brought me here, something in it for you." He flashed her a lascivious grin, ogling her breasts. "Or were you hoping to have my baby? Because if that's the case, all you have to do is lift that tight skirt of yours and spread your legs."

This kind of talk was nothing new, either. Many of the men she dealt with tried to use sex, or what they knew of her past experience with Jasper, against her. Stripped of physical weapons, Garza was poking and prodding, searching for an emotional equivalent with which to destroy her.

Refusing to give him that, she managed a smile of her own. "Actually, I brought you here because we're doing experiments on the biggest assholes in the world — and I needed the perfect specimen."

He'd just been ramping up to act crazy. She could tell. But her response took him off guard. She was pretty sure he'd never heard a mental health professional call him an asshole or behave in an adversarial manner, but she wasn't in the mood to pretend he was anything other than what he'd proven himself to be.

"What do you mean by that?" he asked.

"What we have planned does involve your — er — *equipment.*" She emphasized the word so he'd know exactly what she was talking about. "You've heard of castration, haven't you? It dramatically lowers testosterone levels, diminishing a man's tendency toward violence. I'll admit it's a controversial treatment, but . . . in many instances it has proven effective."

He gave an uncomfortable laugh. "Bullshit! You can't cut off my balls. Not without my permission. That's cruel and unusual punishment."

168

What he said was true. He had to be coming up for parole and be desperate to stop himself from reoffending. It was a choice only an inmate could make. So far, no one at HH had taken such extreme measures. But she wasn't about to volunteer that the procedure was optional.

"Who are you going to tell — way the hell up here?" she asked.

This question wiped the irritating smirk from his face. She'd managed to spook him, which gave her a measure of satisfaction. She'd certainly never tried this approach with an inmate before. But after her meeting with Hugo, she was confused and overwrought. For the first time since coming to HH she'd felt the delicate balance of control shifting — and not in a positive direction.

Besides, appealing to Garza's good side would never work. From every report she'd read about him, he didn't have one. She figured she'd try something new, get what she could from his anger and his arrogance. Psychopaths had an inflated view of their own talents and abilities. They tended to think they were different, special, entitled. She wanted to challenge Garza's opinion of himself.

"That's messed up," he said.

"It is," she agreed. "How do you like being powerless?"

His eyes narrowed into slits. "I see what you're doing. You're trying to show me what a victim goes through. But I'm *not* powerless. You won't do shit to me! You can't. I got rights. I'm protected by the Constitution."

She studied her cuticles. "That may be true, but as long as I'm willing to pay the consequences, I have the same choices available to me that you did when you murdered those women. With the right opportunity, I can do anything. And since I run this place, opportunity is never a problem. The only question is whether I will be punished for it later," she said with a wink. "And, personally speaking, I would consider castrating you a public service, something for which I might risk just about . . . anything."

"You're trying to get back at the guy who hurt you through me. That's all."

"Maybe you're right. We all have our little eccentricities, things for which we'll go a bit too far. Mine is protecting the innocent against predators like you."

"But I've never hurt anybody." It was a throwaway statement, one he'd no doubt made many times.

"Then it's quite a coincidence you had three wives who died in the same manner."

He shrugged. "Some people are just unlucky, I guess."

"One wife *didn't* burn in her bed. What happened with" — she glanced at her note-pad even though it wasn't really necessary — "Courtney Lofland?"

"Nothing. I married her. Then I started fucking the neighbor and things fell apart."

"But she got away. Why? Did she outsmart you?"

"She wasn't a smoker." It was a joke, but even he didn't laugh.

"Have you stayed in contact with her?"

"Leave her out of this," he growled. "I won't talk about Courtney."

His fourth wife was a sore subject; Evelyn made a mental note of that. "Then let's talk about the others."

Feigning boredom, he slouched onto the chair and spread out as best he could. "What others?"

"The women you raped and killed, then posed in erotic positions."

He blinked at her. "So *that's* what this is about? You've hauled my ass all the way up here hoping to get me to confess to the Porn Poser killings?" Dropping his head, he scratched his scalp so rigorously she thought he might make himself bleed, but she did nothing to stop the behavior. She felt

171

certain his self-injury was calculated to torment, trouble or evoke a response, because it was nothing he'd done before being incarcerated. Given that, she decided to ignore it as long as she could.

"You shouldn't have wasted your time," he said when he eventually looked up.

"I'm not trying to get you to confess to anything."

Chains dragging, he got up and began to circle the room like a caged panther.

"You don't have enough humanity to give those poor families the closure they deserve," she explained above the rattle of his movement. "I'm aware of that. I just want to let you know from the outset that you don't fool me. I know who and what you are. And I know what you've done, even if you're still denying it. So there's no need to keep lying."

Stopping at the plexiglass, he gnashed his teeth at her. "Then maybe you can tell me what I'm going to do to you!"

It was her turn to stand. Putting her clipboard on the utilitarian table to one side of her chair, she left her glasses there, too, since they were more for eyestrain than anything else, and approached him. Getting so close frightened her despite the barrier, the video monitoring and the handcuffs and chains. He had eyes like Jasper's, eyes that snapped with evil intent. But she wanted nothing more than to see him get what he deserved.

"Go ahead and try, Mr. Garza," she said. "I guarantee you will be sorry for the attempt. Stop the self-mutilation." She didn't care if that term was no longer politically correct, not when talking to *him*. "Stop the disruptions. And get used to the idea that you are here and will not be leaving, and there's not a damn thing you can do about it."

He banged his head against the glass and laughed when she stumbled back. "And if I don't?"

"If you don't" — a surge of anger gave her power — "you'll be wearing a straight-jacket for the rest of your life and drinking your food through a straw."

"We'll see about that," he said.

"Yes, we will," she responded, and buzzed for the COs to take him away.

They entered the room immediately, but Garza resisted long enough to shout, "That woman who was murdered today? She's just the beginning. Do you hear? I will paint this fucking place red with blood. And then I'll come for you!"

He kept yelling as they escorted him down

173

the hall. Evelyn could hear the echo of his voice but tuned out his words. Allowing Fitzpatrick to badger her into confronting Garza had been a mistake. She'd been hoping to strike back at psychopaths in general — for Lorraine, for herself, for Garza's wives and all the other victims of a psychopath's violence. But every time she confronted such an individual, she felt more powerless than the time before.

She was beginning to wonder what she'd gotten herself into — and to fear that she might never get herself out.

Someone had shoveled her walks. Evelyn guessed it was Kit, the mentally challenged son — who was maybe thirty-five — of her closest neighbor. Sometimes she'd come home to find him standing in the road, staring at her house, doing nothing. If she stopped to ask if he needed something, he'd hunch in on himself and hurry off without responding. If she ignored him, he'd continue to stand there, still as a statue, as if he thought he was invisible.

Normally, the attention he paid her made her uncomfortable. But today she was grateful for his kindness. She was so bone tired she didn't think she could have cleared the walks if her life depended on it, even to get her car into the garage so it wouldn't be buried in snow if it stormed before morning.

The grind of gears sounded as the garage door opened and then lowered behind her, but she stayed in her car, summoning her energy. What a day. What a heartbreaking, terrible day. . . .

After taking a couple of minutes to regroup, she grabbed the files she'd brought home with her and her winter hat, which she'd remembered to take from the office this time, and let herself in through the mudroom.

Sigmund, her cat, was normally waiting to greet her the second she walked in. Tonight, however, he was nowhere in sight. She figured he was napping — or punishing her for neglecting him yesterday when she couldn't get home. Fortunately, his food and water bowls were full, thanks to the refill mechanism, so she didn't have to fret that he'd gone hungry or thirsty.

That was *something* to be grateful for, she supposed.

After removing her boots, she passed into the kitchen, where she peered into the refrigerator. She was hoping to find something quick and healthy to eat so she could drop into bed. But she didn't have a lot of options. She'd left what she and Amarok hadn't eaten of the groceries she'd bought from Quigley's at his place, not that any of it was particularly healthy.

Just as she decided that celery with peanut butter was her best option, the phone rang. Putting the celery on the counter, she picked up the handset. "Hello?"

"You okay?" It was Amarok. She'd left him a message, wanting to know what he'd found out about Danielle.

"I think so. How'd it go today?"

"Wish I could tell you I found the rest of Lorraine Drummond, but nothing has turned up."

Hugo's intimation that he could've saved Lorraine echoed in Evelyn's mind. She felt as if she should tell Amarok that she had a patient who pretended to possess information on the case. But she feared that would only turn Amarok's attention back to HH.

The killer had to be a free man. That was all there was to it.

"Maybe you'll have better luck tomorrow, when . . . when word spreads and more people help search."

"My luck couldn't get any worse than it was today."

"You don't think Lorraine's ex could've killed her, do you? They really weren't getting along there at the last."

"It wasn't Vince."

"How can you be so sure?"

"He's been in Texas, staying with his oldest son since the divorce. I've confirmed it."

Shit. She'd been hoping Lorraine's murder could be solved that easily. With a frown, she took the peanut butter from the cupboard. "Were you able to locate Danielle?"

"I'm afraid I've got bad news there, too." The volume of his voice dimmed as if he was rubbing his face. "I got inside her place, but she wasn't around."

"Did it look like she'd moved out?"

"Not at all. There were dirty dishes on the counter, the remains of a meal. Her makeup, deodorant and toothbrush were in the bathroom. Clothes littered the bedroom floor. I noticed a suitcase in the closet, which she probably would've used if she was going anywhere for an extended stay."

"Oh God." Forgetting about the food she was preparing, Evelyn leaned on the counter. "What could have happened to her? Was there any sign of an abduction . . . maybe a forced entry?"

"None. But I did find her purse."

Danielle would have taken her purse even if she were just making a run to the store. "Anything missing?"

"Not that I could tell. Her money, what little there was of it, was still in her wallet. I got the impression she'd had a nice dinner with someone, someone she was excited to see. And she just . . . disappeared from there."

"What about" — Evelyn had to clear her throat as the dead bodies of her high school friends flashed before her eyes — "blood?"

"I used luminal as well as an alternate light source, but her duplex showed nothing that would lead me to believe anyone was seriously harmed in that space."

She tried to imagine what could have happened but had no idea.

"I did find one thing that might turn into a good lead — or, rather, a lot of leads," Amarok said.

"What's that?"

"She seems to have been well acquainted with the men in these parts."

"And you know that because . . ."

"I talked to her neighbor. He said she was with someone almost every night."

"Maybe she was frightened, didn't want to be alone."

"It's a bit more than that. She kept a very unusual record, one that suggests she had far more than her share of sex partners.

Some days she slept with as many as six guys."

"How is that even possible?" she asked. "For one, there aren't a lot of people living in Hilltop. For another, she's fairly new here. *And* she worked forty hours a week at Hanover House."

"If a girl's determined and not too picky it wouldn't be that hard."

"The threat of venereal disease would be enough to deter most people."

"She must have been some kind of sex addict or something, because she's been with well over a hundred men since she came to town."

"Who are these men?" Evelyn asked.

"I recognize the names of those who hang out at the Moosehead, or have lived here for some time. A few are married, which isn't going to make my visit a welcome one. But the rest . . . Maybe you'll recognize them as correctional officers or other staff at HH who drive over from Anchorage."

"Even if I don't, I can check employee records to help figure out who they are." She pulled a pad and pen out of a drawer. "Why don't you give me the list?"

"Bill Huntington, Tom, Tim —"

She shook her pen; it wasn't working. "What about Tom's and Tim's last names?"

"I have some with two names, some with just a first name and others with just a last name. The information isn't always complete. But I have their dick sizes, if that helps."

"What?"

"I guess we could put everyone in a line and measure them to be sure they all match up."

She straightened. "Are you *joking*?"

"About measuring? Yeah."

"I could tell that from the sarcasm. I mean that . . . that she kept track of penis sizes?"

" 'Fraid not."

She dug through the drawer but couldn't find another pen. "Now there's behavior I've never run into before. And I thought I'd seen everything."

"I could be wrong about the notations she made, but what else could they refer to? They range from three inches — poor bastard — all the way up to eight."

"Who's got eight inches?" She wasn't in a joking mood, but she couldn't resist that one, especially since he'd started it with his "measuring" comment.

"What does it matter? I'll make sure you get everything that you want. There's no need for *you* to look anywhere else."

She let her head fall back against the

cupboard. "How can you say that after last night?"

"At least you tried."

That made her feel a bit better about the situation. "*You're* not in Danielle's book, are you?" She was appalled by the thought but had to ask.

"No."

"Not even once? If Danielle was obsessed with getting laid, I can't imagine someone like you escaped her notice."

"She came on to me a few times. But now I'm not nearly so flattered," he added dryly.

Evelyn couldn't help chuckling. "You turned her down?"

"Wasn't my type."

"I haven't seen you with anyone since I've been here. So . . . who is your type?" She held her breath after she asked. She'd opened herself up, knew he had to understand *she* wanted to be his type — but she'd been so skittish with him. First she'd let him down last summer. Then today she'd told him that what they'd shared was an "isolated incident." Had he taken her words to heart? Did he view their encounter the same way?

"Apparently, I like uptight psychiatrists."

She smiled at his response. "Who are afraid to make love. I hate that I left you hanging. I-I really didn't want to do that."

"It's fine. I'm not afraid of a challenge, Evelyn. Not if it's *our* challenge."

"Meaning . . ."

"We could work on it together — get past it."

She bit her lip. Part of her, a big part, insisted it would be much smarter not to get his hopes up again. But he was the only man she'd met in such a long time who made her want to *try.* "You seemed pretty angry this morning."

"Not over last night," he clarified. "I wasn't angry with *you,* anyway, if that's what you thought. I was angry at the situation."

"A problem you believe *I* brought to town."

"What you'll be leaving me with when you go."

"I'm not going anywhere, Amarok, not anytime soon."

He lowered his voice. "That's good, because I can't quit thinking about you."

She didn't know how to respond. For once, she was as frightened of rejecting someone as she was of accepting him. What if Amarok gave up on her? She didn't want to miss out on getting to know him. "You have more confidence in me than I do."

"Your Ho Hos are here. Why don't you come get one?"

She smiled again, but she knew herself. She wasn't ready to risk a repeat of the frustration they'd experienced last night. Maybe she could if that was all she was dealing with. But in the aftermath of Lorraine's death . . . she didn't have it in her to tackle her sexual problem at the same time. "Maybe another time."

There was a long silence.

"Can you wait?" she asked.

"Yeah. I'll be here when you're ready."

She hoped that was true. She missed the comfort and security she'd felt when she was with him. But she'd be fine here, with Sigmund, she told herself.

Except that Sigmund hadn't put in an appearance yet. Where the heck was he? He was always eager for her company when she arrived home. . . .

Planning to look for her cat, she told Amarok to e-mail her those names, since she had no way to write them down given the dearth of pens in her kitchen. Then she hung up and stripped off her heavy coat. That was when she realized something else was wrong. It was cold in the house. And she didn't think her alarm system had sounded its usual warning signal when she opened the door.

The power had been out for a long stretch thanks to the storm. Maybe the system hadn't been able to rearm itself. Or it was broken. Those were plausible explanations — but she couldn't help fearing it was something other than that.

Reclaiming the cordless phone with one hand, she got her 9mm GLOCK out of the drawer with the other. She had Mace in her purse, but after what'd been done to Lorraine she wanted to be able to use lethal force, if necessary. She wouldn't be attacked again, not without giving her attacker one hell of a fight.

"Sigmund?" She moved slowly into the living room. "Sig, baby, where are you?"

When her cat didn't come, her heart pounded harder. Something was wrong, all right. Part of her insisted the temperature of the house and the missing cat had to be related to the storm in some way, but she wasn't taking any chances.

She hit the light switch in the hall. This elicited no sound, no creak or commotion. But she wasn't sure she would hear such things. If she was about to come face-to-face with the man who'd killed Lorraine, and very likely Danielle, he'd be crouched and ready to spring.

Another uncertain step brought her almost to the entrance of her home office. Sigmund's scratching post and other toys were in there. She hoped to find him sleeping on his mat. But before she could go any farther, she spotted her bedroom door. She always shut it when leaving for work in the morning to keep Sigmund from getting fur all over her new comforter.

That door wasn't closed now. It stood ajar by about two feet.

Someone's been in my house.

Her legs went to jelly; she had to reach out and brace herself. With such a sudden deluge of adrenaline, she was afraid she might slide down the wall and wind up in a heap instead of offering the resistance she'd imagined. But she managed to remain standing.

Was her visitor still around? Watching for her? Waiting?

And what had he done with Sigmund?

She felt the weight of the phone in her hand. She wanted to call Amarok, but she knew whatever was going to happen would happen before he could arrive. She'd be smarter to get out of the house. She could lock herself in her car, call him while she still had the phone within range of its base, then leave.

She turned to do that — and heard a *me-e-ow.*

Sigmund! He was alive. And in her bedroom. Maybe she hadn't latched the door tightly when she left and he'd been able to nudge it open. He was good at that kind of thing, smart. Had she gotten herself all worked up, terrified, over nothing?

It appeared that way.

She inched forward, gun at the ready, craning her neck to see as far ahead of her as possible.

Everything looked normal, exactly as she'd left it. From one vantage point, she could see the swish of her cat's tail. Sigmund was on her bed even though he wasn't supposed to be, but she was so relieved to find him that she didn't care.

If someone were in the room, Sigmund wouldn't simply be lying there. . . .

Still, caution prevailed. She crept through the door and scanned the outer edges of the room.

Nothing. No one.

She checked the closet, the bathroom, under the bed. Everything was as it should be.

Thank God.

Setting her gun on the dresser, she breathed a sigh of relief and turned to scoop

Sigmund into her arms. His name was halfway out of her mouth when the other half froze in her throat. *He* was fine, but what he'd been playing with, the reason he'd been too preoccupied to come when she called, made her sick.

A human arm, cut off at the elbow, lay between the pillows. And that wasn't all. The fingers were taped so that only the middle finger stood up.

10

I don't lose sleep over what I have done
or have nightmares about it.

— DENNIS NILSEN,
MUSWELL HILL MURDERER

Evelyn woke with a start. Oh God . . . *where
was she?*

Heart hammering, she blinked rapidly,
trying to peel away the darkness. She wasn't
in her bed, where she'd expect to be in the
middle of the night.

At first, she was convinced that she was
once again in that remote shack with Jasper, the one they'd visited so many times as
teenagers. The day they discovered it, it had
become their special hideaway, where they'd
made love for the first time, where they'd
go to ditch school and wile away a lazy
afternoon.

But her favorite place on earth had nearly
ended up becoming her grave.

Her neck felt wet. Was her throat cut?

Fear clawed at her chest, growing in power and intensity until —

Her cat mewed and shifted at her side, startled when she reached up to check for blood. And then she remembered. She wasn't in the shack. She was in her living room, separated by two decades and almost five thousand miles from the horrific event that had left such an indelible mark on her life. There'd been terrifying events since then, but nothing quite so bad as that.

Amarok was around somewhere, too. When he'd pressed her to lie down, he'd said he'd stay. She trusted that he would, so she was, for the moment, most likely safe — but she couldn't forget that someone else, the owner of that hand, had just lost her life.

Breathe. Come on, Evelyn, in and out through your nose. You know the routine.

Although it had been a long time since she'd had a panic attack, she'd experienced them often in earlier years. The coping mechanisms she'd developed usually worked, more so recently, but only because of maturity and the perspective she'd gained on all that had transpired in Boston. That severed limb had carried her back, unraveled some of her determined progress. It reminded her that Jasper had popped up again last summer and was still out there somewhere.

Was Lorraine's death and that severed arm his work? That was a question she had to ask herself, especially because the hand had been taped to flip her off. Whoever left it was making a personal statement — and who'd want to give her the finger more than Jasper? The person she'd come to know during those final three days at the shack would never willingly let her go on with her life, no matter how much time passed. He'd proven that by tracking her down five months ago.

"You okay?"

Amarok. There he was. Although she couldn't see him in the dark, from the gravelly sound of his voice he'd been sleeping in the overstuffed chair in the corner. Neither of them was prepared to go back into the bedroom. Since he'd finished processing the scene — and bagging the severed limb, which was in his truck until he could have someone take it to Anchorage — he'd closed the door to that part of the house. In the morning, when she'd had some rest and could summon the nerve, she'd pack a bag and move to Amarok's until they could figure out what was going on. Then she'd decide what to do from there.

When he'd made the offer to let her stay with him, she'd agreed almost immediately. She didn't have anywhere else to go. Nowhere she would feel as safe as she would with him. Jasper — or whoever else — had invaded the sanctity of her home and destroyed her fragile sense of safety, and it didn't matter that she'd had a security system. He'd picked the lock to her back door and dismantled the alarm, and he could've taken all day to do it since she was home only late at night.

Having the sergeant nearby, waiting to help get her things, reassured her that nothing terrible was going to occur in the next few minutes. But the relief occasioned by that thought made her feel selfish. Poor Lorraine. And Danielle. That limb, with its purple fingernail polish, was obviously from a much younger woman than Lorraine. Evelyn had no doubt Danielle was dead, too.

"Evelyn?"

She hadn't answered. Wiping the sweat from her upper lip, she strove for calm. "I'm fine."

"You are?"

"Yes." She'd rather he not know that finding that arm had further shattered the sense of well-being she'd struggled so hard to rebuild, bit by painstaking bit, over the years. She'd done everything possible to overcome her ordeal, to give what she'd suffered meaning by letting it spur her in a direction she would never have chosen otherwise. It didn't seem fair that, after so much time and effort, Jasper could harass her again last summer and follow her all the way to Alaska. . . .

"You didn't sleep long."

Maybe not, but she couldn't take a sleeping pill, as he'd suggested earlier. No way would she do *anything* that could impair her ability to think and move. Amarok didn't understand what she was up against, how important it was that she remain vigilant *always.* Unlike some of the other psychopaths she'd studied, Jasper was armed with effortless brilliance. His agile mind and gregarious nature were partly what had drawn her to him.

He wouldn't get the better of her again. . . .

That reminded her — she'd had her GLOCK in her hand when she lay down. It wasn't there now and, although she patted the area around her, she couldn't find it. *"Where's my gun?"*

"Here. After you fell asleep, I took it away.

I didn't want you to shoot me because I got up in the night to go to the bathroom."

Jostled by her movement and supremely irritated as a result, Sigmund jumped down.

"I'd only shoot you if you tried to harm me," Evelyn said. "After what I've been through, I'd shoot anyone. If only I could kill Jasper."

Her cold determination seemed to take him aback. And she could see why. Her willingness to resort to violence alarmed even her. But she believed the only *sure* way to be rid of the monster who'd tormented her was to end his life. She'd seen far too many psychopaths con their way out of a long prison sentence and achieve parole.

"Why would *I* ever try to harm you?" Amarok asked.

He wouldn't. She knew the difference between him, and Jasper and the other men at HH. At least her *conscious* mind did. What happened in her subconscious she couldn't control, or she would've been able to make love last night.

Briefly closing her eyes, she tried to overcome the fear that had momentarily strangled her internal editor. "Sorry," she said. "Don't mind me. I'm . . . I'm a little freaked out and defensive."

"You have every right to be. I just want to

make sure you can keep the good guys separate from the bad guys."

What you suffered when you were sixteen, and then this last summer, has you so frightened of men you can't trust 'em anymore. He'd said that at his place. And he was right.

"Amarok, I have to tell you something."

"What's that?" He'd been so busy photographing her bedroom, dusting for fingerprints and getting that severed arm out of her house that she hadn't told him the real significance of what she'd found. Unable to cope with the sickening sense of déjà vu that had come over her, she'd been too busy vomiting into the toilet.

"Lorraine. Danielle. This is Jasper's work."

"Whoa, we don't even know Danielle's dead. That hand could have belonged to someone else."

"It's most likely hers. Who else has gone missing?"

"There could be someone. I have to confirm it."

"No. Jasper's here. He didn't get the satisfaction he was aiming for last summer, so he followed me to Alaska."

She heard some rustling, guessed Amarok was getting up. A moment later, he pulled his chair into the soft light filtering in from the kitchen. "Evelyn, if Jasper's here, why didn't he kill you the moment you walked in? Be done with it?"

"After last summer, he's got to be even angrier than he was before. He wants to terrorize me first, make sure I understand who's in charge."

"Why take the risk of letting you get away again?"

She could see why Amarok might not understand. Psychopaths were consistently difficult for anyone with a conscience to relate to. "For the pleasure of it. To feel as if he had the last laugh. To win. You have to remember, people like Jasper — psychopaths — don't experience what we do. They want to prove their superiority. They can't even feel the loss of the love and empathy that eludes them."

"Do they know that they're different?"

"If they do, they celebrate their differences. They view those differences as giving them a leg up in the contest of life. I've met some who claim a sense of 'emptiness,' but most say they feel sorry for the rest of us. They consider us 'suckers,' simply because we can be so easy to manipulate. Our desire to be a good person and to please others puts us at a disadvantage. People are mere pawns to someone like Jasper."

"Pawns . . . winning. You're saying tonight

was all a game?"

She pictured the one bluish finger of that hand pointing up when all the rest were taped down. "Yes, for Jasper it's like chess. He thought he had checkmate when I was sixteen —"

"But you survived, didn't let him destroy you."

"Exactly. I fought back, carried on."

"And you made something of your life. Something that is in direct opposition to what he is."

"I believe that's why he came back."

"Or he could be after revenge," Amarok said. "Living on the run can't be easy. He could blame you for ruining his life, especially because you're still publicizing what he did, making it more difficult for him to avoid detection."

"That wouldn't surprise me. Psychopaths often blame their victims for provoking their behavior, resisting, or merely being available to satisfy cravings for sex, murder, money, drugs" — she lifted a hand — "whatever."

"But Jasper's smart, right? He got away with killing three people, more if you count that woman that was found in a shallow grave not far from where he took you last summer. There's got to be more. So he's having his fun. Why would he keep coming back to you and risk getting caught?"

"Because his desire to beat me, to see me demoralized, shamed and reduced to a quaking mass of fear, is too compelling. After last summer, he's probably even more obsessed with the idea of ultimate victory and has gone to great lengths to plan out how it will go. That's another reason I think it might be him. The staging. The theatrics. The scare before the kill. If what we have going on up here plays out in the media, if it goes public in a big way as this is likely to do if we can't get on top of it quickly, that would only make him feel *more* powerful."

"He's still risking capture. Alaska has never had the death penalty, but —"

"It wouldn't matter even if Alaska *did* have the death penalty. He isn't deterred by fear."

"Even when it comes to his own preservation? I thought psychopaths were narcissistic."

"They are, but they often don't see their limitations realistically. Jasper considers himself too clever to get caught. He's escaped justice before — twice now. He acts out regardless of the consequences because he's too impulsive to let those consequences influence his behavior. You've heard of Dr. Hare's studies. . . ."

"No. I'm afraid that wasn't required reading for becoming a state trooper."

She heard a hint of sarcasm in that statement. Was he taking a jab at her Ivy League education? Or was it merely more evidence of his cynicism toward psychology in general?

Tempted to address that cynicism, she paused but ultimately decided they had more important things to discuss at the moment. "Robert D. Hare has been at the forefront of psychopathy research for more than thirty years. He developed a checklist used by many prisons and mental hospitals to diagnose sociopathic tendencies."

"Diagnosing someone a psychopath is as simple as a *checklist* these days?"

"Nothing in psychology is as simple as a checklist. But having a checklist can help. It gives us certain traits that seem to be common among psychopaths."

He leaned forward. "What happens once someone's been identified? They go in for treatment?"

"There are no effective treatments . . . yet. That's why we need more research." She didn't add that the treatments tried so far only made matters worse. In one study, 82 percent of the psychopaths who'd undergone anger management and social skills training before being released from prison reoffended. Psychopaths who didn't have the training had only a 59 percent recidivism rate.

"So this test you mentioned. What's it like?" he asked.

"It's a manual and rating booklet with interview instructions, and it's designed to assess the presence of twenty different personality traits."

"And these twenty personality traits are . . ."

She ticked them off on her fingers. "Glib charm, sexual promiscuity, callousness, poor behavior controls, denial, a failure to accept responsibility for one's own actions, juvenile delinquency, many short marriage relationships. There are more."

"Most of the people I know exhibit those traits. That doesn't make them psychopaths."

"Your friends, as well as mine, may have *some* of the traits, but not all of them, at least not to a large degree."

"Still, you realize that calling someone a psychopath has huge ramifications. What if the test is wrong? Or the results are taken too far?"

"My own research suggests the PCL-R is probably an oversimplification. There's more involved than it can cover. But it gives us a starting point. Think of all the victims who would never be victims if we could figure out why some people have no conscience. Psychopaths show a great deal of criminal versatility. As far as I'm concerned, knowledge is power against those who could or would destroy human lives without compunction."

"But what are you willing to pay for that knowledge?" he asked. "It's the old paradox — if you want more security, you have to pay for it with less freedom."

"Coming from someone who has never known the terror I've faced . . ."

He dropped his head in one hand and pinched the bridge of his nose. "Which makes it easy for me to say. Point taken."

"Very young children can exhibit psychopathic traits," she said. "I've interviewed as many parents of psychopaths as possible. The majority of them have told me that their child was always different, eerily devoid of compassion, difficult to connect with, prone to be a troublemaker from the beginning. Everyone would like to believe that such individuals must have had an underprivileged upbringing, or were abused. Why else would they harm others for the pleasure of it? But that isn't necessarily the case. Psychopaths come from strong, loving families as well as dysfunctional or abusive ones. And no one can explain why. We need to learn more, to keep attacking the problem."

"But do you honestly think the appearance of these 'psychopathic' traits in children can predict future behavior?"

"It's possible."

"So why not make Hare's test compulsory? Administer it to all kids when they turn a certain age and put away anyone who doesn't score the way we'd like? Think of the crime that could be averted."

He was being facetious. He didn't see the value in any checklist — only the danger of certain zealots taking it too far. Living up here in Alaska, he prized his freedom even more than most other people and resisted anything that might threaten it. It was the old "it could never happen to me, so don't disturb my world" response. But she was living proof that it could and did happen, and far too often.

"I don't think you truly understand what these people are capable of," she said.

"I do. I just don't want the 'cure' to be worse than the problem."

She wrapped her arms around herself. She wasn't in any frame of mind to argue with him, but she felt strongly about this subject. No one could fix the problem without first understanding it. "In one of his early experiments, Dr. Hare had a group of regular people and a group of psychopaths, *as defined by his checklist,* watch a timer. When the timer hit zero, the subjects received an electric shock. Nothing truly harmful, but painful."

"People *volunteered* for that?"

"Fortunately. Because he discovered something that sheds a bit of light on the dark mystery of the psychopathic mind."

"And that is . . ."

She'd captured his interest in spite of his tendency to play devil's advocate. "The regular people would begin to sweat as the clock counted down. They were anticipating the negative result."

"And the psychopaths?"

"Since they don't fear punishment, they had no physiological reaction. That's one reason they are so likely to reoffend. They don't learn from their actions — unless it's to figure out better ways of avoiding detection." Which was why all that anger management training had backfired. "They want what they want, regardless, and their lives are all about getting it."

Amarok rubbed his face. Obviously, he

was as tired as she was. This was the second night they hadn't gotten much sleep. "I get what you're saying. I just . . . I'm not convinced any generalization can adequately cover the diversity of human nature."

"So . . . what? We let it go and hope for the best? Catch whatever murderers, rapists and thieves we can and put them in prison? What happens when they get out? Someone like Jasper would just keep torturing and murdering."

"I admit I don't have the answers you're looking for."

"But you're pissed this is happening, and you want to blame me."

"I want to *protect* you!"

She could hear the scowl in his voice. "Even though you knew better than to let me come to town in the first place?"

He grimaced. "You didn't want this to happen any more than I did."

"What if Jasper followed me here, Amarok? I've pissed him off, taken away the thrill of his kill twice. You saw what he left me, the way he taped the fingers of that severed hand. This is just the beginning."

"Flipping someone off is pretty personal. But why does that mean it *has* to be Jasper?"

"Who else could it be?"

"Anyone. One of the men in Danielle's little black book. Maybe someone who has a complex about being listed as having only three inches."

Although he was joking, she got the point. "What would any of those men have against *me*? Why would any of them want to flip me off in such a-a terrifying way?"

"Because they're angry at something that has to do with you. Hell, when you were building that damn prison, *I* felt like flipping you off. Not like this, of course, but —"

"Why didn't you?" she broke in. He hadn't put much effort into hiding his displeasure, but he had never challenged her outright.

"I let those I cared about — the people here — persuade me that the trade-off would be worth it." He released a sigh. "And then I met you."

There'd been a fatalistic note in his voice. "Why is *that* significant?"

"You honestly don't know?"

She cleared her throat. "If you were attracted to me, you didn't let on — not at the very first."

"I wasn't sure it would be wise to go after what I wanted. Then when you came to town when HH was being built to deal with the vandalism . . ."

"I proved you right. Last night, too."

"I can't complain too loudly, not when I liked touching you, holding you, as much as I did." He fell silent for a few seconds. Then he said, "And there's always the promise of the future."

Her heart began to pound. He still wanted her. But she couldn't risk failing again, *especially* with him. If she did, maybe he'd be convinced, once and for all, that she was too damaged.

Or was she more afraid of success than failure? What if she enjoyed making love with Amarok? What if he enjoyed it, too, and they got into a relationship? That was where they were heading last summer, before she put a stop to it. Romantic relationships weren't easy and would be especially complicated with someone like her. Even if she *could* have sex with Amarok, she couldn't risk her heart. The heartbreak Jasper had caused was the worst aspect of what he'd done.

"I gave it the old college try," she said, skirting the real issue.

He spoke softly, meaningfully. "Maybe next time you'll be able to trust me enough to go through with it."

They would be staying together, so they'd

definitely have the chance. . . .

"Someday I'd like to give you an orgasm," he went on. "More than one. I enjoy thinking about that. I imagine hearing you gasp my name as I feel you shudder beneath me."

The picture he'd just painted made Evelyn short of breath. She was suddenly tempted to make wild, animalistic love with him right here on the living room floor. How better to scream out her defiance than to fulfill her sexual potential in spite of her past? She'd love nothing more than to flip Jasper off in return and to do it in just that way.

But with the thought of Jasper came the memory of that severed limb, which reminded her of Lorraine and Danielle — and that doused all desire in an instant.

"You're a glutton for punishment," she said dryly.

"I was in that bed, too."

"What do you mean?"

"You were *so* close to going through with it."

She couldn't argue that. "Yes."

"And now? Are you still interested?"

If her racing heart served as any indication . . . "Of course," she admitted. "Nothing's changed."

He reached out and took her hand. "We

can work with that — when the time is right."

She was glad he wasn't planning to press her tonight. She'd fail for sure if he did.

"But back to the nightmare of what we're involved in," he said as if he realized he'd pushed her about as far as he could in that direction. "Why couldn't it be someone else who left that hand? If not someone in Danielle's little black book, a friend or loved one of an inmate incarcerated at Hanover House? Or some sick bastard who's vying for his five minutes of fame and feels as if tormenting you, a high-profile advocate for the study and treatment of human predators, will put him in the spotlight?"

"Because whoever did this wasn't just flipping me off," she said. "He was letting me know he could get into my house, could kill me at will. And the posing — that's repetitive behavior." She ran a finger over the scar on her neck. "You know Jasper killed my three best friends. With Agatha, he —" She couldn't bring herself to tell him about Agatha. What Jasper had done was so demeaning that just saying the words felt like a sacrilege. "Never mind the specifics. The bottom line is that he likes to pose his victims in compromising or humiliating positions." And she'd had to be in that room, with her friends dead and posed like that, for three days. . . .

"If it *is* Jasper, I need to know everything you can possibly tell me, Evelyn."

She understood that, but she decided to describe what he'd done to Jessie instead, which would be slightly easier since it was less sexual. "Fine . . . with Jess he . . . he bound her arms across her bare breasts in an *X,* like this" — she moved her arms to show him — "and wired her hand to her face with her middle finger going up her nose."

"He's a bastard, no doubt about it."

"I bet every day I'm alive eats at him, makes him feel inadequate."

"There was no Jasper in Danielle's list of conquests. But, of course, he wouldn't be using that name these days. It's too distinctive."

"Actually, if he knew she kept a record, he would definitely want to be in it, and he'd want me to see his name — the name I would most recognize. What better way to rattle me? So maybe she just never had the chance to add him."

"What I don't understand is how he singled Danielle out in the first place. Is he watching the prison? Following the employees?"

"And if so, what made him pick her?"

"Are you kidding?" he said. "She'd take any man, even a stranger, home. She was playing a game to find the biggest cock in town."

"Interesting behavior."

"Care to explain it?"

"You mentioned sex addiction when you told me about the measuring. Some sexologists claim that's a myth, that it makes a pathology out of normal behavior. Others recommend twelve-step and other addiction treatments. I see it as just another way people try to avoid less pleasant areas of their lives — like habitual drinkers, gamblers, liars and drug abusers. It's not *all* about the pleasure, although the chemicals released in our brains can be drug-like. I never had the chance to talk to Danielle about her behavior, of course, but I once had a patient who was almost that promiscuous. At various times, she worked as a prostitute in the cheapest section of town. After one of the johns she'd slept with tried to kill her, her parents brought her to me."

"What did you find?"

"That her behavior wasn't as complex as I was expecting. She wanted to be loved, wanted to feel desired, and was too dysfunctional to go about it in healthier ways."

"I don't think Danielle was looking for love."

"I'm guessing she got a rush from feeling desired. Sex, in some way, became a substitute. My patient cited that as her main reason. With Danielle, I'd guess she was also excited by the risk."

"She couldn't have jumped out of planes or something?"

"She couldn't afford that." She shifted to get more comfortable. "And she might've been titillated by the sheer carnality of it. Different things turn different people on. I'm just glad *you're* not in that book."

"You and me both. Think how *that* would look, if even the local law enforcement had been taking a turn."

"Your instincts served you well."

"I already had my heart set on someone else." *Her* . . . Although he made that plain, he didn't give her a chance to comment before going on. "But several men I know, some of them people I consider friends, *are* listed and, for a few, I can even understand why. It can get lonely up here, especially for transplants, who aren't used to it."

"You said some are married."

"There's no excuse for those guys, but . . ." He cursed. "That doesn't make this situation any easier. What's happening will wreck relationships, breed fear and invoke criticism and debate. In other words, it'll cost the people here even if there are no more victims."

Evelyn couldn't blame him for being upset. She had indeed brought evil to his hometown, just as he'd feared. To make matters worse, he'd be responsible for fixing the problem, even though he wasn't experienced in homicide — wasn't staffed for it, either. He worked for the Department of Public Safety, so he'd have *some* support, but he'd told her himself that Hilltop hadn't seen a murder in ten years. A decade ago, he'd been nineteen — barely a man. Now, partly because no one would listen to him when she proposed building a correctional facility on the outskirts of town, he was a lone lawman manning a remote post with one or two part-time Village Public Safety Officers to help keep the peace — and he only had that much help during the summer, when the usual influx of hunters and fishermen arrived.

Laughing, so she wouldn't cry, she buried her face in her hands. She'd considered coming to Alaska to be such a good idea. The BOP had provided her with the perfect opportunity to establish the institution she'd long envisioned — one where she'd be free to study psychopathic behaviors and traits in depth and on her own terms. Land here was cheap, which made the facility afford-able. Most residents were eager for the jobs it created. And the overloaded and under-staffed maximum-security prisons in the Lower 48 were more than happy to supply her with subjects, since doing so made their prisons both safer and easier to run.

But she'd unwittingly sent Jasper an invitation to join her. That changed her perspective. Maybe she was free to focus on her work, but she was cut off from the rest of the world, living in a completely unso-phisticated area where the only police pres-ence was a man whose job normally entailed breaking up bar fights, pulling over drunk drivers, following up on hunting infractions and removing animal carcasses from the highway. With the abundance of wildlife in Alaska — moose, caribou, bears, even bald eagles who sometimes swooped down and attempted to carry off small children — the animal issues took up more time than the occasional petty theft or drunken brawl at the Moosehead.

As capable as Amarok was when it came to his regular job, he'd never faced a case involving cold-blooded, premeditated *mur-der*. And once word spread, the whole town would be in a panic, everyone looking to him to put the man responsible behind bars.

When she couldn't quit laughing, he stood up. "You think it's funny?"

"No," she said, sobering. "I'm laughing at the irony."

"And that means . . ."

"The damage might turn out to be even more extensive than you think. I'm afraid I've plunged us both into a fight that will take everything we've got to win."

Had she found it yet? the man wondered.

Surely, by now, she had to have. It was late, late enough that she would have left the prison. He knew she was dedicated and spent long hours there, but it was nearly two in the morning.

He should go to bed, he told himself. Eight o'clock would come far too fast. It was stupid for him to be up pacing the floor with as much sleep as he'd lost the last few nights. Someone might remark on how tired he looked. But the adrenaline flowing through his body wouldn't allow him to relax, especially when he imagined Evelyn Talbot stumbling across that arm. Not only had he put it in her house; he'd put the damn thing *in her bed.*

That was masterful.

And what did she think of the way he'd positioned the fingers? Had she realized the hand attached to that arm was flipping the bird? And that she'd seen that same type of behavior somewhere before?

He hoped so, because that small detail had taken extra effort and been such a pain in the ass to accomplish. The tape he'd used at first wouldn't stick to dead flesh, not very effectively. He'd had to go to the store to get a different kind, even though he didn't really have the time.

Yeah, Evelyn had to have realized that hand was flipping her off, he decided. She had to be remembering.

There was nothing to worry about. All was going according to plan.

11

Violent delights tend to have violent ends.
— RICHARD RAMIREZ, THE NIGHT STALKER

The next day, Evelyn insisted on taking Sigmund and his food with her to Hanover House. Amarok had to get that severed limb to the State Medical Examiner in Anchorage to see what information could be gleaned from it. He'd also told Evelyn he wanted to speak to Kit. Assuming her neighbor's son was indeed the one who'd shoveled her walks, Amarok thought Kit might've been drawn by the sound of the alarm and seen something.

But Evelyn wasn't sure Kit could provide a description, even if he had spotted a stranger or unusual activity. What would he remember? Would the details even be correct?

She had no confidence they would be and couldn't face the agonizing and disappointing process of trying to question him. Besides, she wanted to hurry to HH and call Leon Patton, the private investigator who'd been searching, for the past several years, for some trace of Jasper. Since Jasper had reappeared last summer, Leon felt like he had a chance again and had been working extra hours, trying to dig up some promising leads. He'd even flown down to Aruba, where there had been several sightings.

Not that he'd been able to find anything concrete.

Maybe that was because Jasper was right here in Alaska. . . .

Usually, Evelyn carried her investigator's card in her purse, but she'd taken it out a couple of weeks ago, intending to call then. That was why she had to wait until she reached her office to check in with Leon.

Even if she hadn't been so eager to make that call, she wasn't about to vary from her routine, not when doing so would lead Jasper, if he was back, to assume he'd frightened her as he hoped. She had work to do and she wasn't going to let him stop her from doing it. As effective as the Hare Psychopathy Checklist was in predicting recidivism — those who scored high on the test were three to four times more likely to reoffend than those who didn't — it wasn't enough to stop psychopaths from preying on the innocent. Society needed more definitive ways to spot these individuals and deal with them, and she was going to be part of developing that. Even Hare believed earlier detection was vital so that those with psychopathic tendencies could be socialized. Changing behavior patterns once set had proven impossible.

The COs at Security were understandably somber. They'd lost one of their own — actually two, but they didn't yet know about Danielle since her death hadn't been confirmed.

"Good morning, Dr. Talbot. . . ." "Hello, Doctor. . . ." "Pretty cat, Doc. . . ."

When she spotted Glenn — Officer Whitcomb — near the elevator, she made it a point to pull him aside. "How are you doing?"

He shook his head as if there were no words. "I still can't believe it, Doc. I mean . . . who would ever want to hurt Lorraine? And what he did to her! It's so hard to imagine anyone being that brutal."

She blanched. "So you've heard about that part."

"Yeah. Why didn't *you* tell me?"

"I couldn't."

"After what you've been through, I guess I can see why. Anyway, I wish I could get my hands on that bastard. *Everyone* liked Lorraine."

"She'll be missed," Evelyn said with a nod.

He stroked Sigmund. "She made HH a better place."

"I agree."

"You have to be careful." His eyes, filled with determination and outrage, bored into hers. "Don't go out on your own. If you'd like me to walk you to your car when you leave each night, just let me know when you're ready."

"I'm sure I'll be safe on prison grounds. . . ."

As he lifted his hat to scratch his head, he looked more than rattled; he looked a bit frightened himself. "I don't know if *anyone's* safe."

She squeezed his arm with her free hand. "I'm sorry."

"Don't apologize. You must be as devastated as I am. You loved her, too."

"I did. And thanks for the offer to walk me to my car. I'll take you up on that if you're around when I leave." Even if putting him to the trouble wasn't necessary, it would give them a chance to talk.

"That makes me feel better."

"Me, too." She almost told him that what she really needed was to get his uncle to come from Anchorage to fix her alarm system. There was no one local who did that sort of thing. But she didn't want Glenn or anyone else to know what'd taken place last night, not yet. So she figured she'd have to let the alarm situation go for a while. Although doing so made her nervous, she supposed it wouldn't matter if she was going to be at Amarok's, anyway. She could take care of the alarm later.

With a polite smile, she told Glenn goodbye and nodded to everyone else who addressed her as she carried Sigmund through the facility. She'd felt so fragile last night, so close to the brink of the dark, emotional abyss that had nearly swallowed her years ago, that she was surprised to find herself angry this morning. More than angry — fiercely determined. She'd beaten Jasper this summer, hadn't she? She was no longer an innocent sixteen-year-old girl who knew nothing of his psyche. She was a self-possessed adult, armed with an extensive education on human behavior. And because of his last attack, she knew he was still around, tracking her, watching her, making plans. She would not allow him to drag her back to that shack again, not even figuratively. She'd fought too hard to recover.

"Dr. Talbot, could I speak with you?"

It was Fitzpatrick. From the looks of it, he'd been milling around the reception area, waiting for some sign of her. He seemed upset *again,* but she didn't care. She was ready for her cantankerous co-administrator. She felt ready for anyone.

"Yes, come in." She arranged for Sigmund to stay with Penny for a few days and handed off her pet. Then she led Fitzpatrick into her office. "Please, have a seat." Motioning to the chair he'd taken before, she closed the door and crossed to her desk.

He ignored the chair and kept standing.

Determined not to let him rush her, she set her briefcase on the credenza, the coffee Penny had provided when she took Sigmund on the desk, and stripped off her heavy coat, gloves and hat.

"I have some more tragic news," she announced, getting the jump on him lest he start in on whatever he'd come to talk about.

He made a face. "I hope it's not as tragic as what you told me yesterday."

"I'm afraid so." She wished he'd back up. She remained on her feet because, even with the desk between them, he was so tall and imposing it felt as if he was invading her personal space. "There's been another victim."

His thin, pale lips parted. "Not another one of *us* . . ."

By that he meant someone from Hanover House. HH had only been open for three months, but already an "us" versus "them" mentality was developing — "them" being those among the townspeople who regarded the institution and those who ran it with distrust. It was almost as if Hanover House had become a small country of its own — Israel surrounded by enemy nations. And recent events would only foster more antagonism. Hanover House's opponents would finally be able to point to an actual incident like those they'd tried to warn everyone against.

"I believe it is," she said. "This is just between you and me, since Sergeant Amarok hasn't officially identified the body that's been found, but I'm almost positive it's Danielle Connelly."

What little color there was in his face drained away. "The girl who went missing a couple of days ago? The one who worked in the kitchen with Lorraine?"

"Yes." She wondered if Tim was aware of Danielle's behavior, but she didn't bring it up. She saw no need to destroy the *victim's* reputation — not that Danielle's promiscuity was likely to remain secret for long with Amarok poking around, asking questions. Thanks to the number of men Danielle had been with, it couldn't be much of a secret *now,* at least in some circles.

"Don't tell me it was another decapitation," Fitzpatrick said.

"Possibly. What we found was a severed limb — a hand with part of the arm attached. Nothing more, so far."

He grimaced. "It's not Lorraine's arm."

"No."

"Where?"

Feeling light-headed at the memory, Evelyn sank into her seat in case she was about to pass out. "In my bed."

Resting his knuckles on her desk, he lowered his face. "Not at your cabin!"

"Yes."

After taking a few seconds to digest this, he backed into the chair she'd offered him earlier and perched, in a typically uncoordinated fashion, on the edge of it. "Tell me everything."

She described the events of the previous night — getting home to a cold house with no alarm sounding and finding her missing cat in her bed with that hand and those taped fingers.

"Jasper," he said.

He was almost as familiar with the details of her case as she was. All the doctors on the team had heard her story. She couldn't help but refer to Jasper, since she related everything she learned about psychopaths to her own harrowing experience. "I can't imagine who else it could be."

"This must be . . . *extra* difficult for you," he said. "I'm sorry."

"I'm sorry for Danielle and Lorraine," she responded. "It's bad enough that he killed them, but . . . if it was Jasper, if he followed me here, there will be more victims unless he's stopped."

"What will you do?"

Only when he settled deeper into the chair was she able to relax. He always put her on edge. "What *can* I do? Be careful. Keep my eyes open. Press forward in my studies so that he doesn't take from me what I've managed to establish. And hope that Amarok can catch him before he hurts anyone else."

"The sergeant is . . . young."

No one knew that better than she did. Amarok was in the prime of his life. If she'd had any doubt, getting naked with him had proven it. The body she'd felt against her own when they'd nearly made love had been every woman's fantasy. "Young doesn't

223

equate with stupid."

"I was referring to his *inexperience.*"

Sure he was. She'd heard how patronizing he'd been to Amarok. "He's requesting permission from the Department of Public Safety to contact the FBI, to see if he can get them involved."

He hooked one long leg over the other. "That's great to hear. But you can no longer remain in your cabin alone. You realize that."

"I do. It would be a foolish risk to take, since it's so isolated." And since her alarm had counted for next to nothing. . . .

"You're welcome to stay at my place."

She would *never* go there, not after he came on to her. Just thinking of sleeping so close to him made her skin crawl. "Thanks. That's a very nice offer. But Amarok's taking my stuff to his place this morning. I'll be with him for a few days until . . . until we can figure out what's going on. That's why I asked Penny to care for Sigmund. Amarok has a dog who may not be thrilled to have a feline for company."

He seemed to bristle at this response. "You'd prefer his place over mine, or someone else's on the team?" he added as if to cover for his displeasure.

"He has a gun and he knows how to use it."

"A lot of people have guns, including you. You can shoot. You've told me so. Besides, you barely know Sergeant Amarok. Surely, you won't feel comfortable there. What about Stacy?"

The only female member of their team would be a likely choice, if the circumstances were different. "I called to check on her before I left the house. She's still in a lot of pain."

"I bet she wouldn't mind having you in the house. She could probably use the company."

"She has her husband with her. And her pit bull."

"Maybe you can move to Stacy's once she's feeling better."

Before Evelyn could say she had no plans to do that, he asked, "Any idea when she'll be back in the office?"

"None. My grandmother had the shingles a few years ago, so I know how they can linger. She's on a lot of meds for the pain, told me it'll probably be another two weeks."

"There's always Russ. He has room for you."

"Tim, stop. I'll be fine at Amarok's."

He brushed a spec of lint off his pants. "I'm just trying to help, Evelyn."

Sure he was. "I appreciate that."

"Did you tell Stacy what's going on?" he asked.

"I did. To warn her."

He nodded but stiffly. "That's a good idea, but I still can't believe you'd rather stay with Sergeant Murphy than one of us."

She ignored the censure in his voice. Besides the obvious jealousy, he seemed to feel as if anyone outside their small circle of academics would be too uncouth to associate with. "His place is closer to the prison. I'll be able to stay abreast of the investigation, help with it where possible."

One eyebrow lifted above the other. "Is that all? Or is there something going on between you?"

Her love life was none of his business. She was surprised he would even ask after how quickly he'd backpedaled when she rejected him. "It's the wisest thing for me to do, for the time being," she replied. "Anyway, now that I've delivered the bad news, what did you need to see me about?"

He seemed reluctant to proceed.

"Doctor?"

"It's Hugo Evanski," he finally admitted.

Thank God it wasn't Anthony Garza. "What about him?" She'd missed her session with him this morning. But certainly, after what she'd been through, Fitzpatrick wasn't going to harangue her about keeping her appointments. No one was more dedicated to HH than she was.

"Officer Whitcomb came to see me about him."

"Glenn?" Evelyn clasped her hands more tightly together. "Why would he do that?"

"He's concerned about your safety. He says Hugo spends an inordinate amount of time trying to convince you to meet with him privately."

"I already meet with him privately, three times a week."

He leaned forward again. "I mean while foregoing the usual safety precautions."

Irritation bit deep. "Why did Officer Whitcomb carry his concerns to you?" As much as she liked Glenn, that felt like a personal betrayal.

"He's afraid you might someday agree."

"Then he should've spoken to me," she said. But she could see him thinking he was helping by trying to look after her, to protect her.

"He thought maybe I could have a talk with you, remind you that doing so would be a mistake."

"I'm aware of the danger, Tim."

"Good. Because whatever information

Evanski is promising is merely an attempt to lure you into a compromising situation. You understand how these guys work. You'd be putting yourself in jeopardy for nothing. For lies."

Normally, she would've agreed. But recent events had imbued Hugo's warnings and fears with an air of authenticity. Remembering how strongly he'd cautioned her of danger sent a chill down her spine. At a minimum, his behavior raised some questions.

"What if he does know something about what's going on?" she asked.

"He couldn't." Fitzpatrick replied without even considering the possibility. "Like his fellow inmates, he's particularly adept at ascertaining the vulnerabilities of others. That's all. Don't let him play on yours."

What Fitzpatrick said was probably true. Hugo had never met Jasper, would have no way of knowing whether her old flame was in Alaska. That right there told her Hugo was merely creating drama. Most psychopaths required more stimulation than regular people. Maybe this was how Hugo had decided to create some excitement.

"I can take care of myself," she assured Fitzpatrick.

"Happy to hear it. After that Anthony

trick . . . well, I thought it might be best to go over the rules."

She bit her tongue when he sent that as his parting salvo. She hated rude comments that were delivered with a smile, and Tim used that tactic often. But she refused to take the bait.

Eager to be rid of him, she smiled back. She'd never really liked Fitzpatrick. There were several other prominent psychiatrists she would rather have worked with — but none who were willing to move to Alaska. She'd figured out early on that if she wanted HH to become a reality she'd have little choice in partners.

He headed for the door, but she stopped him. "What are we going to do about Lorraine? We can't limp along without her indefinitely. She was an integral part of the food service program."

"Warden Ferris has placed an ad in the Anchorage paper. He's posted on Craigslist, too. He'll start interviewing as soon as possible."

Evelyn had helped staff the center before it opened. But now she didn't have time to handle the interviews. She didn't care to be involved in finding Lorraine's replacement, anyway. It didn't seem fair that they could simply hire someone else and move on. No one would be like Lorraine; no one *could* be.

Still, Evelyn had to be practical, had to make sure the inmates were fed, and they could only get by with a skeleton crew for so long. *I'm sorry, Lorraine.* She touched her desk where Lorraine would've left a tray for breakfast had she been alive. *I'm going to miss you.*

"One more thing." Fitzpatrick's long fingers curled around the doorframe as he turned back.

Evelyn drew a deep breath. "Yes?"

"That detective from Utah that you've been keeping in touch with?"

"Detective Green?"

"He called earlier."

"He has more for me on the Porn Poser investigation?"

"That's my guess."

But how would Fitzpatrick know that the detective had tried to reach her? It wasn't as if *he* answered the telephones at the prison. "You spoke with him?" she asked in confusion.

"I had a call at the same time and picked up the wrong line."

"I see." She eyed Anthony Garza's file, which continued to rest on the corner of her desk. He'd been at HH for two days, but she hadn't yet had the chance to add her own evaluation. "Did Green say what kind of information he has?"

"No."

"Okay." She took a sip of her coffee. "How's Garza doing, by the way?"

"You don't want to talk about him. Not after what you went through last night," he said, and disappeared.

Evelyn wondered if that meant something had happened with Anthony in her absence. She was almost afraid to find out. At odd moments, the anger that had buoyed her emotions earlier threatened to give way to fear. But she refused to succumb to it, especially where he was concerned. She'd brought Garza to Hanover House for a reason. She'd continue to pursue her goals.

First, however, she had to call her PI and Detective Green. Then she had to get Amarok the contact information for all those names on Danielle's list who could be tied to HH's employee roster.

And after that? She'd meet with Hugo. But as far as gaining any useful information for the murder investigation, it would most likely be a waste of time. He couldn't know anything about that.

Or could he?

12

I was literally singing to myself on my way home, after the killing. The tension, the desire to kill a woman, had built up in such explosive proportions that when I finally pulled the trigger, all the pressures, all the tensions, all the hatred, had just vanished, dissipated, but only for a short time.

— DAVID BERKOWITZ, THE SON OF SAM

While on hold for Detective Green, Evelyn stood at the window, frowning at the storm gathering outside. It was snowing again. Large, crystalline flakes clicked against the glass, blasted there by an increasingly strong wind. Apparently, Hilltop wasn't going to get even a few hours of sunlight today.

The ever-present darkness had been one of the hardest aspects of Alaska to get used to, but the depression it could cause seemed like nothing compared to the other implications of this morning's heavy cloud cover.

How would Amarok find the rest of the bodies if he was battling several more feet of snow? How would he ever capture Jasper, or whoever it was, and see justice done? That was important, because she was pretty sure any arrest, if there was going to be one, hung on him, and it had taken all of two minutes for him to report that none of the leads he'd been following had panned out. She'd told him that Jasper might be in Alaska, and he'd said he'd see what he could find, but she had little confidence it would make any difference. Jasper was too damn smart.

The female officer who'd answered the phone at the Salt Lake City Police Department came back on the line, interrupting the worries Evelyn had been ticking off in her mind. "Detective Green just walked in. I'll put you through to him."

Her call was rerouted before Evelyn could say "thank you." After three short bursts of an annoying, high-pitched tone, Detective Green picked up.

"Homicide."

"Detective, it's Dr. Talbot at Hanover House in Alaska."

"Thanks for getting back to me. I'm sorry about that woman who was murdered. What was her name? Lorraine Something?"

233

"Drummond."

"Hanover House is not that big, so . . . you must've known her, which makes everything exponentially worse."

Evelyn had not expected this. "How do *you* know about it?" she asked, resting her forehead on the cool glass. "Did Fitzpatrick tell you?"

He seemed equally surprised by *her* reaction. "Fitzpatrick? No, it was on the news this morning."

She'd figured it would be on the *local* news, but . . . it had been picked up by the *national* feeds? So soon? If one murder in a place that was almost off the map commanded this much attention, what would happen when word of a second victim got out?

Evelyn straightened and pressed a hand to her churning stomach. Such negative press could cause her to lose everything, especially when they had no leads or information to counter it with. "What, exactly, did the report include?"

"That a woman had been brutally beaten and decapitated in Hilltop, Alaska." He took on an announcer-like tone when he added, "Home of the controversial Hanover House Mental Health Facility for Psychopaths."

"Shit."

"Yeah, they tied it to Hanover House immediately," he said. "And they brought up all the arguments against having such an institution in the first place. But you had to expect they would. The opposition lands a punch whenever they can."

Of course. This provided her critics with a golden opportunity. How many times had she publicly insisted that Hanover House was safe? That they were taking all necessary precautions?

She walked over and dropped into her chair. "But there's no connection — at least, no connection that we know about."

"They're making the most of the location of the crime. And the fact that the victim worked at the prison."

"I have to hand it to them," she said with a humorless chuckle. "They're on top of their game."

"You didn't know the rest of the world was watching?"

"I've been so thrown by what's happened that I haven't sifted through all possible ramifications. I knew it could or would happen eventually, but I thought we'd have a few days to try and learn something. To come up with a rebuttal." They were so cut off up here in every other way. . . . "Not every murder can be reported on the news

235

or there'd be no time for anything else."

"If the killer can be caught soon, and he has nothing to do with your facility, *they'll* be the ones to look foolish. A murder can occur anywhere. The only thing that makes this one remarkable is the gruesomeness of the crime and that she was one of your employees."

But there'd already been a second murder, just as gruesome. And not only was the victim most likely another employee, an arm had been placed *in Evelyn's bed.* That would cement the tenuous connection between this death and her and her work.

"It won't be easy to neutralize such bad press," she told him. "Fads exist, even in psychology. Certain theories receive more support, attention — and funding — than others, all thanks to popular thinking. If what's going on up here turns into a long-running manhunt with multiple, shocking murders —"

"The entire nation will be looking to place blame."

Wouldn't Jasper love making such a big splash? He'd become even more famous — or *infamous,* which was a passable substitute for the average psychopath. "If that happens, if I lose public support, I could also lose my federal funding." Then HH would be forced to close down or, more likely, become a regular penitentiary. Either way, she and her team would be asked to abandon their experiments and case studies and leave. . . .

His voice softened. "I understand how hard you've worked to get that place built, and the necessity for it. That's why I called, to lend you my support. I've seen enough in my line of work to know that some people are pure evil. They're born that way, with no one or nothing else to blame. So put up a good fight, okay? Don't let your opponents win."

That was easier said than done when a percentage of those opponents belonged to her own industry. She doubted very many had stared into the eyes of a homicidal maniac the way she had, however. If they'd known Jasper, maybe they'd be more supportive of her efforts to fight the psychopathy problem.

"I'll do what I can," she heard herself say, but her mind was elsewhere. If Jasper was really behind what was going on, he was even more brilliant than she'd been giving him credit for. Not only would Lorraine and Danielle's deaths terrorize her, they'd destroy her professionally before he destroyed her personally.

A complete coup de grâce.

"I was also calling to check on Garza," Detective Green said. "Did you get him transferred up there?"

Desperate to believe that the killer they were dealing with was anyone but Jasper, maybe someone Danielle had been with who had nothing to do with Hanover House, like Amarok had suggested, or a copycat excited by the media buzz surrounding her efforts, she logged into her e-mail program. "He arrived two days ago."

"There's no chance he could be responsible for what's happening. . . ."

"No. None." She considered telling Green about the severed limb she found on her bed but decided not to. The way she was feeling, it would only bring her to tears, and she didn't want to break down on the phone.

"What do you think of our conscienceless friend?" Green asked.

She pictured Garza's jagged teeth. "I think he's a very dangerous individual."

"Good. Then you'll be cautious."

Right now, she had to be cautious of everyone and everything. Enemies seemed to be sprouting up on all sides. "Always."

"Let me know if he gives anything away, anything at all. I'd love to charge him. As a matter of fact, I'd like to see video of your interactions with him. Maybe I'll hear something that will spark a memory or a connection someone who hasn't been working on the case as long as I have would miss."

"No problem. I can provide the video footage. We tape everything."

She began sorting through her messages, looking for that list of names Amarok had said he'd send. . . .

"What's the local law enforcement like?" Green asked. "They friendly? Supportive?"

She could call Amarok friendly — not necessarily to what she'd created here but to her personally. He was letting her stay at his place, wasn't he? "Nice. But . . . it's just one man, an Alaska State Trooper."

"Are you shitting me?"

"No. They don't have counties here, so there are no sheriffs or deputies. The troopers handle crime investigation."

"I've seen the show."

"He's all they typically need during the winter," she explained. "But . . ."

"Tell me he has *some* experience with homicide."

Unwilling to say anything *too* negative, because it made her feel disloyal, she hesitated.

"Is that a no?" Green pressed.

"He's caught people who illegally kill animals," she said.

"Did you say *animals*?"

She rubbed her temples. "He spends a lot of his time protecting the fish and wildlife."

"That's got to have a lot of crossover." Sarcasm dripped from his words. "Now I understand why you're worried. Is he smart, at least? Dedicated to his job?"

"Absolutely." He was also good in bed, she thought wryly. Although she didn't have much experience in that area herself, she could tell he knew what to do with a woman. But skill in making love wouldn't save her life or her life's work, so she returned her attention to the call.

"I wish you luck up there on the last frontier," Green said, but he didn't sound as if he was holding out much hope she'd get through the coming days unscathed. She would have pointed that out, but she was too preoccupied to answer. She'd found the e-mail she'd been searching for and opened it.

She'd anticipated recognizing a few of the men Danielle had been with — and she did. Some were COs: Dean Snowden and Steve Dugall. That made her particularly angry. Others were clerical support. There was even a "Tim," which was Dr. Fitzpatrick's name — not that she could imagine the stuffy doctor having sex with Danielle. He'd consider a young kitchen helper too far beneath his notice. Besides, there was a maintenance man by the same name who worked at HH.

Then she spotted something that made her slam her hands on the desk and jump to her feet. "Holy hell!"

"What is it?" Green asked.

She'd forgotten she was on the phone. "Oh . . . nothing." Her mind raced as she floundered for something to say to explain her outburst. "It's just a . . . a spider. I've got to go," she said, and hung up. Then she stood there, her breathing ragged, her mind reeling as she stared at the four letters that had hit her so hard.

It couldn't be, she thought. But it *had* to be, didn't it? She'd only ever met one person with the name Hugo.

Evelyn paced behind her chair as she waited for the man who could possibly answer so many of her questions. First and foremost she wanted to know why Hugo was listed in Danielle's little black book and how he came to be there.

Amarok hadn't included any measurements along with what he'd sent Evelyn. He probably didn't see that as relevant. But she was curious to know if Danielle had noted a length for Hugo. If not, maybe she hadn't been intimate with *every* man in that book. She could have been keeping track of those she'd *like* to sleep with, or the ones who had come on to her in the cafeteria. Maybe they'd even exposed themselves. Because she *couldn't* have had sex with Hugo. She couldn't have had sex with any of the other inmates Evelyn had seen listed, either — not unless . . .

Evelyn couldn't bear to consider the "unless." It was the presence of the names of those COs, Dean Snowden and Steve Dugall, in addition to the inmates that made her uncomfortable. It suggested the COs had made some sort of an arrangement with Danielle — like a prostitution agreement where they charged the inmates to have sex with her and then split the money.

Evelyn had heard of inmates bribing guards for cell phones and cigarettes, even drugs. That happened all the time in other prisons, so she supposed it could happen here, too. And if the inmates could bribe the guards for those things, they might also be able to pay them to turn a blind eye to certain sexual activity. But surely the staff wouldn't *participate.* Especially *this* staff. She'd come to know the people she worked with and liked most of them — except Tim.

Hugo's inclusion on that list wasn't the only reason she was eager to speak with him, however. He had been urgently warning her that something was about to happen — and it had. He'd also been afraid that the COs would find out what he was telling her, and now she could see why that might be the case. A whistle-blower was not treated well in prison.

With a sigh, she pivoted and returned to her chair. At the house, she'd been so sure that Jasper was back. Hugo had said that Lorraine's death was all about her — that Lorraine had been chosen *because* Evelyn loved her — and she'd believed him. She'd been particularly susceptible to that suggestion because of her fears and insecurities. But he could've made that up just to frighten her. The men she studied would say almost anything to get a reaction.

Still, how did she account for that arm being in *her* bed?

A taunting smile curved Hugo's lips when the COs brought him in. "Now you wish you would've listened to me," he said with a self-satisfied chuckle.

The door closed and locked behind him

as she took her place at the table on the other side of the plexiglass. "You're going to start off being combative?"

"Why wouldn't I? We're not friends."

This took her by surprise. He'd always been so solicitous of her before. "*I* thought we were. Have you changed your mind?"

He didn't respond. She'd reacted negatively when he'd tried to be her champion, and now he was punishing her.

"How are you feeling today?" she asked, trying to get back on common ground. "Better?"

"I'm great. Why wouldn't I be?" he replied as if he hadn't been the least upset in their last encounter.

"Because of Lorraine," she reminded him.

"Oh, that." He shrugged. "Why would I care if she's dead? That stupid bitch didn't mean anything to me."

Evelyn clenched her jaw. He finally had her at a disadvantage, and he was exploiting it. She couldn't believe she'd ever liked him.

She pretended what he said didn't bother her, but only by looking at the situation objectively. This was just another example of what she'd first observed while reading transcripts of interviews with Ted Bundy. Like Ted and so many other psychopaths, Hugo didn't seem to keep track of the things he said even a few minutes before and often contradicted himself. Most people overlooked these seemingly inconsequential slips, probably because they didn't deal with enough psychopaths to draw the correlation. But this kind of sloppy speech further proved that a psychopath's brain wasn't wired like a normal person's. Although the right hemisphere usually controlled speech, psychopaths were bilateral, meaning both sides of the brain were involved. They weren't the only ones — people who stuttered or had dyslexia were bilateral, too — but bilateralism explained at least one of the reasons Hugo's speech wasn't as well integrated as it should've been.

"I'd like to ask you something," she said.

"About . . ."

"Danielle Connelly."

A Cheshire-type grin spread across his face. "Now *there's* a nice girl. She's been much nicer to me than you have."

"Nicer in what way?"

"She's . . . approachable."

"Did you have sex with her, Hugo?"

His eyebrows shot up. "How could I have sex with her? You know what security's like in here," he said, but his smile never faded and there was no conviction behind his words.

"Perhaps you've worked out a deal with the guards."

"I don't know what you're talking about. And they prefer to be called correctional officers. You'd think you, of all people, so buttoned up and proper, could remember that."

She'd purposely used his lexicon to better connect with him. "You're not going to tell me?"

"Tell you what?"

"How you came to be listed in a certain record Danielle kept?"

"I have no idea what you're talking about," he said with a scowl. "I tried to help you before, but you wouldn't have it."

"And now you won't help."

He jerked his head toward the camera without comment.

Was he saying he *couldn't* tell her, not while others were listening in?

"There's been another murder," she told him.

"There has?" He sat up taller. "No one's been talking about it. Why hasn't anyone said anything?"

She got the impression he was truly unaware, but psychopaths were the ultimate con men, so she wasn't sure she could trust his reaction. "It's not public knowledge yet."

His eyes, bright with interest, latched on to her face. "Who got it?"

"The victim hasn't been identified."

"She has to have some connection to you."

"*She?* You can give me the victim's gender?" Did he know it was Danielle?

"Merely an easy guess."

"Okay. But why does this second murder have to have some connection to me?"

A hint of condescension entered his tone. "Because it wouldn't make sense otherwise. You're the one he hates."

She uncrossed her legs. "Who's *he,* Hugo?"

"Jasper, of course."

"And you know this . . . how?"

Shoving his chair out of the way, he stood. "I'd like to tell you. But . . ."

"But . . . ," she prompted.

"You're too scared to let me. And if that doesn't change, more people will die, and their deaths will be your fault, too."

The memory of the decomposing bodies of her girlfriends rose in Evelyn's mind. She'd never let herself grow so fond of anyone since. She'd been too afraid to invest that much of her heart, for fear of the loss. Jasper had only killed them because they mattered to her, and he was still out there, possibly as close as ever.

She'd cared for Lorraine, and Lorraine had been killed, too. It was hard to ignore the connection. The specific placement of that arm seemed to solidify that he was back, despite the discovery of Danielle's little black book.

"Stop trying to make me feel responsible for what's happened," she said.

"*I'm* not making you feel anything. If you feel responsible, that's on you."

She started to shake her head. He was still trying to coax her to his side of the room.

She wasn't going to fall for that. She'd just told Fitzpatrick that she understood the risks.

But Fitzpatrick didn't know that they were likely facing some serious corruption. And what Hugo said next made her heart jump into her throat.

"Maybe his third victim won't be a woman," he said. "Maybe it'll be that handsome trooper you've been hanging out with."

Amarok! How did he know about Amarok?

Scarcely able to breathe, Evelyn gaped at him. Amarok would not be easy to harm. Not only was he big and strong, he had training and weapons. But she couldn't say that for fear her words would be construed as a challenge. Why draw the attention of Jasper or any other dangerous individual to the sergeant?

Anyone could be hurt or killed if caught at a vulnerable moment.

"Look at your face." Hugo laughed as if she'd just told him the funniest joke ever. "You've gone white as a sheet. So that would upset you. The trooper means something to you. Losing him would be like finding your best friends slaughtered all those years ago. Or is he even closer to you than they were?" He lowered his voice and leaned closer. "Are you fucking him?"

In that moment, she hated Hugo almost as much as Jasper. "What can you tell me about the murders, Hugo?"

He didn't skip a beat. "It'll shock you — but it could also save your life. Are you sure you don't want to hear it?"

Her clothes were beginning to stick to her even though it wasn't remotely warm in the room. "You realize you're being monitored."

"Of course. I'm like a monkey at the zoo with everyone always watching." He grinned. "When I return to my cell, they can watch me jack off while I fantasize about you. But as long as no one hears what I say, it can't get around."

"What's it about?" Would he tell her

249

whether or not he'd slept with Danielle? How it was that so many inmates and COs had their names in that damn book?

"Come on over and find out."

He couldn't say anything while he was being taped. . . .

So how badly did she want that information? How far was she willing to go to make sure no one else got hurt, including the handsome sergeant she so desperately wanted to make love — successfully — with?

Enough to risk her life? Was she putting others in danger because she was too afraid to allow Hugo to whisper a few details in her ear?

"You're thinking about it," he said in a singsong voice.

If she thought too long, she wouldn't do it. She was scared. She was *more* than scared. But if she could save a life, especially Amarok's . . .

Gathering her nerve as well as her clipboard, she stood. "If you try anything, the COs will be on you in seconds."

He spread his hands. "I'd never hurt you regardless."

She didn't believe that. But in most prisons, psychiatrists and psychologists went about their work with nothing except a desk separating them from the inmates they treated. Of course, there were reasons for the plexiglass in this particular prison. But if anything went wrong, help would arrive as quickly as possible.

She just hoped "as quickly as possible" would be soon enough, that giving him a private audience would at least confirm whether or not Danielle was truly sleeping with all the men in that book.

Evelyn's heels clicked on the concrete hallway as she made her way around to his side of the cell. Fitzpatrick's warning ran through her mind like ticker tape, but that didn't stop her. Her colleague had never found any of his friends brutally murdered. Her colleague didn't have many friends to worry about. She wasn't sure he'd risk himself to save anyone, even if he did. She was leaving herself vulnerable, but what if Hugo could provide some detail that would help them capture Jasper — or even another killer?

Fortunately, the CO in the observation room wasn't Glenn Whitcomb. Officer Emilio Kush poked his head out as she came down the corridor. "Shouldn't I go in with you?"

"No." Hugo wouldn't talk if she brought someone with her. He'd made that clear. If she had a CO accompany her, what would be the point of going in at all?

"You shouldn't trust him," Kush warned.

Was he sincerely concerned? Or was he worried that she was about to learn something that would cost him his job? He wasn't on Danielle's list, but that didn't necessarily mean he wasn't involved in whatever was going on. Maybe he'd asked her to keep him out of it because of his wife and kids or was just smarter than the others. . . .

"That's *my* decision," she said.

"I'm afraid Dr. Fitzpatrick wouldn't approve."

He wouldn't. Word would get back to him that she'd broken protocol again, and they'd have another argument. But if she didn't take this chance and later learned that she should have, she'd blame herself. And if she failed at everything she hoped to accomplish, if she let Jasper or any other killer beat her in the end, what would her life matter, anyway?

"Fitzpatrick doesn't control me," she told Kush. "But . . . wait right outside the door."

He dipped his head. "You bet I will."

"I'll be okay." She had no idea whether or not that was true, but Hugo had her firmly on his hook. What could he tell her? Could it really help?

She used her radio to ask the CO in the observation deck at the center of the pod to unlock Interview 4. He gave her a, "Roger that," and a thumbs-up through the bulletproof glass that surrounded him. Then she heard the typical hum of an electric charge, followed by a resounding clang, and the door rolled back.

The exultation on Hugo's face when she stepped into the room nearly stopped Evelyn dead in her tracks. Suddenly she was sure this was all an elaborate game. That she'd fallen into his trap.

But her determination to let nothing stop her or get in her way, that hope against hope that this would provide the results she needed, held her for just a second too long. . . .

13

Take your worst nightmares and put my face to them.

— TOMMY LYNN SELLS, SERIAL KILLER

He was on her immediately. Evelyn managed to get her hands up in an attempt to protect her neck, but he didn't try to strangle her. He grabbed her by the shoulders and slammed her up against the wall. Then he used his body to pin her in place while his mouth came down on hers, hot and wet and invasive.

Twisting her head from side to side, she struggled to avoid his tongue. But that open, seeking mouth seemed to be everywhere.

The door slid wide and footsteps echoed in the room. Kush. Would he peel Hugo off her before Hugo could get her skirt up?

Already Hugo's hands were circling around to cup her ass, but it wasn't until he thrust his erection against her pelvic bone that the real terror set in. She couldn't get away, couldn't move or stop him. And Kush was a thick-around-the-middle family man trying to handle an inmate who spent almost all of his waking hours working out.

Help, she thought. *Now!* But just before Kush gained control, Hugo quit trying to kiss her and put his lips to her ear.

"It's Fitzpatrick," he whispered. "He's a twisted son of a bitch, a true sadist. And he hates you, wants to see you destroyed."

That was all he could get out before Kush started wielding his baton. Evelyn could hear the thud of each blow, the grunts coming from both men as Kush drove Hugo into the far corner. Then the scene turned into a blur of noise and commotion as other COs arrived.

Someone helped Evelyn to stand. She hadn't even realized that she'd crumbled to the floor. She was too busy cursing herself for allowing this to happen, cursing the fact that she could still be so gullible, so hopeful, so damn desperate.

The same guard who set her on her feet — Paul Bramble, a CO not on Danielle's list, thank God — tried to guide Evelyn out of the room, but she resisted his efforts.

"Stop," she managed to say amid gulps

for breath. "Make them . . . stop!"

He glanced over his shoulder at Kush and the others.

"Now!" she cried.

Reluctantly, he called them off. She knew the COs were protective of her, that they would view this as a breach for which Hugo should be severely punished, but she didn't want them to go too far.

When Kush twisted around to face her, his expression confirmed what she'd assumed in that regard and so did his words. "Let us teach this bastard a lesson."

She shook her head. "No. That's enough. See if he needs medical attention. Then take him to his cell."

"It was worth it." Although he was doubled over, with blood running from his nose and mouth, Hugo cackled with glee, supremely pleased with himself. "Hot damn, she tasted like candy! Those few seconds will give me a woody for weeks!"

Feeling like the biggest fool in the world, Evelyn righted her clothes. She'd known better. She'd even been warned. "I won't be meeting with you again," she told him. "I'll assign you another therapist."

She'd thought he would expect as much, let it go at that, but he didn't. His countenance changed completely.

"Wait! *Why?*" Grimacing in pain, he straightened. "I kept my end of the deal. I didn't hurt you. One little kiss! What was one little kiss for a guy who'll be locked up for the rest of his life? It was a small price to pay for the truth, wasn't it?"

Using the back of her hand, she wiped the saliva off her cheek. "You expect me to believe what you said?"

"You have to believe it!" he cried. "I'm trying to help you. It was Jasper, like I said. I swear to God!"

Now he was saying it was *Jasper*? She rolled her eyes. "Get him out of here."

They dragged him away, but even that didn't shut him up. "Just wait!" he yelled. "You'll see!"

Evelyn sat in Amarok's tub/shower, letting the hot water pound down on her. Above her was a rack containing his razor, shaving cream and mirror. It smelled more like Amarok in this small space than anywhere else in the house — and that was the best comfort she could find.

Glumly resting her chin on her knees, she watched the water swirl around the drain. She'd been in the bathroom too long, needed to get out. She was wasting hot water. But she couldn't bring herself to face the world beyond this small room. After that incident with Hugo, she'd had a brief confrontation with Fitzpatrick, then somehow walked out of the prison on her own power, at which point she drove to Amarok's house and used the key he'd given her to let herself in. But once she was safely ensconced in his space — thankfully alone since he wasn't yet home — she'd fallen apart.

She lathered up as if another round of scrubbing would remove all traces of Hugo, especially the memory of that revolting kiss. But it didn't matter how many times she washed herself; she didn't feel any better, couldn't seem to get clean.

Damn him! Damn them all!

What was a nice girl from Boston, someone with a doctorate in psychiatry, doing in snow-buried Alaska, spending all her time talking to men who were, at best, indifferent to her and, at worst, hoping to rape or kill her in the most violent manner possible? Could she really make a difference working with the "untreatable"? Save someone who might've been murdered had she not?

It didn't seem that way. She felt responsible for Lorraine's death and Danielle's, too, if only because she'd brought Hanover House into existence. If she hadn't fought so hard and so publicly, if she'd simply gone on her way and lived her life without starting a war against the conscienceless, maybe this wouldn't be happening — or it would be happening without her.

Closing her eyes, she lifted her face to the spray. *Quit punishing yourself. Block it out.* She'd created the institution, not the monsters who called it home. *Someone* had to tackle the psychopathy problem.

There was a knock on the door. "Evelyn? You okay?"

Shit. Amarok was home, and she wasn't prepared to deal with him. "I'm" — she hated the nasal sound of her voice because it gave evidence of her tears — "fine."

"I heard about what happened at Hanover House."

Although she hoped he wouldn't berate her, as she deserved, sympathy would be worse. Criticism might make her defensive, but sympathy would cause fresh tears. "Who told you?"

"Fitzpatrick. I stopped by to talk to the employees in the dining hall who saw Lorraine last and ran into him on my way out. He said you'd been attacked."

Did he also say it was because of her inability to stop others from manipulating her emotions?

Once again, she heard the harsh whisper of Hugo's voice. *It's Fitzpatrick. He's a twisted son of a bitch, a true sadist.*

She could see where Hugo might come up with such a thing. Fitzpatrick studied pain and how it affected psychopaths. But did Hugo really expect her to believe Fitzpatrick had killed Lorraine?

She'd risked her life, her peace of mind, for more of a psychopath's lies.

"It was my own fault," she admitted.

Amarok didn't argue with her. "What I don't understand is . . . *why?* Why did you take such a risk?"

She'd refused to explain to Fitzpatrick, but she was staying in Amarok's house, felt as if she owed him *some* answer to that question. "Our sessions are recorded. For obvious reasons, he couldn't tell me why he was on Danielle's list in our regular session. He needed privacy. And he claimed to have information on the murders."

There was a moment of silence. Then Amarok said, "Did he share anything important?"

"No."

"I'm sure almost every one of those guys would claim whatever he had to in order to be able to lay hands on you."

But it wasn't *just* the promise of information. Hugo had suggested that Amarok might be targeted, and she'd already lost too many people she cared about, couldn't bear the thought that someone might try to take the first man she'd been attracted to in years. "You need to be careful," she told him.

"Excuse me?"

"Jasper. If he's here, if it's him, he-he kills the people he believes matter to me."

"I can take care of myself, Evelyn," he said. "No one's going to hurt me."

But Amarok didn't understand what Jasper was like. "I'm saying if it's Jasper, and he thinks . . . if he thinks there's something between us, even a . . . a close friendship, he could — he could —"

"Whoa, if that's what you're sitting in there worrying about, stop. I'll be fine."

"But you wouldn't be in danger, if not for me. I should never have come to Hilltop. You were right."

"You would've built Hanover House somewhere else eventually. Do you think the situation would be any better if you were going through it in Texas or . . . or Wyoming?"

A tear plinked into the bathwater. "At least it would be warmer." And they'd be more likely to have an experienced homicide division. But she didn't say that.

"You're tough enough to handle the cold," he told her.

Was she really?

She heard him sigh, even through the door. "I didn't want this fight," he told her. "But . . . now that it's here, it's here. Regrets won't help. And this bastard has pissed me off. I'm going to catch him if it's the last thing I do."

If only she could have faith in Amarok's eventual success. But far more experienced detectives had tried and failed, at least when it came to Jasper. Why would Amarok be any different? "What did Kit have to say?"

"Nothing. He knows who you are, but he can hardly talk. Nothing he said made sense, although I did hear the word 'cat.' "

"Sigmund. He's been fascinated with my cat since I moved in. Sometimes he surprises me by coming into the garage when I'm unloading my groceries. And all he'll say is, 'Here kitty, kitty,' until I get him the cat."

"Are you okay with letting Penny keep Sigmund for a few days? Or should we bring him here?"

"I thought you said Makita might hurt him."

"We could keep them separate. Maybe . . . maybe you need him."

"No, I don't. I feel as if Sigmund is better off staying away from me right now. I'm not sure I can protect him, and I can't face the thought of anything or anyone else getting hurt."

"Right." There was a brief pause. "We'll catch this guy, Evelyn. Maybe I'm not some big-city cop who has a whole forensics unit at his disposal. Hell, I don't even have a crime scene for any forensics people to examine. But . . . this guy's on *my* turf now. No one knows this area like I do."

She shook her head even though he couldn't see her. "I want to believe that — but you have no idea what a psychopath is really like, what Jasper's like."

"Maybe I haven't done the research you've done, but dangerous is dangerous. That's all I need to know. You'll help with anything else. So come on, let's eat. I brought dinner."

"I'll be out soon," she said, but even after she made that commitment she couldn't bring herself to move.

Amarok returned in a few minutes. "Evelyn, the water's still running."

She should apologize. She was being a rude guest. He had only one bathroom. Maybe he needed it.

"I take it you're not getting out," he said

before she could decide how to react.

Hoping her sniffle was indistinguishable from the sounds of the water, she managed a broken, "I'm . . . trying."

After a slight pause, he said, "Why don't you do me a favor?"

She wiped her eyes. She couldn't seem to stop the tears. "What's that?"

"Reach out and unlock the door so that I can get to you, okay?"

That felt far too risky.

"Evelyn?"

She swallowed hard. "I-I can't."

"Why not?"

"I can't reach the door."

"Sure you can."

"And I don't want you to see me," she admitted.

"I've seen you naked before — or felt you. This is nothing new. I won't turn it into a sexual encounter of any kind. I promise."

This made her feel even sillier than she'd felt a moment before. "I meant that I didn't want you to see me crying," she admitted, and heard him chuckle.

"So what if your nose is red? Tears show you care about what's happening. Let me in. I'll get you out of there so you can have something to eat and go to bed."

She squeezed her eyes closed. "I doubt I'll

be able to eat."

"You have to try. And you need some rest."

Listen to him, she told herself. But she was paralyzed by that old, debilitating fear. After last summer, Jasper felt so close — it was almost as if *he* could be on the other side of the door instead of Amarok.

She shouldn't have come here. But where else was there to go? Fitzpatrick's? Would she feel any better if she were with him now?

No. Given the romantic interest he'd assumed she felt toward him when they first arrived, she'd be even more uncomfortable.

"Evelyn, will you let me help you?" Amarok asked. "Please?"

Makita whined as if he was standing at Amarok's heels, beseeching her, along with his master, to cooperate. "I can't . . . I can't quit thinking about Lorraine's head and that arm and Hugo's hot mouth all over my face."

"You're supposed to be thinking about turning the lock. The lock, Evelyn. One click. It's that easy."

Drawing a deep breath, she managed to stand and grab a towel, which she wrapped around her before turning the button. She didn't want to force him to break into his own bathroom.

The door opened slowly. "I'm coming in. . . ."

She didn't answer. She just stood there, clutching that towel, hair dripping down her back.

"Can I get an 'okay'?"

He was trying to draw her out, keep her mind occupied. But she wasn't feeling particularly compliant.

"There you are." Acting no different than if she were fully clothed, he stopped a foot or so away and studied her face. "No bumps or bruises?"

"No. I-I guess I should be grateful for that." She attempted a laugh, but it came out sounding rather choked. "This is embarrassing," she admitted, hugging the towel closed in front but still feeling exposed.

"What's embarrassing?"

"I'm normally not such a crybaby." And, when she did feel like crying, she didn't have to worry about having an audience. Much to her family's chagrin, Alaska had provided a heightened degree of privacy, allowing her to crawl that much deeper into her "cave," as they put it.

You're being swallowed up by your fascination with the soulless, and it can't be good for you, her mother had said just a few weeks ago.

"No one's ever had to drag me out of a bathroom before," she told Amarok.

"We all have our moments." He turned off the water. Then he swung her into his arms and carried her out into the living room. She thought he was going to sit her at the table and insist she eat, even though she'd said she couldn't. But he didn't. He sat on the couch in front of the fire and held her on his lap.

"What are you doing?" she asked. "I'm getting you wet."

"Shh . . . it's okay."

Her heart was pounding in her throat as he pressed her head against his shoulder. "What's okay?"

"To let me hold you. Maybe it'll be good for you."

"I can't — I can't be restrained."

"I'm not restraining you. This is called *comfort.* There's a difference."

Her chest was so tight she could hardly breathe. "I know the difference. I just can't help . . . can't help thinking that, as soon as I lower my guard, you might turn on me."

"I won't hurt you, Evelyn. Maybe if I say it enough you'll believe me."

Makita was milling around. He provided a nice distraction, especially when he came over to lick her toes.

"You sure you're not hungry?" Amarok asked.

She worked to shove Lorraine's death, Danielle's probable death and the Hugo incident into the furthest reaches of her mind, where she'd tried to bury all her memories of Jasper. But every upsetting thing remained very present, and she couldn't help thinking Amarok was partly responsible for that. Attractive or not, he was physically and mentally powerful.

Like Jasper.

"That was a question," he said.

Food. He'd asked about dinner. "I'm sure."

"Are you cold?"

"No." *Not anymore.* She wanted his arms around her, so it was odd that she also wanted to throw them off. Part of her was even tempted to try making love with him again. Maybe she should just go for it. Force it to happen. Punch through that emotional barrier.

The other part warned her to shut him out. She couldn't fail if she didn't try. Fear was costing her a great deal of what others enjoyed in life. But there was as much logic to keeping her distance as there was to giving in. Although he may never turn out to be anything close to what Jasper was, Amarok could still reveal himself to be less than what he seemed. Anyone could.

Even if he turned out to be someone she could love, would he be able to cope with the baggage she carried as a result of Jasper?

"You seem to be relaxing. Are you okay with this?" he asked.

"With being held down?"

He angled his head to see into her face. "With being *held.*"

Not entirely. The weight of his arms caused a flight reflex she overcame only by telling herself, again and again, to ignore it, to override it.

But with more time, the panic began to ebb and she realized she *was* okay . . . for now. He wasn't hanging on tightly. He was merely providing some physical support to go with his emotional support.

"Well?" he prompted.

"It's fine," she admitted. Then she drew a deep breath and added, "You want to try again?"

He ran his fingers through her hair. "Try what again?"

His mind was probably immersed in the case, but she didn't want to think about Jasper or Lorraine or Danielle or Fitzpatrick or Hugo or even Kit. All of that was what had driven her into the shower. "M-making love."

"No."

She hadn't expected such a quick and unequivocal response. "You couldn't at least pretend to be tempted?"

"That's not why I'm holding you, because I'm hoping to get lucky."

"I appreciate that. But it's okay if you are."

"The answer's still no. You're not ready."

But would that ever change? It hadn't so far. Maybe she had to push the issue or she'd never get beyond her own resistance.

She considered ditching the towel, slipping her arms around his neck and kissing him. But she wasn't sure she could get him to change his mind. He had to be stressed and exhausted. He also had to blame her, at least a little, for what was going on in his life.

"Someone who's been emotionally traumatized isn't what you're looking for?" she teased. "I can't imagine why not."

His teeth flashed as he grinned at her, but then his shoulders lifted in a slight shrug. "I'm not counting you out."

"There are plenty of women in Hilltop who don't have my problem. You'd be smart to stick with them."

"Thanks for the advice, but I believe

you've told me that before."

Now *he* was being sarcastic. "I'm serious. Don't let me stand in the way if the opportunity arises."

His arms tightened when she made a move to get up. "Stop it."

She froze. "Stop what?"

"Stop trying to shove me away."

It was plain that he meant that in more than the physical sense. "If you knew what was good for you, you'd be running for the hills."

"I've considered it."

"What's stopping you?"

"I'm not ready to give up."

"Because . . ."

He parted the towel and gazed down at what he'd revealed. "I want you too badly. I've wanted you since the first moment I laid eyes on you."

She felt a crushing disappointment. "I'm sure you regret that now."

His warm hand cupped her breast. "No. You're even more beautiful than I thought. Sweet, too — even if you are stubborn."

Her whole body tightened, but in a good way — the same way it had responded when he kissed her in the hall the other night. She remembered his fingers slipping between her legs, the pleasure he'd brought

271

her almost instantly, and tried to nudge his hand lower. She craved more of the heady, drunken sensation she'd experienced so briefly. There hadn't been enough of that in her life. Maybe then she could forget everything else.

His eyes met and locked with hers, but he very purposefully withdrew. Then he covered her and carried her to the guestroom, where he left her to wrestle with her demons alone.

14

When this monster entered my brain, I will never know, but it is here to stay. How does one cure himself? I can't stop it, the monster goes on, and hurts me as well as society. Maybe you can stop him. I can't.
— DENNIS RADER, BTK KILLER

She was in the trooper's house. The man had followed at a distance, wished he could be a fly on the wall. Had he forgotten anything when he'd chopped up the bodies? Overlooked some piece of evidence? What did the sergeant know?

Curiosity was driving him mad. . . .

But he shouldn't worry. The whole town was in an uproar. The trooper couldn't know much.

Telling himself there was nothing to fear, especially from a lawman who'd probably never investigated a murder before, he drew a deep breath. Amarok wasn't clever enough to outsmart him. He was probably too taken with Evelyn to be concentrating very hard on anything besides getting a piece of ass, anyway.

That she was getting romantically involved with the young trooper, though — that was something he hadn't anticipated. And he definitely didn't like it.

Evelyn woke in Amarok's spare bed. Thanks to the almost constant darkness of the Alaskan winter, she couldn't see a thing — the sun wouldn't appear until much later if it appeared at all — but she remembered the attic-like smell. There was also no question as to what had disturbed her. She could hear Amarok moving around, could smell coffee.

What time was it?

She had no idea. She guessed it was earlier than she had to be up, but she dragged herself out of bed, just in case she was wrong. It wouldn't be easy to show up at the prison after what happened yesterday, but she had appointments.

Once Amarok had carried her to bed last night, she'd put on the footie pajamas her mother had given her. They weren't particularly attractive — she looked like a big kid — but she didn't change. They were practical, and she didn't want to don her work clothes until she'd had a chance to shower.

When she shuffled into the kitchen Amarok looked up from the table and eyed her apparel with disdain. "Sexy."

She was glad he hadn't greeted her with something about the attack last night or the murders. They'd both have to cope with the reality of that situation soon enough. A few seconds of conversation about any other topic would be a welcome reprieve, even if he was making fun of her frumpy-looking sleepwear. "They aren't going to turn anyone on, but . . . they're warm."

"I didn't realize anyone over the age of six ever wore those things."

She shrugged. "My mother bought them. They're perfect for Alaska. And since I haven't slept with anyone in twenty years, I'm not sure I have reason to worry about how much they might or might not appeal to men."

He considered her over the rim of his coffee cup. His bowl was now empty, but there was a box of Wheaties at his elbow. "In case you're confused about where I stand, I'm still hoping to bring that twenty-year hiatus to an end."

She walked over to the coffeepot and poured herself a cup. "If I remember right, you had your chance last night. I made the offer."

Slinging an arm over the back of his chair, he scooted lower and stretched out his long legs. "Why would I want to associate myself with what you were feeling?"

"Sometimes you have to take what you can get."

"Not necessarily." He folded his arms across his chest. "I'll know when the time is right."

His response surprised her. "Really? *How?*" *She* wasn't even sure there would be a time.

His gaze lowered pointedly to her chest before his grin slanted to one side. "When you're crawling all over me and moaning my name, I might consider it."

An unexpected impulse tempted her to straddle him, but she held back. "Is that your plan? You're going to drive me mad with desire? Make me beg?"

"If you're that far gone, maybe you won't bail out."

"You're good with your hands. I think you could've gotten me there last night."

"So I missed my one opportunity?"

"You might not want to turn me down if you get another chance."

He came off as unconcerned. "You're just

mad that I was the one to say no this time."

She added cream to her coffee. "So you *are* holding that night against me."

"Just hoping for a green light next time," he said, and gathered his bowl, spoon and cup. "I've told you before — I won't settle for any half measures, nothing short of unbridled access."

His words excited her. But even if she could make love with him, what would happen after? Did he have any interest in a relationship? Or was he merely hoping to attain the unattainable?

And what did *she* want?

Her gaze settled on his sensuous mouth. "You're cockier than I first thought."

"That's the problem with us young guys."

"A lack of stamina?" she joked.

He laughed as he rinsed his dishes, put them in the dishwasher and took a clean bowl from the cupboard. "Trust me. I can get you off."

"What if you can't?" she asked, serious now. "What if . . . what if we have sex, but I'm not able to . . . you know? You won't take it personally, will you?"

"It might take several attempts, but we'll get there." He offered her the bowl he held. "Cold cereal?"

She loved his patience almost as much as

his confidence. He made her feel so normal. "No, thanks. Coffee is enough. What time is it?"

He put the bowl back. "Almost six."

"And you're already heading to work?"

"*Already?* I'm just grateful I didn't get any calls in the middle of the night. That makes me hopeful I'll have a chance to get on top of this nightmare before the situation gets any worse."

"That would be a relief." She sipped her coffee. "Did you get permission to approach the FBI?"

"I did."

"Were you able to get through to them? Are they sending someone to help?"

"We had a conversation, but they're not getting involved. Not yet."

"Because of the weather?"

"They aren't convinced we have a serial killer in our midst, said they don't want to commit the resources if this doesn't live up to the media hype."

"What do you think of that?"

"I can see their point."

"Which is . . ."

"This could be a jealous lover who acted out of rage and killed both women in a connected event."

"You're hoping it's that simple."

"I am."

"And if it isn't? Will they get involved then?"

"They said they'll monitor the situation and lend a hand if things get any worse."

"Heaven forbid *that* happens!"

"I'm with you there," he said. "So what are your plans today?"

"I'm going to the prison like usual. Before I spoke with Hugo yesterday, I spoke to the warden. He's starting an internal investigation on the employees listed in Danielle's little black book. Maybe he'll find something that can help."

"Tell him to keep it on the down-low as much as possible. For all we know, one of those guys murdered Danielle, and I don't want anything interfering with my murder investigation."

"I made that clear already."

"Great. Did this . . . Hugo shed any light on how he managed to have sex with Danielle?"

"I didn't even get the chance to ask him. Are we sure he *did* have sex with her?"

"There was a measurement by his name — by all the names. He's got eight inches, in case you're curious. The little smiley face after that note leads me to believe Danielle was quite impressed."

"Oh God." She rubbed her eyes. "Just because he's a psychopath doesn't mean he can't be well-endowed, I guess."

"Perhaps the correlation can become a new field of study."

"You wouldn't want me to establish that correlation, would you?" She grinned. "I mean, I didn't have a measuring tape the other night, but you seemed to be well-endowed yourself."

He laughed. "The memory doesn't seem to scare you."

"No."

He stepped closer, rested his hands on her shoulders. "So you'll be able to get through the day? You're over your reaction to that attack?"

She remembered those few terrifying seconds after Hugo grabbed her. "It wasn't really an attack. I mean . . . it was and it wasn't."

Amarok walked over to pour himself another few swallows of coffee and leaned a hip against the counter to drink it. "How can it be both?"

Now that she'd gained some perspective on that event, she realized that it had gone differently than it would have if Hugo had really meant to harm her. "Looking back, I think it was just a ploy to get close enough

280

to steal a kiss. These guys have gone months, sometimes years, without a woman — although, if what you found in Danielle's book is true, I guess it hasn't been that long for Hugo." *Or some of the others . . .*

"I'm sure Hugo would take as much of being with a woman as he can get," Amarok said. "And you're in a position of authority, which creates more of a tendency for him to fantasize about you."

"Cops are often fantasized about, too," she pointed out.

He lifted his coffee. "We don't do it for the pay."

She wondered what it would be like if he walked over and kissed her. She thought she'd like that. "At least not all of *your* admirers are convicts," she said. "It's hard to be flattered by men who are so desperate. But back to my point. There was no murderous intent behind Hugo's groping. He didn't hit me, squeeze me harder than necessary to get me up against the wall, try to choke me. It wasn't even an attempted rape. Nothing like that."

"A kiss and a feel. But isn't that because he didn't have time to do more?"

"He could've inflicted some damage." She carried her coffee to the table to, she hoped, stop all those images of kissing Amarok from crowding in. "He put me in the hospital when he rushed me at San Quentin, in about the same amount of time. That's partly what tells me this was different. I'm not convinced I was ever in real danger. That's embarrassing to admit, after reacting the way I did —"

"Anyone who'd been through what you've been through would've reacted the same way."

"Maybe. But he didn't hit me, or kick me or choke me. He kissed me and thrust against me. Then he told me that Dr. Fitzpatrick is our killer."

Amarok pushed off the counter to come to the table. *"Fitzpatrick?"*

"Can you believe it?"

"That depends. What would make Hugo Evanski choose him as opposed to someone else?"

She shrugged. "Fitzpatrick's the most prominent figure at HH?"

"Other than you."

"Other than me," she conceded.

"Maybe Hugo hates him."

"That wouldn't come as a surprise. Most of the inmates hate Fitzpatrick. His approach is more controversial than mine and some of his experiments are not . . . *pleasant.*"

"Meaning . . ."

"He likes to explore a psychopath's reaction, or lack of reaction, to pain."

Amarok's lips formed a grim line. "More shock studies?"

"Among others. And Hugo has been heavily involved lately. From the way he talks about Fitzpatrick, they've been meeting almost every day."

"Are the inmates forced to cooperate?"

"Of course not. They're incentivized. Most sign up as soon as the option becomes available because there's no other way to get the things they want."

"What's the reward?"

"It varies. Extra yard time, books, stamps, movie nights, a second helping of dessert, access to cigarettes."

"Would Evanski have anything to gain by discrediting Fitzpatrick?"

She'd been asking herself the same question. "Not that I can think of. Most likely he's bored and trying to create drama. The men I study will say just about anything, no matter how outlandish. Usually the stories they spin are designed to paint them in as favorable a light as possible, and Hugo has definitely done that here."

"How so?"

"He's positioned himself as my savior, my

protector, someone who knows more than anyone else about those who would destroy me."

Amarok ran a thumb over his chin as he seemed to consider this information. "How much does Fitzpatrick know about Jasper?"

His words made her slightly uneasy. "He's aware of the posing behavior, if that's what you're asking."

"Because . . ."

"We've discussed my case."

"Down to the last detail?"

She thought of the conversations they'd had over the past five years, the hours they'd spent analyzing Jasper's behavior leading up to the first attack and all the guessing about what brought him back last summer, how long he might hide this time, whether he'd try to kill her again. "Yes."

Amarok didn't look pleased. "You haven't even told *me* the details. You refuse to let me read your file."

"I'd rather you not know *everything* that happened."

"Why?"

She glanced away, suddenly embarrassed. "Because I want to sleep with you."

There was a raw edge to his expression when she looked back, a slight flare to his pupils that suggested he wanted the same.

He didn't move toward her, but his voice was more forgiving when he spoke. "It makes a difference?"

"I don't want to bring all of that into bed with us."

"At least you're serious about this," he said with a decisive nod. "Gives me hope."

"This?"

"Us."

But what did that "us" mean?

She didn't ask. Neither one of them were ready to answer that question.

"So . . . looking at Fitzpatrick regardless of Hugo or anything else, could he be a killer?" Amarok asked.

"No."

He stuffed his arms into the heavy coat on a hook by the front door. "But wouldn't you have said the same thing about Jasper?"

15

I just liked to kill, I wanted to kill.
— TED BUNDY, SERIAL KILLER, RAPIST,
KIDNAPPER AND NECROPHILIAC

Evelyn reached Hanover House before any of the other therapists or administrative help arrived. Breathing a sigh of relief that she'd spotted none of their cars in the lot, she chatted with Glenn Whitcomb, who was on duty at the sally port when she walked in. They were both mourning Lorraine, so Evelyn understood his grief, felt he might need to talk to someone. He showed her a thank-you card Lorraine had given him when he'd fixed her leaky roof, and they reminisced about their friend's bossy but caring ways. Glenn was the only one Evelyn felt truly understood, since they'd both loved Lorraine. But she didn't dare dawdle for long. With a parting smile, she hurried to her office, where she sat with a stack of files and reports.

She was preparing for her morning appointments when Penny Singh arrived.

"Morning, Dr. Talbot."

Penny had removed her heavy coat, but she was still dressed in layers, including a turtleneck sweater, a jacket, a scarf and a nice pair of jeans with furry boots. It was easy to tell she'd just walked in from outside because her cheeks were flushed from the cold and she held the insulated coffee mug she carried to work every morning.

"Hello, Penny." Evelyn smiled at her assistant despite her preoccupation, then waved as Linda Harper, Fitzpatrick's clerical support, came up behind Penny.

Linda didn't bother with "hello." She didn't look happy. "Is it true?" she demanded.

Evelyn focused on her a bit reluctantly. "Is what true?"

"What I heard on the news last night?"

"What'd you hear?" Penny cried, immediately cluing in to her high-pitched tone.

Evelyn hadn't watched the news. She wouldn't have turned on the TV last night even if she'd thought of it. After that incident with Hugo, she'd been in no condition to subject herself to the bad publicity. Public criticism was just one of the many ramifications of her current situation — the least important, which said a lot, considering it could cost her her job and her reputation.

Still, she could easily guess what Linda was talking about. "Yes. There's been another murder."

Penny's jaw dropped and her eyes riveted on Evelyn. "It's not Danielle. . . ."

"We don't know." That *two* people they'd known and spoken to just a few days ago could be gone, and in such a grotesque fashion, was so shocking it was almost . . . unfathomable. "The remains have yet to be identified."

Penny's hand trembled as she anchored a hank of her straight black hair behind one ear, and Evelyn couldn't help wondering if she regretted leaving her parents' house in Fairbanks to accept her position. When Evelyn first interviewed her, before Hanover House opened, she'd said she wasn't cut out for college, couldn't afford it, anyway. She'd been looking for opportunities in Anchorage when she came across Evelyn's ad. Anchorage had more of a social life for "twenty somethings" than the smaller, outlying communities, but HH paid better than waiting tables, which was her other option. HH promised more upward mobility, too. "But . . . it *has* to be Danielle," she said. "She hasn't been seen for days."

"The anchorwoman also said you found part of a *corpse* in your bed," Linda said, blanching.

Evelyn tried to distance herself from the vision that appeared before her mind's eye. But Linda's bald statement conjured Sigmund gnawing on the exposed humerus of that pale, white arm as vividly as if she were looking at it this very moment. She had to cover her mouth to stop the rise of bile, which burned the back of her throat.

Her reaction caused Linda to apologize. "I'm sorry," she said, squeezing past Penny. "That must have been an . . . an *awful* thing to find, but . . . I feel like we need to know. That we deserve to know."

"You do," Evelyn said. "I'm sorry, but . . . it's true."

The color drained from Penny's face. "You don't think these murders could have anything to do with Hugo, do you?"

Evelyn blinked at her. "Hugo?"

"He obviously has a thing for you."

"Hugo is locked up, Penny," she said. "He couldn't be responsible."

Her assistant nibbled at her bottom lip. "But . . . he attacked you yesterday, didn't he? He's never done that before."

"Who told you about the attack?" Evelyn asked. "Fitzpatrick?"

Penny looked to Linda, but Linda was too loyal to her boss to answer. "He told everyone in the office," Penny mumbled at length.

Evelyn could imagine the dogmatic and pedantic Fitzpatrick preaching about her mistake: *Let that be a lesson to all of you.* Sometimes he took great pleasure in proving her wrong, or only human, or no match for the absolutes he held so dear. But being a good psychiatrist, cop, actor, musician or writer — a good anything — meant being able to take a risk when the situation warranted it. And if she had yesterday to do over again, she'd take the same risk. Hugo heard a lot of things she didn't and, if something was going on here at HH, he could most likely let her know — if he wanted to. "Somehow that doesn't surprise me," she said dryly.

If Penny heard the censure in Evelyn's response, she didn't react to it. Her voice sounded small and frightened when she said, "What's going on, Dr. Talbot? It sounds like we have a serial killer on the loose."

Here we go, Evelyn thought. Now that word was out, fear and the tendency to place blame would sock the entire community like one of their many snowstorms — and this storm was bound to get worse the longer they went without an arrest.

She remembered what the investigation had been like when she was sixteen, how upsetting for everyone involved — her family, the families of her dead friends, even Jasper's family, regardless of whether his parents had, as she suspected, helped him escape the country. Many of the students they went to high school with, whether they'd known Marissa, Jessie and Agatha very well or not, had mourned the tragedy of their deaths.

So many people would be impacted here, too. How would Amarok cope with such hopped-up emotions? With frightened citizens barraging him from all sides?

"A serial killer is usually defined as someone who has killed three or more people over an extended period of time, Penny — a month if I remember correctly," Evelyn said.

"Various organizations define the term differently," Linda piped up. "The FBI includes anyone who's killed at least *two* people as separate incidents, with a cooling-off period in between."

Evelyn wished for a cup of coffee to vanquish the terrible taste in her mouth from the cup she'd had at Amarok's, but she hadn't taken the time to put on a pot. Penny usually handled that. "No one can say whether there was a cooling-off period between Lorraine and the second victim," she pointed out, but she couldn't maintain eye contact while saying it. What the perpetrator had done with the bodies convinced her they had a predator on the loose regardless of any technical definition. She would have readily admitted that except she felt she had to do everything possible to stave off the panic that would only make the situation worse.

"So no one incarcerated here could be out killing people," Linda said.

"No," Evelyn replied. "And that includes Hugo," she added to once again reassure Penny. "If an inmate went missing, we'd know it right away."

"There's someone *else* out there, then? Someone who . . ." — Penny could hardly form the words — ". . . who murders women and dismembers their bodies?"

That wasn't all he did. The killer also treated those body parts like trophies by putting them on grotesque display. But Evelyn wanted to keep all she could out of the press — and that meant preventing Penny, Linda and the other HH employees from gossiping about the more gruesome details.

"It would seem that way."

Penny set her coffee on the edge of the desk. "Who could it be? There aren't that many people in Hilltop."

"Personally?" Evelyn said. "I think it could be Jasper."

"Jasper?" Linda echoed.

"The man who attacked me when I was sixteen, and came after me again five months ago. This could be a personal vendetta and not the direct result of what I've tried to accomplish here."

Linda seemed skeptical. "He'd be a stranger in these parts. He'd stand out."

"Not necessarily," Evelyn said. "We're not that far from Anchorage. Other, smaller communities lie between here and there. And who knows who's staying in the various hunting cabins in the surrounding mountains?"

"With the weather we've been having?" Linda scoffed. "There shouldn't be *anyone* there this time of year!"

"It wouldn't be impossible to survive," Evelyn told her. "Not if someone had the proper gear and plenty of supplies." Feeling the constraints of the busy morning looming ahead, she checked her watch. "I'm sorry to cut this short. I know you're both concerned, and so am I, but I've got to go or I'll be late for my first appointment." She also had to meet with the warden on the possible corruption. She'd received a message from him. Before he interrogated anyone, he felt as if they should just keep a close eye on those COs who were on Danielle's list, and after what Amarok had said this morning Evelyn agreed.

Linda went to her desk. Penny reclaimed her to-go cup but didn't actually leave. "You're planning to work as usual despite . . . despite everything?"

Anthony Garza's file drew Evelyn's eye. She wished she hadn't had him transferred here. Not because Fitzpatrick didn't agree with her decision to do so. She just wasn't in the frame of mind to be able to deal with him, not in addition to everything else. She'd had no idea all hell was about to break loose when she'd made the arrangements.

"For the most part I'm carrying on as usual, largely because I believe that what I'm doing is more important than ever." She pulled Garza's file over and flipped it open to find the letter she'd written his last wife on top. "Have we heard anything from Courtney Lofland?"

"Who?"

She showed Penny the letter to jog her

memory. "Garza's last wife."

Penny shook her head. "Nothing's come in. Not yet."

Evelyn supposed it was just as well. She didn't dare leave, even for a few days, in the middle of their current crises, no matter how important the interview might be. She had a terrible feeling that if she didn't stay and defend what she'd created she'd lose it for sure, and she refused to let Jasper or anyone else take more from her than she'd already lost.

"Keep an eye out for it," she told Penny, and closed the file. "Meanwhile, can you check my schedule and find some time I can allocate to our new transfer?"

She pulled a face. "Ugh, everyone hates Garza."

"I'm afraid he's earned that, but there might be important things he can teach us."

Penny held her drink in the crook of her arm while removing her gloves. "How often do you want to meet with him?"

"Every other day."

"Beginning when?"

Dare she put it off? He wasn't going anywhere. . . . "I'm too busy this month. So we'll let him settle in for a couple of weeks and put him on the calendar for February."

"If you want to get with him sooner, you

could have him take Hugo Evanski's slot."

"Hugo's slot?"

"You're not going to continue seeing him after last night, are you?"

No. She'd told him as much. But that meant she'd have to find him another therapist, and she wasn't sure whom to ask. She couldn't ask Fitzpatrick. Even if Fitzpatrick weren't already meeting with Hugo on a regular basis for his own purposes — which exempted him from taking over the general therapy — he wouldn't want to pick up the slack, seeing as he blamed her for causing the problem in the first place.

A light went on in the office across the reception area. The others were beginning to arrive.

"Dr. Talbot?"

Evelyn dragged her attention back to her assistant. Maybe it would be better *not* to wait. Maybe she could get Garza to calm down and solve at least one problem. "That'll work. Give him Hugo's slot."

"So who'll take Hugo?" Penny asked.

"I'll let you know."

Penny shoved her gloves in her back pocket. "This all seems so pointless."

"What seems pointless?" Evelyn asked.

She motioned around them, as if to indicate the whole facility. "Everything. All the work and effort and sacrifice."

"You agree with those who believe we will never find a way to treat psychopaths?"

"I'm leaning that way. I haven't seen improvement in anyone since I've been here."

"What I'm trying to do will take a lot longer than three months, Penny."

"You might not have longer. We could all be brutally murdered in the next few days —"

"No one else is going to be killed." Praying she was right about that, Evelyn stepped around the desk to give her assistant's arm a squeeze. "Just don't go anywhere alone."

Hoping to slip out of the administration area before she could bump into any of the other doctors, Evelyn turned back to gather her files. Then she circumvented her tiny assistant and made a beeline for the double doors that led out into the prison. But Russell Jones nearly bowled her over as he came charging through going the opposite direction.

"Whoa, sorry about that," he said when she barely managed to jump out of the way.

"No problem." She reached for the handle again, but he stopped her.

"You okay?"

"Fine. Just running a bit behind." She

wished he'd step aside instead of blocking the exit.

"Fitzpatrick told me what happened with Hugo Evanski yesterday afternoon. I'm sorry. That sucks."

As casual and sloppy as Fitzpatrick was formal and fastidious, Russ wore a tie with a chambray shirt and wrinkled chinos. A receding hairline made it difficult to guess his real age, but Evelyn had seen his file. He was only twenty-eight — the youngest member of the team. She'd always wanted to like him. With a round, soft body and droopy jowls, he reminded her of a Saint Bernard — a pleasant association but an ironic one given his dark outlook on life.

"Whatever possessed you to trust him?" he asked, his tone full of reproach.

In an effort to minimize the event, so that it would be more quickly forgotten, she manufactured a careless tone. "You know how it goes, how easy it is to like some of these guys."

"Not really," he said. "The men on my roster are pretty scary."

She doubted they were any scarier than the ones *she* treated. But as she'd come to know Russ, she'd decided he didn't have the right temperament for what they were doing. Psychopaths were masters at ascertaining weakness and capitalizing on it, and Russ wasn't nearly assertive enough to oppose that. As a result, he took a lot of verbal abuse and had to adjust his roster more often than the rest of them. It didn't help that he approached life with Eeyore-style gloom:

Bet it's going to storm today. We probably won't be able to get out of the parking lot. . . .

I'd get a dog, but when would I spend any time with him? Hanover House has taken over my whole life. . . .

My girlfriend's not joining me until next month. I bet she bails out again. Why would she want to come to this dreary place?

His negative comments went on and on, which was one of the reasons Evelyn didn't hang out with him after hours. It was hard enough to tolerate the lack of *real* sunshine in this remote corner of the earth. Had he not been a favorite grad student of Fitzpatrick's she would never have hired him.

"Maybe you're immune to their charm," she said. "Or you can see through them more easily than I can." She didn't believe that for a second, but he took her words at

299

face value.

"They don't fool me!"

"Glad we've got you on the team." She hoped that would be sufficient flattery to get him to move his bulk to one side, but he wasn't finished with her yet.

"He claims to be broken up about the fact that you won't see him anymore, but don't fall for it. It's all bullshit. If there's one thing I've learned it's that psychopaths are so full of shit *they* don't even know what's real."

"Have you talked to him?" she asked.

"Who, Hugo? No, I just came from the mail room."

As with any other prison, the mail coming in and out of Hanover House was carefully monitored. A CO went through most of it, but occasionally, if they had reason, the mental health team poked around down there, too. As intrusive as it felt to read someone else's mail, Evelyn had found it to be a necessary evil. Since her recommendation was often the only way these men could be eligible for easier time, a better job inside the prison, transfer to a minimum-security facility, even parole, they had plenty of reason to try to fake improvement. It was worth checking up on what they were sending home. They knew the mail was monitored, so it always amazed her that many slipped and divulged their true thoughts and intentions in spite of that, but they did.

"What did you find in the mail room?" she asked.

"A whole stack of letters Hugo has written to you. Apparently, he was up all night."

She blinked in surprise. She'd never gone down and read the mail of any of *his* patients. "You *read* them?"

His chin puckered with a sheepish, lopsided smile. "Some. I couldn't help myself. I was down there for something else, but when I saw them —"

"What do they say?"

"He apologizes for scaring you, says he acted impulsively. He just wanted a little kiss, never meant you any harm — yada yada." Russell's jowls swung as he shook his head in apparent disgust. "As if you could believe that."

Crazy thing was . . . she *did* believe it. She'd arrived at that conclusion before she'd even known he'd been writing to tell her. "So what's your impression?" she asked. "What's he hoping to achieve with those letters?"

"He makes it obvious. He's begging you to retain him as a patient. He says he'll never ask you to be alone with him again, that he doesn't need to because he already told you what he had to say."

That Fitzpatrick was their killer — what had to be the biggest lie he'd spun yet.

Russell leaned close. "So . . . what did he tell you?"

Evelyn waved him off. "Nothing reliable. Like you said, you can't believe a word that comes out of his mouth."

"You're not going to say?"

She considered repeating what Hugo had whispered, just to see how Russ would react. She was curious to learn if there was some small part of him that might believe Fitzpatrick could be capable of such atrocities. But Danielle and Lorraine weren't just murdered; they were hacked to pieces — and not for purposes of disposal, because they were then displayed. That brought a certain type of killer to mind — one who enjoyed it.

The emergency alarm went off before she could open her mouth, anyway.

"Damn it," he groaned. "It's always something. What the hell's wrong now?"

Anthony Garza had been the reason for the last alarm. Evelyn prayed he wasn't to blame for this one, or Fitzpatrick would do his best to make her feel responsible for whatever Garza had done.

"I'm going to find out," she said, and hurried back to her office so she could call the warden.

Getting through to Ferris took several minutes. By then, the alarm had been shut off.

"What's going on?" she asked as soon as she had him on the line.

"You're not going to like it," he replied.

Her ears were still ringing. "Tell me anyway."

"Anthony Garza just shanked Hugo Evanski."

Stunned, Evelyn felt behind her for her seat. *"How?"*

"With a pen he made into a weapon."

That wasn't what she'd meant. She knew the inmates made homemade weapons out of whatever they could. They even filed their toothbrushes into sharp points. "I mean . . . how was it that they were together?"

"They were exercising in the yard."

This was so unexpected, so unbelievable! It never should've happened. "Hugo's not *dead* —"

"No. Not yet. He's on his way to Medical."

Not yet? "How serious are his injuries?"

"Hard to say. I didn't see him, but from what I've heard he's lost a lot of blood."

Her mind raced as she struggled to sort

out this information. "But . . . Anthony shouldn't have been in the yard." Technically, after attacking her, Hugo shouldn't have been there, either, but she remembered telling the COs to return him to his cell. Since she left the prison right after, without giving instructions for his privileges to be removed, it was conceivable they'd let him carry on as usual.

But Garza? Who the hell had put him in general population? "Why wasn't he on lockdown? He hasn't behaved since he arrived."

"Someone had him transferred out of solitary."

She shot to her feet again. *"Who?"*

"Let me check." There was a pause, then a worried sigh. Obviously, Warden Ferris was as flustered as she was. She could hear him opening and closing file drawers, imagined him searching through the myriad paperwork that crossed his desk and was retained in his office. Finally, he asked someone to help him find the transfer order.

Evelyn had to wait more than fifteen minutes, but she clung to the phone, wasn't about to hang up.

"I've got it right here," he said when he came back on the line.

"Who signed it?"

He cleared his throat.

"Warden Ferris?" she prompted.

"I'm sorry, Dr. Talbot." She couldn't help noticing how much his tone had changed.

"What is it?"

"Maybe you don't remember, but . . . *you* did."

16

I wasn't going to rob her, or touch her, or rape her. I was just going to kill her.
— DAVID BERKOWITZ, THE SON OF SAM

Amarok had a lot of people to interview, but first he wanted to see what Shorty knew about Danielle and her behavior. She had to meet the men she had sex with somewhere, and since Amarok had seen her at the bar himself in recent weeks, he was guessing she'd met them at the Moosehead.

Was that where she had also met her killer?

Possibly. Even if it wasn't, perhaps Amarok would be able to gain information he could use to either corroborate or disprove what he found out when he spoke to those who'd been with her. For starters, he hoped to learn how many people were aware of her activities. It hadn't escaped him that she might have been murdered and cleaved to pieces by an angry wife or girlfriend. But he received a call from Phil Robbins, one of his Public Safety Officers, whom he'd commandeered to help with the investigation by hanging out at the trooper post to man the phone.

"Sergeant Amarok?"

He remained in his truck. The music was so loud inside the building he doubted he'd be able to hear if he didn't. "It's me, Phil."

"I've got the medical examiner's office on the phone — a Dr. Wilson. Says she's the pathologist assigned to look at that head you sent over a couple of days ago."

"What about the arm?" he asked.

"She didn't know about the arm till I told her I dropped it off yesterday."

"And now?"

"She's going to look for it, see if that case was assigned to someone else."

"Did you tell her we've identified the first victim?"

"Course. I told her it was Lorraine Drummond who managed the kitchen at Hanover House. Do you have anything I can pass along on the second victim yet?"

"Not a thing. Tell her I haven't found enough of the second victim to be able to identify her, but a younger employee of HH, a Danielle Connelly, has gone missing."

"And we think it's her, right?"

"That's what we think," Amarok said. "I'm hoping we'll be able to confirm it soon."

"Okay, hang on a sec."

Amarok stared off into the distance as he waited — until movement at the entrance of the bar caught his eye. Shorty was coming out with a large trash bag, which he disposed of at the side of the building. As he trudged back, he caught sight of Amarok and cut over.

Leaving the heater blasting, Amarok rolled down his window. The air outside was cold enough to freeze the balls off a brass monkey.

"What's happening?" Shorty called out as he approached.

"I'm on the radio." Amarok held up the mic. "Everything okay here?"

"Been quiet since the other morning. Thank God. Hopefully, you're here to tell me you've caught the bastard that's scaring the shit out of everyone."

"We need to talk."

Shorty spat at the hard-packed snow. "Am I going to like what you have to say?"

"Can't imagine you will."

"That's what I was afraid of. I'll be waiting."

Phil came back on the radio, so Amarok

lifted a finger to let Shorty know he'd be there in a minute and rolled up the window to block the damn cold. "What was that?" he said to Phil.

"Dr. Wilson says she's got the limb and will take both cases, since continuity could be important."

"I don't suppose she can provide any information from what she's seen so far. . . ."

There was a crackle as Phil relayed the question. " 'Fraid not," he said when he returned a few seconds later. " 'Cept you were right — you got a second victim on your hands. That limb didn't come from no fifty-five-year-old. She said that was for sure."

"Would she say twenty-four sounds about right?"

He waited through the same process.

"If she had to guess," came the response.

"Is there anything else? Can she give me some idea of what the murder weapon might have been?"

Silence. Static. Time. Then Phil said, "There are no gunshot wounds to the head. It's battered enough that she can't rule out blunt force trauma, but that's just one possibility. Without the rest of the body, which could have other wounds, she can't give you anything conclusive."

Amarok was feeling too desperate not to be irritated by the lack of answers. "And it was severed by . . ."

"This is some gross shit," Phil complained, but he went through the relay process again. "I wish it was a meat cleaver," he said at length.

"Why?" Amarok demanded.

"Because that would be easier to find up here than a hunting knife, wouldn't it?"

He had a point. "What did Dr. Wilson say?"

"She's guessing it was a knife. Hell, I coulda told ya that much."

"*She's* the expert, Phil. I have to ask her."

"Sorry," he muttered.

"So have her tell me this. Is there anything about what she's seen that strikes her as strange? Any other cases that've come through her office with the same type of dismemberment?" He sure as hell wished she could tell him where to look for the rest of both bodies. . . .

"Nope," Phil said when he came back again. "She hasn't seen anything like this since she started working at the medical examiner's office — and that was fifteen years ago."

So it was Hilltop's problem and only

Hilltop's problem. *Great.* "What about the eyes?" he asked Phil.

"There were no eyes in that head," he replied.

Amarok bit back a sigh. "There was one. The other was gouged out. Ask Dr. Wilson if she thinks Ms. Drummond's murderer used a knife for that, too."

"She says, now that you mention it, no. There are no superfluous cuts, no gouges to the occipital orb."

"How'd he get the eye out?"

"Probably used his fingers," Phil said when he replied. "She claims it's not hard. And that makes sense since the killer rubbed so much blood through her hair. Shit, I think I'm gonna barf now."

Amarok ignored that. "What tells her all that blood in the hair wasn't incidental?"

"Really?"

"Ask her, Phil."

"Just a minute."

"Well?" Amarok said, growing impatient when this took a bit more time.

"The coverage. It's too uniform," Phil said at length.

Amarok nearly retched himself at the thought of someone gouging out one of Lorraine Drummond's eyes and then combing her own blood through her hair. "Sick bastard."

"Tell me you have some idea who this sick bastard is."

"Not yet," he said. "That's why I need all the help I can get. Tell Dr. Wilson if she happens to notice anything else, anything at all, to give me a call right away, okay?"

"I will."

He hung up and zipped his coat as he plunged into the cold.

Evelyn would never have put Anthony Garza in general population. She hadn't even had a chance to evaluate him. The U.S. Marshals who'd brought him to Alaska had warned her about how difficult he was. She'd had proof when he head-butted an officer and broke the man's nose — not to mention when he threatened her. He wasn't someone who could be trusted around other people.

She paced in her office, waiting for Warden Ferris's assistant to bring her a copy of the order proving she was responsible. She wanted to see that signature for herself, to check the date and time the document was signed, and see if she could guess who might've filled it out since *she* had not. Sure, she'd been stressed lately, but not stressed enough to put a dangerous prisoner, one she was self-conscious about because of the way he'd come to be part of their prison population, in with other men when she had no doubt doing so would create an unsafe situation.

"Dr. Talbot? Dede brought this for me to give to you."

Penny was at her door again. She had the order in hand.

Evelyn met her in the middle of the floor. "Thank you."

Penny stayed despite her dismissal. No doubt she was hoping to be reassured by Evelyn's reaction. For the first time since they'd started working together three months ago, she seemed shaken in her loyalty.

Evelyn tried not to take it personally, but she was so flustered just about everything felt like a betrayal.

"This isn't my signature." She could tell immediately. It was similar enough to understand why the COs had acted on it, but there were significant differences.

"*You* can tell this isn't my signature, can't you?" She held the document out to Penny for verification. The slant was off. So was the size of her *E.*

Penny picked at her cuticles. "If you look *closely* you can tell it's not your usual. But"

— the volume of her voice dropped — "maybe you were in a hurry."

Evelyn grabbed it back. "Seriously? You've seen my signature hundreds of times! How can you say that?"

Her assistant scuffed one of her boots against the other. "That's just what I see."

Evelyn turned her focus to the date and time: January 15, 4:43 p.m. — right after she'd met with Hugo. Unfortunately, she had been at the prison when this was executed. But she hadn't been thinking about any of the other inmates. From what she remembered she'd simply been trying to hold herself together long enough to get out of HH and into her car. She hadn't been making any executive decisions.

Another voice, a deep male voice, caused her to lift her head.

"I just bumped into Dede from Warden Ferris's office. She seemed upset, in a hurry. What's going on?"

For once, Evelyn was grateful to see Fitzpatrick. Maybe he could help her solve the mystery. "Someone forged my name on this transfer order," she told him.

"Why would anyone do that?" He glanced at Penny, probably because she was the only other person in the room.

Penny stepped back and put a hand to her

314

chest. "It wasn't me!"

"I can't imagine *who* would do such a thing," Evelyn said. "But this is *not* my signature." She shoved the proof at him.

His eyes moved as he read over the document. "This is for . . . Anthony Garza?"

"That's right."

He looked up. "Why would you transfer Garza into gen pop when you know it would mean trouble?"

"I wouldn't! That's the point!"

He let go, and the paper fell to her desk. "I would like to believe that, Evelyn. But I never thought you'd circumvent our usual procedure to get him transferred here in the first place."

She massaged her temples in an attempt to ease the tension building there. Fitzpatrick wasn't going to forgive her for ignoring his mandate even though she'd considered it more of a suggestion — at least when it came to her. Never would she willingly have given up her ability to choose her own subjects. That was part of the reason she'd had HH built — so she'd have that kind of freedom — and he knew it. She'd only gone along with the rules he'd been making to allow him to feel he had the kind of power he deserved. That night he'd tried to kiss her and she'd refused, he'd accused her of

315

leading him on just to get him to support her professional aspirations. She'd been afraid he might quit and leave like Martin had, had been hoping to get beyond that little glitch in their relationship and make sure he felt fulfilled in his work, since that was what fulfilled her.

"Let's not argue about Garza's transfer," she said. "This is something else entirely. This is a serious mistake, but it's not *my* mistake." She grabbed the transfer order and held it out to him again. "Check the date and time."

Deep grooves formed on his forehead as he did as she requested. "Yesterday afternoon."

"That's right. *Immediately* following the attack by Hugo Evanski."

"So?" he asked. "What does that prove?"

"That it couldn't have been me!"

"How do you know? You were so upset I'm not sure you were paying much attention to what you were doing."

"I was reeling, I'll give you that. But I wasn't signing any transfer orders, especially for an inmate other than Hugo."

He put down his briefcase. "Maybe your hands were moving without your brain. When I popped in, you were riffling through various files and stuffing your satchel —"

316

"So I could leave!"

"Yes — but if I had to give an opinion on your state of mind, I'd say you were completely distraught."

Even "completely distraught" didn't cover it. But she needed Fitzpatrick's support, needed him to believe her.

"I *didn't* sign this," she insisted. "I wouldn't have signed this no matter what frame of mind I was in. The only thing I did was gather up my stuff and call Officer Whitcomb to ask him to walk me out of the building."

"Okay." He agreed but gestured as if he was only relenting to save them further discord. "Either way, I'll have him moved back into solitary until he proves he can be trusted, and we'll just be glad we caught this before —"

The look on her face must've given away the truth, because he stopped mid-sentence.

"There hasn't already been a problem. . . ."

Penny looked more uncomfortable than Evelyn had ever seen her, as if she was dying to tell him what'd happened, like a child running to her father — a father she'd found too strict only moments before. But, lucky for Penny, since Evelyn wouldn't have tolerated that, she held back and let Evelyn

317

break the news.

"Anthony just stabbed Hugo in the yard, Tim."

Fitzpatrick flushed a bright red. "Tell me he isn't dead!"

She wished she could, for her own re-assurance as much as his, but she had no idea how Hugo was faring. "A lot of blood" could mean anything. "I haven't heard from Medical. I don't want to disturb them when they're in the midst of such an emergency."

Fitzpatrick never cursed. His language was too formal for that. But he muttered some-thing under his breath that sounded a lot like, "Fuck!"

"You weren't here for the alarm?" Penny asked sheepishly.

"*What* alarm?" He kicked over his brief-case in an uncharacteristic show of temper. "I just arrived."

Evelyn watched him stalk to the window, where he presented them both with his back. "Someone forged my name, Tim. I'm *not* responsible for this."

He scowled at her over one shoulder. "I can see why you'd want me to believe that, *Evelyn,* but . . . why would anyone bother to forge your name on something like a transfer order?"

"That's what *I'd* like to know!" she said.

"Listen." When he turned to face her, he seemed to be making an effort to choose his words carefully. "You've been under a lot of pressure. Trying to do too much. Working too long. Pushing yourself too hard. And, let's be honest, it's caused you to make a few poor judgment calls. You've been breaking protocol left and right."

So what? That was *his* protocol. The panic she'd been feeling rose higher. "I didn't do it."

Russell Jones rapped on the doorjamb. "I just checked with Dr. Bernstein in Medical," he announced. "He was about to contact Warden Ferris when I called down to see what was going on. They're trying to decide whether to summon a medevac. Bernstein thinks Hugo Evanski needs to be airlifted to Alaska Regional Hospital."

Evelyn covered her mouth. "No. . . ."

Russell shoved his hands in his pockets, which was how he always stood. "That's what they said. They're afraid the shank nicked his heart. And that's more than we can handle on-site."

"Did Ferris give the okay?" Fitzpatrick spoke as if he had a sour candy in his mouth.

Russell nodded. "I'm sure he did. It might be the only way to save Evanski's life."

Fitzpatrick shot her a dirty look. "This

will be *so* damaging. Think of the publicity. It'll make us look like we've let the power we hold go to our heads. Or that we're being irresponsible or careless with the violent criminals who have been entrusted to our care. I can't believe you did this to me. You got me up here under false pretenses, and now you're running amok."

Evelyn threw up her hands. "What are you talking about? I didn't get you up here under false pretenses!"

"I wouldn't have made such a poor decision otherwise. But I won't embarrass myself by returning to Boston with my tail between my legs."

"You're tempted to give up already? This is our first serious incident —"

"We've only been open three months!" he broke in. "You can't tell me this won't add furor to the reports that are spreading across the nation about the murder of Lorraine and that second victim!"

He was right. She couldn't refute it. "Whoever forged my name meant for something like this to happen," she said. "My work here is being sabotaged."

Fitzpatrick's eyes narrowed. "*Sabotaged,* Evelyn?"

She lifted her chin to let him know she wasn't about to back down. "That's right."

"Who made you go into that cell with Hugo yesterday — *after I specifically warned you not to?*"

"No one, but . . . that isn't what I'm talking about."

He advanced on her. "Okay, who made you transfer Anthony Garza here in the first place?"

She'd done that on her own, too. But bringing a known psychopath to Hanover House, when they already had a prison full of them, didn't change the fact that she hadn't exposed the inmates in the yard to Garza. "I didn't sign this transfer order!"

"You were pretty upset," Penny said softly. "Maybe . . . maybe you were hoping Anthony would teach Hugo a lesson."

"What?" Shocked that this interpretation would come from her own assistant, she whirled around to confront Penny. "That's not true!"

Fitzpatrick took over. "Lorraine's murder has thrown you into a tailspin."

Evelyn felt like she was being attacked from all sides. "And it hasn't *you?* A wonderful woman is dead. Danielle's probably dead, too."

A muscle flexed in his cheek. "While tragic, that doesn't affect me as deeply as it does you. I wasn't nearly as close to Lorraine, and I barely knew Danielle."

He wasn't close to anyone here in Alaska. Maybe that was why she'd been so shocked when he tried to build a more intimate relationship with her. "If you are accusing me of caring about Lorraine, it's true," she said. Lorraine certainly would've shown her more loyalty than Penny just had.

"It's not only your sadness over these tragedies," Fitzpatrick said. "You told me yourself you think Jasper is back."

"He could be!"

"Really?" Russ acted as if he would find that particularly fascinating. "After last summer, I wondered if you had anything to worry about."

Fitzpatrick frowned at their heavyset colleague but spoke to her. "You've been exhibiting some erratic and uncharacteristic behavior, Evelyn. We've all seen it. Maybe" — he paused as if to collect his thoughts and rein in his emotions — "maybe you should take some time off."

And go where? Do what? He was trying to take the lead — to run Hanover House without her — just as he'd been doing since he'd realized they would not be a couple. But she wouldn't allow that. It was *her* energy, *her* initiative and *her* vision that'd propelled them this far. Maybe he'd endorsed her, which had helped at a critical time. As a young psychiatrist relatively new to the field, she'd needed the added credibility in order to get key people to listen to her. But he hadn't worked half as hard as she had, and he didn't care nearly as much — about the men they studied or the innocent people they were trying to protect by doing the research.

"I hope you're kidding," she breathed.

"I'm afraid not. Maybe if we tell the press you signed that transfer order by mistake, and that you are now on suspension, they'll be appeased —"

"It's not up to you to put me on suspension!" That would have to come from Janice Holt, their boss at the Bureau of Prisons, and Janice was in New Zealand, attending her daughter's wedding. Unless she saw a news report or someone from the BOP called to alert her, Evelyn wasn't sure she'd hear from Janice until Janice returned to work next week.

"We have to do something to relieve the pressure until the FBI can figure out who's committing the murders," he said.

Evelyn curled her fingernails into her palms. "The FBI isn't coming, Tim."

"Why not?"

"They aren't convinced they're needed."

He threw up his hands. "Then heaven help us all!"

Evelyn lifted her chin. "Don't act as if everything is lost. Amarok can handle this."

"Sure he can." Fitzpatrick rolled his eyes. "Don't let your infatuation get ahead of you."

"Dr. Talbot's infatuated with Sergeant Amarok?" Penny asked as if that were beyond comprehension.

He didn't answer that question, and neither did Evelyn, but she wanted to. The anger coursing through her was difficult to control. Fitzpatrick was jealous. She could hear it in his voice. For all his pretense of having been only mildly interested in her, in having tried to kiss her merely because they spent so much time together and they were a "logical" match, he was hurt that she'd rejected him.

That realization caused something else to occur to her. "Wait a second," she said. "You were aware that I met privately with Hugo."

He seemed taken aback by the sudden shift in her tone. "Everyone's aware of it. Word spreads fast in such a contained world, especially when you give reason for people to talk."

She ignored that jab. "But I told *you* first.

And I told you why."

"So?"

"You knew he claimed to have information on the murders." She hadn't told him about Danielle's little black book, but he could've stumbled onto the corruption. Was he now afraid that word would get out and put a stain on his life's work? Maybe that was why he regretted coming here. He was afraid of what that decision would ultimately do to his reputation and his prospects.

"I tried to set you straight," Fitzpatrick was saying, "tried to convince you that whatever he said would be nothing more than a ploy to get his hands on you — and he proved me right. He lured you over to his side and attacked you."

Not exactly. He'd kissed her, but he hadn't hurt her. "Did you watch the video of the incident?" she asked.

She could see him weighing the consequences of both possible answers. "Yes or no!" she demanded. "Which is it?" It would be easy enough to do. Thanks to the digital age, the entire library of their sessions could be called up on any computer, as long as the person snooping around had the proper username and password. Only the surveillance video shot in the prison recycled every month, since it required far more storage space.

He buttoned his lab coat. "Of course I watched the video. Part of the reason we record our meetings is so that we have more than human memory to catalogue what transpires. It enabled me to see exactly what occurred and how badly you were traumatized. You hold quite a bit of power here, Evelyn. It's important that you remain capable of wielding it wisely."

That was the second time he'd mentioned power. "Or you'll wield it for me, is that it? If we can't run Hanover House together, as a couple, you'll punish me for refusing your advances and take over alone?"

Something she'd never seen before flickered in his eyes. "Now you've gone too far!"

"Are you the one who signed that transfer, Tim?" she asked.

"You're accusing me of forging your name in an attempt to make you look bad?"

"Or worse. Were you trying to shut Hugo up?"

Fitzpatrick gaped at Penny, then turned to Russ. "Oh my God! Now there's no doubt that the trauma has gotten to her. She's completely lost touch with reality!"

"Tim . . ." Russ made an attempt to calm him down, but Evelyn knew the younger man wouldn't be committed enough to make an impact. He wasn't about to stand up to his mentor, someone more experienced and twenty-two years his senior.

"Do you think *I'm* the one who's out of line?" Fitzpatrick asked Russ. "What have *I* done that's against our policies and procedures?"

Sure enough, that was all it took to get Russ to back off. "I'm just saying we should tread lightly until we know more," he mumbled.

Fitzpatrick confronted her again. "Are you suggesting I had a man stabbed because I was afraid of what he might say?"

Evelyn wanted to support what she'd said by telling him about Danielle's list, but she didn't dare, in case the Tim listed there was the janitor. She'd already caused irreparable damage to their relationship. But she feared she'd done that weeks ago, when he'd tried to kiss her. "If you knew what Hugo told me, you might understand why I'd make that claim."

"And what did he tell you?"

She glared at him. "That you're the one who killed Lorraine."

The shock of her words acted like a tranquilizer dart. Everyone went silent and still. But a second later, Fitzpatrick really let loose. "That's ludicrous!" he shouted.

Russ hurried to get between them. "Come on, Evelyn." He lifted his hands in a soothing manner. "You know better."

Tears were gathering in Penny's eyes. "Why would Dr. Fitzpatrick want to kill anyone?"

"Dr. Talbot didn't mean that," Russ explained. "It's the fear and the tension talking."

But Evelyn wasn't so sure. *Someone* had forged that transfer order. And Dr. Fitzpatrick could've done it easier than anyone else. Maybe he hadn't been trying to get Hugo killed, but it was entirely possible that he'd been hoping to embarrass her, discredit her or make her sorry she ever rejected him.

"I'm not taking any time off, Tim," she said quietly. "And it's not your place to try and make me. You don't have that kind of authority."

He grabbed a paperweight from the top of the filing cabinet and flung it at her desk. "Fine!" he yelled as it hit with a solid bang. "Work yourself to death. We can all see what it's doing to you."

"What it's doing to *me*?"

"You're being completely unreasonable. Accusing innocent people of heinous crimes. Forgetting that you signed certain papers. Refusing to take responsibility for the problems *you've* caused." Even more menace entered his voice. "Or maybe it isn't the stress. Maybe you were never capable of running this institution in the first place and it was a mistake for me to put so much trust in you."

"I'm just as capable as you are!" she snapped, and marched through the middle of them to the door. "I'm going to check on Hugo. At least one of us should be there to monitor the situation. After all, a man's life is on the line."

Fitzpatrick gave her such a chilling look she got the impression even murder wasn't beyond him.

17

I wish the entire human race had one neck, and I had my hands around it!
— CARL PANZRAM, SERIAL KILLER, ARSONIST, THIEF, BURGLAR AND RAPIST

"Tell me you didn't know what was going on."

Shorty wouldn't look Amarok in the face. He wiped down the bar, then turned to throw his rag in the sink.

"You *did* know what was going on," Amarok said. "You're a Public Safety Officer, damn it! Why didn't you say something to me? Tell me there was a girl putting out for everybody who came in?"

An expression of chagrin yanked Shorty's lips down, but he wasn't completely contrite. "Because as far as I could tell, she wasn't breaking any laws. She was of age. I carded her to be sure. She wasn't charging anyone. *And* it was all consensual."

"She was young, new to the area and living alone. That kind of behavior, with so many men cooped up here for the winter, almost all of whom carry guns, is dangerous!"

"I'm telling you, she couldn't get enough! She once asked me to set up a train — even wanted me to tell the boys to play it rough, like . . . like a rape. It was crazy."

Amarok felt his muscles bunch. "Did you do it?"

"Of course not!"

"But you didn't stop her."

"I didn't feel as if I had that right!"

"She was fucking everyone she could *on your property* for Chrissake!"

He poured himself a cup of coffee. "I wasn't using the best judgment, I admit, but we all have to make a living, Amarok. The boys would come out and they'd buy a hell of a lot of booze when she was around."

"You're talking about a girl who's very likely dead, Shorty."

He stretched his neck. "So you said. I feel terrible about that. Wish I would've stopped it now. But it didn't seem to be hurting anything or anyone at the time."

Amarok took a sip of the coffee Shorty had poured for him when he first sat down. "Can you tell me how often this went on?"

"Whenever she came in — and she came in whenever she could."

"Did she have regulars?"

"I don't know if you'd call them regulars, but they'd sure as hell get back in line."

"Any strangers around when that shit was going down?"

"Of course. We always have hunters and trappers and survivalists and people filming documentaries coming through here, even in the winter. I didn't make them sign a logbook."

Amarok slid the picture of Jasper he'd pulled off the Internet across the bar. Evelyn's attacker hadn't been seen since his murderous rampage in Boston. And she hadn't gotten a look at his face when he attempted to kidnap her last summer. So this picture was an old likeness, and no one knew how his looks might've changed. But it was all Amarok had. "What about this man? Do you recognize him? Has he been here?"

"You mean *boy*?"

"He's not a boy anymore."

Shorty shook his head. "Naw, I don't think so."

"That's too bad." Reluctantly, he put it back in his coat pocket. "Did anyone ever get too possessive of Danielle — or think he had more of a right to get in her pants than the next guy?"

"No, Sarge. I swear it. It was all in good fun or I would have come to you straight-away."

Amarok rubbed his chin. He couldn't believe this had been going on right beneath his nose. It was just too sordid. "I need you to make me a list."

"A list?"

"Of every guy you know who touched her."

He scowled. "You can't be serious."

"I'm dead serious. We're talking about murder here."

"But some of the guys, they're . . ."

Amarok played innocent. "What?"

"Married. If what they did with Danielle comes to light, it could break up their fami-lies."

"Glad you pointed that out. Start with the ones who have the most to lose." He had Danielle's little black book and planned to speak to everyone, but Shorty didn't know that. Amarok figured it wouldn't hurt to see if Shorty's list contained all the same names — or a few new ones.

"This is terrible bad." Sorrow filled Shorty's voice as he smoothed his apron. "Terrible bad for everyone."

"So's having a crazed psychopath running around," Amarok told him.

"Is that what we got?"

"Until I can prove Lorraine Drummond and Danielle Connelly were murdered in a jealous rage — or come up with some other scenario — we can't rule it out."

"Wait." Shorty gestured toward Amarok's coat. "Now I know why you showed me that picture and said that kid was no longer a boy. He's the bastard who slaughtered Doc Talbot's friends all those years ago, right? The one who slit her throat and left her for dead when she was just a teenager? Surely you don't think *he's* come to town."

"It's possible. He came after her again last summer, didn't he? And considering he probably no longer looks anything like this picture" — he patted his pocket — "how would we know?"

Shorty whistled as he shook his head. "Holy shit."

Hugo had his eyes closed and wasn't moving. Evelyn stood by his side, feeling . . . she didn't know what. Confused by her own emotions, maybe even disappointed in them. She knew too much about what he'd done before being incarcerated not to despise him for it, at least to some degree.

She'd been a victim of someone like him, which made it difficult to experience the compassion that would normally attend a man who'd just been stabbed. And yet she wanted to feel more than panic for how this might threaten her own situation. Praying for him to live only so that she wouldn't come under criticism and possibly lose her grip on HH made her almost as narcissistic as he was.

The nurse and doctor who bustled around the room had acknowledged her with a nod when she walked in but hadn't taken time to address her. Their daily grind consisted of handing out meds — for depression, high blood pressure, high cholesterol or other chronic ailments — and taking care of minor injuries, like the broken nose suffered by a CO thanks to Anthony Garza. This was their first major emergency, and Evelyn could tell they were feeling the seriousness of it.

"How bad is he?" She finally posed the question that was on her mind, despite her fear of their response.

Dr. Bernstein glanced over. Originally from Seattle, he'd accepted the position as head of their medical staff because he loved the wilderness and wanted to hunt and fish in Alaska. He'd once told her it was like getting invited to work where he most wanted to play. Almost all the management and medical staff came from the Lower 48, or Anchorage, including the warden. For the most part, Hilltop had only provided employees who could be trained on-site: some of the COs, administrative assistants, kitchen help, janitorial and maintenance crews.

"He's sustained two stab wounds," he replied. "One in the upper right quadrant of the heart, the other in the lower sternum. The blade's lodged in there, possibly causing a tamponade."

Evelyn had been to med school. Although she'd never practiced as a medical doctor, and definitely wasn't a surgeon, she understood how serious a cardiac tamponade could be. Hugo needed to have his chest opened, his aorta cross-clamped and, if necessary, his pericardium opened to relieve the fluid gathering in the sac around his heart. "You've removed the shank?"

"No, I don't dare. Not here. I'm afraid it would do more harm than good."

"So . . . where's the handle?" They'd covered Hugo with a blanket to keep him warm, but she would've expected to see some evidence of the knife protruding from his chest.

336

Bernstein maneuvered around the nurse. "Gone. Broken off."

Another one of the many downsides to homemade weapons.

Evelyn tightened her grip on the railing of Hugo's gurney. "Is there any danger of him bleeding out?"

"We're doing our best to make sure that doesn't happen. I've already given him six liters."

Shit. That was all a human body typically contained.

With a sigh, Evelyn read the chart the nurse had left on the table: *Pt verbally responsive, HR 82, RR 28, AE clear bilaterally, HS1 + 11 clear, no neck vein distention, ECG Lead QQ NSR, SP002 96% on Fi02 1.0.* "Will he be able to hang on until he arrives at Alaska Regional?" she asked.

Bernstein had been too busy preparing Hugo for transport to stop working while they talked. But at this, he paused. "Maybe."

"Did he tell you anything about the incident?"

"No."

"Did he speak to *you?*" She turned to the nurse, since it was the nurse who'd noted that the patient had been verbally responsive when he arrived.

"He told us who did it," she replied as she

337

added more tape to Hugo's hand to prevent his IV from coming out should the tube get snagged.

"Let me guess — Anthony Garza," Evelyn said. "Is that what he said?"

"If that's 'the new bastard.' "

"That's him." But what she wanted to find out was . . . *why?* And how did the stabbing come about? She could see Anthony shanking someone in the yard, but it was too coincidental that the victim of that attack would be Hugo. What connection did they have?

None that she knew of. She could only guess, as she'd just said in her office, that Fitzpatrick had put him up to it. Or maybe it was Dean Snowden or Steve Dugall, one of the COs on Danielle's list who would lose his job for allowing the inmates to have sex with her. That there were other possibilities made her regret accusing the one person who'd helped her bring Hanover House into existence. She couldn't really believe he'd do such a thing, and yet . . . someone had signed that transfer order. Would Dean or Steve dare be so bold?

Tough to guess. She didn't know them that well, but they both had families, so it said something about them that they'd have sex with Danielle.

"It doesn't make sense," she mumbled.

The nurse was too busy to comment. Evelyn was talking to herself, anyway.

"Evelyn."

That wasn't the doctor's voice. Hugo was looking at her with those strange, flat eyes of his. Even while he was fighting to survive she could find no real warmth in them. In her mind, that was probably the most distinguishing characteristic of psychopaths. Not only had she noticed that commonality herself, she'd heard about it many times from other victims: *There was something with his eyes. They were so devoid of emotion.*

"How are you?" she asked.

"Not so . . . good." He groaned. "Did you . . . did you get my letters?"

She hadn't technically received them, but, thanks to nosey Russ, she knew the gist of what he'd written.

"Yes."

"Will you . . . will you forgive me?"

When he reached for her hand, she let him take it. Chances were he wouldn't make it through the night. No matter what kind of individual he was, she couldn't bring herself to treat him poorly on his deathbed, especially when she was feeling partially responsible for his plight. Maybe she hadn't put

339

Garza in the yard, but, as Fitzpatrick had so emphatically pointed out, she was the one who'd brought him to HH.

"Of course." She battled the despair that tugged at her like gravity. "Why did this happen, Hugo?"

He wet his lips as he gathered the strength to answer. "No clue. Don't . . . even know the guy."

"There was no insult or reproach? No demand for something you wouldn't give?"

"None. He came . . . out of nowhere."

"We're ready to take him up," Bernstein announced.

Evelyn put out her free hand to hold the doctor off. The helicopter couldn't have arrived yet. They were merely making sure they had Hugo in place for when it landed. This was the first time they'd ever had to use the helipad. Just before the medevac unit was due to set down, Bernstein would push the button that would cause the cover on the roof to roll back. She hoped the groundskeepers had kept that cover clear of snow, since it was their most important responsibility.

"There has to be a reason, a trigger," she told Hugo, trying to keep him focused.

Bernstein touched her arm. "He really shouldn't exert himself, Dr. Talbot."

She understood the risk. But she also understood that she might never have another chance to get the answers he could give her. And she had to have them. This went far beyond her job. If they didn't figure out what was going on, even more people could die. . . .

Ignoring Bernstein's disapproval, she continued to cling to the bed but bent close to make it easier to hear Hugo's broken speech. "Think!" she whispered to him. "Why did he come at *you*?"

"Maybe because . . . I told you . . . about . . ."

"Fitzpatrick?" she prodded.

The way he gasped for breath made her fear he'd go into cardiac arrest and that would be the end of him.

"Dr. Talbot!"

The rebuke in Bernstein's voice caused fresh alarm. As intent as she was on getting answers, she didn't want to make matters worse.

"It's okay, Hugo," she said, straightening. "Don't try to talk. We'll . . . we'll cover this later, when you get back."

They both knew it was highly unlikely he'd be coming back, so he fought to speak despite her words. "It . . . had to be Fitz-patrick. He . . . he wants to destroy you.

I . . . swear it!"

Chills rolled down Evelyn's spine. For all Hugo knew, he wouldn't live more than a few minutes. Would he confirm such an outlandish lie on his deathbed? And so emphatically — when he had nothing to gain by it?

Could he despise Fitzpatrick that much?

"How do you know?" she asked.

Bernstein had had enough. Forcing her to step back, he started rolling the gurney away. But Hugo grabbed her arm.

"You believe me . . . don't you? Tell me . . . you . . . believe me. You're not safe."

She moved with them so she wouldn't slow them down. "It's not Jasper?"

"Who's Jasper?"

In Hugo's more lucid moments, he would know. He'd said it was Jasper right before the COs pulled him out of the cell after he attacked her. He'd made a study of her life, found it funny to return the scrutiny she gave him. He often told her psychiatrists were worse than psychopaths.

"Never mind," she said. "Just . . . pull through, okay? Hang on. We're going to get you taken care of."

"Evelyn?"

When he used her first name for the second time, Bernstein's scowl darkened.

"That's 'Dr. Talbot' to you," he said, but she let it go. In light of what Hugo had suffered, what he was *still* suffering, she figured she had to put everything in its proper perspective. It was upsetting that Lorraine and another woman had been killed. It was upsetting that someone had forged her name and Hugo had been stabbed as a result. It was upsetting that a man she relied on and trusted might be to blame for all the trouble.

At the moment, having an inmate call her Evelyn didn't even rank in the top ten.

"What?" she said to Hugo.

"I know . . . you don't think I'm . . . capable of love. But . . ."

His eyes closed and she thought he'd stop right there. She was more than happy to let him. This sounded like further proof of his infatuation — or, rather, his *fixation* — with her. She feared what he was about to say would only make her uncomfortable. But the nurse stopped pushing the gurney to double-check the flow coming from the IV bag and that gave Hugo the chance to continue.

"But if I've ever loved anyone or anything . . . it was you," he finished.

Evelyn felt like crying but refused to let herself. "I appreciate that."

"I hope . . . you'll miss me." He managed a grimace that passed for a smile. "At least a little," he added, and then the doctor and nurse wheeled him into the hall, moving quickly toward the elevator.

Evelyn stayed in the emergency bay and gazed through the small slit that passed for a window, wondering if the helicopter coming from Anchorage would be able to land. It wasn't snowing, but large gusts of wind swayed the trees beneath the bright perimeter lights along the fence.

The mental image of the helicopter crashing into the side of the building made her shudder.

Please, God, don't let that happen. No way did she want to feel responsible for any more loss of life.

"Maybe I won't miss you, but . . . I'll certainly never forget you," she muttered to Hugo, finally answering his question even though she now stood alone.

18

What I did is not such a great harm, with all these surplus women nowadays. Anyways, I had a good time.
— RUDOLF PLEIL, GERMAN SERIAL KILLER

Archie Rubin sat inside Amarok's truck, which he'd left running to help ward off the cold. This wasn't an interview Amarok felt comfortable conducting inside the man's home. His wife was there and his kids would soon be back from school. But Amarok couldn't afford the time it would take to drive him down to the trooper post, not when he had so many people to interview.

"What's going on, Amarok?" Archie looked nervous. "Mia's got to be wondering why you'd want to talk to me."

Archie's wife stood at the kitchen window, gazing out at them, making her curiosity apparent.

"For your sake, it's better to let her

wonder than to allow her to listen in on our conversation, Archie," he said.

He began to fidget. "Am I in trouble?"

Amarok didn't answer. Archie would probably be in trouble with his wife but not necessarily from the law. "I need you to tell me the last time you saw Danielle Connelly."

He didn't hesitate. "Down at the Moosehead a week ago last Friday, why?"

"You haven't heard?"

"She's gone missing. Everyone in town is talking about it. But I didn't do anything to her. I swear. I'll take a lie detector test or whatever you want to prove it."

Amarok studied Mia through the window. "It's not that easy. Did you have sex with Danielle?"

He cursed as his gaze fell to his boots.

"Is that a 'yes'?"

A sheepish expression stole over his face. "I'd had too much to drink. And I was with Bill Tate. You know how Bill is."

"Everyone knows how Bill is." A boisterous, barrel-chested man with a long beard, Bill was the life of any party. "Problem is . . . I wasn't asking about Bill."

"I know you weren't. But he said all the guys were doing it, that she put out every time she showed up at the Moosehead." He sighed as he raked a hand through his hair. "She liked getting down and dirty, liked it rough. What I did with her, though . . . it didn't mean anything."

"But you did have sex with her."

"Mia and I have been having problems since I hurt my back and can't work. We're struggling to pay the rent, buy groceries, gas . . . and that's causing some strain. You understand how it is. I hadn't had a woman act like she wanted me in" — he let his words fade before starting up again — "in a long time. That was a powerful temptation. But I love my wife," he added. "I-I want to work things out with her if I can."

Amarok frowned. "I doubt this will help."

His hands flexed and released. "Does she have to find out?"

The pleading in his eyes made Amarok uncomfortable. "The way this is going? The whole community will probably learn what's been going on."

"But . . . I got kids, man."

Amarok didn't comment on that. He hated to see one stupid act destroy a family, but Archie's employment record was another strike against him. He worked as a roughneck when he could get on with one of the oil companies that drilled nearby, but it seemed as if injuries, or personality differences, always got in the way.

"Who else spent time with Danielle that night?" Amarok asked — and how the hell did *he* miss that nearly the whole male population of his hometown were screwing the new girl?

He'd been too focused on his love-hate relationship with Dr. Talbot and HH, he supposed. He'd been watching them both from afar, blind to everything except his own desire and frustration — desire for the doc and frustration that he'd allowed a prison housing the worst humans in the country to be built so close to his home.

Archie chuckled without mirth. "You're kidding, right? Almost everyone at the bar. I didn't want to be the only one to miss out. Some of the other guys were married, too."

"I know." Amarok had them on his lists — both the one he'd culled from Danielle's and the one Shorty had provided. They were adulterers, for sure, but Amarok couldn't believe that any of the men he'd known for so long had suddenly turned into a cold-blooded killer. He was more suspicious of what might have changed in Hilltop over the past several weeks — the new folks who'd entered the area — and hoped the men who'd been with Danielle could tell him what was different. "Were there any strangers at the Moosehead that night? Anyone you didn't recognize?"

"There were a couple of COs from Hanover House who sat in the back room with her, watching the whole thing."

"They didn't participate?"

"Maybe before I got there. When I went in, they were just coaxing her to have another drink."

"Would you say they acted like they were orchestrating the whole thing?"

"No. They didn't charge any of her . . . partners, if that's what you're getting at. Or, if they did, I didn't hear about it. No one asked *me* for money, which is why I thought it wasn't that big of a deal and it could just . . . fade into the past."

Amarok adjusted the heat before checking the house to see that Mia was still looking out at them. Even if Archie hadn't been charged any money, there'd be a price. . . . "Participating in a train is pretty disgusting. You weren't worried about catching a venereal disease?"

"They had condoms — a whole bowl of them. But she was wearing a birth control patch on her arm — plain for all to see — so a lot of the guys didn't bother."

More proof of her addiction to risk, to adrenaline. A birth control patch didn't protect her from AIDS and other venereal diseases. "What about you?"

"I wore a rubber. I didn't want to bring anything home to my wife — especially after I heard Danielle joking about getting it on with the inmates at Hanover House."

"She was *joking* about that?"

"She said none of us could fuck better than they could."

Hanover House. Again. As far as Amarok was concerned, it was a cancer to the whole area. "Those men are locked up, Archie. Did she say how she was spending private time with them?"

"The COs must be helping. They were getting quite a kick out of it all. One chimed in that the inmates would do *anything* for a few minutes with Danielle."

"Do you remember the names of those COs?"

"Kush. One was Kush. I can't recall the other. I'm not sure I ever heard it. He wasn't from around here."

Amarok rested his hands on the steering wheel. "Is there anything else I should know, Archie?"

He shook his head. "It was a quick bang and that was it. Except . . ."

Amarok eyed him, waiting for him to continue.

"Except before she'd let me touch her, she insisted on measuring my . . . my cock. She said she was looking to screw the biggest one in Alaska."

"She was that open about it?"

"She had no shame — none whatsoever. And I was too drunk and horny to care."

Amarok took a picture out of the manila folder sitting between them. "We've found part of another body — a hand. Does it look familiar to you?"

"I wouldn't be able to recognize —" he started, but fell silent the moment he saw the picture. Then he opened the door and stuck his head out as if he might vomit.

"You okay?" Amarok asked.

He seemed to overcome the impulse, but he left the door hanging open as if he was eager to get the hell out of the truck and away from that image. "No, I'm not. That's got to be *her* hand. She was wearing the same purple fingernail polish when she . . . when she brought out the damn ruler."

Evelyn was functioning on pure adrenaline. She hadn't spoken to Fitzpatrick, the psychologists she worked with or Penny, not for the three hours since she'd left them in the administration center, but she'd kept in touch with Warden Ferris by radio. The

351

medevac had landed safely on the roof and carried Hugo off to Anchorage. At best, he had a ten-minute flight — at worst, twelve- or thirteen. She didn't see how he could last another quarter of an hour with a homemade knife broken off in his chest. A cardiac tamponade, if he had one, put too much pressure on the muscles of the heart.

But she was hoping he'd pull through — for his sake *and* hers.

Officer Emilio Kush poked his head into Interview Room #6, where she paced in an effort to help soothe her nerves.

"Where is he?" she asked when she realized Kush hadn't brought Anthony Garza as she'd requested.

The CO came inside. She met him at the edge of the desk.

"After last night's attack, I . . . um" — he shifted on his feet — "I thought maybe I should mention to Dr. Fitzpatrick that you were hoping to have a session with Garza today."

"You *what*?" Since when did anyone have to clear her instructions with Fitzpatrick or any other member of the mental health team? Had Fitzpatrick ordered the COs to report on her actions? Or had Kush taken it upon himself to go around her?

He hurried to finish what he had to say.

"Garza's our most dangerous inmate. After stabbing Hugo Evanski in the yard this morning, he's on lockdown, anyway. He's not scheduled to come out for over a month. Fitzpatrick doesn't believe he should have the privilege of interacting with anyone, especially you, since that's what he most wants."

She folded her arms. "Obviously, you agree with him."

His voice grew more strident. "This guy needs to be taught a lesson, Dr. Talbot. He needs to understand that we won't tolerate such behavior."

"So you took it upon yourself to go to Fitzpatrick instead of fulfilling my request?"

He cleared his throat. "I'm sorry. But . . . but it's my responsibility to protect you and everyone else here at Hanover House."

"Insubordination is not the way to go about it," she said.

Growing uncertain beneath her challenging glare, he stood taller. "I'm surprised, after yesterday, that you really want to see him."

"You're afraid I could be hurt even if I'm behind the plexiglass?"

"That's just it." A hint of defiance entered his eyes. "I'm afraid you won't *stay* behind the plexiglass."

Evelyn felt her jaw clench. Kush's rank put him in charge of a handful of other COs, but it gave him no power to defy her authority. "I'm sorry to hear you say that," she said. "Apparently, we have a different interpretation of what your job entails."

"Excuse me?"

He'd made a gross miscalculation if he thought she'd allow him to overstep his authority. "Either you get Anthony Garza for me *immediately,* without consulting anyone, or you will be dismissed. Questioning direct orders will not be tolerated at Hanover House, Officer Kush. Especially now, when we are going through such difficult and challenging times."

His mouth opened and shut twice before any sound came out. When he finally found his voice, he said, "Dr. Talbot, you can't be serious."

Getting right in his face, she spoke low and mostly through her teeth. "I am *absolutely* serious. And even if you decide to comply, you'll be written up for your actions this morning. Do you understand?"

He blinked several times. "Dr. Fitzpatrick agreed with me."

"Great. Feel free to rely on him if you think he can save your job."

It was a bluff. She wasn't sure she could

prevail if she and Fitzpatrick came to loggerheads regarding Kush's employment. Now that the man she'd once thanked for helping her get Hanover House off the ground was grappling for control of the institution, she had no idea who'd wind up at the helm.

Kush was beginning to sweat. She could see beads of it glistening on his forehead. "I didn't mean to . . . to cause a problem, Dr. Talbot."

She pretended to be supremely confident — while clutching her arms so tightly she was almost cutting off the blood-flow. Internal discord could cause the destruction of Hanover House far more quickly than anything else, especially now. They needed to present a united front — but she had no idea if she and Fitzpatrick would be able to get beyond what had occurred in her office. She feared the roots of that stemmed back to December and his accusation that she'd led him on — led him to hell on earth — to gain his support.

Regardless of how he interpreted their relationship, she'd never given him any indication that she might be interested in him romantically. And she wouldn't allow him to monitor or dictate her actions now. "Then don't," she told Kush.

"Yes, ma'am." With a sharp nod, he turned on his heel. "I'll get Garza."

After he left, Evelyn sat down and slumped over. She was exhausted, and it wasn't yet noon. She felt like Jeremy Renner in *The Bourne Legacy,* standing on the frozen tundra waving a burning stick at all the snarling wolves that were circling, looking for a chance to dart in for a quick bite.

Her radio went off. "Dr. Talbot?"

It was Warden Ferris. She recognized his voice, but she was almost too afraid to respond. Was he about to inform her that Hugo had died en route to the hospital?

Fortunately, when she forced herself to reply he told her the opposite.

"Hugo Evanski has reached Alaska Regional."

"Alive?"

"For the moment."

She covered her face. "Thank God."

"I thought you'd be relieved."

"I am." She drew a deep, calming breath. "I appreciate you letting me know."

"No problem."

She was about to set her radio aside when she heard the warden say, "There's one more thing."

Puzzled by the change in his voice, she straightened in her seat. "What is it?"

"Dr. Fitzpatrick just paid me a visit."

Her heart started to pound again. "What did he want?"

"An update on Hugo."

That wasn't so unusual. Like her, he had to be concerned about the ramifications of this morning's tragic incident. So . . . why did she get the impression there was more to it? "Is that all?"

The warden made a sound that suggested he was struggling with what he was about to say. "Not quite."

"What is it?"

"He indicated that . . . from now on . . ."

"Yes?"

"He'll need to approve any transfer orders you submit."

Evelyn couldn't believe her ears. Her hands began to shake as she wondered what she could do to counteract this brazen attempt to seize control. She was young, and she'd been through a lot. Maybe he thought she wouldn't put up much of a fight. That in the midst of the painful and frightening investigation of Lorraine's death, and the attempt to identify that second victim, she would be too distracted and upset to stand her ground.

But she wasn't about to let him take over.

"What did you tell him?" she asked, carefully modulating her voice so that the warden wouldn't hear her panic or anger.

"I didn't tell him anything. He didn't give me the chance. He stated the directive as if I had no business questioning it and left."

Typical, arrogant Fitzpatrick. "That's fine, Warden. I'll handle it from here."

There was a significant pause. "Is . . . everything okay between you?"

"Of course." She tried to sound positive, but when the door banged open on the opposite side of the room and Anthony Garza swaggered in, chains dragging, she knew her day was likely to get even worse.

19

One thing I know for sure. It was a definite
compulsion because I couldn't quit.
— JEFFREY DAHMER,
THE MILWAUKEE CANNIBAL

Evelyn fixed a placid expression on her face.
"Please, have a seat."

Garza glared at her. She guessed he wasn't
going to comply. But then he sat down
without argument, as if to prove he could
be as civilized as she was.

She slipped on her glasses, opened her
notebook and picked up a pen. Wanting this
interview to seem like any other, she hoped
her professionalism would disarm him, at
least to a degree. He'd met with prison
psychiatrists before. She'd read their notes
in his paperwork. If she was lucky, he'd
settle into the routine of it and abandon the
theatrics that'd marked his earlier behavior.

But she wasn't counting on it. She hadn't

been very lucky of late.

"I hear you've had a busy morning," she said.

A satisfied smile revealed those jagged teeth. "I prefer to think of it as . . . *productive.* Did that piece of shit I stabbed die?"

He didn't seem very invested, either way. If he'd attacked Hugo out of anger, or because of a personal slight, she felt he would've shown some sign of it. "Fortunately for you, no."

"You mean fortunately for *you.*" He tilted his head, mocking the way she was sitting and looking at him. "I'm in prison for life. There's nothing more you can do to me."

"You enjoy solitary confinement?"

"I won't let the threat of it control me. I won't let *anything* control me."

She adjusted her position. Worry and upset ran like acid through her veins, especially after that radio conversation with Ferris. But she could show no sign of it. The information she received from Anthony Garza would depend on how well she played him. As always, it was a chess game and she had to outsmart her opponent.

"Is that why you stabbed Hugo Evanski?" she asked. "In some misguided attempt to lash out at *me?*"

Because his wrists were cuffed, he had to

raise both hands to pick something out of his teeth. "Stabbings get reported in the papers."

She wished she could wipe that smug look from his face. "Not always."

"This one will." His smile widened. "And you can't afford the publicity."

"Why not?"

"Come on, you don't need me to explain it to you. I may be a psychopath according to that Hare quack and his ridiculous test, but I'm not stupid. I heard about the murders, *Evelyn.*"

"That's 'Dr. Talbot' to you," she said coolly.

"It's whatever I want it to be. You can't stop me from talking."

"I can stop meeting with you and leave you in your cell alone indefinitely. Is that what you'd like?"

Ignoring the question, he continued to taunt her. "Pretty soon you'll be hanging on to this pile of bricks by the hair of your chinny chin chin. People are already spooked by its existence." He moaned like a ghost and wiggled his fingers at her. "So many hobgoblins all in one place. Sort of gives you the creeps, doesn't it?"

His laughter did sound ghoulish. "You've

launched a personal vendetta against me, then?"

"Why not? At least it'll make my life here in Alaska interesting. If I can't have a lover, I might as well have an enemy. I doubt you'll be tough to destroy, but . . . we'll see."

She pretended to have some emotional detachment, as if she found what he had to say only slightly amusing. "And all of this hatred is coming from . . ."

He threw up his hands. "If you're going to lock me up in the middle of this godforsaken wilderness and poke and prod and study me like some kind of lab rat, I'm going to get my paybacks any way I can."

Sliding her chair back, Evelyn crossed her legs. "Has someone been poking and prodding you that I'm not aware of, Mr. Garza?"

He rolled his eyes. "Not yet. But that's what's coming."

"You don't have to participate in our studies if you'd rather not. Our research programs operate on a volunteer basis. They provide you with opportunities to acquire goods and services you would have little or no access to in a regular facility. Most of the men are eager to sign up."

"They're idiots. Just because you're offering me a prize, like some dumbass kid who gets a sucker at the doctor's office, doesn't

362

make it right. Am I supposed to be *grateful* for your generosity as you pick me apart piece by piece?"

"A dumbass kid getting a sucker at the doctor's office. That's an improvement over your lab rat analogy."

"It's all demeaning!" He leapt to his feet and smacked the glass, moving so fast, so explosively, she experienced a burst of panic, as if he could reach her. It took a second to realize he couldn't — and in that second Officer Kush hurried into the room.

"Everything okay?" he asked, his hand on his baton in case he had to subdue Garza.

Part of Evelyn wished Kush would use it. No one deserved a few blows more than Garza. But Kush was *hoping* she'd need his help. He wanted to feel vindicated for trying to derail this interview before it ever happened. Maybe, if he had to intervene, he'd even report it to Fitzpatrick.

"Mr. Garza, are you ready to calm down?" Evelyn asked. "Or would you like to accompany Officer Kush back to isolation?"

Nostrils flaring, chest rising and falling as rapidly as if he'd been exerting himself, Garza cursed. "I won't let you mess with my mind, *Dr.* Talbot," he said. "I'm not interested in your theories, your judgments or your high-handed self-righteousness. Are you really that sure you're so much better than me?"

When she raised her eyebrows as if she wasn't impressed enough to even formulate a response, he grumbled, "I'd rather have your abhorrence."

"You most certainly have that." *He* hates *feeling impotent,* she realized. Most psychopaths were quick to take offense, quick to react to any hint of reproach. Their tempers could flare with little or no provocation. But she believed this went a bit deeper than those typical reactions. Even more than most psychopaths, Garza dreamed of being a big man, someone others treated with respect and admiration.

"So are you going back to solitary now?" she prompted. "Or would you like *me* to make the decision?"

Again, he didn't answer. "Tell me something," he said instead. "How do you know *I'm* the one who's not right in the head? How do you know it's not *you*? Or this asshole?" When he jerked a thumb at Kush, Kush lifted the baton, but Evelyn waved him out.

Kush didn't move. Only when she insisted did he return to his post, but he stood right outside the door, staring in at them through the viewing slot.

"For starters, *I* haven't murdered anyone," she told Garza.

"Neither have I." He spoke flippantly, obviously expecting her to react with outrage. When she refused to take the bait, he shrugged and added, "At least no one who didn't deserve it."

"Your ex-wives deserved to die?"

Suddenly as calm as he'd been angry, he shrugged. "Hell yeah."

"But not your last wife."

His eyes narrowed until he was glaring at her so intently she thought he might start banging the glass again. "I told you I won't talk about her."

Did that mean she should let it go? Or push the subject? There was a greater chance he'd reveal more about the stabbing, his past deeds and the type of person he really was when overcome by emotion. But with the echoes of her argument with Fitzpatrick still ringing in her ears, and the angst of knowing Hugo might die on the operating table, Evelyn wasn't in any shape to deal with what could happen if she antagonized Garza. According to a battery of tests his exasperated parents had paid a specialist to administer to their "difficult child" when he was a young teen, he had a decent IQ. She needed to be in better control of her emotions when she dug that deep.

But she couldn't send him back to his cell, couldn't miss this chance to hear his thoughts while the stabbing was fresh in his mind. Maybe she could find out if Fitzpatrick, or someone else who had access to the transfer orders, was involved. According to one of Garza's former psychologists, one who'd interviewed him several times when he was first incarcerated, he liked to talk, liked to be the center of attention. She figured she should at least shine the spotlight on him, let him brag, taunt, tease, say whatever he liked — in case she could discover some tidbit that would help her unravel the mystery.

"Fine," she said. "We'll talk about something else."

"Like?"

"Where would you rather serve your time than here?"

For the most part, his calm returned. "*Now* you're asking? Send me back to Colorado. I had conjugal visits there."

"I didn't realize you were married." That hadn't been in any of his paperwork.

"Just tied the knot two weeks ago."

"With . . ."

"Some fat chick," he said.

So the marriage had taken place *after* his file had arrived. . . .

"You don't know her name?" As illogical as it seemed to most people, serial killers received a great deal of romantic attention. The more notorious they were, the more offers of marriage and/or sex they received.

"What does her name matter?" he asked. "I only married her because she was stupid enough to come to the prison and spread her legs for me. And she had nice tits." He curved his hands as if he were hefting them. Then a thoughtful expression overtook the lascivious one. "I wonder if she's pissed that I gave her herpes."

Evelyn folded her arms. He was trying to get a reaction. "Why would she be mad? Doesn't every woman want herpes?"

Although he laughed at her sarcasm, he quickly sobered. "See what you did to me? There's no way she has the money to fly up here. S-sh-i-t," he said, drawing out the word. "Chances are slim I'll *ever* get another piece of ass. I mean, I'll take guys if that's all I can get, but" — his eyes moved over her body — "I prefer women."

She felt sorry for *anyone* he came into contact with, even the other psychopaths at HH who might not be capable of standing up to him. He didn't care who he dominated so long as he dominated *someone,* which meant he'd be as much a predator inside prison as he was out. Those in charge tried to watch for that type of behavior, to protect the victims, but most inmates refused to report sexual assaults. They couldn't. Prison justice was too quick and ruthless. The consequences for divulging what slipped past the watchful eyes of the COs could be worse than the abuse the prisoners were hoping to avoid.

"And if they're pretty, like you, that's all the better," he added softly.

She managed a benign smile. "Thank you."

His eyebrows shot up. "For what?"

"For the compliment."

He hadn't meant to flatter her. He'd meant to intimidate her. She knew the difference. But she also knew it would be a mistake to let him feel as if he'd been successful.

"You're not afraid of me?"

She got the impression he was wondering if she might prove to be more of a challenge than he'd first thought. The idea of that seemed to intrigue him. "Why should I be?" she replied. "You'll live the rest of your life in a cage the size of my closet. And there's nothing you can do about it."

"Someday you'll see what I can do." That voice, threatening and low, brought back memories of Jasper: *Hold still or I'll cut you. You don't want me to scar that pretty face, do you? Then no one will want to look at you, except me.*

"I say something wrong?" Garza jeered.

She blinked and regained her focus. "No. You can't reach me. That's all that matters."

"Like I said, I'll have my chance."

Nausea welled up, making Evelyn long to dash from the room. But now was not a time when she could show weakness. Forcing herself to remain right where she was, to tell herself she would *not* be sick or back down, she folded her hands in her lap so he wouldn't notice how they trembled. "Was Hugo someone you'd hoped to add to your list of conquests, Mr. Garza?"

Maybe Anthony had approached Hugo in the yard and Hugo had rebuffed him. Maybe Hugo getting stabbed had nothing to do with Fitzpatrick. If only it was all a big coincidence — but that didn't account for the forged transfer order.

"I wouldn't have turned him down if he wanted to give me a blow job. But then I don't turn anyone down who wants to suck my dick," he said with a laugh.

Working among such men, Evelyn had

heard worse. A lot worse. She hated how crude they could be. But she'd learned not to let on. Otherwise, they'd talk that way nonstop. This was, basically, a fishing expedition. Garza was assembling his arsenal for future combat, and she was assembling hers.

"It was a little early to be propositioning Hugo, wasn't it?" she said. "Had the two of you even been introduced?"

He scratched his head — an awkward endeavor with handcuffs. "I heard him bragging about touching you, kissing you. That was enough."

"Now you're saying you stabbed him out of jealousy or possessiveness? I thought you were trying to punish me for bringing you here by making me look bad."

"You're the shrink. You figure out my motive."

In a last-ditch effort to obtain *some* shred of useable information, she got up and walked to the glass. She also lowered her voice so whoever might listen to the video of this interview later wouldn't be able to tell what she said. "What do you think of Dr. Fitzpatrick?"

"Who?" Garza got up, too, and came as close as he could. For a change, this was what she wanted. Then she wouldn't have to speak any louder.

"Fitzpatrick."

"Never heard of him."

"You haven't visited with any of the other doctors?"

"Just a tall, skinny one who thinks he's God."

"That's Fitzpatrick," she said wryly.

"You said *you* were my shrink. I don't know why I had to deal with him. He looks like a fucking cadaver."

She ignored the cadaver part, although she could see how Garza came up with the comparison. "Did Fitzpatrick, or anyone else, mention Hugo to you? Draw him to your attention? Try to make you angry with him?"

He leaned against the glass. "Are you saying you don't trust your own staff?"

"I'm saying they might have inadvertently created a target without realizing the danger they were putting him in. There has to be a reason you chose Hugo and not someone else."

"I told you. I did it for you." With that, he kissed the glass as if he were kissing her, moaning and thrusting against it at the same time. "Anyone who touches you is a dead man," he whispered when he pulled back.

The sight of the glass, smeared with his

saliva, turned her stomach. "You're an animal."

"That's right," he said. "You'll be *begging* Colorado to take me back before I'm through."

She already regretted bringing him here. Satan couldn't be any worse than this man.

"Guard, get me the hell out!" Garza yelled, using his cuffs to bang on the plexiglass.

Kush entered the room, and this time, when he looked at Evelyn, she nodded.

20

It wasn't as dark and scary as it sounds. I
had a lot of fun . . . killing somebody is a
funny experience.

— ALBERT DESALVO,
THE BOSTON STRANGLER

Hugo Evanski didn't die in surgery. The
sharpened pen Anthony Garza jammed into
his sternum had nicked his aorta and caused
a pericardial tamponade, just as Dr. Bernstein had guessed. How Hugo's heart had
held up under the pressure no one could
really say. But after five hours of surgery,
he'd been deemed "stable." Unless he suffered a setback, Evelyn expected him to live.
With any luck, he would be back at HH in
a few weeks.

She'd received this update around dinnertime. That report had brought her a measure
of relief — but by no means solved all her
problems. Those problems seemed to crowd

close now that it was growing late and she was alone with her thoughts. But at least she'd managed to outlast the rest of the mental health team. After what Fitzpatrick had done, going to Warden Ferris and also overriding her request to see Anthony Garza, she had to come earlier and stay later than everyone else just to protect her interests.

Although she'd passed Fitzpatrick in the halls twice since that less-than-friendly encounter in her office, they'd avoided making eye contact. They hadn't even nodded hello. She was glad he hadn't tried to engage her. She wanted a chance to see if she could figure out who'd signed her name to that transfer order before she and Fitzpatrick had another conversation, even a conciliatory one. She had to be decided on her position, so she wouldn't fall victim to the anger and fear that had caused her to speak so impulsively last time. There were moments when she was horrified by her own lack of faith in him, was certain she owed him an apology. Accusing a prominent psychiatrist of murdering two people was no small matter.

But . . . there were also moments when she wondered if, somehow, Hugo could be telling the truth. Fitzpatrick had easy access to all the forms they used. He was almost as familiar with her signature as she was. And who else would be so brazen?

There were the COs who had to be hoping to save their jobs, she reminded herself. She and the warden were keeping the investigation so quiet Snowden and Dugall and the others on that list didn't even know they'd been discovered. But they had to have heard that Danielle was missing. If they were aware of her black book, they could realize what was at stake if it was found.

Still, Hugo had been so damned convincing, gasping with what could've been his last breath that Fitzpatrick was a danger to her. . . .

Then there was the matter of Fitzpatrick's actions *since* the stabbing. They seemed to indicate she couldn't trust him. He was staging a takeover, was grappling for control of Hanover House. But whether that was because he felt she was truly unfit to continue performing as she had in the past or he was moving in for the kill on some well-executed plan to punish her for rejecting him she couldn't be sure.

The telephone rang. She considered letting it go to the answering service. Since it was coming through to the administration offices, it had already been routed through Corrections and could wait until Penny returned to sift through messages in the morning. If anyone on the secure side of the institution needed Evelyn — if Garza was acting out again, for example — she had her radio.

But then she thought it might be Glenn Whitcomb. She'd taken a break and gone down to speak with him earlier, asked him to see what he could find out about that transfer order. Maybe there was some rumor or other detail floating among the COs — about Fitzpatrick or even someone else — that Glenn could make himself privy to.

He'd promised he'd do all he could to help.

Her caller could also be Amarok, looking for the reason she wasn't home. She'd spoken to him once, around three. They'd had a brief conversation in which he'd asked some additional questions on Lorraine's routine and habits — he was still searching for the rest of her body. Then he'd gotten interrupted and had to go before Evelyn could even tell him Hugo had been shanked.

The phone had rung four times already. Gathering what remained of her mental fortitude, in case it wasn't Glenn or Amarok but Fitzpatrick wanting to have a heart-to-heart, she picked up the phone. She'd been expecting one or more of her colleagues to request a meeting or phone call. That was how they handled their disagreements, mild though they'd been in the past.

The voice on the other end of the line didn't belong to the sergeant, Glenn or a colleague.

"I just heard the news!" her mother cried. "My God, are you okay?"

Evelyn cringed. She didn't want to have this conversation, wasn't sure she could withstand the emotionality of it, not in addition to everything else she was going through. "I'm fine."

"Why haven't you called? Didn't you realize we'd be worried?"

"Is Dad there, too?"

"Of course he's here."

"Hi, honey," he called out from somewhere in the background. It was the same words he always used, but tonight they sounded stilted. Obviously, Grant was as upset as Lara.

"He doesn't understand why you haven't called us, either," her mother said.

What was so difficult to understand? Evelyn saw no need to upset them. They'd only start pleading with her to leave Hanover

House and return to the Lower 48. They'd barely stopped that a few weeks ago, when she'd finally told them she wouldn't stay in such close contact if they couldn't accept her life choices.

"I'm sorry," she said. "I've been meaning to get in touch, but . . . I was hoping to have some answers before we talked, something to . . . to explain what's happening and put your minds at ease." She stared at the digital clock on her desk, watched the numbers flip from 8:08 to 8:09.

"How could you ever put our minds at ease about a *murder*?"

Evelyn didn't answer that question. It was rhetorical, anyway. "How'd you hear?" They never watched the news. After what'd happened to her, they couldn't tolerate the crime reports. Even relatively mild stories could cut them like a razor; no way could they handle the really bad stuff.

"The neighbor," her mother said. "Can you believe that? Your father and I were just getting home from having dinner with your sister when Chad pulled into his drive. He said he'd been at a fund-raiser where that busybody on the corner had mentioned two people were recently murdered in Hilltop."

"Theresa? *That* busybody?"

"Of course. Who else?"

Her parents still held some of the things Theresa had said twenty years ago — when Evelyn went missing — against her. Judgments Theresa had had no business making about Evelyn "reaping what she'd sown" by getting so intimately involved with a boy before marriage.

"Chad wanted to know if you were okay and that blindsided me — because, of course, we feared you might not be. We haven't heard from you in over a week, since before —"

"Mom, stop getting yourself worked up." Evelyn wished she *had* contacted them, but even if she had she doubted their reaction would've been any less severe. "I'm sorry I wasn't the one to tell you. I really am. But as you can imagine, this has thrown *me* for a loop, too."

"Of course it has! Chad said one of the victims was Lorraine Drummond. She was your friend, right?" Her voice broke and she cried through the rest. "I've heard you mention her many times. She stayed with you not long after you moved to Alaska, when she was separating from her husband."

Evelyn dropped her head in her hands. This wasn't helping anything.

"Evelyn?"

Fighting the lump rising in her own

throat, she said, "Yes, I knew her well."

"We can't face another nightmare like the last one," she responded with a sniff.

"It'll be okay," Evelyn promised, which sounded absurd. How could anything be okay when two people were dead? There was no way to return them to life.

"Tell me Jasper hasn't followed you up there!"

"At this point, we know very little. It could be *anyone.*"

"Not someone so fixated on you!"

Apparently, the neighbor hadn't heard, or hadn't relayed, the part where a portion of a human limb had been found in Evelyn's bed. *Thank God.* "I'm with you on that."

"So when will you be leaving that place?"

"Excuse me?"

"What are you waiting for? Lorraine's head was cut off and one of her eyes was gouged out! You have to get out of Hilltop. Right away, do you hear me? I don't know why you ever went up there to begin with. The wilderness is no place for a girl like you. With your education, you could go anywhere."

Her parents had never liked that she'd decided to use her psychiatric degree to study psychopathy, and they'd liked that she was moving so far away from them even less.

I don't see how you can put the past behind you if that's all you ever think about, her father would grumble. Then her mother would add, *Don't you think psychopathy is all a bit . . .* depressing?

Both parents seemed content to label Jasper an "evil man" and let it go at that. They didn't mind that "evil" could be so inexplicable. They just wanted to forget and get on with their lives, as if drawing a curtain would make what was on the other side disappear.

Evelyn wished she *could* live like a normal person. But Jasper had made that impossible. He'd opened her eyes to a problem she might never have encountered otherwise, at least not personally. And now she was determined to do something about it. If she could stop just one person — be it a sixteen-year-old girl, a fifty-year-old woman or a nineteen-year-old boy — from suffering as she had, it'd be worth all the sacrifice. She didn't want Jasper, or anyone like him, getting away with more pain, degradation and murder.

So what if you're back? she thought, picturing his preppy-looking face as she remembered it from high school. He hadn't even been capable of growing a beard when she knew him, had seemed so innocent. *I'll fight you. I'll fight you till my dying breath — just like I did last summer.*

She'd fight Fitzpatrick, too, if necessary.

"I'll pay for your plane ticket," her mother was saying. "Just go to your house and pack up."

Her parents had been through an unimaginable ordeal when Jasper did what he did. For three days, Evelyn and her friends had been missing. Everyone, and no one more so than Lara and Grant, had feared the police would discover her body. Or that they wouldn't find anything at all — no trace of her. Her mother had once said the possibility that they'd be left to wonder for the rest of their lives had probably been the worst of it. Lara couldn't bear to go through anything like that again. And Evelyn couldn't blame her.

But she'd started Hanover House, still believed in it. She couldn't pack up and walk away. That would be conceding to the opposition, conceding to *him.*

"Calm down, okay?" She changed the phone to her other ear. "We both know that terrible things can happen in Boston, too. I'm proof. Remember last summer? Jasper will come wherever I am."

"Not if he can't find you. What you're doing now is *courting* trouble!" Her mother sounded almost hysterical. "Rubbing elbows with *known* sadists. When we welcomed Jasper into our lives he seemed like a sweet seventeen-year-old boy. What happened wasn't our fault because we didn't know to keep you away from him. But we're fully aware of the type of people you're with up there — and they're some of the most notorious killers in America!"

"At least I know they're dangerous. These men can't surprise me the way Jasper did." Even as she said that, Evelyn couldn't help flashing back to the moment Hugo had slammed her up against the wall yesterday. That had been a close call, could've gone very differently.

Her mother wasn't satisfied with her response, anyway. Evelyn could tell by the sudden silence. She almost thought they'd lost their connection. "Mom?"

"And your father wonders why I need anti-anxiety drugs," she mumbled.

Evelyn's breath hitched. Had she heard correctly? "You're on medication? Since when?" And did Evelyn's sister know? If so, Brianne hadn't mentioned it when they'd spoken just a day or two before Lorraine was murdered. "Mom?"

There was no reply.

"Answer me!"

"I can't deal with this," Lara finally responded.

Evelyn tightened her grip on the phone. "Let me talk to Dad."

"He just walked out of the room. I-I'll have him call you tomorrow," she said, and hung up.

Evelyn sat staring at the phone. She couldn't bear worrying about Lara on top of everything else. She was about to call back, to try to offer her mother some comfort and achieve reassurance in return. But the phone rang before she could.

"Hello?" She tensed as she waited to hear her mother's or father's voice. But it wasn't either of them.

"Hey."

Amarok. She rested her head against the back of her chair. "Hey, yourself," she said, striving for calm even though her stomach was in knots. Maybe she'd needed to get away from her family. Maybe that was another reason she'd come to Hilltop. They were as damaged as she was. But that also made her feel obligated to return and take care of them. "You home?"

"Not yet. I stopped by the Moosehead so I could give you a call. I'm on my way to check something out."

"Something?"

384

"Bill Jenkins' dog has found some bones. But don't get your hopes up. Chances are they're the remains of some animal."

"Any word on Danielle?"

"Yes. That's primarily why I'm calling."

She stiffened again. "You've identified that . . . that arm? It was her?"

"DNA will have to confirm it, and that takes time. But some of the guys who were with her recognized the unusual purple fingernail polish."

Evelyn closed her eyes. "I guess it's better to know." Except Danielle's murder confirmed that both victims were employees of Hanover House.

"It's a step in the right direction."

"Did you get the contact information for those HH employees I e-mailed you?"

"I did. But what about the others? The ones you left blank?"

"If there's no contact information it's because we don't have anyone on our roster by that name."

"I was afraid you were going to say that. Shit. Now I'll have to track those guys down some other way, if I can." There was a brief pause in which he yawned or scratched his face or something. "I just wish there were more hours in the day."

"You sound exhausted."

"So do you. You ready to leave work?"

"Not quite."

"Will you do me a favor?"

"Of course."

"Call my trooper post when you pack up? I want to know when you leave and when you get home."

"Okay, but . . . it might be a while."

"Why? After the past couple of nights, you shouldn't be putting in such long hours. You need to conserve your strength. I'm afraid this is going to turn out to be more of a marathon than a sprint."

She didn't want to hear that; she wanted it to be over *now*. "I'm just waiting for the cleaning crew."

"Why do you need to do that?"

"They're the only ones with a key to Dr. Fitzpatrick's office."

There was a slight pause. Then he said, "Why do you need to get into his office?"

"I'd like to take a look around."

"I'm not sure that's a good idea, Evelyn. What if he were to catch you? Or find out about it later?"

"Fitzpatrick is up to something, Amarok. I have to get to the bottom of it — to save my job, my career, my sanity. Maybe even my life."

"You could be taking an unnecessary risk."

"He's diligent about locking his office for a reason. The rest of us usually don't bother. Our offices are inside a prison, for God's sake. Which tells me he doesn't want me or one of the other doctors poking around in there."

"So what's your plan?"

"Since the janitors are the only ones with a key, besides him, I'm hoping to put some tape or gum on the door so it won't lock again when they leave."

"Your relationship with Fitzpatrick seems to have deteriorated."

"We've been at each other's throats all week, and the situation grew a great deal more . . . tense today." She told him about Hugo getting stabbed, the forged transfer order and the accusation she'd launched that Fitzpatrick was behind the murders.

"Holy hell, Evelyn. Don't provoke him. I don't trust that bastard."

"Maybe the accusation will rattle him enough that he'll panic and make a mistake."

"Or he'll try to hurt you in some way."

"Don't tell me you're starting to believe Hugo!"

"I'm keeping an open mind. If psychopaths are as common as you say, there's no reason Fitzpatrick can't be one."

"Not all killers are psychopaths."

"To do what this killer has done, he'd almost have to be."

"I agree. But . . . it's crazy that I'm even considering taking the word of a convicted killer over the psychiatrist I work with."

"There's some basis for it. You mentioned yourself that Fitzpatrick might've had Hugo shanked because he was talking. And there *is* a Tim in Danielle's book."

"I saw that. But, as I noted, we have a maintenance man here by the same name."

"Tim Hancock."

He'd looked over what she'd sent. "Right. So I'm not sure we can draw any conclusions from that piece of the puzzle."

"I'll go visit Mr. Hancock as soon as possible, probably in the morning. See if I can determine if he was ever with Danielle. If not, I'll be visiting Fitzpatrick next."

"I wish I could be there to see that. You two are as compatible as oil and water."

"I told you, I don't trust him."

"I don't anymore, either. But even if Mr. Hancock says he isn't the Tim in Danielle's book — that doesn't mean Fitzpatrick is."

"What are the chances it could be someone else? We're not a big community, especially this time of year."

"The chances aren't huge, but I can't

imagine any prosecutor being willing to build a case on a first name."

"That wouldn't be the entire case. We could line up both Tims and bring out a ruler."

In spite of everything, the mental image of that nearly made her laugh. "If Dr. Fitzpatrick was one of her partners, he'll be mortified when he finds out she recorded that information."

"I wish it could've been the length of their noses or something. Then maybe we *could* measure."

"A last name would've been nice. She put that down for some of the men — like Snowden and Dugall. Why couldn't she have done it for all?"

"Maybe because this one was such a central figure it felt redundant?"

"Or there would be scandal involved, some reason to keep it more private than the rest."

"Either scenario points to Fitzpatrick over a janitor."

"True."

"Tell me, does Fitzpatrick have much interaction with a CO by the name of Emilio Kush?" he asked.

"We all do," she replied. "Why? Emilio wasn't on the list you sent me. I would've recognized his name — first or last — immediately."

"He wasn't on the part I kept, either. But he was aware of Danielle's activities."

The hair stood up on the back of Evelyn's neck. Emilio Kush was the sergeant who'd gone to Fitzpatrick when she'd asked him to bring Anthony Garza from his cell. "How do you know?"

"He and one other CO — Eddie Petrowski — were in the back room, lining up a train for Danielle and placing bets on whether or not she could make it all the way through."

Evelyn shook her head in disappointment. "I can't believe any of my COs would be involved. Especially Emilio Kush. He's so . . . by the book."

"Several of Danielle's partners gave me the same names. I can't imagine there could be any mistake."

She blew a strand of hair out of her face. "Were they charging to have sex with her?"

"Not when they were with her at the Moosehead. But several of the men I spoke to reported hearing them make statements that suggested they had some type of arrangement with her when it came to HH inmates."

"Which means . . . what? They're only charging the incarcerated?"

"That's what it sounded like to me."

"But putting her in a cell with almost any of these guys — that's dangerous. If she were to get hurt or killed, it'd be their fault. Why would they be so foolhardy?"

"Because prostituting her to the inmates could be very lucrative. Since the inmates can't get a piece of ass any other way, I'm sure they'd pay a lot — and do whatever they can to raise what they don't have."

"So why would Kush be stupid enough to divulge what he did?"

"It was actually Eddie Petrowski who did the talking. He was drunk and couldn't resist the urge to brag a bit, I suppose. Kush tried to claim he was full of shit, but, as far as I'm concerned, that's what lends it so much credibility."

Evelyn pictured Emilio with the pretty woman he'd brought to the Christmas party — his wife. They had three small children. Eddie Petrowski was single and about ten years younger than Kush, maybe thirty. On the surface, they didn't seem to have a lot in common. Emilio was five-foot-ten or so and stocky, with dark hair and eyes. Eddie was tall and stringy with red hair and blue eyes. But they'd been almost inseparable since the day they first met when Hanover House opened.

Had Kush proven to be Petrowski's downfall? Kush had to be the leader. No way could it be Eddie. Eddie just didn't have that sort of thing in him. "The warden's brought in a few of his most trustworthy COs to keep an eye on the other officers."

"I hope he can come up with some answers. I could use a break."

She glanced at the window. It'd started snowing earlier in the afternoon. Now the wind was picking up, too. "The weather certainly isn't cooperating."

"Not entirely. But this storm isn't supposed to be a bad one. It's the next one I'm worried about. The one that's coming over the weekend."

She sighed. "Sometimes I wonder why I don't let my parents talk me into going home."

She hadn't really been thinking when she made that statement, not about the implications about her feelings for him. But when he made no immediate response, she could tell he'd taken it personally that she could be so cavalier about leaving him behind.

"Really?" he said at length. "We don't have anything here you like?"

"I didn't mean it that way," she said.

"Come on. You're a short-timer. I've always known it." He suddenly acted as if it didn't matter to him either way, which made her wonder if she'd hurt him. She couldn't imagine she held that much power with the handsome trooper, but . . .

"Amarok —"

"Don't worry about it," he said. "Of course you'll go back to Boston. That's where you belong."

His defenses had gone up again. She'd all but heard them snap into place. She didn't like that — but she had no right to try to bring them down again. She *was* a lousy bet, and because she really did care about him she didn't want to disappoint him. "My family needs me. They ask me all the time to come back. I'll have to go eventually," she told him. "Because of that, it's better not to count on me."

"So you've said," he responded, his voice flat.

"I'm sorry."

He changed the subject back to business. "Is the warden still there?"

She wished he was. After what she'd just learned, she wanted to talk to Ferris right away. "No, he's gone for the night."

"Maybe I'll stop by his place after I check on those bones, if it's before ten."

"I hope you won't be out *too* late. You need to get some sleep as badly as I do."

"I'll get home when I can."

"Okay." She started to hang up, but he stopped her.

"If you don't get out of there in the next hour, wait for me to come get you. I'd rather not have you driving in this mess."

She smiled at the grudging way he'd stated that. He couldn't help looking after her. That was just the kind of man he was. "If I were normal . . ."

"You wouldn't be able to resist me. I know," he joked, and hung up.

21

I am deeply hurt by your calling me a
women hater. I am not. But I am a monster.
I am the "Son of Sam." I am a little brat.

— DAVID BERKOWITZ

Evelyn listened to be sure no one was approaching the administration office. The COs knew she hadn't left. She checked out when she did. So there was always the chance that someone might come by to get an update on Hugo, to report on Anthony Garza or for a number of other reasons. Sometimes, when she was working late, various COs came by just to talk. She was, after all, a psychiatrist, and their job could be difficult.

But all was quiet. Even the cleaning crew, a team of two — at least in this part of the institution — was gone. Before they left, she'd taken their key. That hadn't been as hard to do as she'd imagined it would be, since they hung their ring on their cart in the reception area while vacuuming the individual offices. The most difficult part had been sorting through the twenty or so other keys on the same ring, since they all looked alike. She'd had to try one after another, hands shaking and heart racing, until she managed to unlock her own door.

Once she had the master, she'd slipped it into her pocket before replacing the rest.

If they'd caught her, she'd planned to say she'd accidentally locked herself out and was merely trying to get back in. But if something was left askew in Fitzpatrick's office and he happened to notice it or get suspicious in the morning, he might ask the janitors, and they might remember that she'd had the keys in her possession for a few brief minutes. So it was better, *much* better, that they had no clue. By the time they realized their key was missing it would probably be tomorrow night. They wouldn't be able to get into the mental health offices, but Evelyn didn't see where missing a night or two of janitorial service would be a big deal. They would just have to get a locksmith to change the locks and provide a new master.

Fitzpatrick's office smelled musty, like he did. There was an ornate coatrack in the back corner, where he hung his heavy wool overcoat, hat and umbrella. A mahogany desk and leather chair held court on the opposite side of the room. His degrees hung on one wall; bookshelves filled the other. But instead of a credenza, like hers, he had a tall filing cabinet.

Evelyn had always assumed he kept files from previous patients in there, or bits and pieces of research. He didn't need that big of a filing cabinet for his work at HH. They were supposed to use the file room off the reception area. That way, if a member of the team got sick or couldn't come to work someone else could pick up that doctor's caseload and would have immediate access to the patients' most recent assessments and histories.

The psych team didn't always meet that ideal. They carried various files around instead of putting them away or left them on a desk or in a briefcase because they had yet to finish a report. But Evelyn didn't think anyone else on the team crowded his or her office with such a big filing cabinet. . . .

So what was in it?

She tried to find out, but it was locked.

Fortunately, the desk wasn't. Although she went through it, she didn't find anything of interest, except a small key. She thought it might open the filing cabinet — but it didn't.

"Damn!" Where else would Fitzpatrick keep the key? Did he take it home each night? Surely there couldn't be anything *that* secret in those drawers. And if there was — the question was *why*?

Stymied, she went through his garbage, which was the reason she'd wanted to get into his office in the first place. She was hoping to find evidence of the same kind of practicing she and her sister had done on their mother's signature in high school. Evelyn doubted he'd be dumb enough to leave ten different attempts at "Evelyn Talbot" in his trash can; surely he'd shred that. But she thought she might find the imprint of her signature on his writing pad or blotter, even another sheet of paper. She'd seen that type of thing on forensic shows. A detective would scrape pencil lead across what appeared to be a blank piece of paper to reveal what had been written on the one before it.

She examined everything she could find that wasn't shredded — and came up with nothing more incriminating than a note to Russ about her "erratic behavior." She was just reading that when a noise made her freeze. Someone had come into the offices. . . .

"Dr. Talbot?"

Fear gripped her like a tight fist that would hardly allow her to expand her rib cage enough to breathe as she flattened herself against the wall. Had she been seen through the frosted glass? She'd left the door to her office open to make it look like she'd just stepped out and locked this one. Whoever it was wouldn't be able to get in.

But the light was on. . . .

Was it too much to hope her visitor would assume the janitors had forgotten to turn it off?

"Dr. Talbot?"

Glenn Whitcomb. He probably wanted to follow up with her on whether or not he'd been able to learn anything about the transfer order. But she couldn't let anyone know she'd been in Fitzpatrick's office, even Glenn. She preferred he be able to answer honestly if he was ever questioned about her.

When a knock sounded, she was sure he'd found her — until he moved on past Fitzpatrick's door and continued to call out.

"What am I doing?" she whispered, and slid down the wall to crawl into the footwell of Fitzpatrick's desk, where she for sure couldn't be seen.

She could hear Glenn's footfalls and the curiosity in his voice as he looked for her. Then he returned and jiggled the doorknob, making her curl into a tighter ball. She really didn't want to explain her actions; they wouldn't reflect well on her. This was going too far, even for a friend like Glenn to understand.

"Dr. Talbot? Hello? Doc, you in there?"

Covering her mouth with one hand, she struggled to remain calm and still. *He'll be gone shortly,* she promised herself, and, after a few minutes, that seemed to be the case.

She waited a bit longer, to be sure. Then she forced herself to abandon her hiding place. She needed to get out of Fitzpatrick's office as soon as possible, before Glenn could come back when he didn't find her elsewhere. But just as she was about to stand up, she spotted a flash of silver out of the corner of her eye.

It was another small key, only this one was taped to the underside of Fitzpatrick's desk drawer.

Amarok was worried. He hadn't heard from Evelyn, and she wasn't answering at the prison. Surely she hadn't tried to drive home in the blizzard they were having and gotten stranded somewhere.

He studied every car he passed, but even with his windshield wipers moving on high it wasn't easy to see.

"Damn it." He was risking getting stuck himself. He hadn't had a chance to fix the hydraulic plow on his truck. But he drove out to the prison, anyway. He wasn't going home without her.

He breathed a sigh of relief when he saw her car in its usual spot, mostly buried by snow despite the parking cover. It didn't appear that she'd been out of the building. But that didn't mean she was okay. There was possibly more danger *inside* than out, given all the shit that was going on.

Fitzpatrick better not have harmed her, Amarok thought as he parked under the portico at the main sally port and hopped out.

The cold nearly stole his breath. But it was plenty warm inside. The COs greeted him and put him through the standard security measures before he took the elevator to the second floor.

The usual sounds of such a place seemed muted, which made him anxious. He hoped Evelyn was working at her desk, knew she often stayed late. What she'd said about searching Fitzpatrick's office had him on edge, however. What if she'd been caught?

Those fears escalated when he couldn't get into the mental health offices. Her office light was on, but everything else — the entire reception area — was dark. Why would the place be locked up if she hadn't yet left the prison?

"Evelyn?" He pounded on the glass doors.

When there wasn't an immediate response, he turned, planning to get someone to let him in. But as he started walking away, he heard a noise and went back to see her approaching those glass doors from the other side.

"I'm here." She didn't turn on the light, but she poked her head out.

"What's the matter?" he asked. "Why's the place so dark?"

"I'll explain in the truck. Can you watch this area for a second? Don't let anyone past."

"Why?"

"Hang on." She disappeared again. He saw her office light go off and another office light go on and off before she let herself out.

"All set," she said.

With only partial lighting it was too shadowy to see her face clearly, but he could tell she was anxious. "Everything okay?"

She pressed a finger to her mouth, signaling caution, but spoke plenty loud — almost too loud — when she responded. "Of course. Thank you for the lift. No way could I have made it home in this weather."

"No problem," he said.

"Did you make it past Tim Hancock's?" she murmured as they got into the elevator.

"Not yet. It got too late."

"And those bones?"

"Part of a bear."

She frowned to show her disappointment, then cursed right before the elevator doors opened.

"What?" he said.

"I hope Officer Whitcomb isn't down here."

"Why?"

"He came up earlier to deliver a brownie to me, and I never acknowledged it, which will seem strange. I was too busy making copies."

"You're worried about a brownie?"

"He also left me a note that no one seems to know anything about the forged transfer order."

"Who'd he ask?"

Once again she indicated silence as the elevator doors opened. Then they stepped into the main lobby. Fortunately, Officer Bramble was stationed there instead of

Glenn Whitcomb.

Amarok knew that was a good thing, although he wasn't entirely sure why.

Evelyn gave Bramble a polite smile, and Bramble wished her a good night. It wasn't until both she and Amarok climbed into the truck and he pulled away that she let that smile fade.

"Now what's this about Whitcomb and that forged transfer order?"

She cast a final glance over her shoulder at the prison as he rounded the circle and headed down the long drive. Hanover House had their own grounds crews who kept the driveways on the property clear, which made this part easy to navigate. But once she and Amarok got out onto regular roads it would be slow going with all the snow. "Don't worry about that. I'll explain later," she said.

"You're not going to tell me now? What's going on?"

"I found something in Fitzpatrick's office tonight," she announced. "In a locked file drawer."

He shot her a look. "If it was locked, how'd you get into it?"

"I sort of . . . stumbled onto the key."

"Which you put back, I hope."

"Of course. But the cleaning crew is going

to have a hard time getting in tomorrow."

"They won't suspect you. . . ."

"No."

"What'd you find?"

She pulled a manila folder out of her satchel. "This."

Slowing to a stop before he could reach the guard tower, he turned on the interior light and flipped through a stack of photocopies. "What is this stuff? Some kind of background check?"

"On me!" she exclaimed. "It looks like Fitzpatrick was having me followed, watched."

"Why would he do that?"

She shook her head. "I have no idea. It's an invasion of my privacy. Look at this picture someone took through the window of my cabin when I was changing. That's here in Alaska!"

He studied a blurry shot of her in her bra. "You don't lower the blinds?"

"Usually, yes. But I live out in the middle of nowhere. The few neighbors I have can't see into my bedroom — not unless they're creeping around, like someone obviously was. And I'm guessing that day I just wanted to quickly change my shirt."

He glanced at a few more pages. These seemed to contain information on her family — her sister and parents and their addresses. "Did you find any files like this on the rest of the team?"

"There was a file on each of us, but the others barely contained anything besides their résumés — maybe a list of awards and accomplishments, notes from their first interview, that sort of thing. I can understand him keeping that on hand in case he has to do a write-up on the team. I keep that sort of thing available for when I go after a grant or other source of funding. But their files didn't contain anything of a personal nature — certainly not any half-dressed pictures!"

"That's true even for the other woman on the team — Dr. Wilheim?"

"Stacy? The only picture Tim has of her is a professional head shot."

He picked up another list of names and addresses. "Who are these men?"

She rubbed her hands together to ward off the cold. In her preoccupation with what she'd found, she hadn't put on gloves. "Those are the men I dated in Boston. *All* of them."

"You've got to be kidding me." It wasn't a long list. But, as reluctant as she was with romantic relationships, he wouldn't have expected it to be.

"Actually, some wouldn't even fit into that category," she clarified. "Mostly they're professional associates who attempted to get to know me on a more personal basis, people I would occasionally meet for lunch."

He thumbed through more sheets and found a copy of her driver's license. "How far back do these documents go?"

"Five years — from the time I first met Tim. No, actually he's dug up stuff from even longer."

"What's this?" He held up an advertisement.

"I used to live at that address. You're looking at the flyer the Realtor gave out when I was selling my condo."

"Which has the diagram of the floor plan on the back." *Was that why Fitzpatrick had taken it?*

She grabbed something else. "And look at this — this is the announcement from when I opened my last practice."

Amarok shook his head at that but was especially surprised by what he found next. "Are these your college transcripts?"

"Yes! Who can say how he got hold of those!"

Amarok noted all the As. "I would've guessed you'd have marks like these."

She grabbed the transcripts. "All I did was

study! Of course I had good grades."

"We don't have too much in common," he muttered.

"You didn't do well in school?"

"Not particularly. But I didn't apply myself. I hated it. Didn't have the money for tuition, anyway. That's why I left. I wanted to become a trooper."

"How old were you?"

"Twenty."

"There's nothing wrong with working instead of going to school, especially if it's in your chosen profession."

"I just don't see a guy who's had to live by his wits his whole life getting with a woman who had the kind of privileged upbringing you did. You have an MD-PhD from Harvard. What are you even doing way the hell out here?"

"That's how you've seen it all along."

"You said yourself that you have to go back to your family eventually."

She seemed about to say something significant. He hoped she would, because he really wanted to believe she was committed to seeing what she'd started in Hilltop through, with Hanover House *and* with him. Was she planning to go back in five years? Ten?

When she looked away, he knew she'd

decided against that moment of honesty or transparency or whatever. "The odds are stacked against us."

"Fuck the odds!" he said.

Her eyes darted back to his face. "I don't know what you want from me."

"I'm pretty sure you do."

"Sex?"

He tossed the file aside. *"Seriously?* If that's all I wanted, I think I'd have a better chance with just about anyone else."

"So why aren't you *with* someone else?"

What answer could he give? Besides the obvious, the fact that she was a beautiful woman, there was no way to explain why he was so attracted to her. That sort of thing couldn't be put into words.

He needed to back off, somehow quash the desire he felt for her. "Forget it."

"Amarok —"

"We have enough to worry about right now. I'm sorry I said anything. We just need to catch our killer," he said, and held up the folder she had brought. "The most recent item in here — when is it from?"

She hated to let their more personal discussion end on a sour note but didn't know what else to do. "That picture of me in my bra couldn't be more than two months old. You can see a sweater on the bed my mother sent me right before Thanks-giving."

"Have you ever felt as if your esteemed colleague might have a thing for you?"

She gave him a helpless look. "Yes, but that's not what this comes down to. It can't be."

"Why not?"

"Because I've never acted remotely interested in him. Never given him any reason to think I might be attracted to him or . . . or open to getting involved with him in that way."

"But he *has* hit you up."

"After we got here, he . . . he came into my office one night, late. Tried to kiss me. I was so surprised I shoved him, and he knocked his head against the wall. In retrospect, I could've reacted in a gentler fashion, but . . . he's almost the last man on earth I'd want to touch me. Although I admire what he's accomplished professionally, I've *never* even found him particularly likeable. Besides, he's too old for me."

Amarok grimaced. "Why are you so hung up on age?"

"Most people would agree that a decade is a lot, and he's quite a bit more than that."

"Age is just a number."

"Every older woman who's ever gotten

involved with a younger guy tells herself the same thing. But I doubt very many of those marriages last, probably a lot less than the national average, which isn't impressive to begin with."

He might've argued that that depended on how big the age difference was. But the fact that he was younger wasn't the only thing he had going against him. There was a big disparity in their professions, their backgrounds, their education level. And he lived in a harsh and unforgiving part of the world that she would eventually want to leave.

Like his mother . . .

"You're not going to respond?" she asked.

"No." Amarok drew a deep breath. "This storm is getting bad. I better get us home before we can't get anywhere. Put that stuff in your briefcase until we're past the guard tower."

She did as he asked, but he could tell she was upset.

"What are you thinking?" he asked once they were beyond the gates.

"The truth?" she demanded, her words a challenge.

He glanced over. "Always."

"That I want to be with you — probably worse than you want to be with me. But I

411

don't know how, okay? I can't build a bridge — between me and anyone, really, but especially a man like you."

"A man like *me*?"

"Someone I find so . . . appealing."

Seeing her tortured expression made him feel bad. He had no business adding to her grief. He should've stayed away from her. He'd known that from the beginning — and he'd been trying, especially after she backed away from him last summer. But then she'd gotten stranded at Quigley's and it seemed as if fate took over. No normal man could've been expected to refuse what she offered him when they met up in the hall later that night.

"Don't worry." He slung one arm over the steering wheel as if he wasn't as emotionally invested as he'd made himself sound. "We'll take it one day at a time. Figure it out. No pressure either way."

She seemed relieved. "My trust is shot," she admitted. "And this" — she tapped what she'd found in Fitzpatrick's office — "isn't helping. *Again,* it looks like I've trusted the wrong person."

"Yeah, well, *I* wouldn't be the wrong person. But I wouldn't sleep with you now, anyway," he added.

She arched her eyebrows. "Really?"

He winked at her. "Turned you down last night, didn't I?"

22

I don't feel guilty for anything. I feel sorry
for people who feel guilt.
— TED BUNDY, SERIAL KILLER, RAPIST,
KIDNAPPER AND NECROPHILIAC

Evelyn was glad when they reached Amarok's. It had been a slow, arduous ride home. He'd had to dig out the tires twice, the snowdrifts were so high. But Makita was there to greet them and, as usual, Amarok's house felt warm and cozy. She liked it there.

He told her good night almost as soon as they walked in. Then she went to bed and he spent some time with Makita, taking him out before playing with him in the living room.

As tired as she was, Evelyn figured it wouldn't be difficult to fall asleep. But then she heard the shower go on — and the image of Amarok standing naked beneath the spray popped into her mind.

Stop! Why would she put herself through the torture of wanting something she couldn't have? Why would she put *him* through it?

But her heart began to pound like it had the night she'd gone to him in the hallway.

She wasn't sure she was ready to commit to intercourse, exactly, but there was no doubt she wanted to be with Amarok, to feel his arms around her, to give and take both comfort and pleasure. She was so tired of the constant isolation, the aching loneliness.

But would she only disappoint them both a second time?

Telling herself not to even answer that question, she got out of bed. She wouldn't think of failure. If he rejected her as he had last night, so be it. She'd never get beyond where she was right now if she didn't keep trying.

At least, that was the dialogue going through her mind when she knocked on the bathroom door.

"Yes?" he said.

She swallowed. "I-I'm coming in."

"I'll be out soon."

"I don't need to use the bathroom."

There was a slight pause. Then he said, "So . . . what do you want?"

"What do you *think* I want, Amarok?"

"We've already made this decision. Go back to bed, Evelyn."

He didn't think she was ready. He'd said so before. But maybe he was wrong. Or maybe he just didn't want to set his expectations too high. What if she pushed him a little? Pushed herself, too? What would happen?

"Unlock the door."

"Evelyn —" His voice was more of a warning growl than anything else, but she ignored it.

"I" — she hauled in a deep breath — "I want to feel your naked body against mine. If you don't want to try to . . . to make love, it's fine. We don't have to do that."

There was no answer.

"Amarok?"

"It's already unlocked."

Her hands were shaking as she turned the knob.

When he heard her, he poked his head out of the shower. He was scowling, still acting as if he'd send her away. But she wasn't about to make that easy for him. Before he could say anything, she pulled off her nightgown.

His nostrils flared as his gaze moved down over her. She could tell that her act of bravery had the effect she'd been hoping for. But his voice remained stern — maybe even gruffer than it'd been before. "It's not a good idea, Evelyn. Not tonight."

"Because . . ."

"Because I'm not capable of being the kind of lover you need. I'm exhausted and —"

"I know." She was so short of breath she could barely speak. She was exposing herself emotionally as well as physically. And yet she felt empowered by her own actions, by the fact that she was once again taking the initiative. "You've been working long hours. And you're under a lot of pressure. I'll understand if you can't . . . you know . . . get it up. Maybe you can just hold me. That was nice last night."

"Get it up?" He barked out a laugh. "That *definitely* isn't the problem. I don't have the control I'm going to need to do this right. To go slow. To be gentle. To make sure you aren't ever frightened or . . . or uncomfortable."

"Last time, in so many words, you said you didn't want to make love to me as if I were a glass doll."

"I remember what I said. But I'll do it if that's what you need. It's just . . . tonight I'm too wound up and frustrated and . . ."

"And?" she prompted. Had he lost complete confidence in her ability to overcome the past? She hadn't given him any reason to hope.

"And hungry to know you trust me enough to let me be with you in that way. It wouldn't be wise to approach something that needs so much patience and care when I'm on edge. You understand?"

She nodded and picked up her nightgown, and he closed the curtain as if that was that. But she couldn't make herself leave, couldn't even make herself get dressed. Not while success seemed so obtainable.

Once again tossing her nightgown aside, she stepped into the shower with him.

He didn't back away, but his eyes narrowed. "You're only making it harder," he warned, but before he could say more she slipped her arms around his neck.

She heard him suck air in between his teeth, saw him close his eyes. But he didn't move, didn't react until she pressed herself fully against him and fisted her hand in his hair to bring his mouth to hers.

When their lips met, she kissed him as passionately as she'd wanted to kiss him since that night in his bed, and he moaned and slid his hands down her bare backside, anchoring her to him.

"That's it," she whispered, but she wasn't just encouraging *him*. She was celebrating her victory in coming this far. "I guess you were right."

"That this isn't a good time? God, I hope not." He spoke against her mouth in between kisses.

She pulled back long enough to smile at him, feeling oddly powerful for a change. "I mean about getting it up."

"I'd have to be dead not to be able to get hard for you."

He licked the water from her skin as his mouth moved down her neck. The steam was so thick it felt like a blanket, like the only blanket they needed as he bent her over one arm to suckle her breast.

"You taste so good," he murmured, turning his attention to her other breast.

When she wrapped her hand around him, he lifted his head to look at her in surprise. But she didn't give him the opportunity to question her. She dragged his mouth back to hers while she explored his thick shaft. She wasn't afraid of him, she told herself. She was simply going to embrace the desire burning through her veins, let it goad her on, give her strength — strength instead of fear.

As they kissed, he explored her body, too,

and manipulated what he found with his fingers until she hardly had the strength to remain standing, until she wanted to feel him inside her so badly there was no room for fear.

When she laughed, giddy with relief that she could even be having such thoughts, he gazed down at her. "What?" he whispered, his eyelids half-closed, his voice hoarse.

"I'm ready. If we weren't covered in water you'd be able to tell how wet I am."

"I know the difference," he whispered. "I can feel the slickness."

"So what do I have to do to get you to go further? Crawl all over you and beg?" she teased. But she wasn't sure he even remembered saying something to that effect. He seemed too caught up to be thinking clearly.

"Let's go into the bedroom."

She didn't want to leave the shower. There'd been no running water in that shack where Jasper had taken her. She didn't associate the shower with anyone except Amarok.

"I could do more for you," he coaxed, "if we were lying down."

"No. Please." She gripped his arms, trying to convey how important it was that they not change anything. She didn't want to have to explain, didn't want to drag her most tragic memories into this bathroom with them. And, after a moment, he seemed to understand.

"Okay. Don't worry. Everything's fine. I like showers." When he lifted her against the tile and she wrapped her legs around his hips, she was pretty sure he held his breath as he started to press inside her.

"You all right?" He obviously expected her to refuse him at the last second, but she tightened her legs, pulling him the rest of the way.

"What do *you* think?" she replied.

"I'm in," he murmured, his voice full of awe.

"And you feel good there," she told him. "You make *me* feel good. Full. Complete. Part of you."

"Talking like that . . . you're going to make me come too soon," he said with a ragged laugh.

She kissed his jaw, his cheek, pecked his lips. "You warned me that you didn't have any control tonight."

"That wasn't the kind of control I meant. But with you so warm and tight around me . . . now I'm seriously worried."

Somehow feeling wild and suddenly free of all that had held her back, she laughed. "Don't worry about anything. The difficult part's over."

"Not really," he said. "What happens next is even more important."

Unsure of what he meant, she said, "I'll let you finish. That's what I'm saying. I won't back out on you now. I'm fine."

"But I want you to like it." He nipped at her mouth. "I want you to experience how amazing it can be. Is that possible? Can we try?"

"It probably would never happen in this position. And you'd have to pull out in order for us to move. I don't want that. I wish we could stay joined all night."

He kissed her lips so softly and gently that it was her turn to look at him in surprise.

"Then maybe you'll let me do it again sometime," he said.

She closed her eyes. "Let's just enjoy *now*. Now is all that exists," she said, and threw her head back, feeling the heat of the steam and the pounding of the water on her face and shoulders as he began to thrust.

Amarok had never dreamed this would happen tonight. He'd just decided that maybe it should *never* happen. As fascinated as Evelyn was by the monsters she'd brought to Hanover House, he didn't see how she could stick around Hilltop for long — not with everything that was going on and her family hoping she'd return to Boston. He couldn't even feel good about encouraging her to stay when he knew it might only traumatize her further. If Jasper had followed her to Alaska — if he had some elaborate plan to continue tormenting her, as she feared — the smartest thing for her to do would be to get out of town. She should disappear, set up a nice private practice in a brand-new state and, this time, stay out of the damn media.

He'd been considering that while he was showering, had been planning to suggest it — until she came in. Then he couldn't think about anything except the feel of her slick, wet skin, her mouth, which was open for his tongue, and the little gasps she made when he touched the right places. He couldn't refuse this, he decided, not when he wanted it as badly as he did.

He was *so* close to climax. He could feel the tension building, feel the surge of pleasure tightening every muscle. He wanted to hold off, make it last. He wasn't confident he'd have another chance to be with her. But as her hands held his face and she kissed him even deeper, moaning as if she could tell he was hovering on the brink, there was no way he could hold back. He barely remembered to pull out before it was too late.

Several moments passed. He was breathing hard, could no longer kiss her with any skill, and his arms were beginning to shake at the strain of bearing her weight, but he didn't want to let her go. Somehow she'd overcome her fear enough to create this incredible moment, and he felt so lucky to be the one to share it with her.

"You did it," he said, resting his forehead against hers.

"*We* did it," she responded. "And it was . . . nice. *Really* nice."

Afraid his knees might buckle, he put her down, but he didn't release her. "Let me make you come," he whispered above the rush of the water.

She shook her head. "Not tonight."

"I can do it." He began to lick the water off her shoulder, her breasts, her belly, but she stopped him.

"Maybe no one can do that for me. Maybe it's not possible."

"Of course it is! Have you ever had a man's mouth on you before? I mean . . . since . . . all that?"

"It didn't even happen then. Jasper was . . . a clean freak and . . . rather put off by the idea."

"I'm glad. Because I don't feel put off by it at all. I *want* to taste you."

She stopped him again. "I'd rather not take the risk. Not right now."

"*Why?* You didn't think you could allow a man penetration, either. But you let me inside you. We're beyond that."

"It's not so simple, Amarok. You mentioned earlier that making love requires a great deal of trust. It does. But letting go to . . . to *that* extent while making love requires even more, maybe more than I'm capable of. And if that's the case, I'd rather not know right now. Let me celebrate my success, enjoy it for a while."

Once she said that, he couldn't argue. "I loved it," he said. "Every second."

She grinned up at him. "Good thing you're so young and strong. An older man might not have been able to hold me for that long."

He frowned as he stared down at her.

"What?" she said.

"I don't want to hear any more about my age. If it didn't bother you, I wouldn't care. But I know it does."

"My assistant openly gushes about you, as if she's *that* sure I could never be interested in you myself."

"Maybe her attitude has nothing to do

with our respective ages. Maybe you've just made it clear that *no* man is a possibility for you."

"You think so?"

"*I* do. But we don't need her approval, anyway. I don't give a shit what she thinks."

A smile tugged at the corners of her mouth.

"What?" he said.

"I can't believe we did it. I feel like I just punched Jasper in the face."

He couldn't help chuckling. "Anytime you want to punch him again, you let me know. I'll help you with that whenever."

"We'd better get some sleep," she said, and started to get out, but he caught her hand.

"Are you moving into my bedroom?"

Her eyes searched his. "That's a little scary, don't you think?"

God, she was skittish. "*Why?* You've slept there before."

"There's an emotional side to this, you know."

"Is that why you're withdrawing? Because you're afraid of what you're feeling?"

"It's a bit overwhelming."

"But I'm feeling it, too. Isn't that the important part? That we're in it together?"

Doubt clouded her eyes. "I don't want to

fall in love with you."

"Because of my *age,* Evelyn? Really?"

"No, because love is the biggest risk of all." She got out of the shower, grabbed a towel and left the bathroom.

After that, Amarok assumed he'd be sleeping alone. He stopped at her door as he came down the hall and considered trying to talk to her about it again. After what'd just passed between them, he wanted her by his side. But she'd overcome a lot tonight. Maybe she needed some space to regroup, to feel safe despite allowing him such intimate access to her body.

She'd come to him in the shower, he told himself. Maybe, in a day or two, she'd come to him in his bed.

But he didn't have to wait that long. Although he was too tired to even turn on the lights before dropping onto the mattress, it didn't take more than a second to realize Makita wasn't the only one there waiting for him.

For Evelyn, morning seemed to come in the blink of an eye. When Amarok's alarm went off, he silenced it right away, but he didn't roll out of bed. He gathered her to him and kissed her shoulder. "I have good news and bad news," he said.

She liked the feel of his sinewy body wrapped around hers. "I've had enough bad news; what's the good news?" she mumbled, still half-asleep.

"It's Friday. Weekend's almost here. That should make a difference for you, even if it doesn't for me."

"I spend most my weekends working, too. So what's the bad news?"

"You don't have a car here, which means . . ."

She pulled herself further into consciousness. She'd left her Beamer at the prison last night and taken a ride with him. "*I* have to get up, too," she finished.

He shoved himself onto one elbow so he could look at her. "Unless I can talk you into taking a sick day and staying right here."

"With you?"

"I wish. I've got to work. We both know I can't avoid that right now."

She gave him a sleepy smile. "Then why would *I* stay?"

"Because, at the moment, Hanover House is a toxic atmosphere for you. That file you found in Fitzpatrick's office — it has me concerned. I didn't like him to begin with. But now that I believe he's obsessed with you I like him even less."

"I can't hole up, Amarok. I have to go in."

With a sigh, he climbed out of bed. "I was afraid you'd say that."

"Just so you know, Sergeant, I plan on fighting for what I've established here," she told him, sitting up.

His gaze dropped to what she'd inadvertently revealed, and an appreciative smile curved his lips. "What'd you say?"

"Stop it!" She laughed as she covered herself with the blankets. "I said I'm not going anywhere. You and I — we'll fight through what's happening, put a stop to it."

Although he'd grabbed his pants, he paused before pulling them on. "And then?"

"And then . . . what?"

"You'd be open to a relationship?"

"With a man nearly ten years my junior?"

"Ten?"

"Seven?" she clarified.

"I can't change how old I am, Evelyn," he said, and finished dressing.

As he went to put on some coffee, Evelyn dragged herself out of bed and into the bathroom to have a shower. Just turning on the water reminded her of last night, of what it had felt like to finally make love after so long. Amarok was everything a woman could want. But that was part of the problem. She had so little faith a relationship between them could actually work. She was too damaged, and he had too much to offer other, healthier women.

What would stop him from looking elsewhere the second things got difficult? And they would get difficult. She and Amarok had differing opinions on so many subjects, the most divisive being her work, which she loved. He was slightly misogynistic and didn't even know it. He loved Alaska, would never leave it, but she wasn't committed to this place in quite the same way.

If she allowed herself to embrace him as more than a temporary lover, where would it lead? And where would it end?

He banged on the door. "You coming?"

She wiped the water from her face. "Yeah. I'll be right there."

23

I wish I could stop, but I could not. I had no other thrill or happiness.

— DENNIS NILSEN,
MUSWELL HILL MURDERER

When Evelyn arrived at Hanover House, she wondered if maybe she should've taken Amarok's advice and stayed home. She'd been hoping to talk to Glenn first thing, to thank him for the brownie and to tell him to continue to keep his ears open in case he heard anything about that forged transfer order. She would've called him up to her office first thing, except Penny told her she was wanted in the conference room.

Other than Stacy Wilheim, who was still out sick, the entire mental health team was there waiting for her — all three of the psychologists along with Fitzpatrick. He paced up front, near the wipe board, while the others sat around the table, sipping coffee.

There was a plate of donuts in the center of the table. The fact that no one had touched them indicated this was not the usual staff meeting.

Evelyn thought of the key she had stolen from the janitors. She'd thrown it into the snow last night the first time Amarok climbed out to get them unstuck. By the time spring came and the snow melted and uncovered it, no one would know what that key went to. If it was ever discovered. But she was still afraid that Fitzpatrick had found her out — that, even though she'd made copies of the contents of that file and carefully replaced it, he was somehow aware she'd been in his office.

If so, she would divulge what she'd found. Fitzpatrick had no right to be collecting so much personal information on her. That he was doing it secretly made her even more uncomfortable. Before leaving Amarok's this morning, she'd looked through all of those documents again. Besides the more intrusive items she'd noted before, he'd recorded every detail of anything she'd ever said about Jasper and even had pictures of Jasper from their high school yearbook.

Although she received a few less-than-enthusiastic greetings, no one jumped up to accuse her of snooping through Tim's office. That was the one bright spot. She figured out pretty quickly, by the way Russell Jones looked up and then glanced away, that this was about the Anthony-Hugo stabbing and the accusations she'd subsequently launched. Russ would not be behaving so sheepishly if he had fresh fodder for the type of self-righteous anger Fitzpatrick was nursing.

She wished Stacy could've made it in this morning. She'd called to ask after Stacy before she left Amarok's, but the pain of shingles had not yet subsided. Without her only ally, Evelyn would have to stand alone against Fitzpatrick, his protégé Russell, and the anti-confrontational Greg. Preston Schmidt was a wild card. He could align himself with either side, depending on the issue. But Evelyn could guess, by the way Fitzpatrick had behaved in her office yesterday, how he was going to present his complaints. Given that, she was willing to bet Preston would join the opposition today.

"I see you're prepared for my arrival." She spoke to the room at large as she took a seat at the other end of the table and put down her briefcase.

"It's time we get some perspective on what's going on here at HH," Fitzpatrick

433

responded. "We need to put the welfare of the institution above our own egos."

That sounded noble in theory, but Evelyn knew Fitzpatrick wasn't speaking about himself. He was telling her to put the good of the institution above *her* ego and do whatever he said.

She rolled her eyes. "And that includes what, exactly? Why have you called this meeting? So we can talk about how out of line I've been? Go over my reckless behavior and then take a vote on whether everyone else agrees that I'm no longer fit to run HH? That I'd better take some time off before I completely crack up?"

He blinked at her, obviously surprised that she'd be so transparent in her disdain. "We need to discuss your emotional stability, yes."

"What good is a discussion if you're not willing to take in new information?" she asked.

He raised his eyebrows. "Excuse me?"

"You're trying to railroad this meeting like all the others of late."

"Evelyn," Greg warned, "don't make this any worse."

"Can it get any worse?" She shifted her focus to him. "We have two Hanover House employees who've been *murdered.* Part of

Danielle's body was placed in *my* bed. I'm doing the best I can to figure out what's going on, and instead of supporting me as he should, Tim is trying to take control of what we've both created."

"Listen to yourself!" Fitzpatrick snapped. "Since when did *I* become your enemy? I'm merely asking that you take some time off, get some sleep, figure out if you can handle working with . . . with the memories this must be conjuring. That's all."

He was being far more diplomatic than she'd expected, but when his gaze riveted on Preston she understood why. Fitzpatrick hoped to gain Preston's support but wasn't quite sure he'd managed it.

"Tim, Emilio Kush went directly to you when I asked him to bring Anthony Garza to be interviewed, and you both decided that I shouldn't be allowed to speak to him."

"See?" Fitzpatrick responded. "Even the COs are beginning to question your judgment."

"They wouldn't if you weren't encouraging them to do so," she retorted. "You *are* the one who contacted Warden Ferris and asked him not to act on any of my orders, aren't you?"

"Yes! But only because you're not yourself these days and we can't suffer another incident like that stabbing in the yard."

Evelyn could hardly speak for the anger that welled up. "I told you. Someone forged my name on that transfer order. Whether you believe me or not, that's the truth. No matter how distraught I was, I would never have transferred Anthony into gen pop. Not in a million years."

Fitzpatrick took a copy of the document in question out of a folder on the table. "And yet we have proof," he said, holding it up for all to see.

"I didn't sign that," she repeated.

"You think it was *me.*" His words were more of a taunt.

She managed a shrug despite the tension in her body. "I don't know for sure. But I plan on finding out."

Spit shot out of his mouth with the hard consonant of his second word. "I can't believe you would even consider it a possibility!"

She looked from Tim to Greg to Preston. "At this point, I don't have the luxury of ruling out *any* possibilities. That's what murder investigations are all about."

Fitzpatrick gripped the back of his empty chair. "You're not leading the investigation. Sergeant Murphy is. And yet, yesterday, you accused me of murder!" Fitzpatrick eased up on that chair long enough to gesture at his old grad student. "Russell heard it."

"It's Hugo who claims you are behind the murders," she said.

"But you believe him."

"I have yet to find proof either way."

"He's a psychopath, for crying out loud!"

"And yet he sounded quite credible," she responded. "Especially when he reiterated the same thing on what could've been his deathbed. I find it highly suspicious that someone moved Anthony Garza out of isolation and into gen pop, that it happened almost as soon as you learned Hugo had been talking and that Hugo, of all the people Anthony could've attacked, was the one who got stabbed."

Fitzpatrick threw up his hands. "Listen to her. I told you. She's lost her mind."

Russell turned his coffee cup around in its saucer. "Evelyn, I hate to say this, but I agree with Tim. You're sounding more and more unstable. Why not take some time off? You can't be thinking clearly if you believe that he had anything to do with what happened in the yard. I've known him for nearly a decade. He would *never* do anything like that."

"You'd rather think *I* caused that stabbing?" Evelyn asked. "That I couldn't take a little groping from Hugo and went after revenge?"

"It *is* your name on that transfer order," Russell said.

"Are you sure about that?" she asked. "Have you looked at it? Compared it to my usual signature? If you will, I think you'll see the difference."

"So you won't let me take the lead until you're feeling better," Fitzpatrick said.

Evelyn's heart was pounding when she stood. She'd never dreamed she'd have to take on the team she'd helped create. But she knew in her heart she'd never have the freedom to study what she intended if she let Fitzpatrick take over. "No."

Fitzpatrick looked to Preston, but when Preston remained mute — merely rocked back in his seat and crossed his legs — Fitzpatrick rounded the table. "You may not have any choice."

She lifted her chin. "I can always fight back." She motioned to the transfer order. "I'm going to find out who signed that and why. And then we'll talk about who will or won't be working here."

Fitzpatrick whirled to face Greg. "Don't you have anything to add?"

"I'm afraid I have to support Tim on this one, Evelyn." Greg frowned as though he was at least *trying* to be objective.

"This one?" she echoed with a laugh. "Let's face it, Greg. You support him on *every* issue. You've decided he's the stronger horse in this race and don't want to back a loser."

Greg scowled. "You're hanging on by a very thin thread. It would be better for everyone, including you, if you would just —"

"What?" she cried. "Step down? Let Tim take over my position just because he thinks his way of running HH is better than mine?"

"Yes!" Greg responded. "Get some rest and a new perspective on your work —"

"Losing Evelyn, even for a short time, would be a tragedy," Preston broke in, finally entering the conversation and causing everyone to gape at him. "I personally think you're barking up the wrong tree," he said to Fitzpatrick.

"Because . . ." It was Russell who spoke, and his surprise that Preston would take her side was apparent in his expression.

"Evelyn would never do *anything* that would threaten HH," Preston said. "We all know that."

"She may not have realized what she was doing," Fitzpatrick retorted.

"So you've said," Preston went on. "I still

can't believe she'd sign that transfer order. Doing so would risk everything she's created. Why would she want Hugo to be hurt?"

"Because he attacked her!" Fitzpatrick said. "You saw it for yourself. We watched the video."

Evelyn curled her fingernails into her palms. Fitzpatrick had done his homework, but all his preparation didn't seem to be having the desired effect — not on Preston.

"On which I saw a traumatized woman get back on her feet almost instantly and retain control of a difficult situation," Preston said. "If she wanted Hugo to be punished, why would she risk her career by transferring Garza into gen pop when she could simply have delayed calling off the COs? Instead, she stopped the violence before much of anything could happen. Someone who does that isn't going to send Anthony Garza out into the yard to shank Hugo Evanski, especially when she knows she'll get the blame. It makes no sense."

There was an uncomfortable silence during which Fitzpatrick turned to Greg and Russell. Evelyn thought he might address the real issue — who had forged her name. But he didn't. He kept pushing his agenda. "I still say she should take some time off.

440

You two agree with me, don't you?"

"I don't believe it matters one way or the other who agrees — at least in this room." Preston spoke before they could. "You don't employ her; the federal government does. And even if this *were* a voting matter, I'm fairly certain Stacy, if she were here, would argue in favor of Evelyn's sterling reputation and her dedication, insightfulness and self-sacrifice when it comes to this institution. That splits the team right down the middle."

"*That's* what you have to say?" Fitzpatrick cried. "What about the way she transferred Garza here as if . . . as if her opinion was the only one that mattered?"

"As far as I'm concerned, if she wants to work with Garza, she has that right. The bureau doesn't mandate that we agree on our subjects. That was something *you* put forward, and we went along with it because it's a good rule of thumb. Collaboration makes us more cohesive as a group, but . . . this is the first facility of its kind. That's partly what drew each of us to this particular job — the chance to branch out, do something new. If we weren't willing to step out of the norm once in a while we wouldn't be here. So, as far as I'm concerned, it's not a crime that she cut through the red tape *you*

441

put in place." He stood. "I can understand you being slightly irritated, of course, since you're so big on policies and procedures, but you're taking it too far. Now, I have a busy day — and I'm sure Evelyn's eager to get on with finding out who put her name on that paper. So if we're finished here, I'd like to start work."

Fitzpatrick intercepted him. "I'll go to the Bureau of Prisons."

"That's your prerogative," Preston said, but as he spoke he gestured toward Evelyn. "I wouldn't start a 'me' or 'her' type of battle, if I were you, though. You have no idea how passionate she is about this place if you think you could ever beat her. Should it come to your job or hers . . ." He didn't finish. He just gave a shrug and walked out.

Evelyn had never expected Preston to defend her. He was so preoccupied with raising his four teenage boys, whom he and his wife had brought up here for a home-steading experience, Evelyn hadn't realized he'd noticed her level of dedication. But she was grateful to him. For once, he'd gotten behind her on an issue that really counted.

"As Preston mentioned, I have pressing matters to attend to," she told the others as if that was that and grabbed her briefcase.

They said nothing when she left, but

Penny waved her down before she could reach her office. "Courtney Lofland is on line one."

Evelyn didn't immediately recognize the name. Her mind was too preoccupied with what had just taken place and how she might go about discovering who was behind the forged transfer order. She hoped Glenn might still be able to uncover something. Working over on the prison side, he heard and saw things she didn't. "Courtney *who*?"

"Anthony Garza's last wife?"

"Hold all my other calls," she said, and closed the office door behind her.

There was a guard posted at Hugo Evanski's door. Were he in any better shape, there would be two. It was a testament to how poorly he was doing that the government had decided against expending the additional man-hours.

Amarok showed his ID, received a curt nod and shouldered open the door.

Hugo had his eyes closed and didn't move at the sound of Amarok's entry. Amarok felt bad for disturbing a man who was barely hanging on to life; Hugo was almost as pale as the sheet he was lying on. But Hugo's poor condition was part of the reason Amarok had made the trip. He felt as if he should talk to Hugo while that was still an option.

"Mr. Evanski?"

There was no response. Amarok gave Hugo's arm a gentle shake. If he was going to drive all the way to Anchorage despite the myriad things he needed to be doing in Hilltop, he couldn't wait for Hugo to rouse on his own. The time Amarok spent here had to count. "Hey."

Finally, the other man opened his eyes. They didn't seem particularly clear or focused, but he was on a lot of medication, so Amarok couldn't expect too much.

"I'm Trooper Murphy from Hilltop." He rested his hands on the bedrail. "I drove over here to speak to you because I think what you know might be important."

Hugo's throat worked as he swallowed. Then he said, "Sergeant Amarok."

Amarok had never met him, so he was surprised by the recognition. "How do you know me?"

"You're the law in Hilltop. That means you get mentioned now and then at Hanover House. Besides, you're popular with the ladies. Especially Danielle. You were all she could talk about. She was dying to fuck you. You were the unattainable."

Amarok scowled. "She didn't even know

me. Not really," he said, but if he'd learned anything about Danielle, it was that knowing a man didn't matter. He just wanted to keep Hugo talking.

"She'd seen you. That was enough. She was convinced you had the biggest cock in Alaska."

"She didn't seem to have any complaints about yours."

"You know about that?" He managed a feeble smile. "Some things are just God given and can't be taken away, I guess."

Amarok pulled over the only chair in the room. "You had sex with her, then?"

"Not as often as I would've liked," he replied. "The bastard guards charged too much."

"So you had to pay."

"Course. The only free sex I've ever had in prison is called rape."

Amarok didn't ask if he was the victim or the perpetrator. Hugo didn't seem capable of having a long conversation, so Amarok wasn't about to veer off the subject. "How and where did these encounters take place — with Danielle, I mean?"

"It wasn't complicated. I paid the guards a hundred bucks, and —"

"Where would an inmate get that kind of money?" he asked, shocked at the amount.

"We manage, when we want something bad enough."

"How?"

"I have an uncle who puts a couple hundred bucks on my books every now and then. Some take what they need from others. Some save up, but that's the hardest route to go, given the wages we're paid."

"So you'd come up with the money and then . . ."

"Kush or Petrowski would pull me out of my cell or call me over if I was out in the yard."

"And?"

"They'd take me into a pantry or a toolshed. Something like that where they could guard the door and she'd be waiting."

"Danielle wasn't scared of you? Wasn't scared of how dangerous it was to be putting out for a known killer?"

"Hell no. She loved the adrenaline rush. One time she even had Kush tie her up." He grinned. "I loved that."

Leaning back, Amarok folded his arms. "What happened after you had sex with her? You'd just slip back into the prison population?"

Hugo was tiring out. It took several seconds for him to be able to gather the breath to speak. "It wasn't quite that simple. For an added price, we could get . . . other things."

"Like . . ."

"We could . . . do a line of coke beforehand. Or . . . take a friend in. You name it. She was . . . open to anything, which was fortunate for . . . for Kush and his buddies. They could put a high price on the kinkier shit."

"You never said anything to Dr. Talbot about what was going on?"

His eyes closed, then opened, and Amarok could tell he was once again summoning his strength. "Why would I?"

"I'm under the impression you care about your therapist. If she gets fired, she moves away, and you never see her again." Neither would he. . . .

"I didn't want to blow a good thing."

"So why are you talking about it now?" Amarok asked.

He wet his lips. "Party's over. Danielle's dead."

"Maybe, given enough time, Kush and his friends would've tried to replace her with someone else."

"Who?" Hugo scoffed. "It isn't . . . like they could . . . smuggle in some prostitute. Danielle worked . . . at the prison. No one . . . questioned her presence. That's what . . . made it all possible."

Amarok hadn't expected Hugo to be quite so forthcoming. "So now that Danielle's gone, you want to see the guards get what's coming to them, is that it?"

He lifted a hand to his chest, touched it gingerly. "Why not? I" — it took a second for him to continue — "owe them."

"Are you suggesting they could've stopped you from getting shanked?"

"Sure. Instead, they . . . put that animal in the yard . . . with me."

"How do you know they did it on purpose?"

"Garza . . . the guy who stabbed me . . . didn't even know me. He had no . . . reason to want me . . . dead."

Amarok shifted on the hard seat. "Who else spent time with Danielle?"

"Anyone who . . . could afford it."

"Including the COs? Did they ever participate beyond collecting the money?"

Sweat was beginning to pop out on his face. "Kush would . . . sometimes take her from behind while . . . someone else was in front. She thought it was . . . funny to have a guard and an . . . inmate at the same time. That's the type of . . . wild shit that really . . . turned her on."

"What about Fitzpatrick? Did he ever

come out to play?"

"Not when . . . I was there. But I bet he was involved . . . at the top."

Amarok covered a yawn, then rubbed his face. He wasn't bored, just feeling the effects of getting so little sleep the past few nights. "Who killed Danielle?"

"Not an inmate. I can" — he had to wet his lips again — "promise you that. None of us . . . wanted her dead."

"A CO, then?"

He shook his head. "They were making . . . too much money and . . . having too much fun. That'd be like . . . killing the goose that . . . laid the golden egg."

"You think it was Fitzpatrick."

Hugo threw renewed effort into his side of the conversation. "Yes, he must've . . . feared I'd tell Dr. Talbot what was going on."

"Murder's a big step for a prominent psychiatrist to take."

"I'm guessing he wasn't about to . . . go down for . . . simple prison corruption."

"That doesn't explain what happened to Lorraine."

When his eyes closed, Amarok worried Hugo was fading into unconsciousness. "You still with me?"

"I can't explain that." He forced his

eyelids open again. "Except" — his breath rattled in his chest — "he knows that Dr. Talbot . . . loved Lorraine, and this . . . was also a way . . . for him to strike out at her."

"Why would Fitzpatrick have anything against Dr. Talbot?"

Hugo couldn't respond right away. That required a laborious swallow. "He . . . hates her."

"For no reason?"

"Because she'll . . . never love him, not the way . . . he loves her."

The file Fitzpatrick had put together on Evelyn revealed a certain level of fascination. But was it *love*? "Wouldn't she have some inkling of it if he was upset that she wouldn't get involved with him in that way?"

Hugo shook his head. "You don't understand how . . . Fitzpatrick works."

"And you do?"

"As well as anyone. He's been . . . having sessions . . . with me almost since . . . Hanover House opened."

"What are those sessions about?"

"He . . . claims he's . . . studying my sexual response to . . . women. But the only woman . . . he ever shows me pictures of . . . is Evelyn. He knows . . . that's what really . . . excites me."

"What kind of pictures are they?"

"Pornographic ones."

Amarok felt his jaw clench. "And where does he get those?"

"I think he makes them . . . on Photoshop. Her head . . . other women's bodies — bodies that are engaged in . . . sex acts."

So why weren't they in the file Evelyn found?

Because he had to take them to the sessions. They were probably in his briefcase.

Amarok was almost afraid to hear the answer to his next question. "What does he say when he shows you these pictures?"

"He talks about how good it would feel to fuck her. What do . . . you think?"

"*That's* why you're convinced he loves her?"

Again, Amarok had to wait. He wasn't sure how much longer Hugo would be capable of talking; it was sapping his energy.

"Partly," he said at length. "I think . . . he came up here believing . . . she'd eventually see that they were . . . meant to be together. That loneliness and a . . . a love for the same kind of work would . . . lead to a relationship. But . . . shit, even the isolation of this . . . remote place hasn't . . . been enough to drive her into his arms, and . . . it's my guess that he's realizing nothing . . . ever will."

"That makes him angry."

He nodded. "Fills him with rage."

"Enough to commit murder?"

"Look how he's been . . . disrespecting her. If he could do that . . . why not more?" He attempted another chuckle. "Besides, murder isn't as . . . difficult as you might think."

This man would know. "Dr. Talbot wasn't that close with Danielle," Amarok pointed out.

"He killed Danielle . . . to protect his reputation, like I said, and to . . . to torture Evelyn — make her believe her worst fears are coming true."

What Hugo said sounded plausible. The evidence supported the scenario he'd described with Danielle. But could Fitzpatrick be the cold-blooded killer Hugo made him out to be? Or was Hugo trying to destroy someone he hated?

Evelyn admitted that the inmates had no love for her fellow psychiatrist. She'd also mentioned how well they could lie — not that Amarok would've assumed otherwise.

"What do *you* feel for Evelyn?" Amarok asked.

Hugo's eyes grew more focused as they riveted on his. "I'd kill you this instant if . . . if I thought doing so would . . . make her want me instead."

Instead? Amarok stood. How did this guy know the lead psychiatrist at Hanover House had any interest in him? Hugo had been behind bars since arriving in Hilltop, had never seen them together, and that wasn't something he guessed she would mention. "What makes you think I mean any more to Dr. Talbot than anyone else?"

His smile turned sly. "Fitzpatrick told me."

Amarok thought of that picture of Evelyn in her bra taken from outside her window. Was her fellow psychiatrist following her? *Stalking* her?

"*And* you're the only reason she . . . let me get close . . . enough to speak with her in private the . . . other day," Hugo added.

"She told me you lured her over by telling her my life was in danger," Amarok said.

Hugo seemed to study Amarok intently. "I wasn't . . . making that up."

Amarok leaned close. "Fitzpatrick is no threat to me."

"That's where . . . you're wrong." He struggled for more breath. "Fitzpatrick is a threat . . . to everyone."

After shoving his hands in his pockets, Amarok fished out his keys. He had to return to Hilltop, had an appointment with Tim Hancock. "Thanks for your time."

"Or it could be Jasper," Hugo called after him as he turned to go. "You can't rule him out . . . just in case."

Amarok sidestepped a rolling tray. "Do you know anything about Jasper being in Alaska?"

Once again Hugo closed his eyes, but this time Amarok didn't get the impression he was going to sleep. The deep grooves in his forehead suggested he was continuing to battle his weakness and fatigue. "No, but we both . . . know it's possible," he said. "Far as I'm concerned . . . it has to be one or the other. My bet's on . . . Fitzpatrick. You have no idea how . . . sadistic that son of a bitch can be. The shit . . . he's said and done . . . to me. But you'd be a fool to . . . to ignore that there was . . . another man who wanted to destroy her long . . . before he did."

"I'll make a note of that." Irritated he'd come all this way for confirmation of the obvious, where Danielle was concerned, and a few vague warnings, Amarok stepped into the hall. But he held the door open because he had one more question. "Why would Fitzpatrick want to work with psychopaths if he was one?" he asked.

Hugo managed to laugh but winced at the same time. "You're kidding, right? Where else . . . could he get away with . . . so much?"

24

In my lifetime I have murdered 21 human beings, I have committed thousands of burglaries, robberies, larcenies, arsons and, last but not least, I have committed sodomy on more than 1,000 male human beings. For all these things I am not in the least bit sorry.

— CARL PANZRAM, SERIAL KILLER, ARSONIST, THIEF, BURGLAR AND RAPIST

"Courtney? Can you hear me?" Evelyn gripped the phone so tightly she was almost losing the feeling in her left hand, but she had to get through to Garza's ex, enlist her cooperation.

"I'm here," came the reply. "It's just . . . I can't help you. I admire you. I really do. And I'm sorry for . . . for what you've been through in the past. When I got your letter, I went on the Internet to look you up, and I read about your . . . experiences. What you're trying to do at Hanover House is admirable. But I want . . . I want to forget Anthony Garza, to pretend he was never part of my life."

"I understand," Evelyn said. "He's a very difficult and dangerous individual. I'm sure he caused you a lot of pain and degradation, but . . . if you are *truly* sorry for what I've been through — and you'd like to stop other women from suffering the way we *both* have — I need you to tell me everything you can about him."

"*Why?*" she said. "Why go back and revisit that? He's in prison for the rest of his life. It's over."

"For you, maybe. But I believe he's committed far more murders than the ones he's been charged for. The detectives investigating the Porn Poser are convinced he's their man. That's at least six more deaths right there. But they can't give the families of those victims any closure without proof."

"Proof won't resurrect the dead."

That was justification and fear talking. "It will answer their questions. Allow them to stop fighting for the truth. Give them more peace than they have now."

"If I get involved, if I talk, Anthony will kill *me*! I'm the only wife he's had that he *hasn't* murdered."

457

How could Evelyn convince her?

While she searched for just the right approach, she toyed nervously with the note Glenn Whitcomb had left with that brownie he'd tried to deliver to her last night. Besides letting her know he hadn't been able to learn anything about the transfer order, it said he'd brought a treat up from the kitchen because Lorraine wasn't around to do that type of thing for her anymore, which was thoughtful. She needed to call him next. "Anthony will never get out of prison, Courtney," she said. "You said so yourself."

"If only I could rely on that. But he's not quite forty. He's got a lot of years left to live. And you know how things go with prison sentences. Maybe Hanover House will get too crowded, and they'll let him out. Anything can happen."

Evelyn understood those fears probably more than anyone else. She shared them. But she had to convince Courtney to come forward. "He's a convicted serial killer. He won't ever go free."

"Says you. I can't stake my son's life on that!" she cried, and hung up.

Letting go of a long sigh, Evelyn shoved that note and the accompanying brownie away and sank deeper into her seat. But she didn't put down the phone. She kept staring at the handset, willing Courtney to come back on the line. The statement she'd made — *if I talk* — had grabbed Evelyn by the throat. Courtney knew something, something important. . . .

"Dr. Talbot?"

Evelyn shifted her attention to Penny, who'd poked her head in.

"The hospital called a minute ago. Hugo Evanski tried to escape and wound up going into cardiac arrest."

Oh no. Not this. "Is he dead?" she asked.

"The doctors are fighting to save him."

She gave a single nod to acknowledge that she'd heard. She preferred Penny leave her to cope with the news alone, and Penny did — albeit hesitantly. Her assistant didn't know how to interpret her subdued response. Evelyn probably seemed strangely distant, but she was screaming inside. Somehow, someway, she had to get on top of what was going on and put a stop to it!

Finally setting the phone on its cradle, she checked the schedule, saw that Glenn wasn't due to come in until after noon and called him at home.

"I had no idea any of that was going on," he said, sounding shocked once she told him about Danielle and Kush and

Petrowski. "How could they be doing that right beneath our noses — and keep it so hush-hush?"

"They were careful, I guess."

"Those bastards! They probably got Danielle killed. Maybe Lorraine, too. I swear to God, if that's the case —"

"Glenn, don't even think that way. Let the law handle it, however it turns out."

"It would just be so wrong!"

"Who knows what all was going on. But . . . will you do me a favor?"

"Anything. You know that."

"Will you continue to keep your eyes and ears open? Now that you know what's been happening, maybe you'll pick up on something."

"Of course. It's just . . ."

Surprised by the reluctance in his voice, she hesitated. "What?"

"I hate to even bring this up, but . . . you don't think Dr. Fitzpatrick could be involved. I mean, from what I've seen, *he's* the one who's been acting strange."

Her stomach tightened into knots again. Where had he gotten Tim's name? She hadn't led him there, hadn't mentioned anything about her fellow psychiatrist. "Strange in what way?"

"It could be nothing, which is why I

haven't mentioned it. But when I went to escort Hugo back from one of their sessions together, it just . . . felt very odd, as if something had been going on that shouldn't be, you know? I heard Hugo say, 'God, it was good to finally get a piece of that ass.' Then Dr. Fitzpatrick saw me and silenced him with a quick shake of his head. That makes me wonder if . . . if he wasn't aware of the whole thing."

It made *her* wonder, too. But she'd already been wondering about Fitzpatrick's culpability — even in the murders. "There's no telling who's involved. Only Kush and Petrowski are for sure busted. They're about to be suspended. Hopefully they'll talk and we'll find out more. But, in case they don't finger everyone, let me know if you learn anything."

"I will."

"Thanks," she said, and disconnected before coming to her feet. She had a meeting with the warden to talk about the forthcoming suspensions, since neither Kush nor Petrowski were working until later, and to discuss who else Ferris felt might be involved. Then she planned to view the videotapes of Fitzpatrick's sessions over the past few weeks. Doing so would keep her from her regular work and it was a shot in the dark — those tapes might not reveal anything important — but she had to go through them, just in case. At least they'd give her a glimpse into his recent life, show her who he'd been talking to and what he'd been saying, even how he'd been acting — with some of the COs as well as the inmates.

"Dr. Talbot?"

Penny was back at the door. "Yes?"

"Warden Ferris is waiting for you. He said you left an urgent voice mail that you needed to meet with him this morning."

"Tell him I'm on my way," she said. But she caught Penny before Penny could leave, asked her to let Ferris know it'd be another fifteen minutes and called Courtney back.

The phone rang so many times Evelyn assumed it would go unanswered. Her heart sank — but then she heard a timid, "Hello?"

Renewed hope charged through her. She had another chance. "Courtney?"

"Yes?"

"I'm sorry to bother you again. I really am. I don't like upsetting you. But someone has to fight Anthony. Do you understand? If that has to be me, I'm willing. But in this instance, I can't do it alone. I need you to take a stand with me, to help me put a stop to the terror that is Anthony Garza."

"And what about my son?" she asked,

breaking into tears. "Danny's only eight. Imagine how I'll feel if he gets hurt or killed!"

"I can't promise you that won't happen." Evelyn had to be honest; Courtney needed to be aware of the chance she'd be taking — especially since, in the fervor of her desire to get Courtney to help, Evelyn had stated so unequivocally a few minutes earlier that Anthony would never get out. "But if Anthony Garza succeeds in intimidating you, in keeping you silent, he wins. He gets away with killing those poor women. And here's the thing. We don't really have a choice. We *have* to stop him and others like him."

"You have no idea what he's like," she responded. "How strong and determined he can be. After what I've learned over the past two years, I wouldn't put *anything* past him."

"Is he the Porn Poser?" Evelyn asked.

There was a long silence. Courtney *wanted* to talk; Evelyn could sense it. "Courtney, *please*. Help me."

"I have something here," she said at length.

Evelyn sat up straight. "What is it?"

"A . . . oh God, I swore I'd never do this, never put myself in Anthony's sights again."

463

Evelyn could hear the waver in her voice. "I understand why you'd make yourself that promise. No one understands better than I do."

"If he ever gets out —"

"He'll be a lot less likely to get out if what you know ties him to another murder — or, better yet, a string of them."

After a protracted silence, Courtney said, "It's a credit card."

"A credit card?" Evelyn repeated.

"Before Anthony went to prison, he showed up at my house, out of the blue. I don't even know how he found me, which is partly why I'm so scared. Once I reached Kansas, I thought he was out of my life for good. But he knocked on my door one day and asked to see my son."

"Your son isn't his son?"

"I had Danny before Anthony and I got together. But Anthony considers himself Danny's stepfather and claims to love him."

"So what happened?"

"I'm ashamed to say I let Danny go with him for the day. He has an anger problem, but he's never hurt Danny, Danny was begging to go, and I hadn't yet heard about the murders. I didn't even know that Anthony had had so many other wives, let alone that they were dead. I was still blaming myself for most of the stuff that went wrong in our marriage — he was good at making me feel responsible."

"Psychopaths have a knack for that," Evelyn broke in. "So how'd Danny's day with Anthony turn out?"

"Luckily, fine. But when Anthony brought Danny home, Danny had a sack of candy with him. It was close to dinnertime, and I didn't want him eating any more of it, so after Anthony drove off, I took it away. I was going to toss the wrappers and save the rest. That's when I found the credit card."

"It wasn't Anthony's. . . ."

"No. It was" — she paused as if she almost couldn't say it aloud — "it had a woman's name on it: Elaine Morrison."

Elaine Morrison! She was one of the victims of the Porn Poser.

"Did he come back for it?"

"He didn't. I never saw him again. I'm not sure he's even aware of where it went. He's not the most organized person in the world."

Penny popped her head in again to remind Evelyn that the warden was waiting, but Evelyn waved her off. "What did you do with that credit card?"

"I have it here. I figured it belonged to whatever new woman was in his life. So I put it in the cupboard in case he asked about it. I'm just lucky he didn't, and that I didn't have a number for him, or I would've called to let him know. I had no idea he was accused of murdering someone by that name. It wasn't until a week or so later that my cousin told me he was being charged for killing three women who had all been married to him at one time. And right about then, the news broke about an Elaine Morrison's body being found at the ski resort not far from where Anthony lived. It just . . . gave me chills. I can't explain how, but I knew in my heart that he was to blame before that detective even started calling me."

"Detective Green has reached out to you?"

"On several occasions."

"You never told him about the credit card, though?"

"I couldn't! I didn't dare. Anthony was going to prison. I figured that was good enough."

"But it's not," Evelyn argued gently. "You understand why."

"I do. In my heart I've always known."

"So will you come forward? Tell Detective Green what you told me?"

There was no response.

"Courtney, let's hold Anthony accountable for his actions. Will you do it?"

Still nothing.

"Don't let him beat you — beat all of us!"

At last, Courtney sniffed and muttered, "Okay."

Evelyn leaned on her desk, nearly spent from the adrenaline coursing through her body. "Thank you. I can only imagine how grateful Elaine's family will be. And the other victims, too. This might be the link Detective Green needs to charge Anthony with all six of the Porn Poser murders."

"Will Anthony find out I'm the one who came forward?" she asked in a small voice.

Evelyn wished she could say no, but . . . "I'm afraid there isn't any way to avoid that."

"He's going to wish he'd killed me."

"How is it that he didn't? How were you any different from the women he'd been with before?"

"I've asked myself that so many times," she said. "But I have no idea. He was having an affair with our neighbor when I left him. And I didn't try to take anything — no money, no furnishings. I'd seen his temper. To me, fighting over that stuff wasn't worth the rage it would evoke. I was just glad to get out with my son. So maybe it was that I never made him mad enough. Or he let me live for Danny's sake."

"What are Anthony's parents like?" Evelyn asked.

"That's the thing," Courtney replied. "They're *really* nice. They don't deserve a son like him."

Evelyn got up to stand at the window. "No one deserves a son — or a husband — like Anthony Garza. Don't worry, Courtney. He'll never be able to hurt you again," she said, and got Detective Green on the line.

Amarok's meeting with Tim Hancock proved enlightening, enlightening enough that he headed over to Hanover House next. It was time to talk to the other "Tim" in Danielle's book — Dr. Fitzpatrick.

Evelyn's chief colleague tried to put him off by citing how busy he was and how he couldn't be late for his next appointment or it would throw his schedule off for the rest of the afternoon. But Amarok wasn't about to accept that. He had a murder investigation on his hands, and he was doing everything he could, as quickly as possible, to solve it. So he threatened to drive Fitzpatrick down to his trooper post for the interview, pointing out how much more time *that* would require, and only then did Evelyn's colleague agree to a quick sit-down

468

in his office.

"So here we are," Fitzpatrick said from behind his big desk.

Amarok noted the locked cabinet Evelyn had described as containing the file that held so much information on her. "Thank you for your forbearance," he said as he claimed one of the two seats directly opposite the desk.

A muscle moved in Fitzpatrick's cheek; he could tell Amarok was being facetious. "Apparently, what you have to say to me can't wait, so what is it you need, Sergeant?"

"I'd like you to give me a little information about your relationship with Officer Kush and Officer Petrowski, if you would."

"My *relationship* with them?" He seemed genuinely puzzled.

"That's right. You know both, don't you?"

"Of course. They work here."

Apparently, he hadn't heard they were about to be suspended. Evelyn had done an admirable job keeping that under wraps. "Are you any more familiar with these COs than the others on staff?"

"No, why?"

Amarok didn't answer his question. He merely moved forward with his own agenda. After what Hugo had told him, it was difficult to even look at Fitzpatrick without punching him in the face. "You don't associate with them outside of work? Never spend any time with them after hours — at your place or theirs?"

"No. Never," he said as if that would be too far beneath him.

"Can you say the same about Danielle Connelly?"

Caution entered his tone. "Excuse me?"

"Did you have a relationship with Danielle outside of the prison?"

He straightened several items on his desk. "What makes you ask *that*?"

Amarok narrowed his eyes. "Why don't you answer the question?"

"Of course not. Danielle was young and . . . and uneducated. What would *we* have in common?"

"You're saying you weren't interested in her romantically."

"Not at all."

"You only saw her at work."

His gaze met Amarok's, but only briefly before it skittered away. He shuffled some papers. "That's correct."

"You've *never* had sex with Danielle."

"Do I really have to tolerate this?" he asked, coming to his feet.

"Since I'm determined to figure out who killed her, yes."

"But this is crazy. The next thing I know you'll be blaming me for her death!"

"That's an interesting comment." Amarok rubbed his chin. "Would there be any reason for me to consider you a suspect?"

Looking supremely uncomfortable, he smoothed his lab coat. "No! You're only here because you don't like me."

"You're halfway right," Amarok said. "I *don't* like you. But that's *not* why I'm here."

Fitzpatrick gestured toward the window. "There are so many other people out there you should be questioning."

"Out there . . ."

"In Hilltop. Wherever."

"You mean besides you."

"Yes, besides me!"

"So . . . if I told you that Danielle's neighbor saw you at her house, you would say . . ." Amarok crossed his legs and looked up. Lloyd Hudson hadn't seen anything; this was merely a hunch. But when Fitzpatrick fell back in his chair as if he'd been shot, Amarok knew his hunch was correct. Hugo had started Amarok thinking that there wouldn't be many places for a man like Fitzpatrick to find physical satisfaction in Hilltop, not when the woman he really wanted wasn't interested. With those pictures he was showing Hugo, he had to be

471

looking for a sexual outlet. That, taken together with the evidence of Danielle having made such a fancy dinner and the fact that Danielle probably wouldn't have gone to so much trouble for just any man, made Amarok wonder if her dinner guest could have been someone she meant to impress, someone she considered important — like a member of the mental health team from the facility where she worked.

"Dr. Fitzpatrick?" Amarok prompted.

He unbuttoned the collar of his shirt and loosened his tie. "I had dinner with her. That's all."

"Does that mean, if I were to measure your cock, it would come up as something other than five inches?"

His mouth dropped open. "Measure my — is that your idea of a joke?"

Amarok couldn't help smiling; it was hard not to laugh outright. "Not really. Although, in my mind, it *is* a little funny. In case this is news, Danielle Connelly made a record of most of the men she slept with, and she made a note of each man's . . . size." Amarok didn't mention that she hadn't mentioned Tim's last name. He didn't want Fitzpatrick to realize he had the chance to lie — not until it was too late to do so.

A single vein popped out in the psychia-

472

trist's forehead. "She . . . she wrote that information down? What kind of woman does that?"

What kind of psychiatrist shows a convicted felon, a known psychopath, pornographic pictures of his female colleague? "Maybe she was performing her own study." Amarok wasn't nearly as relaxed as he hoped to appear. He needed a confession. Tim Hancock hadn't even been in Alaska on the date Danielle had recorded the encounter in question. But, as Evelyn had pointed out, that didn't mean — at least with absolute certainty — that the Tim in Danielle's book *had* to be Dr. Fitzpatrick. "You didn't warrant a smiley face," Amarok added. "But there were others with less to offer, if that makes you feel any better."

He clutched his chest, but Amarok could tell he wasn't in physical pain; he was shocked and embarrassed.

"You don't remember her measuring?" Amarok went on. "Because I'm thinking that would stand out — no pun intended, of course."

"I have no idea what you're talking about. She-she didn't measure me. She didn't even mention that sort of thing . . . mattered."

"It shouldn't when your brain is big enough to compensate, right? Maybe for you she made an educated guess. She certainly had the experience to do so." He shoved the hems of his jeans more securely into his snow boots. "But you *did* have sex with her, did you not?"

Fitzpatrick looked around as if he were drowning and couldn't find a rope.

"You wouldn't want to lie and then have your DNA show up on the body," Amarok said, using a cautious tone that, he hoped, demanded the truth.

"What body?" Fitzpatrick responded, pouncing on the only thing he could. "You mean her *hand*? Last I heard you hadn't found any more of her — and you won't, running around questioning the wrong people."

"Finding a body can be a bit difficult when we're surrounded by such a vast wilderness. The wildlife around here can devour remains pretty quickly. But the pathologist has scraped under Danielle's nails — and found some very interesting evidence." Although her nail filings were on the way to the lab, Amarok had no idea if the technicians would find anything. He was still bluffing — bluffing for all he was worth.

Fitzpatrick mumbled something Amarok couldn't hear, so Amarok leaned closer. "What'd you say?"

"I said she was . . . constantly flirting with me. And she . . . she made me feel as if . . . as if our time together would be discreet. A simple release, if you will."

"She was merely servicing you."

"Yes," he barked with supreme irritation, "if you have to state it that baldly."

"Did you pay her?"

He shoved his chair back, slipped out from behind his desk and began to pace. "Of course not. She was . . . lonely, too."

"Then you weren't aware she was also sleeping with everyone else?"

"Everyone else?"

"Kush and Petrowski, several of the inmates and most of the men who frequent the Moosehead. The list is quite extensive." He was learning it wasn't quite *exhaustive,* however. Somehow Kush and Petrowski had managed to keep their names out of that book — if what Hugo had told him about them taking part was true.

Fitzpatrick covered his eyes. "Lord help me."

Amarok doubted he'd receive any sort of divine intervention, but he waited to let his words sink in before pressing further. Fitzpatrick was beginning to crack. If he was guilty of the murders, maybe he'd let it *all* out, relieve his conscience, and Amarok would be able to arrest him. After what he'd learned about Fitzpatrick, Amarok didn't want him around Evelyn anymore.

Fitzpatrick was the first to break the silence. "Does Evelyn know about this?" he asked, dropping his hand. "Is that why . . . why she believes what Hugo said?"

"That you hate her?"

"I don't hate her," he said, coming to a stop at the window.

"Then why did you use her likeness in your sessions with Hugo? Make her out to be a whore for him? For you both? So you could get off in the name of research? Or punish her for bringing you all the way out here and then disappointing you in the worst way?"

He glanced over his shoulder and blanched. "What I did with Hugo, it was . . . for my work. I was . . . I was performing studies on —"

"You were fulfilling your own sexual desires any way you could. You must've liked seeing Hugo crave her as badly as you do, liked creating that same frustration, knowing he'd never be able to assuage it, either."

"Stop. You don't know —"

"As far as I'm concerned, it all comes down to one thing."

He pivoted and began to pace again. "And

that is?"

"You're obsessed with Evelyn."

"See?" He threw up his hands. "That's not true!"

"It is," Amarok said. "And there's a file in the cabinet behind you that proves it."

What little color remained drained from his face, and he came to a dead stop. "How do *you* know?"

"About the file? I've got a copy of the contents."

He shook his head. "What she must think of me."

"She used to admire you." Amarok got up. "But tell me this, Doc."

The slope of Fitzpatrick's shoulders made him look defeated.

"Were you involved with Kush and Petrowski in charging the inmates to have sex with Danielle?"

His dismay cleared and a spark of anger flashed in his eyes as his sharp chin came up. "No! I knew *nothing* about that."

"You didn't kill Danielle to hide their corruption?"

"Of course not! I swear it! I had sex with her, yes, but . . . but then I left. And that was it. I haven't seen her since Saturday night."

"You didn't go back for more and get

angry when she refused or you learned about the other men?"

"No! And I certainly didn't harm Lorraine Drummond. If you think I could hack two women to pieces . . ." His words fell off as if he couldn't even say it, let alone do it.

"I never dreamed you could do what you've done to Evelyn. That doesn't give you a great deal of credibility. Maybe you were afraid that news of your involvement with Danielle would get out, that you might be disgraced, lose your job —"

"I'm embarrassed!" he snapped. "That's the reason I lied, the reason I didn't come forward to tell you I'd been with Danielle that once. But as bad as having lied makes me look, and all that business with . . . with the file I've got on Evelyn and what I did in those sessions with Hugo, I didn't kill anyone, Sergeant. It would take a lot more than having sex with the wrong person to drive me to murder."

"Even if the discovery of your actions meant losing Evelyn's respect?"

He crossed over and threw himself in his seat. "I admire her. I'd rather she not know — about any of this. But she's already lost respect for me."

"Then maybe we can make a deal."

"A deal?" he echoed with a spark of hope.

"If you willingly hand over the file I mentioned, the one in the cabinet behind you, I won't tell her about your sessions with Hugo. Maybe that's one thing she won't have to find out about — since I'd rather she not have to hear it." Amarok could only imagine how that would make her feel.

Without another word, Fitzpatrick took a key from under his desk, opened the filing cabinet and handed over the documents Evelyn had copied.

Amarok glanced through it to make sure everything was there. "Thank you. I'll do what I can to spare you both news of . . . those sessions. But you realize I'm going to be asking Kush and Petrowski if you were involved in the prostitution."

"Of course."

"If they implicate you, all promises are void."

He looked shell-shocked as he rubbed his forehead. "If they implicate me, they're lying. I would never condone such actions, and I think they are both fully aware of that."

"We'll see what *they* say," Amarok said.

His eyebrows knitted together. "You're not the right man for her, you know. You might have certain . . . assets, a handsome face and maybe other . . . things. But you don't get what drives her. And you're not nearly smart enough for her."

Amarok refused to let his smile fade. "Maybe you don't realize it yet, but I was just smart enough for you."

25

What's one less person on the face of the earth, anyway?
— TED BUNDY, SERIAL KILLER, RAPIST,
KIDNAPPER AND NECROPHILIAC

Evelyn adopted a pleasant expression as Anthony Garza glared at her. "There've been some interesting developments," she said.

"That bastard I shanked has died?"

"Not yet. But he tried to escape from the hospital, got into a tussle with the man guarding his door and wound up in cardiac arrest."

Garza flashed her those jagged teeth. "So this is *good* news."

"Not entirely." She crossed her legs and brushed a speck off her skirt. "I took a moment to call the hospital before coming here. The doctors were able to save him. He's in stable condition."

"What a dumbass." He clicked his tongue. "I can only imagine what that must've looked like — him trying to run away with his bare ass hanging out his hospital gown."

"He's putting up a good fight — on every front. I thought if anyone could admire his determination, you could."

"I don't admire anything about him. The fact that he's still breathing ruins a perfectly nice morning."

She grinned at Garza.

"What?"

"I'm afraid I'm about to ruin far more than that."

"Oh yeah?" He leaned close, his eyes more watchful than before. "What else can you do to me?"

She yawned, as if she was no longer impressed with his "tough guy" routine, and opened the folder she'd brought in with her. "Does the name Elaine Morrison ring any bells?"

"None," he said with an indifferent shrug.

He lied so quickly, so effortlessly — with none of the nervous habits that gave away most other people. Evelyn might have been tempted to believe him.

Except she knew better.

She took out the picture Green had faxed over while she was meeting with the warden and held it to the glass. "Elaine was one of the victims of the Porn Poser. She was a pretty lady, wouldn't you say? A schoolteacher, only twenty-eight."

He gave the photograph a cursory glance. He didn't care what he'd done, felt no regret, no remorse. "So?" he said. "Why would I give a shit about any of that?"

"Because you're about to be charged for her murder, and maybe several others."

Making an exaggerated show of it by slapping his leg, he laughed, then abruptly stopped. "No, I'm not. They can't connect me to her murder, or they would've charged me before."

"Here's the thing," Evelyn said. "I've managed to come across an important piece of evidence."

"*You* managed to find this evidence?" He was still skeptical.

"Yes."

"Way the hell up here?"

She shrugged. "All it took was a phone call — and the right sort of appeal."

His hesitation suggested he was getting worried. "Who'd you talk to?"

"I could say, but . . . I'd rather let you sweat it out." She put the picture away and got up.

"You're lying," he said. "They have nothing on me."

"We'll see, won't we?"

He jumped to his feet. "Where are you going?"

"I'm done here."

"I'm not! *What do they have?"*

"Maybe if you give me the name of whoever told you to stab Hugo Evanski" — she covered another yawn as if she didn't much care either way — "I'll share, too."

"You can go to hell!"

She feigned surprise. "You'd rather protect whoever it was out of spite? You *can't* care about them. You just arrived here."

"Maybe I like having something you want."

Leaning forward, she planted a kiss on the glass, leaving a perfect imprint with her lipstick. "And maybe I like having something *you* want," she said, and headed for the door.

"I'll find out eventually," he called after her.

"True, but the way these things go, it could take months to get the information from whatever public defender they wind up assigning to your case," she said as she moved.

"I'll be in here forever, anyway. What does time matter?"

"It *doesn't* matter — not to me." She made a careless gesture with one hand. "Forget I said anything. The COs will be here to take you back to your cell in a few hours."

"What are you talking about, *hours*?" he cried. "You can't leave me in here that long. There isn't even a bed."

She paused with her hand on the knob. "There's a chair. Use that."

"This ain't right!"

"Consider it part of your therapy."

"The cruel and unusual punishment part?"

She laughed as if he were being silly. "This hardly qualifies. Anyway, who's going to care? There isn't a person in this world who gives a damn about you."

"My parents do!" he insisted.

"Too bad they'll never hear about it, then."

"I'll write them!"

"Don't waste your time. That letter will never leave the premises."

"You bitch!" he screamed, kicking the plexiglass. "Someday I'm gonna slit your throat and drink your blood."

"Now stop." She added a laugh. "You're getting me excited and I have to work."

"Wait!"

Halfway out the door, she froze — then

485

turned slowly back to face him. "Yes?"

His expression changed, grew indifferent. "You're right. I don't give a shit about anyone here."

Or anywhere else, she thought. She could've added that but felt she'd antagonized him enough. "So . . ."

He used his hands — both, since they were shackled — to rub his shaved head. "It was that dickhead Kush."

She caught her breath but refused to let her surprise register on her face. "You expect me to believe it was a *CO*?"

"If you think COs never do anything wrong you're even more naïve than I thought," he said.

"Was it *just* Kush? Or was there someone else who encouraged you to stab Hugo?" *Maybe someone like Petrowski? Or Fitzpatrick?* She wanted to know but didn't want to suggest any names.

"Someone else? Like who?"

"I'm asking *you.*"

"No. And if there was, I'd say. What do I care if Kush loses his job and goes to prison? Maybe it'll do him some good to be on the other side, for a change. Maybe it'll imbue him with a little *empathy.*"

An ironic statement, coming from a man for whom empathy was a complete mystery.

Adopting a neutral expression, Evelyn went back inside and allowed the door to close. "Or you could be looking for some sort of revenge."

"You're the only one I'm dying to hurt."

She believed that. "Fine. But there must've been *something* in it for you."

"Why? I like to kill. I did it for the fun of it."

She didn't believe him. "Okay" — she tapped a finger against her lip — "I'll have your cell tossed, see what we can come up with —"

He called her a bitch again. But when she started to go as if she really was done with him this time, he hurried to catch her. "Drugs, okay? Kush said he'd get me an eight ball of coke and a few explicit pictures of the girl who was killed screwing the guy I was supposed to shank."

Kush again. God, how could he be that *depraved?*

No doubt he'd loved showing Anthony what he could get away with at Hanover House, who held the real power in this prison.

"Did you make the weapon?"

"There was no time for that. He provided it. Then he pointed out the guy who needed to dance on the blacktop."

Was this true? She'd hoped Kush's crimes stopped at prostitution. But if he'd go *that* far, maybe he'd go even further. "Did he deliver on his promises when it came to the dope?"

"It's all in my cell if you don't believe me. Are you going after it?" he added as if that would be highly unfair.

"Of course." Those pictures were evidence. "But . . . if you're cooperative, I'll make you a deal."

He glared at her. "I don't like dealing with you."

"Even if it's in your best interest?"

He idly kicked his chains around. "What do you want?"

"If we go back to your cell together, right now, and you turn over those illicit pictures, I'll wait to order the search."

"Until . . ."

"Next week." By then, the drugs would be gone — they'd probably be gone if she gave him any time at all — but the eight ball was the least of her problems. The pictures were what mattered. She couldn't risk not being able to find them or having them destroyed. "You know how busy it can get around here."

"Maybe you're not a *total* bitch," he said. "I'll take that deal. But now it's your turn to give me the information *I* want."

She'd made the only concession she could make today, which was partly why she'd offered it — to be as fair as possible. "I will as soon as I can confirm that what you've told me is true." She didn't see how Anthony could ever hurt Courtney or her son, but she preferred to wait until Detective Green had Elaine Morrison's credit card so that harming Courtney wouldn't benefit him, anyway. "I'll meet with you again when I have what I need."

"Hell no!" he cried. "Tell me now!"

"Waiting a few days is still better than waiting months to hear from your lawyer," she pointed out.

"I swear to God I'm going to kill you!"

She tilted her head. "If that's the way you're going to be, I guess I'll have the COs toss your cell right now, find the pictures, remove the drugs and use the fact that we discovered contraband to order a body cavity search — which will need to be repeated twice daily *indefinitely* to make sure you're clean."

He banged his head on the glass so hard it started bleeding. But she didn't react, didn't jump back in fear or rush to get him help. This time, she'd been prepared for his temper.

They both stood their ground, glaring at each other.

"What's it going to be?" she asked calmly. "And if you think knocking yourself silly might help you decide, feel free to bash your head all you like. It doesn't hurt *me*."

"You're no kind of shrink."

"Because I won't allow you to manipulate me through my humanity? I guess that's too damn bad."

His nostrils flared as he continued to try to intimidate her. But then, when he realized he wasn't going to get the upper hand, not today, he said, "Fine. I'll give you the damn pictures. But you'd better hope you *never* find yourself alone with me."

She wrinkled her nose as she looked him up and down. "You think that scares me? I've been attacked by much bigger and stronger men than you."

Evelyn marched along with the pictures from Garza's cell tucked under her arm, so angry with Kush and Petrowski she could hardly see straight. As if two murders weren't tragic enough, she was dealing with some significant corruption and, if Hugo died, a third death.

Was Kush behind Danielle and Lorraine's murders, too?

She supposed it was possible, but she couldn't see Kush doing what had been done to Lorraine. That had been a rage-filled attack, a classic lust killing. Was he really *that* kind of man?

Although . . . if Garza could be believed, Kush *had* ordered Hugo shanked in the yard.

She entered the administration area intent on calling Amarok to report what she'd learned, but the moment Penny and Linda saw her they hurried over.

"Fitzpatrick's gone," Penny announced, reaching her first.

Evelyn came to a halt and looked from one to the other. "What do you mean, *gone?*"

"He packed up his things and left while I was at lunch," Linda said.

"*I* was here," Penny told her. "He made several trips."

"And he did this *with no explanation?*"

"None. He has appointments this afternoon, too. I checked the master calendar and tried to remind him that he had a busy afternoon. I even asked if I should tell Linda to cancel those appointments. But he wouldn't speak to me. The way he was rushing around, I could tell he was upset, but he wouldn't say why, where he was going or if he'd ever be back."

Evelyn's gaze strayed to the open doorway of her office. She considered calling down and having the COs stop Tim before he could drive off the premises, but she had a sinking feeling it was too late. "When, exactly, did this happen?"

Penny checked her watch. "About an hour ago."

"He left before I could even get back from lunch," Linda complained.

Circumventing both women, Evelyn strode to Fitzpatrick's office. Sure enough, it was bare. Even his degrees had been removed from the wall. He wasn't just taking off early so he could enjoy a long weekend. . . .

The filing cabinet she'd broken into had a drawer hanging halfway out. He hadn't bothered to remove most of his files. Perhaps he figured they were so heavy they'd take too long. But the file on her was gone. She noticed that right away.

She crossed to the window and gazed out, hoping to spot his Escalade below.

Unfortunately, since most of the parking was covered, she couldn't tell if it was there or not.

"Dr. Talbot?" Linda said from behind her.

"Yes?" she replied absently, still straining to see.

"Can you tell us what's going on? Is it that Dr. Fitzpatrick and you have decided you can no longer work together, or . . . or what?"

What Linda really wanted to know was how this latest development would affect her job. Evelyn heard it in her voice. But she couldn't provide an answer. She didn't know. "I'm afraid I can't clarify what he's doing," she replied. "I have no idea. He didn't say a word to me."

Keeping the pictures she'd collected from Anthony Garza with her, she hurried to her own office. She called down to the sally port from there, but the COs told her Dr. Fitzpatrick was long gone. When she couldn't reach him at his house, either, she tried to alert Amarok by calling his trooper post.

Phil Robbins answered. "Sergeant Amarok's office."

"Phil, this is Dr. Talbot."

"Hello, Doc. How are you?"

God, it was hard to get by without the use of cell phones. It was hard to believe that the rest of the country used to be this way — except the rest of the country didn't get snowed in quite so often. "Fine, thank you.

Listen, Amarok isn't there by any chance, is he?"

"No, hasn't been in all day, which is why I'm stuck on the blasted phones."

"I'm sure it's a big help to have you there," she said. "Can you tell me where he is?"

"Last I heard he was over at Hanover House. You haven't seen him?"

Both Penny and Linda had gravitated to her office. She'd been too preoccupied to bother closing the door.

"No," she told him. "But I haven't been in my office for most of the day."

"Hang on. I'll get him on the radio."

"Thanks." She waited two or three minutes. Then Phil came back on the line.

"He's with the warden, arresting Officer Kush, but he'll stop by soon."

"Is it true what Dr. Fitzpatrick said?" Penny asked when she was off the phone.

Evelyn frowned, her mind going in a million different directions. "What?"

"That you're infatuated with Sergeant Amarok?"

She rocked back. "Would that be so hard to believe?"

"Not really," Penny replied. "I mean . . . I guess I just never imagined you as . . ."

As being anywhere close to his age? Was

that what was coming next? Evelyn braced for it, just in case. "As?"

"As having any interests outside work," Linda supplied.

Evelyn hadn't — until she'd met Amarok. That was what frightened her. She was falling in love with entirely the wrong person, someone she could never hope to keep even if she remained in Alaska. She had trust issues. Getting with a younger man, one so many other women desired, wasn't going to help.

"Sometimes things change," Evelyn said.

"We all need outside interests," Penny said. "You can worship at his feet along with the rest us," she added as if that were all Evelyn could ever hope for.

Evelyn glanced away. Little did Penny know she was doing a little more than that. . . .

26

The more I looked at people, the more I
hated them.

— CHARLES STARKWEATHER,
TEENAGE SPREE KILLER

Anthony Garza lay awake in solitary confinement, staring at the ceiling while waiting for the man he was expecting. That man
had promised to let Anthony out of "the
hole," out of the entire prison, so that he
could do what he wanted to do more than
anything else in the world — which was get
his hands around Evelyn Talbot's throat.

He rested his arm over his eyes as he
listened for footsteps. Where was the bastard? Couldn't be much longer now. The
note Anthony had been passed had indicated it wouldn't be late when it happened,
and he had no reason to doubt the promises
in that message. For one, he'd since been
provided with a guard's uniform. For an-

other, he'd received directions to the place Evelyn was most likely to be when she wasn't at the prison — the Alaska State Trooper's house where she was currently staying. Why would he be given those things if he wasn't really going to be freed?

Besides, the person he was dealing with had an exemplary track record. Anthony had been asked to shank Hugo Evanski and had been shuttled out of solitary and into the yard, hadn't he? Why would this be any different?

There was some serious shit going down in this prison. . . .

He remembered Dr. Talbot glaring at him when she said, *I've been attacked by much bigger and stronger men than you.* How dare she taunt him! He'd show her just how minimal her previous experiences had been. And he couldn't wait. He'd kill her slowly, enjoy every moment. He could already feel her pulse weakening beneath his fingertips as he crushed her windpipe, which caused his own heart to race with excitement.

She'd tell him exactly what Detective Green had on him — with her last breath. That would be good information to have in case he was ever caught again. But he didn't plan on returning to prison. He'd be gone by the time they found her body, and the guy who was letting him out knew it, said he needed the diversion. With one of the guards fudging the morning count, there should be just enough lead time.

The footfalls, when Anthony heard them, sounded steady and confident. This was a man who knew what he was doing, a man who could get things done.

Anthony could respect a dude like that.

Evelyn seemed far more remote than Amarok had expected, after last night. He'd been dying to see her again, but when he tried to catch her eye, to get her to smile at him, she wouldn't even meet his gaze. After he walked in, she closed the door and gave him a wide berth as she circled to her desk — very professional, all business, as if they'd never slept together.

"Phil said you wanted to see me," he said. "What's going on?" He'd hoped it was for personal reasons. Despite all the pressure he was under, he'd been anxious to catch a glimpse of her. But he could tell this wasn't an "I miss you. Last night was great." It was something else, something far less welcome.

"Did you know that Dr. Fitzpatrick has packed up his office and left?" she asked.

He felt himself stiffen as he bit back a curse. "When?"

She glanced at her watch. "About an hour and a half ago."

Shit. "What'd he say?"

"Nothing. He did it while I was on the prison side. Penny told me when I came back — and I checked. His office is empty, except for a number of files on old patients that couldn't be very valuable to him, anyway. He took the one on me."

Amarok shoved a hand through his hair as he tried to decide how this might impact his case. What was going on with Fitzpatrick? Was he running? "Actually, I've got that file. I spoke to him earlier, made him give it to me."

She seemed to breathe a little easier. "What'd he say when he found out you knew?"

"He was humiliated. He has a lot of pride. Have you tried to reach him?"

"He's not answering at his house. Penny mentioned to me —"

"Penny's your assistant, right?" He had so many names, places and people in his head right now, and he was going on so little sleep. . . .

"Really?" she said. "As crazy as she is about you?"

Evelyn didn't act like she was teasing. Amarok got the impression that Penny's admiration wasn't working in his favor where *she* was concerned.

"Why would I remember *her*?" he asked. "She has nothing to do with this case. And she's not the woman I'm interested in."

She looked up at him then, *really* looked at him for the first time since he'd walked into her office. "Who *are* you interested in?"

"Who do you think? I want *you,* Evelyn." He was tired of messing around, of second-guessing what she might be thinking or feeling or what she might do if he revealed the level of his interest. He didn't want to scare her off, but as far as he was concerned, it was too late to pretend it wouldn't sting if she rejected him. When he thought of her, he felt something he'd never felt before. And if last night had shown him anything, it was that there was something about Evelyn Talbot that fit him perfectly — despite all the reasons they could both list as to why that should be otherwise.

"Even if we could get past the age difference —" she started.

He lifted a hand. "Don't even bring that up. Just answer me this: Do you want to come home to me at night?"

She bit her lip.

"You look scared," he said. "And that scares me. It's a simple question. Yes or no?"

"We've got so much going on right now, Amarok. Why don't we wait until —"

"I'm not waiting for anything," he broke in. *"Yes or no?"*

When she covered her mouth, he scowled at her. "Is it that hard to figure out?"

"No. It's not!" she snapped. "It's hard to say."

"Because . . ."

"Love hurts!"

He lowered his voice. "Not always, Evelyn. Give me the chance to prove otherwise."

After briefly closing her eyes, she nodded.

His heart was pounding. He hadn't meant to come in here and lay it all on the line like this, wasn't sure what had gotten into him. They had been spending time together for a few days. But somehow he'd known even before she'd come to stay with him that he wanted her. "So you'll move in with me on a more permanent basis?"

"That's a big step."

"There's no reason to wait."

She fiddled with her belt. "What about my cat?"

"Sigmund's invited, too."

"Makita might not like it. . . ."

"I say we introduce them, see if they can get along. Makita will adjust."

She studied him for several seconds.

"What do you say?" he asked.

"Okay."

He drew a deep breath, hardly able to believe that, in the end, she'd capitulated so easily. "Then we'll start there. I don't know what you're going to do, how long you'll even stay in Alaska. But I want to be with you while you're here. It's that simple."

Her eyebrows gathered. "It won't stay simple. Romantic relationships never do —"

"It's simple right now," he said. "And we're going to leave it at that."

She seemed taken aback. "I didn't expect this. Not so soon."

"I figure if I want you to lower your defenses, I have to lower mine first. One of us has to take the lead. I can't put that on you, not after all you've been through."

"So you're going to be our fearless leader?" she teased.

"I'm going to fight for what I'm feeling," he said. "In spite of Jasper. You already mean too much to me. I don't want to lose you."

He wasn't sure how she would've responded because Penny knocked before leaning into the room. "Dr. Talbot, I've tried Dr. Fitzpatrick's house a dozen times. If he's there, he won't pick up."

"Thank you, Penny. You can give it a rest."

Her assistant's gaze traveled to him. Then she blushed and ducked out.

He ignored her interest and was grateful when Evelyn did, too.

"Did Fitzpatrick leave because of that file?" she asked. "Or is he involved in something else, something worse?"

"I can't answer that quite yet. What I can tell you is that Tim Hancock isn't the Tim in Danielle's book."

"You're sure?"

"Positive. He has an airtight alibi. On the date his name shows up, he was in California, attending his mother's funeral."

Her eyes widened. "You're not . . . I mean, there's no way *Fitzpatrick* slept with Danielle. . . ."

"He did. He admitted it." Fortunately, Fitzpatrick hadn't realized he could lie. . . .

"I can't believe that." She shook her head. "Or maybe I can. I talked to Glenn Whitcomb, one of the COs I'm friendly with. He said he overheard Fitzpatrick saying something strange to Hugo. Tim's name seems to be popping up a lot."

When she explained what Glenn had told her, Amarok said, "I'm not surprised."

She tucked her hair behind her ears. "So . . . Fitzpatrick must've quit, right?"

"Looks that way to me. I'm guessing he

couldn't face you. And, from his perspective, there's not much point in waiting to be fired."

"I wonder what Janice will do when she finds out what he's been up to."

"Janice?"

"My boss at the BOP."

"You haven't talked to her?"

"She's been out of the office."

"When will she be back?"

"Next Wednesday."

"That doesn't give us a lot of time to get the answers she's going to demand."

"I know. It feels like I'm strapped to a time bomb. But first things first. Shouldn't we stop Fitzpatrick, in case he's trying to flee? He could be guilty of more than having sex with Danielle."

" 'Could be' is the key phrase."

"It's looking more and more likely. I wouldn't want him to go on the run, Amarok. We have to catch whoever is behind these murders. I can't live with Lorraine's death ending the way my other friends' did. It'd be like having another Jasper out there."

Amarok wished he *could* arrest Fitzpatrick, hold him at least until they sorted everything out, but it was impossible. They had nothing solid on him. "I understand. I'd have Tim watched, if only for the manpower. But I don't have the help, and I can't do it myself. I have to keep digging. There's still the chance he's not the one."

"Everything seems to be pointing his way."

"I'm not completely convinced. There's one thing that bothers me."

"And that is . . ."

"He admitted to having dinner with Danielle on Saturday night —"

"That means he was the last person we know of to see her alive!"

"But when he left, she was fine."

She moved a stack of files off to one side. "How do you know?"

"She had the chance to put him in that book of hers. And I don't think she'd risk adding his name while he was there. If he'd been aware of that record, he would've taken it."

"I agree."

"He was surprised when I told him about her size obsession and the number of other men she'd been with."

"But she was killed sometime between Saturday night and Tuesday, when her arm showed up in my bed. He could've gone back."

"What would've triggered his return? He considered her beneath him, which gives me the impression he'd only be with her if and when he desperately needed a woman. I doubt he'd feel the need to see her again that soon."

"Maybe he told her not to tell anyone they'd been together and they got into an argument over it."

He shook his head. That didn't seem to jive with the feeling he'd gotten, talking to Fitzpatrick. "I'm not sensing enough anger. He believed their encounter was a simple, private 'release.' You should've seen him. He was stunned when I revealed what she'd been doing with other guys. I guess he thought she had a thing for him and him alone."

"He's arrogant enough to believe that. But we can't rule him out. Hugo insists Fitzpatrick is twisted, dangerous."

"Hugo's been convicted of strangling fifteen women. His word doesn't count for shit."

"Yet he seems like the hero in all of this," she said. "Sometimes the lines can get so blurred."

Amarok knew exactly what she meant. "Believe me, if I could detain Fitzpatrick I would. But I have nothing to hold him on."

"What about that file on me? It proves stalking. Isn't that illegal?"

"That file would help you get a restraining order. Not much more, since he never hurt you or even threatened to."

With a sigh, she shoved a manila folder across her desk. "You need to take a look at this."

When he opened it, he saw explicit pictures of Danielle Connelly having sex with some guy. "Just what a dead person hopes to leave behind."

"Actually, given her obsession with sex, in this case it might be true."

"Who's she with?"

"You don't recognize Hugo?"

"Not from his ass. Where'd you get these?"

"Anthony Garza."

"That's the inmate who stabbed Hugo, the one who's such a bastard."

"Yes."

He took a closer look, then asked, "What made him cough them up?"

"*I* did. Miracle of miracles, I was able to get something on him I could use for leverage."

"Nice work."

She flashed him a brief smile. "He claims Kush put him up to shanking Hugo and gave him those pictures and an eight ball of coke as payment."

"Perfect. The word of another reputable witness."

He knew she'd heard the sarcasm in his voice when she said, "Garza's testimony might not be worth a whole lot — he could blame anyone — but those pictures are proof that Danielle was indeed servicing the inmates."

"I was kidding. These will come in handy."

"Where's Kush now?" she asked. "Phil told me you were here, arresting him."

"He's locked up downstairs, waiting for me to take him over to my trooper post so I can book him."

"Has he told you anything?"

"Just that Danielle came to them and suggested the idea."

"Him and Petrowski? What about Dean Snowden and Steve Dugall? They had to be aware of what was going on, since they were listed in Danielle's book."

"Kush insists Snowden and Dugall never received any money, that they were clients."

"You mean they paid to have sex with her?"

"According to him, they caught wind something was up and were included in the fun now and then so they'd keep their mouths shut."

"So they had sex with her for free. They're still going to lose their jobs." She had to be disgusted that so many of the men on her correctional force had gotten involved in the corruption and that none of them had reported what was going on — and this statement confirmed it.

"But they'll probably receive a lesser penalty as far as the law goes," he added.

"Did Kush mention any other names in connection to this mess?"

"No. He insists it was just him and Eddie. That all they did was make the arrangements for the encounters and split the proceeds with Danielle."

"Sadly, I believe it probably *was* her idea," Evelyn said. "Why she'd take such a risk is hard to fathom. But maybe she was getting bored with regular men, men she was fairly confident wouldn't hurt her. So she decided to step things up."

"Nice guys really do finish last," he teased.

She stretched her neck. "Did you ask Kush if he forged my name on that transfer order? Because, according to what Anthony told me, it had to be him or Petrowski. If Snowden and Dugall weren't on the business end, I doubt they'd be invested enough to do something that bad."

"I was only talking to Kush about the prostitution. I've got to come up with something that lends credence to Garza's claims before I hit him with the transfer order. He'll never cop to instigating that shanking, otherwise. That'll carry a far stiffer sentence than the year or two he'll likely get for pandering, if he gets that much."

"Pandering?"

"The legal term for acting as a 'procurer.' "

"I've never heard that before. What will happen after he's booked?"

"I have two cells at the trooper post. He'll stay in one until the Anchorage police can come get him. With the size of the storm that's due tomorrow, it might be a few days."

"What about Petrowski? Is he in custody, too?"

"He didn't show up for work today and he lives in Anchorage, so they'll arrest him there."

"When?"

"Maybe it's already happened. It was getting so late I had to let Phil go home, but there could be a message for me on the answering machine." Or maybe Petrowski had gotten wind of what was going on and bugged out. . . .

Amarok hoped not.

"Nice of Anchorage PD to pitch in," she said.

"A little cooperation between police forces

never hurt anybody. They're aware of what I'm facing out here."

She looked glum as she propped her chin on her fist. "It feels as if this place is tumbling down around me, Amarok."

He wished he could wipe the worry from her face. "We might be able to save it."

"*We?* I thought you didn't want HH here."

"I'll put up with it if that's what it takes to make you stay," he said wryly.

His support seemed to cheer her up, to a degree. "Maybe if I watch some of the videotape shot in this place after Garza arrived but before Hugo was shanked I'll find something to corroborate what Garza told me."

"That could prove helpful. Did Fitzpatrick record his sessions, too?"

"Yes. We all do. It's standard operating procedure."

"I'd like to see those myself."

"Tonight? I can access them right here, on my computer."

"No. I'd better take care of Kush. We'll do it in the morning."

She nodded. "For what it's worth, it felt like Garza was telling me the truth."

"Interestingly enough, it felt like Hugo was telling me the truth this morning, too,"

Amarok said.

"You spoke with him?"

"At the hospital."

She made a face. "Was that before or after he tried to escape?"

Amarok hadn't heard about this. "Must've been before. What happened?"

"He fended off the guard, then dropped to the floor with a heart attack."

"He didn't die?"

"No, but he still could."

Amarok glanced through the window, at the perimeter lights that glowed eerily in the darkness. "I guess I can't blame the poor bastard."

She blinked at him. "*Poor* bastard?"

"I'd rather die than be locked up." He felt claustrophobic just entering Hanover House.

"He has only himself to blame. If you get caught, murdering people tends to restrict your freedom."

"I'd better go." He crossed to the door. "When will you be home?"

"Late. It'll take some time to view all that videotape. I can't gain access to the general security tapes, not with the warden gone. But I can take a look at Fitzpatrick's sessions, pare down what you'll have to watch tomorrow. It's not like you'll be home tonight, anyway. I'd rather not be there alone if I can avoid it."

He realized there could be something in those sessions that revealed what Fitzpatrick had been doing with Hugo. But he couldn't conscionably stop Evelyn from viewing them — not when they could reveal more than he knew about the murders and he couldn't take the time to view them himself. Finding whoever had killed Lorraine Drummond and Danielle Connelly took precedence over everything. "Call me if there's anything . . . upsetting."

"Okay."

"And don't try to drive that car of yours home. The roads are too slick. I'll come back for you when I'm done."

"I'll wait."

He reached for the doorknob, then cursed under his breath and went back. He didn't care if they were at the prison, playing their respective professional roles. He wanted to kiss her. But he'd barely put his mouth on hers when Penny came in again.

"Oh! Yikes! I'm sorry! I didn't realize!" she cried, and ran back out.

"Whoops," Amarok murmured, but he didn't let go of Evelyn. "I hope you don't mind that Penny knows we're together."

"We're together?" she echoed. "I'm not

merely worshiping at your feet?"

He scowled. "What are you talking about?"

"Never mind." She pulled him back in for another kiss. "All your other fans will just have to suffer the disappointment."

He laughed, but he wasn't laughing a minute later, when he left her office and learned what Penny had been so anxious to tell them.

Hugo Evanski had made a second attempt to escape from the hospital — and this time he'd managed it.

27

I'm as cold a motherfucker as you've ever put your fucking eyes on. I don't give a shit about those people.

— TED BUNDY, SERIAL KILLER, RAPIST, KIDNAPPER AND NECROPHILIAC

Taking a break from all the video she'd been viewing, Evelyn rubbed her eyes. She'd spoken to her father earlier, but their talk hadn't gone much better than her last conversation with her mother. He pleaded with Evelyn to come home, said it would bring her mother a great deal of peace. Evelyn felt the added guilt his words dumped on her but assured him that there was nothing to worry about, that no one else was going to get hurt. And they'd ended at the typical impasse, except that her father had confirmed that her mother was on anti-depressants and anti-anxiety medication. Evelyn hated that they thought she could ease Lara's struggles and wouldn't. But she honestly didn't see how going home would fix them. Jasper could attack her in Boston as easily as anywhere else. He'd proven it last summer. And what happened when she was sixteen had happened. There was no returning to the innocence they'd enjoyed before. Her mother had to overcome the impact of Jasper's actions just like she did.

Fortunately, she'd spoken to her sister after, who'd tried to make things easier. Brianne had promised to take care of their mother and had encouraged Evelyn to stay in Alaska and do what she had to do. That helped. Brianne had always been so calm and supportive — a blessing to the whole family.

Now that it was getting late, however, that phone call with her father was bothering Evelyn again. Probably because she was so tired. Her thoughts cycled through the same worries over and over and then stalled, as if she might fade to sleep in spite of the need for diligence. She'd been functioning on caffeine since Amarok left, but coffee didn't seem capable of sustaining her any longer. She'd expected him back long ago.

Where was he? She guessed he was interfacing with the Anchorage police on Hugo's escape in addition to seeing that Kush was booked and jailed at the trooper post. But surely Hugo was in custody by now. He couldn't get far in his condition. He had two knife wounds in his chest, he'd just had a heart attack and, as far as she knew, he didn't even have a coat. . . .

"Come on, come on," she muttered, eyeing the phone. Why hadn't Amarok checked in with her? She was starting to get a headache.

She took some medication to fend it off. That enabled her to work a bit longer. But after another thirty minutes the phone still hadn't rung — and when she tried calling Amarok at the trooper post his voice mail came on.

With a sigh, she got up to stretch her legs. The weather seemed to be taking a turn for the worse, which made her think that the big storm they were expecting tomorrow might be a bit early. Or maybe not. It was nearly midnight. She supposed that meant that the storm was right on time. It was Amarok who was late, and waiting for him meant she wouldn't be able to get to his place on her own. . . .

Patting her cheeks to revive her flagging energy, she returned to her desk. As concerned as she was growing at Amarok's long absence, there were a lot of legitimate reasons he could be delayed. It didn't shorten the wait or do any good to pace and worry. She figured she might as well push through her fatigue and continue viewing the recordings of Fitzpatrick's most recent sessions.

But when she clicked on the next file, she noticed something odd. The recording didn't seem new. She'd viewed it before. It was from right after they opened Hanover House, when they were all carefully watching one another for training and critiquing purposes, or she probably wouldn't have remembered it.

How strange. That couldn't be. The date on the file indicated it was taken five days ago.

She closed out of it to be sure, checked the file name and brought the footage up again. Maybe she was so fatigued she couldn't trust her brain. It wasn't as if the background on the tapes varied by a great margin. And Fitzpatrick's voice did tend to drone on. . . .

When he mispronounced an inmate's last name and the inmate corrected him, however, it felt like déjà vu. She recognized him saying that name in exactly the same way. Besides, he would have to know the proper pronunciations of his patients' names by now. He'd been meeting with most of them for three months. . . .

"This is from our first week," she mumbled, her pulse spiking. Fitzpatrick must've deleted this file and replaced it with a copy of the earlier session so he'd have something taking up that storage space. She was pretty sure he never expected anyone to look. Even if someone did, whoever it was would likely never realize the file was a duplicate, not unless he or she started at the very beginning and sifted through all the files, which would take forever.

She'd almost missed it, hadn't she?

What was he trying to hide?

She opened more of his files. Several of those with a recent date had been replaced with sessions from November, too.

Why?

The obvious answer made her sick. He was doing something in these sessions he shouldn't, and yet he pretended to care so much about their work, about what they'd created with Hanover House.

"You bastard." She searched back to find out how long this had been going on, but when she reached January 3 there was no file at all. It had been deleted without another one uploaded to replace it — until she tried again a few minutes later. Then a file was there — the same duplicate session where he mispronounced the inmate's name.

Fitzpatrick was replacing the files right *now,* she realized. He was out there, somewhere, trying to cover his tracks. So he couldn't be on a plane. He had to have access to a computer and an Internet connection.

"Damn you!" she cried. "I bet you're at home. You just won't pick up the phone."

She wished she could lock him out of their database, but her boss was the only one who could change the password — a safety precaution they'd decided to engage in case one of the team grew angry and tried to lock out all the others.

Evelyn clicked on a few more links, hoping to get ahead of him, but he was working too fast.

Switching over to her e-mail system, she sent him an instant message. *How can you be such a complete fraud?*

She guessed he wouldn't write back. But she was wrong. After only a short delay, his answer appeared.

We all have needs.

I trusted you. And you've destroyed everything.

You think I'm *not disappointed?*

You have only yourself to blame!

For wanting more than work to fill my life?

I never promised you more than a chance to further your research.

You don't know what you're missing, how devoted I would have been to you. Maybe I don't look like your young trooper, but I would've loved you better — and much longer.

Much longer . . . He was striking at the heart of her insecurities where Amarok was concerned, but she was determined not to react to that.

You don't know how to like someone, let alone offer more. What are you trying to hide by deleting all the videos of your sessions?

There was a long delay. Then he wrote: *Since they're gone now, I guess you'll never know.*

That's where you're wrong.

She smiled when a question mark popped up in his response space. He'd never been particularly savvy when it came to technology. She'd had to teach him how to use their patient software, convince him that it was more convenient to pay his bills online and help him set up a Facebook page to keep in touch with his extended family back in the Lower 48. She was astonished he'd been able to figure out how to delete, copy and replace files, but that was pretty easy.

These computers are routinely backed up, she wrote. *I have the password. I can access the cloud.* Which was exactly what she did. It didn't take her ten minutes, since she knew the dates of the files she most wanted to view.

She wasn't feeling so smug a few minutes later, however. What she saw when she called them up turned her stomach. Hugo was being shown pictures of her face with some other woman's body — a woman with the biggest breasts Evelyn had ever seen — who was using a dildo, or performing oral sex or touching herself. . . .

Evelyn turned it off; she couldn't make herself watch any more.

How dare you! she wrote.

When he didn't send a reply, she figured that was it. She'd once been so grateful for him, so grateful that he'd been willing to lend her his support. Now she couldn't believe she'd put up with him and his prickly personality for the past five years. Why? For *this*? For the sick way he'd used her image in those sessions with Hugo?

Even if Amarok could catch Lorraine and Danielle's killer, Evelyn wasn't sure she'd be able to rise from the ashes. What was her boss going to say when she returned to the states next Wednesday? When she learned that two Hanover House COs had been pimping out a female member of the staff? That Fitzpatrick had been creating pornographic pictures of her and showing them to Hugo and possibly other inmates?

Evelyn had had enough nasty surprises in the past week to last a lifetime. But she got another one when Fitzpatrick's next message arrived. The two words he sent didn't formulate the apology he owed her or the angry retort she'd expected in its place. But they were a little disquieting: *hugo's out*

It wasn't like Fitzpatrick not to use punctuation, and without a period or question mark she couldn't tell if he was making a statement or asking a question. Either way, how did he know Hugo wasn't in the hospital? Had he called over there? Or was someone at Hanover House keeping him informed?

If Fitzpatrick wasn't going to be involved in Hanover House any longer, why would he care? It seemed odd that he'd address Hugo's situation in the middle of the night, especially when he'd just learned that she was able to view the video footage he'd been trying to hide.

She was about to ask what he meant when one more word appeared.

Then her disquiet gave way to bone-chilling fear.

help

Again, he hadn't used his customary punctuation, but that was what made it so damn believable.

Evelyn wasn't about to try to drive her BMW into town. Thanks to the weather, she'd never get beyond the prison. But *someone* had to check on Fitzpatrick. If he was really in danger, she couldn't sit idly by no matter what he'd done or how she felt about him. So when she couldn't get him to respond to any more instant messages or pick up his phone, and she couldn't reach Amarok, she knew she had to track down a more reliable vehicle before leaving the prison grounds.

After bundling up in the snowsuit she'd worn over her clothes when she came to work today, she braced against the snow and wind and ran to her car. She'd left her gun under the seat the day she moved out of her cabin.

Once she was assured her GLOCK was loaded and resting on top of the seat where it was more accessible, she started her Beamer to get the defroster working while she used the shovel in her trunk to dig out the wheels. The wind had blown snow onto her car despite the parking cover. The drifts were especially deep since she hadn't moved her car for a while, which meant she also had to clear the windshield. She had to be able to see well enough to drive around the prison and find a member of the grounds crew. There wouldn't be many working this late. Those who were would be busy in this mess. But she needed to borrow a truck — one with a shovel on it.

She watched for headlights as she unburied her car. She was hoping Amarok would come. But she wasn't optimistic she'd be able to spot his vehicle even if he did turn in at the entrance — not from where she was and with so much snow whipping around.

Maybe it would be better to go it alone, anyway, she told herself. *She* was the one who'd pioneered Hanover House. *She* was the reason both Hugo and Fitzpatrick were in Alaska. It wasn't fair to expect Amarok or anyone else to risk life and limb to clean up the mess HH was turning out to be.

While she worked, the thought crossed her mind — as it had several times — that this could be a trick. If Fitzpatrick had killed Lorraine and Danielle, he could be luring her out to his place, intending to do the same to her. That would give him the last laugh, let him go out with a bang — which could be exactly what he was after. He had to be mortified that she knew what he'd been doing, that she'd seen evidence of it. He'd essentially ruined his career, so he didn't have much to lose. The resulting despair could make him very dangerous.

But she kept imagining him at the mercy of someone who'd murdered fifteen people, someone who hated him, and couldn't pretend she hadn't received that cry for help. If Hugo had made his way back to Hilltop, it wouldn't be hard to learn where Fitzpatrick lived. Pretty much everyone in town could provide that information, and they wouldn't hesitate if Hugo had a weapon.

She *had* to respond to Fitzpatrick's plea, but she wouldn't go unprepared — for the weather or what she might find once she arrived.

Although she was soon out of breath and her head was pounding, despite the two ibuprofen she'd swallowed earlier, she refused to ease up. Timing could be critical. Even with all her effort, it required more than ten minutes to get the job done.

As soon as she felt she might be able to get out of her parking space, she threw the shovel and scraper in her trunk, put the

Beamer in reverse and punched the gas pedal, hoping to barrel through or go over whatever snow might still be in her way.

The car spun out, but she drove forward and then back, this time giving the motor even more gas, and managed to reach the main section where the plows kept it fairly clear.

"That's it; here we go," she muttered, but the roads were so slick she was afraid she'd crash into half a dozen cars before reaching the lot outlet. She could feel her tires struggling for traction as she drove.

Come on. . . . Making sure the windshield wipers were set on high, she hunched over and peered through the storm as best she could. A little property damage, if she caused it, was preferable to a murder. She wouldn't allow Fitzpatrick or anyone else to be harmed by Hugo or the other psychopaths she'd had brought here.

Hopefully Hugo hadn't been able to make it this far. She couldn't imagine anyone picking him up, but she supposed he could've stolen some clothes and a truck. Enough time had elapsed since he escaped that he *could've* reached Hilltop if he did get transportation, and that was reason enough. She had to act simply because the possibility existed. A human life could hang in the balance. . . .

And if Hugo wasn't there? If Fitzpatrick was lying in wait?

She'd use her gun to defend herself. She didn't like the idea of having to resort to violence, but if she was going into this situation despite the danger she wouldn't have the luxury of being timid or squeamish. She'd always promised herself that if she ever came up against another predator like Jasper she'd do whatever it took to kill him before he could kill her — and she meant it.

Progress was slow, even though the perimeter road had been plowed more recently than the parking lot. But when she reached the far side of the institution, she saw yellow lights flashing through the falling snow. That had to be one of the plows.

She turned her headlights off and on, trying to signal the driver, and was grateful when he stopped.

As he climbed out to see what was going on, she grabbed her purse and her gun and met him in the middle of the road. "I need to use your truck!" she shouted above the gale-force winds.

"What?" he called back.

"Dr. Fitzpatrick could be in trouble! I have to reach him!"

"I can't let you drive off with prison property! I have work to do. We're in the middle of a storm!"

"This prison, and that truck, wouldn't even be here if it wasn't for me. Would you rather someone be killed?"

His face was too sheltered to be able to ascertain his reaction, but after another reluctant pause, during which she was fairly certain he'd noticed her gun, he waved her on, and she left her car for him to drive back to the sally port. She wasn't sure what he would do while she was gone since he wouldn't be able to clear. But, at this point, it didn't matter. Reaching Fitzpatrick's house was the priority.

Fortunately, the truck was in four-wheel drive and the switch that raised and lowered the shovel was obvious. She raised it, for the time being. The roads on-site were cleared well enough that she could make quicker progress without trying to plow.

Once she drove out of the prison, however, it would be an entirely different story.

28

I have always wondered myself why I don't feel more remorse.

— JEFFREY DAHMER,
THE MILWAUKEE CANNIBAL

Despite his heavy coat, boots and hat, Amarok was numb with cold. He'd come upon a car accident while trying to get back to the prison. Fortunately, no one had been seriously injured, but he'd had to tow the vehicles off the road so they wouldn't be a danger to anyone else and deliver the people inside those vehicles to safety.

It'd been a long day, and now he was worried about Evelyn. He'd stopped to call, to let her know why he was running late, but that call had gone to the HH message center. He hoped she'd just fallen asleep in her office and that she hadn't tried to drive herself home. . . .

When he reached the prison he asked the

tower guard if Evelyn had left, but the officer stationed there said he was covering another guy's break and had barely come on. So Amarok drove inside to check her parking space — and found the stall empty.

"Damn it!" He hadn't seen her along the road. Had she somehow managed to reach his place in spite of the blizzard?

He almost turned around and went after her. But then he decided to go in and see what time she'd left. He thought he'd also try to reach her at his house. Maybe she'd pick up.

Leaving his truck under the portico, he jogged around to the entrance and was greeted by two COs — Pellier and Levine — as soon as he walked in. " 'Lo, Sergeant."

Amarok stamped the snow off his frozen feet. "Hey."

"What are you doing out so late — and in this?" Levine asked. "Don't tell me there's been another murder."

"No," Amarok replied. "I'm looking for Dr. Talbot. Have you seen her?"

Levine turned to Pellier. "How long ago was it that she came through here?"

Pellier ran a thick, callused finger over his chin. "I'd say it's been . . . forty minutes or so."

"Do you have any idea where she went?"

Amarok asked.

"Home, I would think," Pellier replied. "Considering the weather, she'd be crazy to go anywhere else."

"Wherever it was, she seemed to be in a hurry," Levine added with a whistle.

She was probably irritated that he hadn't come back for her. "Is there a phone I can use?"

"Of course." Pellier took him into a small guard station, where he dialed his own number. But there was no answer at the house, which led him to believe she was still in transit.

He called *her* house, too, just to be sure she hadn't gone there, but didn't achieve any better results.

"Thanks!" he called out as he left. Then he jumped in his truck and, as soon as he turned out of Hanover House, drove very slowly, hoping to come upon her little Beamer.

When Evelyn saw the light through the trees, she couldn't believe she'd made it clear across town. She never would've been able to do that, not without the shovel on the truck she'd borrowed. It didn't seem as if Phil had been out at all, clearing the streets. She'd barely crept along the entire way, and once she'd turned down the long drive that wound around to Fitzpatrick's cabin it was even worse. She almost got stuck twice, despite having four-wheel drive.

Fortunately, all of that was behind her now. She'd arrived at last. Although it was too dark and stormy to see much detail, if she stopped in the right spot she could make out a faint glow through the trees. She wondered if it could be headlights but didn't think so.

What am I going to find here?

She hoped it wasn't Fitzpatrick's dead body. But she also hoped he wasn't lying in wait — *for her.*

Did he possess the kind of rage required to do what had been done to Lorraine and Danielle?

If so, he cloaked it well.

After parking down the hill — she felt it wouldn't be wise to announce her arrival — she trudged on foot the last hundred yards. The snow was so deep in places it came up to her thighs, making her grateful for her snowsuit. She was cold enough as it was.

Soon she could see Fitzpatrick's house peeking out from behind the trees that separated her from it. He had an SUV in addition to his sedan. She figured both vehicles must be in the garage, because they weren't out front.

There *was* a commercial vehicle parked haphazardly, however. The light she'd seen turned out to be a high-powered commercial pole to one side of the property, so she could make out that unfamiliar truck as clearly as the storm would allow.

After taking a moment to watch the area, during which she saw nothing to alert her as to what might be going on inside, she slid the handle of her purse over her head to be able to wear her purse across her body, held her gun at the ready and approached the house.

The blinds were down, making it impossible to see through the windows.

She listened at the door, trying to figure out what might be happening. But that didn't help. She couldn't make out a thing above the howl of the wind.

Shit. With a deep breath for courage, she tried the knob.

The door was locked. Should she knock? Would Fitzpatrick hear her? Even if he could, she wanted to know what she might be walking into before landing in the middle of a bad situation.

Her heart seemed to be ten times too big for her chest as she trudged around to the back.

It was darker here. There were no lights, except the flashlight she pulled from her purse. Fortunately, that thin beam was enough to reassure her that she was alone — and to see the gleaming shards of a broken window.

Given the truck out front and this, she was beginning to believe Hugo *had* made his way to Hilltop. But she couldn't imagine how he'd found the strength.

Still afraid of letting her presence be known, she decided to sneak in and have a look around. Her gloves and snowsuit were thick enough she was fairly certain she could climb through that broken window without getting cut. . . .

After hoisting herself up, she pushed the blind over and crawled inside. Due to the wind, she wasn't overly afraid the small noises she made would alert anyone to her presence. It wasn't until she moved away from the window and the sounds of the storm dimmed that she became aware of someone deeper inside the house cursing and ranting.

Was it Fitzpatrick? What was being said didn't sound like him. The words were filled with vitriol instead of his usual tight-lipped scorn. But the voice . . .

Although she couldn't be sure, she

thought it *might* be him.

So where was Hugo or whoever had broken that window?

She crept around the corner. She intended to take a quick look before slipping back out of the house. But what she saw froze her to the spot.

Amarok drove between his house and the prison twice before he thought about checking his messages. He'd been so intent on believing that Evelyn had just given up on him and decided to head home, that he'd find her on the side of the road since there was no way she could make it all the way in her Beamer, that he'd never dreamed she would leave him a message — other than to ask where he was. The phones were out at his place, anyway. He had to stop by the trooper post to be able to access his voice mail, but what he heard turned his blood to ice.

"Amarok, I hope you get this soon. Fitzpatrick just instant messaged me on the computer, saying something about Hugo and asking for help. Now he won't respond. No clue what it means, but it's very strange. I realize it could be a trap, but with Hugo on the loose it could also be a legitimate cry for help. You know how badly Hugo hates Fitzpatrick. I have to go out there and see what's going on. Come if you can."

"No," Amarok muttered, closing his eyes. "Tell me you didn't." He didn't want her anywhere near Fitzpatrick, let alone risking her skin to save his life, especially after how Fitzpatrick had treated her. If only Amarok had known she might do something like this when he decided not to tell her about Fitzpatrick's sessions with Hugo. Maybe she wouldn't have gone. . . .

Scooping his keys off the table where he'd dropped them before calling his voice mail, Amarok rushed out to his truck. He'd managed to switch vehicles with Phil earlier in the evening, so he had a working shovel. That made him wonder how the hell Evelyn thought she'd be able to get to Fitzpatrick's in that car of hers.

"You'd better not have hurt her." He skidded around the corner going much faster than he should've been and upped his speed from there. He didn't have a second to waste. All he could think of was Lorraine's severed head — with that one eye gouged out.

Fitzpatrick was holding an iron fireplace poker and had blood spatter all over him — on his face, his clothes, in his hair. Hugo —

if the man lying on the floor was indeed their escaped convict — was wearing ill-fitting clothes and his head was bashed in. Evelyn was pretty sure he was dead. He wasn't moving, was no longer a threat, yet Fitzpatrick wasn't trying to call for help. He was pacing and cursing, and every once in a while he'd strike the inert body.

"You think I'd hurt her?" he'd shout. Then he'd mutter, "How dare you do this to me. This is . . . not right, not right at all. I don't deserve this; I never have."

Seeing him so out of control turned Evelyn's stomach. She'd feared he might not be able to defend himself — or that Hugo had brought a knife or a gun. Weapons were everywhere in Alaska. He could've taken a hunting rifle from a pickup or an empty house. He'd obviously found clothes. But whether he'd had a weapon or not, Fitzpatrick had dealt with the problem.

The memories of stumbling onto the bodies of her dead friends welled up, causing her to break into a cold sweat. *This is different,* she reminded herself. As crazy as Fitzpatrick was acting, he wasn't necessarily a homicidal maniac. She didn't know who'd killed Lorraine and Danielle, but what she saw here was a clear case of self-defense. It wasn't as if Fitzpatrick had *invited* Hugo to his home.

So why had he come? He'd escaped. He could've gone anywhere. . . .

Evelyn decided she'd rather ask those questions tomorrow, when Amarok was around. Maybe this was self-defense, but that file she'd found in Fitzpatrick's cabinet — and what she'd seen on those videos — made her hesitant to confront her former associate. She didn't want to be here, with this. She wanted to get out of the house and put some distance between her and another death, whether it was a justifiable one or not.

She was backing away so she could return to the living room and quietly let herself out when someone came up behind her.

"Evelyn?"

Startled, she whipped around and aimed her gun.

"Whoa!" Russell Jones lifted his hands. "Don't shoot. I-I didn't mean to startle you."

He was shaking, had tears streaking down his face.

Almost automatically, Evelyn lowered the muzzle. She was frightened, but Russ seemed more traumatized than she was. What'd happened here?

Before she could ask, Fitzpatrick came

rushing around the corner, eyes wide, mouth hanging open. "*Evelyn? What are you doing in my house?*"

She cleared her throat, tried to remain calm. "What do you mean what am I doing in your house? I crept in because you sent me an instant message saying you needed help!"

"I can't believe you came."

He seemed touched by her effort, which made her uncomfortable. She had no interest in mending their relationship, not after what she'd viewed in those video sessions. She'd never be able to look at him the same, never be able to trust him again. "Of course I came, in spite of the many reasons I shouldn't have. I didn't know you had Russ here."

"I didn't. If Russ hadn't shown up when he did, I'd be dead right now." He touched a slash in his neck she hadn't noticed for all the other blood. "That son of a bitch tried to stab me."

"I didn't see your truck," she told Russ. The one in front wasn't his. Had it been stolen by Hugo? Hugo had had to get here somehow. . . .

Russ barely seemed capable of coherent speech. "I-I came on my snowmobile. It's parked out back."

Of course. Russ lived only half a mile from Fitzpatrick, and a snowmobile parked off to the side would've been easy to miss in the dark and stormy night. By the time she'd rounded the house, she hadn't even been looking for a vehicle. She'd been too afraid she'd run into a man bent on murder.

"Why did Hugo come *here*?" she asked. "If he managed to escape, why wouldn't he make good on it?"

"He thought *I* was behind having him shanked," Fitzpatrick told her. "And he was convinced I was a danger to you."

Was he a danger? "He couldn't have been in good shape. . . ."

"He could barely stand," Fitzpatrick said. "But he had a knife, so it didn't matter — not as long as he could slash. He kept telling me I didn't know who I'd been fucking with and that he'd teach me once and for all."

"I heard him screaming," Russ jumped in, covering his ears as if he could *still* hear it. "If I hadn't snuck up on him, grabbed a lamp and . . . and" — he blanched — "hit him over the head, he would've murdered Tim." Russ stared at his hands as if he couldn't believe they belonged to him. "How did I do that? I hit him so hard."

Evelyn wasn't sure what to think or feel.

541

She gulped for breath, trying to get her pulse to settle into a regular rhythm. "So then you . . . then you beat him with the fireplace poker?"

A sheepish expression claimed Fitzpatrick's blood-spattered face. "It was the adrenaline," he explained, his voice pleading with her to understand. "When he went down, I grabbed this" — he looked at the poker, seemed to realize there was no reason to still have it in his hands and dropped it — "and-and went a little crazy."

"I watched him die," Russ marveled, his words disconnected from the conversation. "It's my fault he's dead."

"Have you tried to reach Amarok?" she asked. "To get help?"

"How?" Russ cried. "Thanks to the storm, the phones are out.".

Evelyn wasn't sure she'd ever get through this terrible winter. Feeling dizzy, as if she was about to pass out, she bent over to get some blood to her head and struggled to push back the darkness that seemed to be closing in.

"Are you going to be sick?" Fitzpatrick asked.

"I think so."

"Then give me that gun before you hurt yourself or someone else."

Grabbing her arm, he wrenched it from her grip as she ducked past him for the bathroom. She hadn't cared for Hugo the way he was convinced he cared for her. Not even remotely. But at times it had been almost impossible not to like him. He was a human being, at any rate, and the sight of his head . . . the image of his brains spilling out on the carpet wouldn't leave her. Neither would the memory of Fitzpatrick striking him, even though he was dead.

As she leaned over the toilet, she could hear Russ and Fitzpatrick fighting about moving the body outside. Fitzpatrick didn't want it in the house any longer. But Russ didn't seem capable of coping with its removal. He was talking about how heavy Hugo would be, that moving him would get blood all over. He said they should leave Hugo until morning when they could get Amarok over and kept repeating himself as if he was in shock.

He probably was.

Evelyn hummed a song to tune them out. She already felt like death warmed over, didn't need to hear *that* conversation. As soon as she could gather the strength, she was going to walk out of the house and drive home before the storm made travel, even with a four-wheel drive that had a shovel, impossible.

Soon there was nothing left in her stomach to throw up, so she wiped her mouth, closed the toilet lid and gingerly lifted herself onto it. But as she sat there, struggling to regain her equilibrium, she happened to notice that the shower curtain was pulled back just enough to reveal part of a curious blob-like object in the tub.

What was *that*?

Sliding off the toilet seat and onto her knees, she pulled the shower curtain back even farther and bent close. Then she nearly screamed and fell back.

It was a clear plastic bag filled with frozen body parts.

29

I have no desire whatever to reform my-self. My only desire is to reform other people who try to reform me. And I believe that the only way to reform people is to kill 'em. My motto is, Rob 'em all, Rape 'em all and Kill 'em all.

     — CARL PANZRAM, SERIAL KILLER, ARSONIST, THIEF, BURGLAR AND RAPIST

Her gun! Fitzpatrick had taken it. Why hadn't she refused to let him, insisted on keeping it with her?

Because, at that point, she hadn't been prepared to shoot anyone and her revulsion and sickness were getting the best of her.

Maybe it wasn't too late to reclaim it. . . .

Reaching for the wall, she braced herself to stand. She had to find out where Fitz-patrick had put her GLOCK. But Russ came to check on her before she could even climb to her feet. And he could tell instantly that something was wrong. She saw it in his face, in the way his eyes moved from her to the tub and back again.

She scrambled to get as far away from him as possible, which wasn't easy in such a small bathroom. She couldn't dart out the door. Even if she'd had the strength and agility, he was blocking it.

"Did you know?" She could hardly get the words out for the terror building inside her.

He wiped more tears from his face. He didn't look dangerous; he looked rattled. But that didn't necessarily mean anything. Was he in on the murders? Or had he not seen — or understood — what was in the tub? "Know what?"

"That Tim killed Lorraine and Danielle." Her hand was shaking when she gestured. "That's got to be the legs of one or both of them right there — or another victim. Can't you see the foot? The painted toenails?"

The thought of another victim caused goose bumps. Had Tim been killing for a while? Since before he'd come to Alaska? Maybe he'd only helped her get Hanover House off the ground because he craved the freedom he'd have here. Alaska wasn't just a good hunting ground for moose, caribou and other animals. There were a lot of people who went out alone. Most of those who didn't come back were presumed to be killed by wildlife, the weather or a fall. That file of information Tim had collected on her, and those pictures he'd shown Hugo, could be some type of ritual he performed in advance. Maybe he'd been putting special effort into re-creating what Jasper had done by killing her friends. Lorraine, at least, had been close to her. . . .

"Wait — you . . . you're . . . getting the wrong idea," Russ said.

Was she? Suddenly it all seemed so clear.

Fitzpatrick came up behind his former grad student. "She still thinks I killed Lorraine and Danielle? Is *that* what she said?"

Russ lifted his hands to calm them all. "She found what I . . . what I brought over and it has her a little spooked. That's all."

"*You* brought that bag over?" Evelyn cried.

Fitzpatrick seemed bewildered when he looked at it. "What is it?"

With his forearm, Russ mopped the sweat glistening on his face. "I think it's the . . . it's the rest of Lorraine and Danielle."

"What are you talking about?" Fitzpatrick asked.

He hurried to explain. "That's why I came tonight. I-I was getting ready for bed when I realized I was low on wood. So I decided to-to go out to the woodshed and stock up before the storm could get any worse. And when I went out there, I found that bag. Can you imagine what a shock stumbling across that would be?"

Since she'd just stumbled across it herself, Evelyn could relate.

"I dropped the wood I'd picked up and-and almost smashed my toe."

It was hard to care about his near miss on the foot injury when she couldn't figure out if he was telling the truth. Was it all an act? Could he be murdering people with Tim? Or helping hide the evidence?

It wouldn't be the first time two friends teamed up in crime. Charles Ng and Leonard Lake were one example of a killing duo. Nathan Leopold and Richard Loeb were another, arguably the most famous. But there were others. Those relationships seemed to crop up mostly when one friend dominated the other to an extreme degree, which was exactly how she perceived Tim's control of Russ.

They weren't being aggressive with her, though. Was it because they weren't sure who she'd told that she was coming out here? Were they waiting to see what they could get away with?

"How-how'd it get in your shed?" She

hated that her teeth were chattering. Her past created such a handicap despite her determination to overcome it. A full-scale panic attack seemed to be hovering just below her skin. But she couldn't let it break free and overtake her. Then she wouldn't be able to think clearly, and if she couldn't think clearly she couldn't defend herself.

"That's what *I'd* like to know," he replied. "I tried calling the-the trooper post to tell Sergeant Amarok what I found, but I didn't have a working phone. So I jumped on my snowmobile and brought that bag over here to show Tim. Except when I arrived, I saw the b-broken window and heard the shouting, so I just . . . dropped it in the living room."

"You dropped it," she repeated.

"I never wanted to touch it in the first place!"

"When did you put it in the tub?"

He blinked at her as if he thought that question was irrelevant, and then he seemed to catch on to why she'd ask. "Fitzpatrick was so shocked to see me I wanted to tell him why I'd come — but we were both in such a state. I couldn't even form complete sentences. So I carried it into the bathroom before it could thaw on the rug. I don't know why I thought of that. It was just . . .

what my mother would have me do, I guess. I didn't want him to get angry with me for being thoughtless. And when . . . when I came back out, there *you* were, peering around the corner at him."

"You didn't" — she curled her fingernails into her palms — "think to mention it to me right away?"

"Who would? I was completely freaked out!" he said. "Not only had I just found body parts in my shed, I'd helped kill a man! And I wasn't expecting you, so that added even more surprise."

Was he responsible for putting those body parts in his shed? Had he killed Lorraine and Danielle as well as contributing to Hugo's death? She said nothing, just stared at them both. She had no weapon, was completely defenseless. They could do whatever they chose to do to her.

"Are you okay?" Russ asked as if he wasn't quite sure.

She didn't bother to reassure him. She couldn't get past what she'd seen. "Who could've left that bag in your woodshed?"

He shook his head. "I told you. I don't know. It could be anyone. I'm not home very often."

"Don't you lock it?"

Shivering and sweating at the same time,

he rubbed his arms. "No. I don't like having to track down the key when *I* want to get into it."

"Someone could steal your wood —"

"If they need it that badly, I'll replace it. It's not as if I'm leaving thousands of dollars lying around. We're talking a few hundred, and even then any would-be thief would have to get his pickup back there to haul it away, which isn't likely to happen in winter. I don't care if someone runs off with a couple of sticks. But" — he scratched his head — "why are we talking about firewood? Am I dreaming? Is this just a terrible nightmare?"

Fitzpatrick spoke up. "I feel devastated, physically weak." He studied his hands as if they no longer belonged to him. "I have to shower, have to get this blood off me. It's everywhere."

He was going to *shower*?

When Evelyn's eyes cut to that bag in the tub/shower next to her, he shook his head. "Not in this bathroom. I'll never be able to use this bathroom again."

Russ came in and slid the curtain closed. "That might help. I'm sorry it scared you. It scared me, too."

"The person who left it has to be a friend or . . . or associate of yours," she insisted.

"Not necessarily," he said. "Come on, let's get you out of here. You'll be more comfortable on the sofa."

"Next to *Hugo?*" She shrank away when he tried to touch her.

"That's the study."

Determined to stand on her own power, she used the vanity for support. "I'm going home."

"Not right now you're not," he said, growing adamant. "You're in no shape to battle that storm. Look at you. You're nearly hyperventilating."

And she'd thought having a headache was bad. Right now, she couldn't even feel the pain. "I *can't* stay here."

He scowled at her. "Then I'll take you back to my place, but I'm *not* going to let you leave."

Amarok never did find Evelyn's BMW. He discovered a truck parked at the bottom of Fitzpatrick's drive with the Hanover House logo on it, however, and figured out that she wasn't driving her car. *Thank God.* He didn't know where the Beamer was, but he was grateful she'd abandoned it in favor of more reliable transportation.

Or maybe he wasn't so glad. He didn't want her to be *here.*

After parking in the driveway, he grabbed his rifle, just in case, and hurried to the house. He couldn't see through the windows, couldn't hear anything, either. Was she safe?

He'd never been more frightened to find out the answer to a particular question in his life.

"Fitzpatrick?" He banged on the door. "Open up! Police!"

It was a testament to the fact that he didn't really expect a response that he was moving along the side of the house, intent on going around, when the door opened and Russell Jones poked his head out. "Sergeant Amarok? Am I glad to see you! You're never going to believe what's happened here tonight."

Seeing the blood on Russ's shirt caused Amarok's breath to shorten. "Where's Evelyn?"

"She's here. Come on in."

Amarok didn't move, and he didn't lower his weapon. "Bring her to the door."

Tears welled up in Russ's eyes. "But it's freezing out, and I just . . . I just got her calmed down —"

"Now!"

Russ's eyes flared wide, but he seemed to understand that Amarok would shoot him if he didn't do exactly what he'd been told. "Okay," he said. "But . . . don't worry. She's fine. Just a little rattled, so I made her lie down. We're all traumatized and upset and not thinking straight."

"You'd better not have been traumatized and upset enough to harm her," Amarok ground out.

Russ's cheeks flushed and grew mottled, but when he followed Amarok's gaze he realized what was on his shirt. "Oh! This isn't *her* blood. It's *Hugo's.*"

"Let me see her." Only if she was really okay would he be willing to hear about Hugo. She was all that mattered to him at the moment.

Russ started to close the door, but Amarok stopped him. "Leave it open. . . ."

Russ's Adam's apple bobbed as he swallowed, but then he lifted his hands to show submission and lumbered away. A minute or two later, he returned — with Evelyn.

"Amarok!"

The relief that washed over him was so powerful it sapped some of his strength. "Thank God." He held his gun away while she hugged him. Then he fisted his hand in her long hair so that he could look down into her face. "Are you hurt?"

"No."

Tears were filling her eyes, so he pulled her even closer. "It's going to be okay. I've got you."

As she pressed her face into his coat, he breathed in the scent of her. He'd been so sure he wouldn't make it in time. . . . But here she was. *Here* she was. "I won't let anyone hurt you," he murmured.

"I know," she said, and yet she clung to him as if she couldn't bear the thought of letting go.

"Everything will be fine. We'll get you home soon. But . . . what happened to-night?"

After another moment she lifted her head. Then she turned to look at Russ. "Hugo tried to kill Fitzpatrick," she said dully.

Amarok scowled at them. "Why?"

"Revenge," Russ volunteered. "And he was convinced that Fitzpatrick was a danger to Evelyn."

"Are we sure he's not?" Amarok had to ask; he still didn't trust Tim.

"Of course not," Russ said, but Evelyn spoke at the same time.

"We can't rule anything out. We were never alone tonight, so that could've changed what might've happened other-wise."

"Where's Fitzpatrick now?" Amarok asked.

"In the shower," she replied.

"And where's Hugo? Has he been subdued?"

She wiped the tears from her cheeks. "He's dead."

It had been one fucking cold night and Anthony was *not* in a good mood. He'd been released, as promised, but he hadn't been provided with much to help him survive. If he got the chance, he'd kill the bastard who'd left him so vulnerable. He should've done it not long after he'd been marched through the front doors of Hanover House as if he were a guard. That was one ballsy plan, though, man. It had his adrenaline pumping, was terrifying and exhilarating at the same time. He'd never dreamed it could be that easy, but the sheer audacity of what he'd done was probably why it worked. Who'd ever think he'd put on a guard's uniform, pull his hat down over his eyes and walk out with someone who was so well-known that no one would pay him a speck of attention?

The moment they cleared the perimeter fence he'd been so excited, so filled with anticipation, that he hadn't even minded when he'd been dumped off only a mile or so from Hanover House with just twenty bucks to buy a bite to eat when he reached town. He'd been grateful for his freedom and knew his "partner" was eager to be rid of him. But he wouldn't have had *that* much in his pocket if he hadn't demanded it. He would've been left to forage on his own with nothing. Not that he'd been too concerned about that at first, or he would've insisted on more. He'd figured he could steal whatever else he wanted.

Town was a lot farther away than he'd been told, however. And he couldn't steal money, food, weapons or a car unless he could find someone who had those items. This godforsaken town rolled up its streets at night, and everything was so spread out, so far from the damn prison. It'd been a miracle he'd managed to find shelter, such as it was, before his feet got too numb to walk any farther. He'd thought for sure he'd freeze to death before he ever reached the trooper's house.

But people were up and starting to move around now. It wasn't light, but it didn't get light in Alaska very often. At least he could see headlights in the distance as he came out of the abandoned woodshed where he'd spent the coldest part of the night. All he had to do was spruce up his uniform so it didn't look as if he'd been sleeping in it and make his way over to the road.

Once there, he'd just stick out his thumb. Who wouldn't stop for a stranded prison guard?

By the time Evelyn woke up the following morning, her headache was gone and so was Amarok. She felt bad for how hard he'd been working. It was more than any one man should be called upon to do. But she was proud of his dedication. He was stepping up, trying to deliver for his community. He loved this place, loved the people and his job, and it showed.

He'd followed her to his house last night and gone to bed with her. He'd been too exhausted to do anything else. But now he was driving Kush to Anchorage since he had to go back to the State Medical Examiner's, anyway. Those body parts she'd found in the shower and Hugo's body were in his truck.

She pulled the blankets over her head as she recalled the moment when she'd first spotted that bag in the shower. The memory of it made her weak. Poor Lorraine. She missed her so much. But she was also embarrassed that she'd jumped to such terrible conclusions when it came to her fellow team members, especially Russ, who'd never done anything to hurt her.

She was getting paranoid, she decided, letting fear take control of her life despite all her efforts to fight it. When Fitzpatrick had gotten out of the shower last night, he'd seemed just as harmless as Russ, especially now that he was so contrite over what he'd done in those sessions with Hugo.

With a yawn and a stretch, she sat up. Then she pulled Amarok's pillow to her face and breathed deeply. "I'm falling in love with you," she mumbled into it, "and that's terrifying enough."

The way he'd kissed the scar on her neck last night when they'd gone to bed made her smile — and thinking of him reminded her of his dog. Where was Makita? She would've expected him to be in the room.

"Makita?"

Amarok had left the bedroom door open, but the dog didn't come trotting in.

"Makita!" She planned to take him out for an extra potty break and to spend a little time with him. It was Saturday. She didn't have to go to work until later. Technically she didn't have to go to Hanover House at all, but she felt like she should reassure everyone, especially Warden Ferris, that she was still at the helm. With all the arrests and Fitzpatrick's resignation, her employees and work associates had to be on edge.

We'll pull everything back together, she told herself. But her boss wouldn't even be in the office for four more days. She had no idea what Janice was going to say — or who she might decide to blame. Until recently, Fitzpatrick had done a superb job of pretending to be everything a distinguished psychiatrist should be.

"Makita?" she called again.

Still no response.

She got up to search for him, but he wasn't there. Amarok must've taken him, she decided. Amarok hated that his dog had been spending so many hours shut up alone, hated having to rely on his closest neighbor to come over, let Makita out and feed him.

Knowing Makita would like nothing better than to spend the entire day with his master, she relaxed and put on some coffee. Makita rode with Amarok quite often when Amarok was patrolling the area and doing his regular thing, so it wasn't unusual.

After she had breakfast and showered, Evelyn decided to drop by her cabin before heading to work. She hadn't brought nearly enough clothes with her, was missing a few articles required to finish off certain outfits. And, more important, she'd forgotten her hair mousse. She figured it would be smarter to head that way while she had a four-wheel drive with a plow at her disposal. She couldn't expect Amarok to take his valuable time to drive her over once he got home. It would be late by then — too late to mess with such an errand.

The wind had died down and the snow had stopped falling, but it was as cold and dark as ever when Evelyn left Amarok's house. "If I didn't know better, I'd think it was midnight," she grumbled. But she couldn't help grinning when she saw that Amarok had taken a few minutes to scrape off her windshield.

"I'm in trouble." Love had never been part of the equation when she'd promised her family she'd return to Boston. But it was still early to be worried about those kinds of decisions.

Tucking her hands under her arms, despite her thick gloves and the heater blowing full blast, she let the engine warm up. Then she lowered the shovel and plowed the street, thinking that would give Amarok less to do later. She was still plowing when she reached her own street. She could tell it hadn't been done since the last big storm.

Her headlights illuminated a man standing off to one side with a hand shovel. Sight of him startled her, made her tense. But she chuckled as she drew closer. That mysterious individual was Kit, attempting to do what he did best — clear the snow from the driveway of his house.

God, there was that fear again. It was exactly what whoever was terrorizing Hilltop, someone like Jasper or the psychopaths she worked with, would want her to feel. Jasper would probably love knowing it was difficult for her to return to her own house. She couldn't let him or whoever had murdered Lorraine and Danielle dictate what she could and couldn't do, couldn't let that person control her in such a way. She had to go on living her life. She just had to be careful, to be prepared — and she had her gun with her, just in case.

She doubted Kit could see her in the dark, so she didn't bother waving. But she was slightly reassured to find him out. At least she wasn't entirely alone.

"It'll take two minutes," she told herself. "I'll run in, grab everything and run out." But even after psyching herself up, she stared at her cabin for several long seconds before grabbing her GLOCK, getting out and approaching the front door. Her garage clicker was in her car and her house key was on the ring that contained her car key at the prison, but she had a spare hidden by the front door.

Because she hadn't left any lights burning, she used the small flashlight from her purse to be able to dig the key container out of her front planter.

She found it without any problem, but when she let herself in she was so intent on her purpose it didn't register when she first threw the light switch that there was a strange pair of snow boots in the entry. A split second later, she looked down. But by then she'd already lost the chance to run.

30

Murder is not about lust and it's not about violence. It's about possession.
> — TED BUNDY, SERIAL KILLER, RAPIST, KIDNAPPER AND NECROPHILIAC

Evelyn tried to get out the door, but the arm that went around her waist, hauling her back, felt like iron. She remembered her gun. She'd thought it'd be easier to use. But the surprise of having someone fly at her so fast, before she could even get a glimpse of his face, hadn't given her the opportunity to fire. And now whoever had ahold of her was trying to wrench her GLOCK away.

She screamed. That was all she could do. She screamed as loudly as possible and began calling for Kit to get help. She had no idea if he could hear her or if he would understand and be able to convert her cries to action. But she was determined to do all she could to save herself. This was Jasper, she thought. It *had* to be Jasper. Just like last summer. If he managed to subdue her, she'd be in for only God knew what.

Don't let him win, Evelyn! Now's your chance to fight back!

She gave the struggle everything she had, used all the pent-up anger she'd felt toward him, not only for the last five months, for the last two decades. The surge of energy that came to her rescue was born of desperation — and the desire to vanquish her greatest enemy. And not just for her sake. For her mother's sake, her entire family's sake, her best friends' sakes. She would finally overcome him. Or she'd die trying.

Clawing and kicking, she fought like she'd never fought before. She could tell her ferocity surprised him. When he cursed, she tried to remember his voice, tried to match it to what she'd heard last August — and couldn't. Still, she was so convinced it was Jasper that she was stunned when she twisted around enough to be able to see her attacker's face.

Then her strength gave out and she went limp. "Glenn!"

"Shut the damn door!" he yelled, but he accomplished it himself by dragging her to one side, out of the way. After that, he let go of her but lashed out with a vicious kick, causing her thigh to explode in pain.

Fortunately, he didn't continue to assault her. He began to pace, curse some more and wave the gun he'd taken from her. *"What are you doing here?"* he ground out.

She blinked at him. "What do you mean? This is my house!"

"You're supposed to be living with Sergeant Amarok! You told me you moved in with him. I saw you go there myself."

"How?" she cried. "Have you been *following* me?"

"I needed to know certain things."

"Like what?"

"Never mind. Why'd you come back? I was just about free of this town, free of it all."

Her mouth was so dry she could barely swallow. "I needed some . . . clothes. That makes sense. What doesn't make sense is finding *you* here. What could possibly have possessed you —" She didn't even get the question out before the answer came to her. "Oh! You're part of the prostitution scheme!"

"Danielle came to *us*," he said. "And it would've been fine — if Kush and Petrowski hadn't been stupid enough to parade her around town and brag about what we had going."

"That puts you in good stead," she said, hurrying to capitalize on his words. "It means no one knows you're involved. You could get away with it."

"*You* know."

She heard that fatalistic note in his voice and did what she could to combat it. She had to offer him hope. "No! I won't say a thing to anyone."

He rolled his eyes. "You won't have to. They'll offer both Kush and Petrowski a deal trying to get Snowden and Dugall, who weren't really involved except to fuck her now and then, and one of them will roll over on me. It's only a matter of time."

So he knew he was going to lose his job. But . . . why this? Why was he hiding out at her house? "How'd you get in?"

He shoved his free hand through his hair, causing it to stick up and make him look even more like a madman. "I broke a window," he said, but the nervous way he spoke and the way he'd glanced around before arriving at that answer indicated otherwise. He was lying. Given the temperature outside, the house was far too warm for there to be a broken window.

She remembered how cold Fitzpatrick's

had been last night. . . .

Glenn must've picked the lock on the back door — like the person who'd delivered that severed arm to her bed.

She blinked at him, stiffening. It was Glenn's uncle who'd installed her alarm system. Before she'd hired Glenn at the prison, he'd worked for that uncle. Who would know how to disarm a system better than the person who'd installed it?

Holy shit. . . . He'd put in an alarm system for Lorraine, too. And at her recommendation, he'd done one for Russ, could easily know about the unlocked woodshed.

Glenn narrowed his eyes. "What are you thinking?"

"Nothing," she replied, but her mind was busy conjuring up the note Whitcomb had left her with that brownie the other night. She'd been so preoccupied when she'd read it — first when she'd been in such a hurry to copy the file she'd found in Fitzpatrick's office and then when she'd been on the phone with Garza's ex-wife — that the handwriting hadn't registered. She'd thrown it away before ever really studying it. Whitcomb was her *friend:* she'd never dreamed there'd be any reason to take a closer look at anything he gave her. But now she recalled the way he'd written her name. The

E was distinctive. It was overlarge and slanted to the left — *like the one on that forged transfer order.*

"Don't lie to me!" He could tell that *something* had become apparent to her. Maybe it was Kush who'd met with Garza and offered him the drugs and pornography to shank Hugo. But it was Glenn who'd taken care of the transfer order, which meant he was behind the stabbing every bit as much as Kush and Petrowski.

"I'm not," she said. "I'm just . . . wondering what you're doing here."

Clearly not convinced, he aimed the gun. "I'm waiting."

"For . . ."

"A friend at the prison to get off work and bring me some money. I have to have money. I can't go anywhere without it." His eyes shifted to the contents of her purse spilled across the floor, and he kept the GLOCK trained on her while squatting to dig through it for her wallet.

Evelyn's thigh was aching. So was the wrist he'd bent back when he forced her own weapon from her grip. Cradling her hand in her lap and using her good leg to propel her, she scooted to the wall so she'd have some back support — and a bit of distance between them, not that five feet would help against a bullet. "Pandering, which is the charge for what you, Kush and Petrowski have done, doesn't carry a stiff sentence, Glenn. If you don't do anything else, you won't serve more than a few months, if that."

After riffling through her cash, he shoved it into his pocket. "Fifty bucks? That's all you got?"

She rested her head against the wall, hoping to look defeated, hoping to lull him into believing she'd been that easily subdued, so she could have some time to think. "My ATM card is there."

"I can't use your card. They can trace that shit."

She ignored his complaint. "Glenn, *why* are you doing this?"

"Believe me, this isn't how I hoped things would turn out. I didn't plan for any of what's happened!"

"Then don't *let* it get ahead of you. Think!"

"It's too late. There are certain things I've put in motion that I can't stop."

"What does that mean?"

He nudged her compact and wallet aside. "It means I won't let them take me in. I know what prison's like. No way will I spend the rest of *my* life there."

The rest of his life? Did he even realize what he'd just said? Those words confirmed what she'd already guessed, but she couldn't let on. That would be the death of her. "It won't be the rest of your life. Aren't you listening? It'll be a few months, at most."

"Oh, stop pretending." He waved her words away in disgust. "I can tell you've figured it out. But it's not what you think. It's not like I *meant* to kill Danielle — either one of them. This whole thing . . . it got out of hand, is all."

A fresh wave of fear swept through Evelyn. That he would make such an admission so easily wasn't a good omen. "She probably provoked you," she said in an effort to reassure him. "You're not the type that would hurt anybody."

"I'm not," he agreed. "I'm not a killer, especially a *serial* killer. You have no idea how hard it was for me to cut up those bodies." He shuddered as if he was reliving the dismemberment in his mind. "But I knew you'd connect that type of murder to Jasper. That's all I ever hear you talk about when you analyze the men you study — how they compare to the monster who killed your friends and slit your throat. That's why I put Danielle's hand in your bed. I figured if I could make what I'd done *look* like it was Jasper, or one of those crazy-ass psychopaths at Hanover House, no one would ever suspect it was me. That gave me a way out, a way to put what I'd done behind me."

She scrambled to come up with a question, anything to keep him talking. "Was Kush in on it then?"

"He knows I took care of the transfer order."

"Why was he the one to approach Garza?"

If Glenn was surprised she knew, he didn't show it. "He didn't want to do that, but I had pictures of him with Danielle. His wife would never stay with him after learning he'd been sleeping with a whore on the side, especially once he was fired and brought up on criminal charges. He was desperate. And it wasn't fair for me to have to do everything."

She sucked in a lungful of air, trying to get her pulse to settle. "So Kush isn't aware that you killed Danielle or Lorraine?"

"No." He kept blinking and wetting his lips, looked as if he hadn't slept in days.

"You've got some money," she said, focusing on the practical. "Why don't you take off?"

"*Fifty bucks?* You want me to leave with only fifty bucks? There's no way. I have to wait, get more."

"Then wait for whoever's coming, but . . . after that you'll leave, won't you? Without hurting me?"

He rubbed his face, then pressed three fingers to his forehead. "Of course."

Evelyn had been praying he'd speak those words, but as soon as they came out of his mouth she knew it was a lie. He couldn't let her go, couldn't allow her the opportunity to tell what she knew. Because she would tell. There was no question about that, in either one of their minds. She was the ultimate victims' rights advocate, had spent her life fighting those who victimized others.

He had to kill her. If he did and made it look like Jasper's handiwork, as he'd done with Danielle and Lorraine, anyone searching for the responsible party would be chasing a man no one had been able to catch in two decades — instead of a disgraced prison guard who had no experience at evading the police. By leaving her brutally murdered, even if he didn't take the time to hack her to pieces like Lorraine and Danielle, he'd throw Amarok and everyone else off his trail. No one would go to much trouble to track down a man guilty of pandering. If she was out of the picture for good, he had a much greater chance of slipping away and establishing himself somewhere else without the past ever coming back to haunt him.

And he'd already killed twice. She doubted one more time would matter to him.

"So when's your buddy going to get here?" she asked.

He seemed disheartened when he checked his watch. "Probably not for another hour. Cooper's always staying late to help out with something."

She knew Elias Cooper. She could only hope he'd come sooner rather than later — and that he'd help her. But even if she was still breathing when he arrived, she doubted Glenn would let him see her. "Does *he* know?" she asked. "About Danielle and . . . and everything else?"

"Cooper? You think I'd bring Dudley Do-Right in on this? Hell no. He's just a nice guy, willing to loan me a few bucks and drop it by while I fix your alarm system."

"He has no idea you're about to disappear with his money."

"He's still got a job, doesn't he? He can live without a few hundred bucks."

She winced against the ache in her thigh, which wouldn't subside. "You've thought of everything."

"I was sure of it, until you showed up."

He scrubbed a hand over his face, released a sigh and shook his head. "Damn it! I don't want to do this."

He spoke as if he was talking to someone else, but she answered. "Do *what*? You said you'd let me live."

"I wish I could, Doc. I really do."

"Glenn, you don't need to hurt me. . . ."

He didn't seem to be listening. He was too busy trying to summon the nerve. "If only I hadn't killed Dani to begin with! Why'd I do that?" he cried, pounding on his head.

Evelyn's chest grew so tight she could feel her heart bumping against it with each bass-like thud. "That's what I'd like to know."

"I didn't mean to," he said. "When she didn't show up for work on Monday, I dropped by to see why. She was just lying around, listening to music and doing her nails — had no good excuse. When I told her she'd lose her job that way, she told me it wasn't gonna happen, not now that she was sleeping with Fitzpatrick."

"So you argued."

"Hell yeah, we argued. That pissed me off. I tried telling her how foolish it was to get involved with him, how it risked us all, but she didn't care as long as she got to indulge her sick fantasies."

Evelyn guessed he'd been quite titillated by Danielle's fantasies when he'd been making money off them, but she couldn't afford to be critical. "Were you jealous?" she asked. "Is that it?"

"No! Aren't you listening? There was too much at stake. I couldn't let her screw Fitzpatrick. What if she said something to him that gave us away? Or he started paying too much attention to her and figured it out on his own?"

Evelyn could easily imagine the scene. "This argument must've come to blows eventually —"

"I didn't hit her. I'm not a violent man."

He seemed adamant. "Then . . . how'd she die?"

"I just wanted to shut her up, you know? She kept yelling that she was going to call Amarok, that she'd love an excuse to get him over to her house, anyway. I was afraid her neighbor would hear and call him for her. So" — he winced — "I got my hands around her throat and squeezed to get her to stop, and-and it worked. It brought instant relief, so much so that I . . . I couldn't let go."

Evelyn wondered if she could somehow reach the kitchen, get a knife. But she didn't see how. He had her cornered. A knife was no match for a gun, anyway. "That doesn't explain what happened to Lorraine," she said.

"God, Lorraine. You know how much I loved her. I didn't want to hurt her, but she walked in out of nowhere and saw Danielle dead on the floor while I was standing there, trying to decide what to do with the body. She started screaming, tried to run. I had to act fast."

So it *was* the fact that Evelyn had asked Lorraine to go by Danielle's that'd gotten her killed. Evelyn felt terrible about that. But she couldn't allow herself to focus on it. She had to keep Whitcomb procrastinating the moment he pulled the trigger. "Why was there no blood in Danielle's house?"

"I told you!" he cried, belligerent. "I strangled her. It's not like I shot her! I didn't go there intending to kill her or anyone else. I strangled them both."

"But only Danielle's hand showed up in my bed."

He calmed down. "Oh, that. I cut both her and Lorraine into pieces in the barn behind my grandparents' house. But I told you why I had to. I was only trying to make it look like it was a serial killer."

"Which was brilliant," she said. "Effective. I *did* think it was Jasper."

He nodded, gratified by the praise. "I watch TV, know what overkill suggests. But how any man could *enjoy* murder — that I don't understand."

"What you did isn't the same," she told him. "It was merely a means to an end."

"That's it. That's it entirely. I had no other choice." He gave her an apologetic look but raised the gun. "And I'm afraid it's the same here. I don't *want* to do this, Evelyn. I've always liked you. Probably more than I should have. It's just that I'm in too deep and there's only one way out. You're the last hurdle standing between me and the chance to start over. If only you hadn't come home . . ."

Evelyn tried to shrink into the wall. That was all she could do. She wished Amarok would come to her rescue, but she knew he wasn't going to. He was in Anchorage, miles away, taking care of Kush and delivering Hugo's corpse and what was left of Lorraine and Danielle to the medical examiner. Chances were he wouldn't even think to check on her, wouldn't realize she wasn't at home or at work until much later in the day.

He fired once. The bullet went into the wall beside her, shocking her, making her panic. This was *real.* She had to *do* something. So she quit cowering and launched herself at Whitcomb.

The reversal in her behavior took him by surprise. The gun went off again, deafening her, but the bullet must've landed in another wall, or the ceiling — she wasn't sure since he'd pulled the trigger while falling back.

He hit his head on the travertine, which stunned him long enough that she managed to get her hands on the gun. The shock wore off before she could gain control of it, however. Then they were wrestling. This time, if he gained the advantage Evelyn knew it would all be over. He'd fire as soon as he could turn the muzzle on her.

He surprised her by firing before that. This bullet definitely went into the ceiling, because a sprinkle of Sheetrock dropped onto her face.

The next bullet was going into her head. Grabbing her by the hair, he pinned her down with the weight of his body. She could feel the cool metal of the barrel when it touched her cheek and didn't have the strength to turn it away.

"Glenn, no!" she whispered — and then, out of nowhere, the door hit them both as someone forced it open.

Assuming Kit had finally brought his father to her rescue, Evelyn felt a brief flash of hope — which was instantly quashed by the report of a gun. Help had arrived too late. Glenn had pulled the trigger.

Because Evelyn was expecting to feel pain, it came as a shock that she didn't, especially when the pressure on her cheek fell away and Glenn went limp on top of her.

Her mind struggled to process what'd really occurred as she tried to shove him off. But one thing seemed clear. *She* wasn't shot; someone had shot *Glenn.* She could feel his blood soaking her shirt, feel the heaviness of his body in a completely different way.

He was dead. She knew it instantly. But how? *Kit* couldn't have shot anyone. . . .

Was it Kit's father? Or Amarok? Could he have come — somehow, miraculously — after all?

Filled with an instant and overwhelming gratitude, she managed to summon the strength to lean up on her elbows despite Glenn's weight so that she could see — only to realize that she hadn't been saved at all. It wasn't Kit or Amarok who'd shot Glenn. Anthony Garza stood in the entryway wearing a grin that indicated he had plans for her Glenn would never even have dreamed of.

31

I was born with the devil in me. I could not help the fact that I was a murderer, no more than the poet can help the inspiration to sing.

— H.H. HOLMES, SERIAL KILLER, CON ARTIST, BIGAMIST

Garza was terrifying enough when a thick plate of plexiglass separated her from him. Without that protection — with nothing between them — Evelyn could scarcely breathe. "What are you doing here?" she gasped.

He curled his lip, revealing his sharp teeth as he advanced on her. "There've been a few changes in the power paradigm."

She tried to scramble away, but Glenn was still lying on the lower half of her body, and he was so damn hard to move.

"Now that we're on a more even playing field, I'm hoping our relationship can prove to be far more . . . satisfying," Anthony said.

She shuddered at the way he looked at her. "How'd you get out?" Surely the alarm had been sounded at Hanover House and there were people looking for him. Maybe Amarok had even been called. Since Kit hadn't responded to her cries, that seemed the best chance of help she could hope for.

"How do you think I got out?" He lifted Glenn and tossed him aside — as if he were no more than a sack of wheat. "This bastard let me out last night. Said he'd gotten himself into some trouble and needed to create a diversion." He studied Glenn's inert frame. "Too bad things didn't work out for him. I guess he wasn't as smart as he thought."

What was she going to do? What *could* she do? "He-he wanted you to run?"

"Soon as I killed you. Said he could only buy me enough time to make it to Anchorage. Guess he thought that would get me out of Hilltop sometime today and send everyone who was anyone after me. But how could he expect me to go anywhere without a car?"

Evelyn tried to keep her eyes from flicking to the gun Glenn had taken from her. It lay on the floor not far away, but Anthony would be on her the second she reached for it. "If you don't have a car, how-how'd you get here?"

"CO by the name of Cooper saw me an hour or so ago and tried to offer me a ride, thanks to my smart uniform and all."

Glenn had provided him with a CO's uniform. Until he opened his mouth and showed those strange teeth, he could easily be mistaken for an employee. "That was a stroke of luck," he said, "since he happened to know right where you lived."

Her mouth was so dry she had a difficult time speaking. She kept thinking about what Anthony had done to Elaine Morrison and his other victims. By the time he was finished having his fun with her, she'd be found dead, with her body positioned in the most humiliating manner possible. She wouldn't put it past him to strip her and Glenn both and shove Glenn's genitals into her mouth or something equally disturbing.

She couldn't stomach the thought of Amarok discovering her like that, couldn't bear the idea of her parents hearing about it. "He-he was coming here, bringing Glenn some money," she managed to say.

"Yeah, well, he didn't quite make it all the way and won't be doing much of anything from here on out."

Evelyn squeezed her eyes closed as images

of the shack where Jasper had kept her for three days paraded through her mind. She'd been treated worse than an animal there, could easily guess that what she faced with Anthony wouldn't be much different. "You should leave," she said, sliding away from him. "Right away, if-if you hope to escape."

Emboldened by the quaver in her voice, he rested his hands on his hips as if he had all the time in the world and let his gaze range over her. "I'll go when I'm good and ready. I have a few things I'd like to accomplish here first."

Frightened on a level Glenn could never have achieved, Evelyn began to tremble. Glenn had been normal. He hadn't been a *good* person. He'd been a selfish bastard not much better than the psychopaths she studied. He would probably even score fairly high on Hare's test. But at least she could understand Glenn's actions and motives and follow his logic.

She couldn't count on logic or reason to understand or influence Anthony. He wasn't thinking about self-preservation; he was only thinking about how much he was going to enjoy torturing and killing her. After all she'd learned in her studies, she recognized the overinflated view he possessed of his own abilities. That type of thing characterized so many psychopaths. No doubt he thought he could get what he wanted and *still* walk away in the end.

Sad thing was, with Amarok in Anchorage for the day, he probably would be able to escape.

"I'm sure you realize this now, but they won't be charging me with those Porn Poser killings," he said. "They'd have to find me first. But I'd still like to know what they have on me."

She struggled to remain calm, to take advantage of the opportunity to stall. "It doesn't matter if you won't be around, does it?"

When he stepped on her ankle to keep her from being able to move any farther, she barely stopped herself from crying out. "I'm curious. So I suggest you tell me. Otherwise, I can promise you'll be begging to tell me anything I want to know in about fifteen minutes — if not less."

"Your last wife —"

"Courtney."

"Yes." Evelyn pressed a hand to her chest, hoping it might help regulate her breathing. "You-you accidentally delivered Elaine Morrison's credit card to her with the candy you bought her son."

"No kidding." He put more pressure on

her ankle, grinding it into the travertine. "You contacted Courtney?"

Evelyn was having a difficult time controlling the quaking of her limbs. The pain from her ankle didn't help. "Yes. And she-she's turned that evidence over to police."

"Because of you," he reiterated.

When she didn't confirm it, couldn't confirm it for the panic flowing through her, he leaned close. "Because of *you?*" he repeated.

The look in his eyes told her she *had* to answer, and there was only one answer she could give. Her heart seemed to lodge in her throat as she nodded.

"Great. Then I'm happy for this chance to express my gratitude." His hand fisted in her hair and he jerked her head back so hard she thought he might break her neck. Then his mouth came down on hers, and his tongue shoved its way through her lips.

Evelyn gagged. But it wasn't until he broke away, set the gun aside and started undoing his pants that she understood just where he planned to start this painful odyssey.

Bile churned in her stomach. She couldn't endure what was coming next and she knew it — even if she survived it physically.

Again, she marked where her gun had

fallen. She wasn't sure she could grab it and turn it on Anthony in time to preserve her own life. But if making the effort didn't work and she died, at least she'd be more likely to die a quick death.

She wouldn't give him the pleasure of torturing her, of making her scrape and beg and humiliate herself. She'd been through that once with Jasper and had promised herself she would never go through it again.

He didn't seem surprised when she lunged forward. He seemed to expect it, to be ready. He would've shot her right then if he hadn't heard what she heard — the door opening and a voice saying, "Here, kitty, kitty!"

Kit. The gunfire a few minutes earlier must've finally drawn him to the house. But her poor neighbor wasn't the least prepared for what he was walking into.

"Run!" she screamed.

He didn't. He remained in the doorway, gaping at them. Anthony wasn't about to let him get away, regardless. He turned to fire — and that gave Evelyn the split second she needed to grab her own firearm. She pulled the trigger as soon as she could — and kept firing until there were no more bullets. Then, shaking and gasping for breath, she watched as he fingered the holes she'd put in his chest as if he couldn't believe the red stains spreading out on his shirt could really be his own blood.

"You bitch!" he cried, and lifted his weapon.

Evelyn raised her arms — a futile gesture. But he fell before he could take aim. And then he didn't move.

Tears rolled down Evelyn's cheeks. Was he dead?

She had no idea, and she didn't dare get close enough to check. It wasn't until she heard Kit whimpering on the doorstep that she forced herself to move. She needed to see if he was okay. She couldn't quit shaking, her hands were bleeding where she'd broken several of her nails and she could hardly walk on the ankle Anthony had tried to crush. But she was alive — and she needed to help her neighbor, if she could.

Because her legs were too rubbery to support her weight, she fell back when she tried to stand. But she managed to drag herself over to the door and was relieved to find Kit curled into a ball, very frightened but unhurt.

"Kitty," he moaned, over and over.

Evelyn forced herself to get close enough to Anthony Garza to retrieve his gun. Then she set both firearms to one side, yet still within reach, put her arms around Kit and pulled him close so he no longer had to see the lifeless bodies a few feet away. "I'm sure Sigmund misses you, too," she said. "I'll bring him by to see you as soon as I can."

32

After my head has been chopped off, will I still be able to hear, at least for a moment, the sound of my own blood gushing from my neck? That would be the pleasure to end all pleasures.
— PETER KÜRTEN, GERMAN SERIAL KILLER CALLED THE VAMPIRE OF DÜSSELDORF

"What are you thinking about?" Amarok asked.

Evelyn kissed his bare shoulder and snuggled closer to him in the warm bed. "Dean Snowden and Steve Dugall."

"Why are you thinking about them?"

"They performed the morning count when Anthony Garza wasn't reported missing."

"How do you know?"

"The warden e-mailed me earlier to see if I was okay and to let me know that he'd discovered the breakdown there. They were both dismissed on the spot."

"You were going to fire them anyway for having sex with Danielle and not reporting the corruption."

"True, but I was hoping to be able to wait a couple of weeks. I didn't want to lose too many correctional officers at once. We still have a prison to run."

His hand came up to cup her breast. "So will you have enough manpower?"

"I'm sure we can limp by. Ferris says he'll get some more help as soon as possible. Our current situation just isn't . . . *optimal.*" She adjusted the blankets. "How are you even awake after the long hours you've put in this past week?"

"Who knows? At least we can sleep in tomorrow, enjoy our Sunday."

"I can't believe what's happened is over."

His hand left her breast and his fingers moved through her hair. "Neither can I. Are you sure you're all right?"

"I told you — I'm fine."

"You'll probably be black-and-blue tomorrow."

She shifted so she could rest her head on his chest. "I've got a few bumps and bruises, and my ankle's swollen and sore, but that's it." She remembered the look in Anthony Garza's eyes. It could've been so much worse. . . .

"Is that all we have to worry about?" he asked. "The physical side of your injuries?"

She hesitated before answering, searching for the answer to that question herself. "I think so," she said at length. "Coming up against Garza was frightening, but it was sort of empowering, too." She drew a heart on his chest. "I won that struggle."

"You were just starting to trust men again."

"No." She lifted up to peck his lips. "I was starting to trust *you,* and I still do."

Makita got up from where he'd been sleeping on the floor and walked over to stick his nose in the bed. He hated to be left out of anything. Evelyn laughed out loud when he jumped in a second later.

Amarok didn't seem to mind. He moved over to make room and pulled her with him. "I like the sound of that."

"What happened with Garza — that was minor compared to Jasper," she explained. "I didn't love Garza, so it wasn't such a personal betrayal. It ended before he could torture me. And he's dead, so he can't come after me again. Those are important distinctions." The thought that Jasper was still out there somewhere cast a shadow over her relief and happiness, but she shoved that shadow away. She was still looking for him. She'd find him eventually, and she'd see justice done there, too. "I'm relieved, more than anything — that Kit wasn't harmed, that Glenn also got what he deserved and that the nightmare is over. Now all of Hilltop can rest easy," she finished.

"Does that include me?"

Evelyn leaned on one elbow. They'd left the light on in the hall so that Makita could come and go as he pleased, which meant she could see Amarok's profile. "What do you mean?"

"Are you planning to move back to Boston after everything that's happened here? Maybe in the spring?"

She thought of that last call with her father, wasn't sure how to ease the strain her refusal to return to Boston was causing. But she wasn't ready to go back. "No."

"Will you give me that same answer after you've talked to your folks?"

That was what had him so pensive? He thought what they had might be over before it ever really got going? "I'll call them first thing in the morning and assure them they don't have to worry any longer. I would've called tonight, but it's been a long day, what with getting Glenn and Garza's bodies to Anchorage. Besides, it's so much later there.

I didn't see any point in waking them just to assure them they'll now be able to sleep at night."

He rolled onto his side, too, facing her, and punched up his pillow. "What will you tell them about me?"

"I'll say I'm dating an Alaska State Trooper who'll look after me while I'm here."

"Will you add that we're living together?"

"Not yet. I figure it'll be better to start with the fact that I'm finally dating someone," she said with a chuckle.

Closing the gap between them, he ran his lips over the curve of her cheek. "How do you think they'll react to that news?"

"They'll be shocked and excited. They might even quit bugging me to come home," she said wryly. "They've been pushing me to move on, to find a man, since forever."

"Just not in Alaska?"

"Exactly. Closer to Boston," she admitted. "But you're my first boyfriend since Jasper. That makes you significant."

"Let's see if I can become a little more significant," he said, and rolled her onto her back.

She caught his face. "You want to make love?"

"I want to bring you to climax, and I think

now's the perfect time."

The fear of failing at something so integral to being a woman welled up again. "We can do it later," she said. "You're too tired tonight."

"Quit being such a chicken," he said. Then he showed her that he had all the stamina he needed — and that she'd been worried for nothing: her body could perform as well as any other woman's.

The following morning, Evelyn called her parents, who were so relieved that the killer had been caught they managed to muster a little support for her continued presence in Alaska, especially once they learned about Amarok.

After she hung up with them, she rode with Amarok and Makita to Anchorage, where they met his father, Hank, and his father's wife, Joanna, for dinner. Evelyn liked the old guy. Hank was a weathered fisherman, a man of few words, but she could tell that Amarok respected him. She respected him, too, sensed a great deal of strength in his quiet reserve. She especially enjoyed witnessing their father-son dynamic. She even liked Amarok's stepmother. Evelyn had been worried that his father might not be pleased with the age difference between her and Amarok, but he didn't act as if he even noticed.

Maybe he hadn't. She seemed to be the only one hyperaware — and hypersensitive — to those seven years. It wasn't like she was robbing the cradle. Most people wouldn't be able to tell there was much of a difference, just those who already knew. Anyway, Hank and Joanna had been much more captivated by her injuries and the story of what'd happened the past week than they were critical of her relationship with their son.

Once she and Amarok returned home, they cozied up in front of the fire for a while before tidying the cabin, doing laundry and getting ready for another workweek. Evelyn felt guilty for not going into the prison over the weekend. She'd meant to show some leadership, to reassure HH's employees. But after that struggle with Glenn and Anthony Garza, she'd needed the chance to recover.

Besides, there'd never been a time like this, when she so thoroughly enjoyed being with a man. She didn't want to miss out on a single moment.

On Monday, Amarok insisted on taking her to work so that she wouldn't have to drive her Beamer. As they passed her car, which they'd parked in the drive next to his truck, she noticed that he'd stuck a For Sale sign in the window.

"You're selling my car without my knowledge?" she asked.

He patted Makita, who was coming with them. "That's my way of notifying you."

"If I sell my car I'll be more likely to stay. Is that your thought process?"

"My story is that I won't be able to quit worrying about you as long as you're driving that thing" — he shot her a grin — "and I'm sticking with it."

"So it has nothing to do with getting me to stay."

"I'm not sure I can *completely* deny that, but a small sedan, one that doesn't even have snow tires, is too impractical either way. Can't you get something else?"

"To be honest, I've already come to the conclusion that I should," she admitted. "But I can't imagine I'll have any luck selling this kind of car here."

"No one in Hilltop would buy that pansy-ass thing," he agreed. "But" — he winked at her — "now that I have your permission, I'll place an ad on Craigslist for Anchorage."

"We might have better luck if we wait until spring," she pointed out.

"You need a four-wheel drive even if the

Beamer sits parked in the driveway for the rest of winter."

He was right. "I guess I could swing another payment," she said, especially because she was going to sell her cabin. No way could she live there after finding Danielle's arm in her bed — and fighting Whitcomb and Garza for her life in the entryway. She hoped one of the psychologists she hired to replace Brand or Fitzpatrick might be interested in it. But, depending on how long she lived with Amarok, she should save more than enough on mortgage payments to pick up some added car expense. "What should I get instead?"

"An SUV would be nice."

They talked cars until Amarok pulled under the portico of Hanover House to let her out. "What time should I pick you up?" he asked.

"I'll call. Will you be at your trooper post?"

"For a change."

She gave Makita a scratch as she leaned over for a quick kiss from Amarok — and felt happier than she'd ever been.

With a final wave, she hurried inside and spoke to everyone she came across to let them know that, no matter what'd happened last week, Hanover House was going to be just fine and so were they.

Penny glanced up the second Evelyn walked into the mental health section. "Hi."

"How are you?"

"Good," she said. "You still coming over to get Sigmund tonight?"

"I am. Six thirty okay?"

"Fine with me, but . . . I'm going to miss him."

"I hope he and Amarok's dog will be nice to each other."

Penny blushed but made no comment about Evelyn's new living arrangements. "You have two messages," she said, turning to business. "One from a Detective Green in Utah. He said to tell you he has the credit card, whatever that means."

That didn't matter quite as much now that Anthony was dead. "And the other?"

Penny bit her lip. "Janice Holt with the BOP wants you to call her right away."

Evelyn's heart skipped a beat. "She's back from New Zealand?"

"Not yet. She must've checked her voice mail or caught the news, though, because she knows about the murders. She sounded pretty upset."

Some of Evelyn's optimism faded. Was her program headed for the scrap heap?

She hurried to her office, piled everything on her desk and stared down at the phone.

Then she drew a deep breath and dialed.

Janice answered on the first ring. "Evelyn?"

"Yes?"

"What the hell's going on up there?"

"It's been a . . . a rough week." She explained everything about the murders, Danielle having sex with the inmates and what happened with Fitzpatrick, how he'd been disappointed when she rejected him and that disappointment had smoldered into resentment.

"But he quit?" Janice said when she was done.

Evelyn slid her skirt up a few inches to study the bruise she'd gotten when Glenn kicked her. Her ankle actually seemed to be healing faster. "Yes, he walked out on Friday."

"Thank the Lord."

Evelyn went into a bit more detail, about the file she'd found in his office and what he'd done in his sessions with Hugo.

Janice listened silently, so silently that Evelyn was afraid to stop talking for fear of what she might say in response. But that moment had to come at some point and, when it did, Evelyn braced herself.

"You've had one hell of a time," Janice said.

"As if the weather up here isn't bad enough," Evelyn joked.

"So what now?"

"I'd like to replace Martin and Tim and keep working. Of course, Warden Ferris will take care of the job openings on the prison side."

"The media has had a field day with this," she mused.

"I'm aware of that. I'm sorry."

"What they don't understand is that corruption can happen in any prison."

A ray of sunshine came through the window, and it was so rare for this time of year that Evelyn got up to look out and enjoy it. "True. But what Fitzpatrick did will cost the mental health team a great deal of credibility."

"I haven't seen Fitzpatrick on the news. Does anyone besides us know about what he did — in his sessions, I mean?"

Surprised by this question, Evelyn forgot about the sun. "No. I mean, Hugo did, but —"

"Hugo's dead."

"Yes." Amarok knew, too, of course, but she wasn't about to mention that. He wouldn't tell anyone.

"You said Fitzpatrick deleted the files that were stored there at the prison, so it's unlikely any of the rest of the team will ever look back."

"There's still the cloud —"

"Which no one will have any reason to bother checking. It's not like we have to fire him and worry about showing cause. He quit."

"True. . . ."

"Then, from my perspective, the whole Whitcomb/Kush/Petrowski thing has nothing to do with you, the other mental health professionals or the patients you're studying. Those were correctional officers, so it's a prison matter, something I should be discussing with the warden."

Evelyn opened her mouth but wasn't quite sure what to say.

"Ferris has to get a handle on his staff," Janice continued. "We can't afford this type of negative publicity at any prison, but least of all at Hanover House. Tell him he can expect to hear from me when I get back to the states."

Too shocked to respond right away, Evelyn covered her mouth. She couldn't believe it. She was being left alone to continue as she'd been before?

She'd been so sure there would be severe repercussions!

There probably would've been, had Janice

learned what was going on any sooner. . . .

"Dr. Talbot?" her boss said. "Hello? Are you still there?"

She cleared her throat. "Yes, I'm here. How was the wedding?"

"I'd enjoy the festivities a lot more if I liked my son-in-law," she said. "Good luck finding the right people to fill the vacancies on your team."

"Thank you. Have a safe trip."

Janice had disconnected when Penny walked in, but Evelyn was still in a state of shock.

"Dr. Fitzpatrick called while you were on the phone."

Evelyn couldn't help grimacing. "Don't tell me he asked to speak to *me.*"

"No, he knew you wouldn't want to talk to him."

"So . . . was he after the files he left behind, or what?"

"He asked if I'd deliver his sincerest apologies, for everything, and tell you that he'll be moving back to the Lower Forty-eight as soon as possible."

Grateful that he had the integrity to at least acknowledge his mistakes, Evelyn nodded. "Thank you," she said, and waited for her assistant to go back out before calling Detective Green.

603

"You have the credit card?" Evelyn asked without preamble.

"I do," he replied. "Now that it will no longer do us any good as far as convicting Garza."

"At least his victims will know he was the one, and that he's gone. That should bring them some closure."

"And save the government a pile of money. I owe you a drink, Dr. Talbot. Maybe someday I'll come up there and take a peek at Hanover House."

"I'd like that."

"I also wanted to tell you Elaine's daughter is having a baby — and plans to name it after you."

That made a good morning even better. A baby brought hope, healing, especially because Evelyn wasn't sure she would ever have a child herself. "How nice."

"You deserve that and more."

"I only did what I should've done." She was just saying good-bye when the warden knocked on her open door. "Morning," she said, and waved him in.

He eyed her carefully as he approached the desk. "*Is* it a good morning?"

Curving her lips into a smile, she gestured toward the window. "It is indeed. Haven't you seen the sun?"

EPILOGUE

"I had a compulsion to do it."
— ED GEIN, SERIAL KILLER
(INSPIRATION FOR *PSYCHO*
AND *SILENCE OF THE LAMBS*)

Jasper Moore, who was now going by the name of Andy Smith — he'd used several aliases over the years — sat at the table with his wife's two little girls while she made them all breakfast.

"What are you reading, Daddy?" Miranda, the oldest at eight, leaned over to see the newspaper.

He looked up from the piece he'd read twice already. "An article about a lady who's running a prison in Alaska."

"Where's Alaska?" Chelsea, Miranda's younger sister by two years, got up on her knees.

"It's a place that's far away, where it's really cold," he replied.

"Colder than here?" she asked.

He chuckled. "We live in Arizona. Almost every place is colder than here."

Her little heart-shaped mouth puckered. "Not today. It's raining."

He took a sip of his coffee. "Even we get a storm every once in a while."

"How many people live in Alaska?" Chelsea asked.

"Not a lot," he replied. "It's the last frontier."

"What's a frontier?"

He should've known that question was coming next. "A vast wilderness with lots of animals and wide-open spaces."

Miranda frowned as she studied the picture of Evelyn. "Why would such a pretty lady want to start a prison, especially where it's so cold?"

"This is a new kind of prison, one where they like to peek inside a man's head," he explained.

Chelsea scrunched up her nose. "Can they do that?"

"They like to try."

She seemed horrified. "Wouldn't it hurt?"

Hillary, his wife, carried a skillet over from the stove. "I don't think a place like that is meant to be pleasant. That's where they put bad people, honey."

"A prison doesn't sound like a very nice place," Chelsea said.

"It wouldn't be uncomfortable for Evelyn Talbot," Jasper pointed out. "*She* isn't locked up. My guess is that she likes her work, that she thinks she's really doing something."

"You don't agree?" Hillary asked.

The lines that were already forming in his wife's face bothered him. He wished she'd get some Botox or something. She didn't have a whole lot to offer besides a willing body whenever he demanded sex and the living she made as a nurse. Her income was the only way he could get by when he was out of work, and he was more often out of work than not, which was part of the reason his first wife had left him. "Psychiatry is all hocus-pocus to me. How can you tell what a man's going to do by giving him a test?"

"A *test*?" she replied. "Psychiatrists study behavior. As screwed up as so many people are, *someone* has to try and dig for answers."

She always acted as if she knew more than he did. That bothered him, too. But he let it go. He'd learned which people were important, if only for practical reasons and the creature comforts they could provide, and which were expendable enough to fulfill certain . . . other appetites.

Miranda gave a little shiver. "I wouldn't want to go to a prison in Alaska."

Hillary peered over his shoulder as she dished up his eggs. "Why are you so interested in Hanover House? If anything on that place ever comes over the news, you're riveted."

She had *no* idea. . . . "I'd like to visit there someday."

"The prison?" she asked in horrified surprise.

"Alaska," he said with a benign smile.